BATTLE STATION PRIME

ESCAPE FROM FORTRESS CITY

AN UNOFFICIAL GRAPHIC NOVEL FOR MINECRAFTERS

CARA J. STEVENS

ILLUSTRATED BY SAM NEEDHAM

SKY PONY PRESS
NEW YORK

Copyright © 2019 by Hollan Publishing, Inc.

Minecraft® is a registered trademark of Notch Development AB.

The Minecraft game is copyright © Mojang AB.

Sky Pony Press books may be purchased in bulk at special discounts for sales promotion, corporate gifts, fund-raising, or educational purposes. Special editions can also be created to specifications. For details, contact the Special Sales Department, Sky Pony Press, 307 West 36th Street, 11th Floor, New York, NY 10018 or info@ skyhorsepublishing.com.

Sky Pony® is a registered trademark of Skyhorse Publishing, Inc.®, a Delaware corporation.

Minecraft® is a registered trademark of Notch Development AB.
The Minecraft game is copyright © Mojang AB.

Visit our website at www.skyponypress.com.

10 9 8 7 6 5 4

Library of Congress Cataloging-in- Publication Data is available on file.

Cover design by Brian Peterson
Cover and interior art by Sam Needham

Print ISBN: 978-1-5107-4136-2
Ebook ISBN: 978-1-5107-4141-6

Printed in China

#1

BATTLE STATION PRIME
ESCAPE FROM FORTRESS CITY

MEET THE

NAME: Pell
ROLE: Doer of Good Deeds

A boy with a talent for getting lost and for making the best of every situation.

NAME: Logan
ROLE: Possibility Curator

Pell's best friend who likes collecting junk, hacking, and getting into trouble.

NAME: Maddy
ROLE: Knowledge Keeper

Logan's intelligent and annoyingly charming little sister.

CHARACTERS

NAME: Uncle Colin
ROLE: The Overseer
Pell's mysterious uncle
who may or may not
need to be rescued.

NAME: Ned

A homesteader in a
prison jumpsuit.

NAME: The Professor

Homestead resident
who's helping to plan
the rebellion.

NAME: Mr. Jones

Former government
employee, now part of
the rebellion.

NAME: James

A Mr. Jones lookalike,
he's the overseer of
Base 10.

INTRODUCTION

Sometimes, the only thing you can do is hope for an escape route.

Everyone wants to live in Fortress City, where hostile mobs never spawn and lightning never strikes—as long as you're part of the ruling class. In a world where everyone is judged by their wealth and enchanting power, Pell, Logan, and Maddy can't keep up, no matter how hard they try. When a mysterious letter arrives with instructions on how to break out of Fortress City, Pell, Logan, and Maddy decide to take their chances and set off into the unknown.

Our story begins as our fearless, powerless, and clueless heroes are seeing just how difficult things can be in an unfair world.

CHAPTER 1

BULLIES AND TRASH

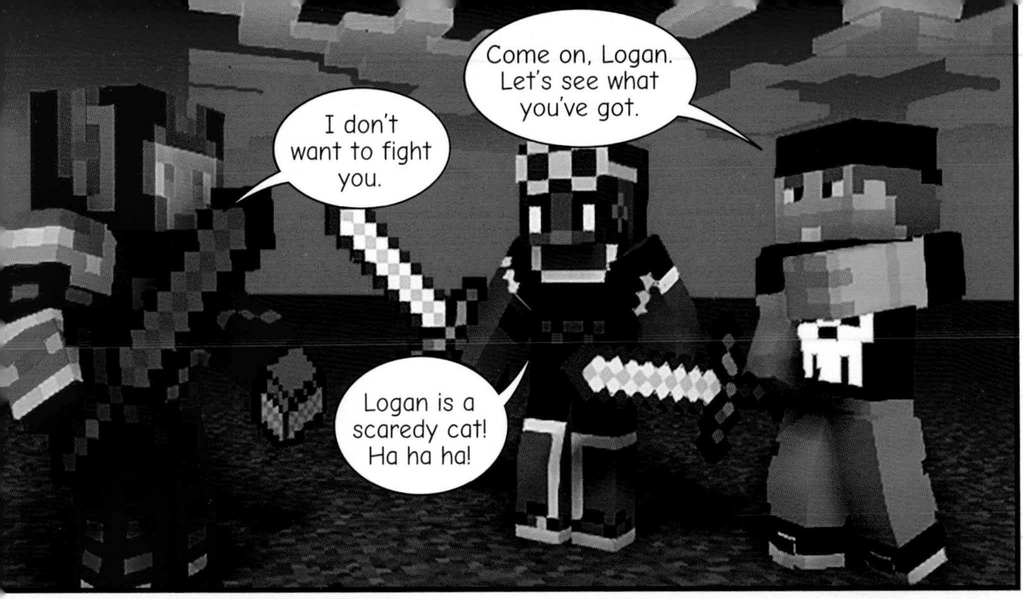
Come on, Logan. Let's see what you've got.
I don't want to fight you.
Logan is a scaredy cat! Ha ha ha!

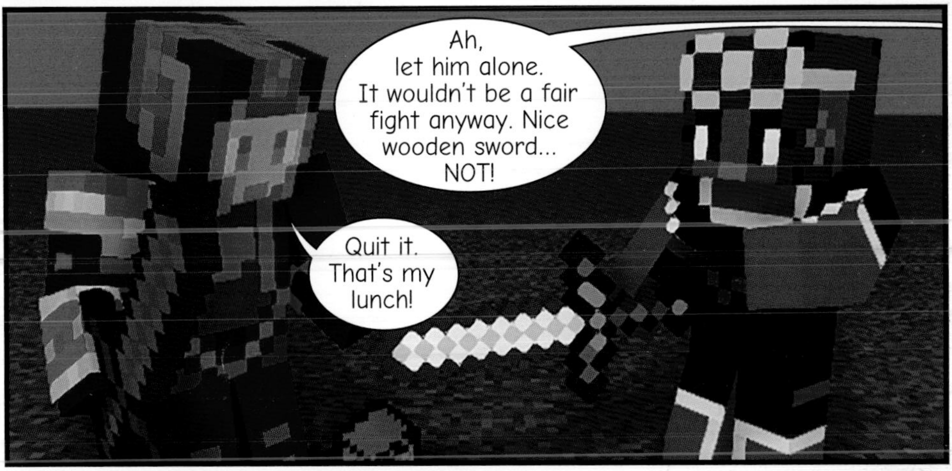
Ah, let him alone. It wouldn't be a fair fight anyway. Nice wooden sword... NOT!
Quit it. That's my lunch!

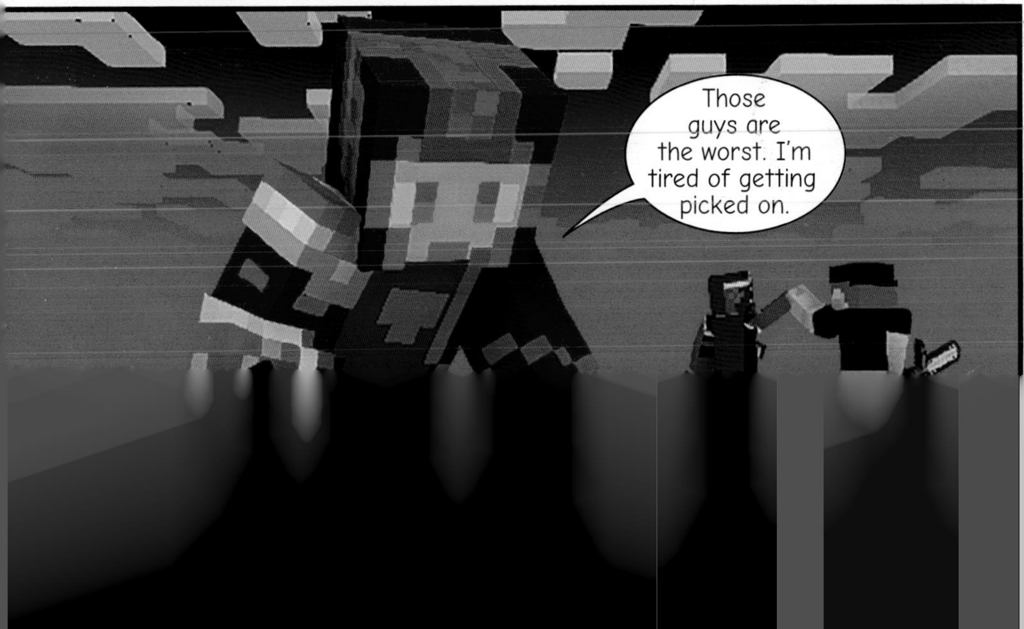
Those guys are the worst. I'm tired of getting picked on.

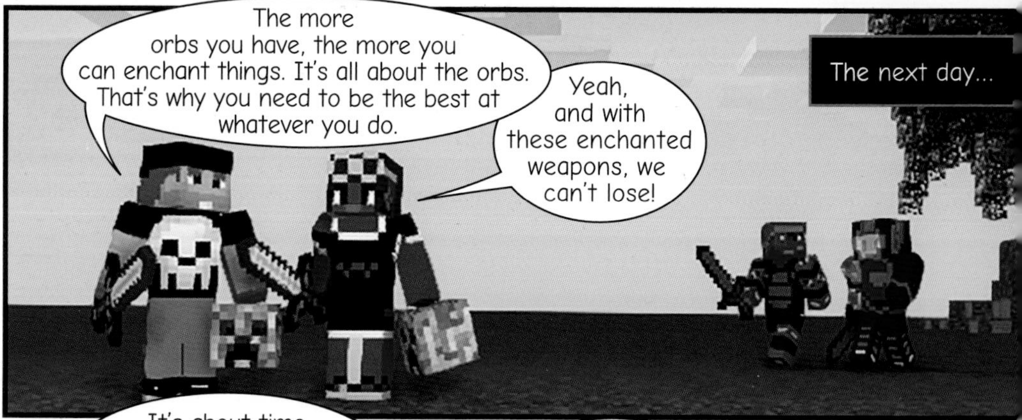

The next day...
The more orbs you have, the more you can enchant things. It's all about the orbs. That's why you need to be the best at whatever you do.
Yeah, and with these enchanted weapons, we can't lose!

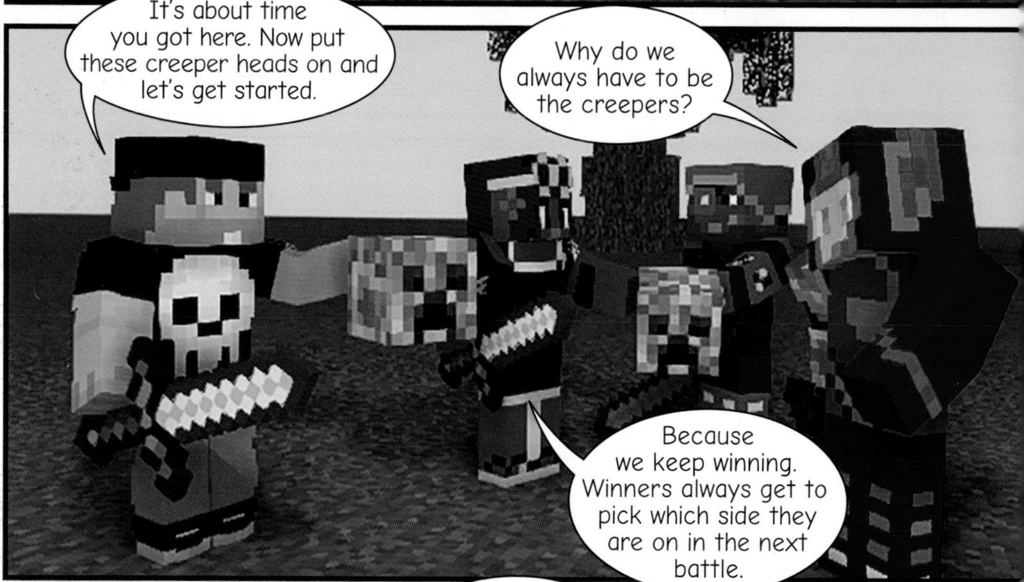

It's about time you got here. Now put these creeper heads on and let's get started.
Why do we always have to be the creepers?
Because we keep winning. Winners always get to pick which side they are on in the next battle.

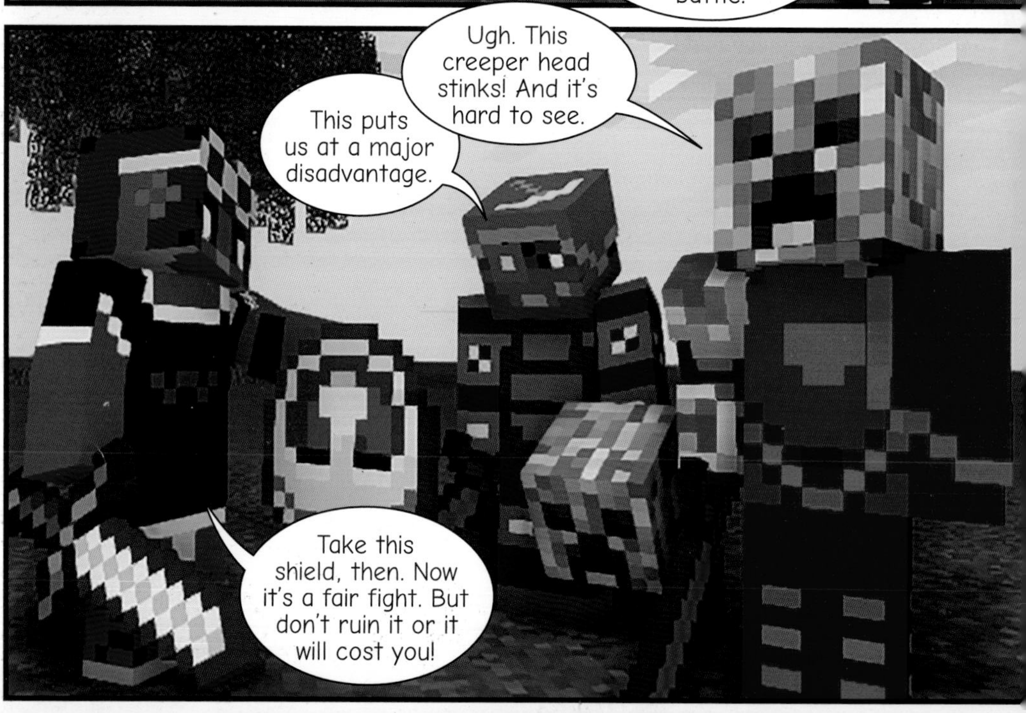

This puts us at a major disadvantage.
Ugh. This creeper head stinks! And it's hard to see.
Take this shield, then. Now it's a fair fight. But don't ruin it or it will cost you!

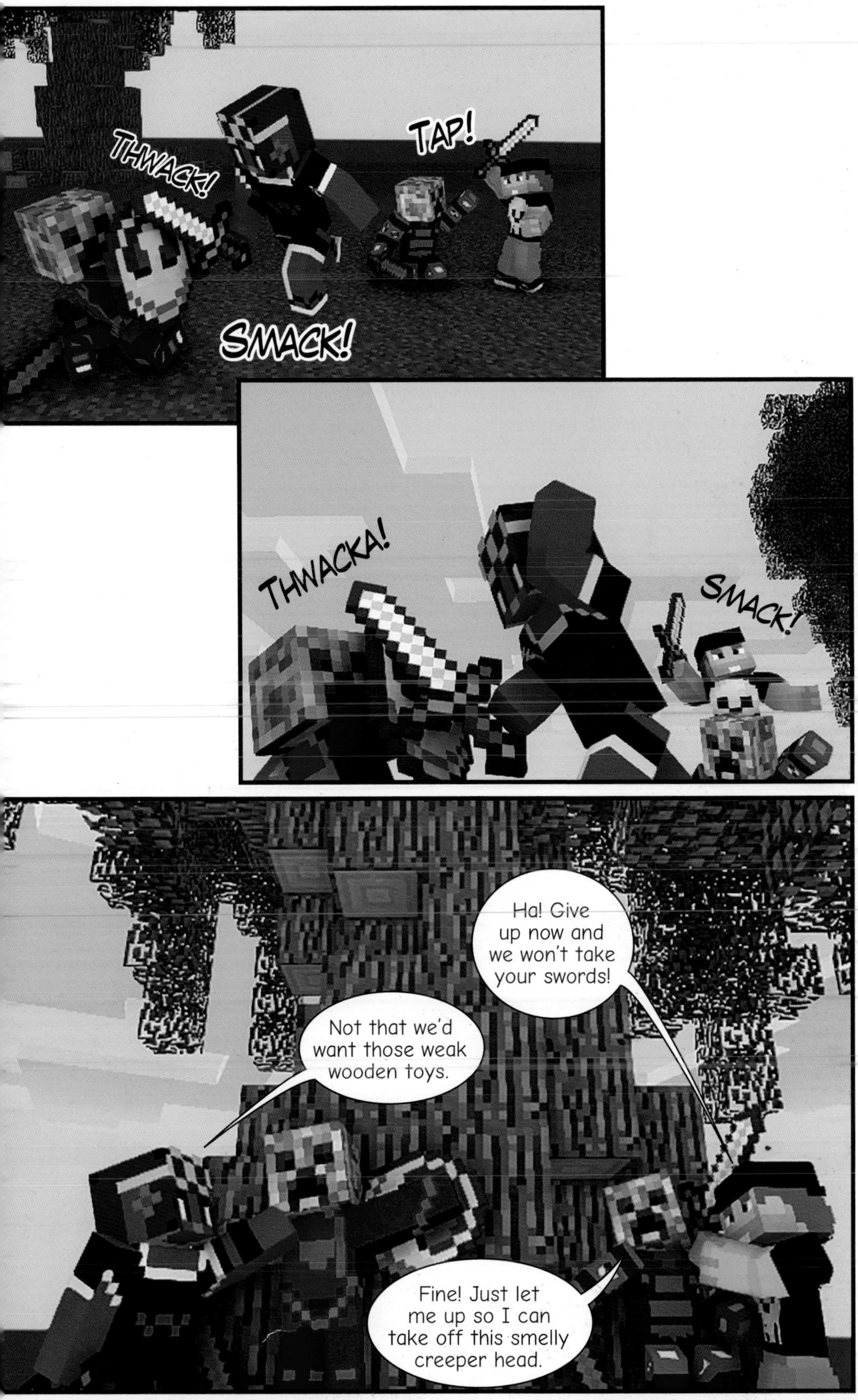
THWACK!
TAP!
SMACK!
THWACKA!
SMACK!
Ha! Give up now and we won't take your swords!
Not that we'd want those weak wooden toys.
Fine! Just let me up so I can take off this smelly creeper head.

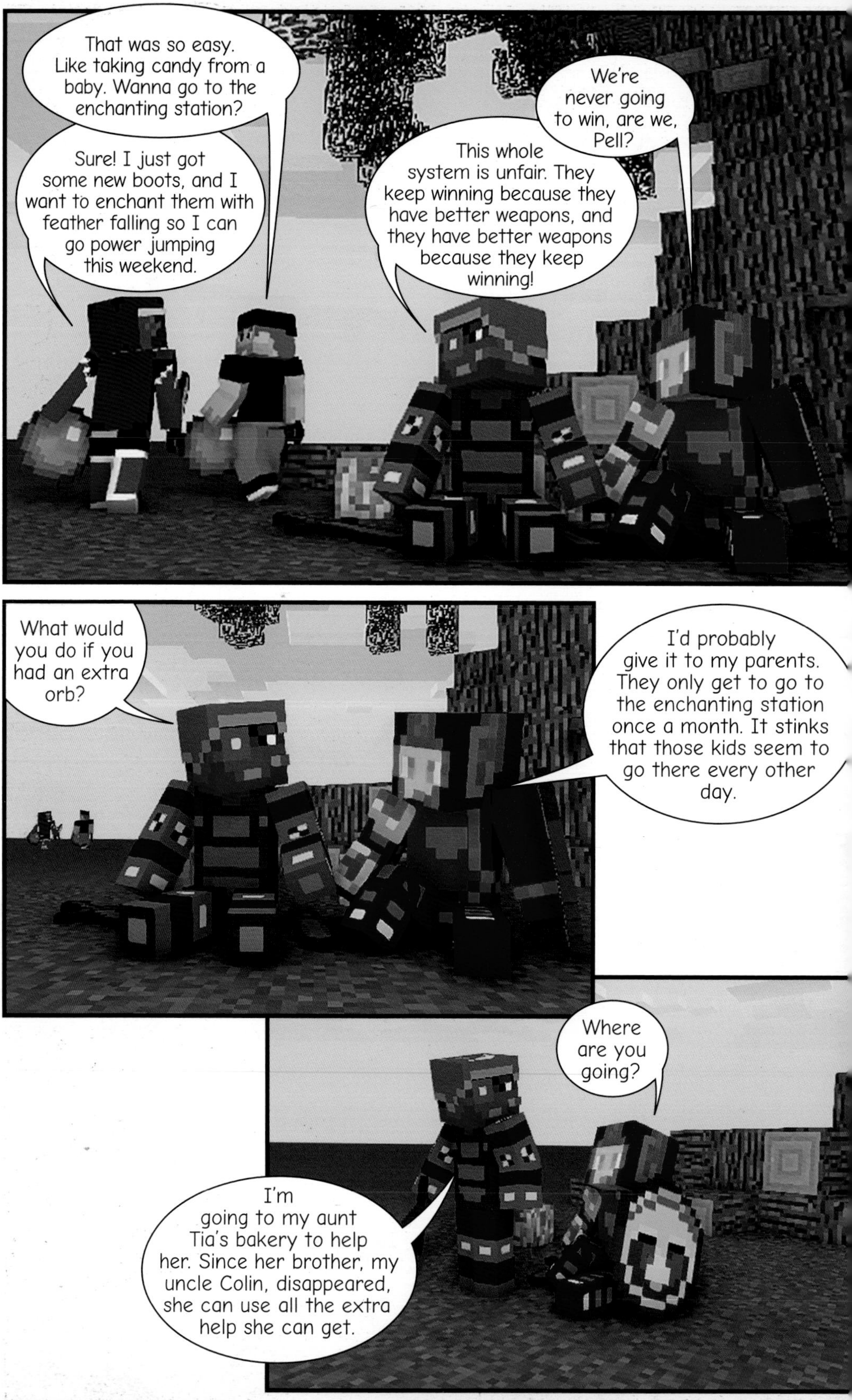
That was so easy. Like taking candy from a baby. Wanna go to the enchanting station?
Sure! I just got some new boots, and I want to enchant them with feather falling so I can go power jumping this weekend.
This whole system is unfair. They keep winning because they have better weapons, and they have better weapons because they keep winning!
We're never going to win, are we, Pell?
What would you do if you had an extra orb?
I'd probably give it to my parents. They only get to go to the enchanting station once a month. It stinks that those kids seem to go there every other day.
Where are you going?
I'm going to my aunt Tia's bakery to help her. Since her brother, my uncle Colin, disappeared, she can use all the extra help she can get.

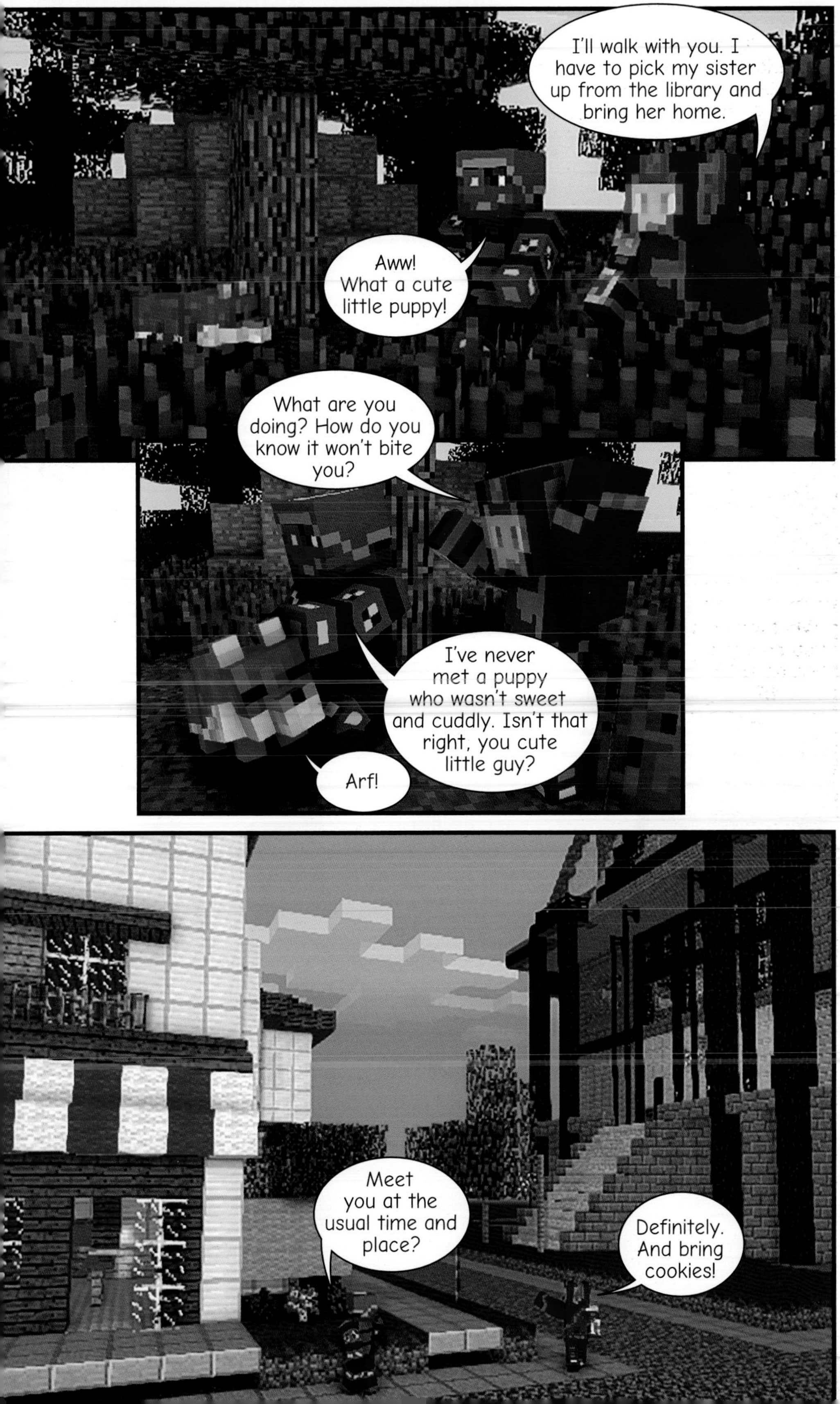
I'll walk with you. I have to pick my sister up from the library and bring her home.
Aww! What a cute little puppy!
What are you doing? How do you know it won't bite you?
I've never met a puppy who wasn't sweet and cuddly. Isn't that right, you cute little guy?
Arf!
Meet you at the usual time and place?
Definitely. And bring cookies!

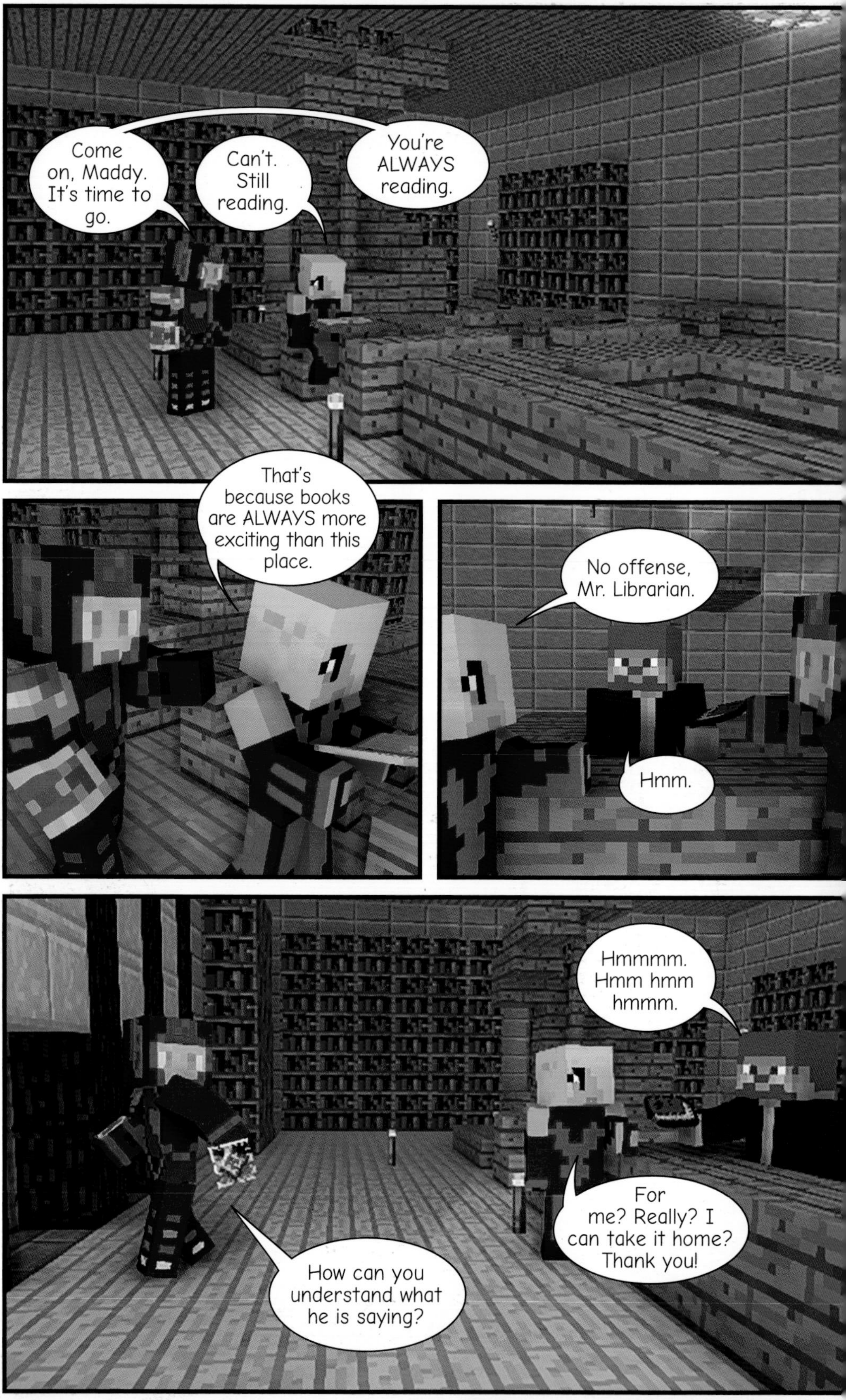
Come on, Maddy. It's time to go.
Can't. Still reading.
You're ALWAYS reading.
That's because books are ALWAYS more exciting than this place.
No offense, Mr. Librarian.
Hmm.
Hmmmm. Hmm hmm hmmm.
For me? Really? I can take it home? Thank you!
How can you understand what he is saying?

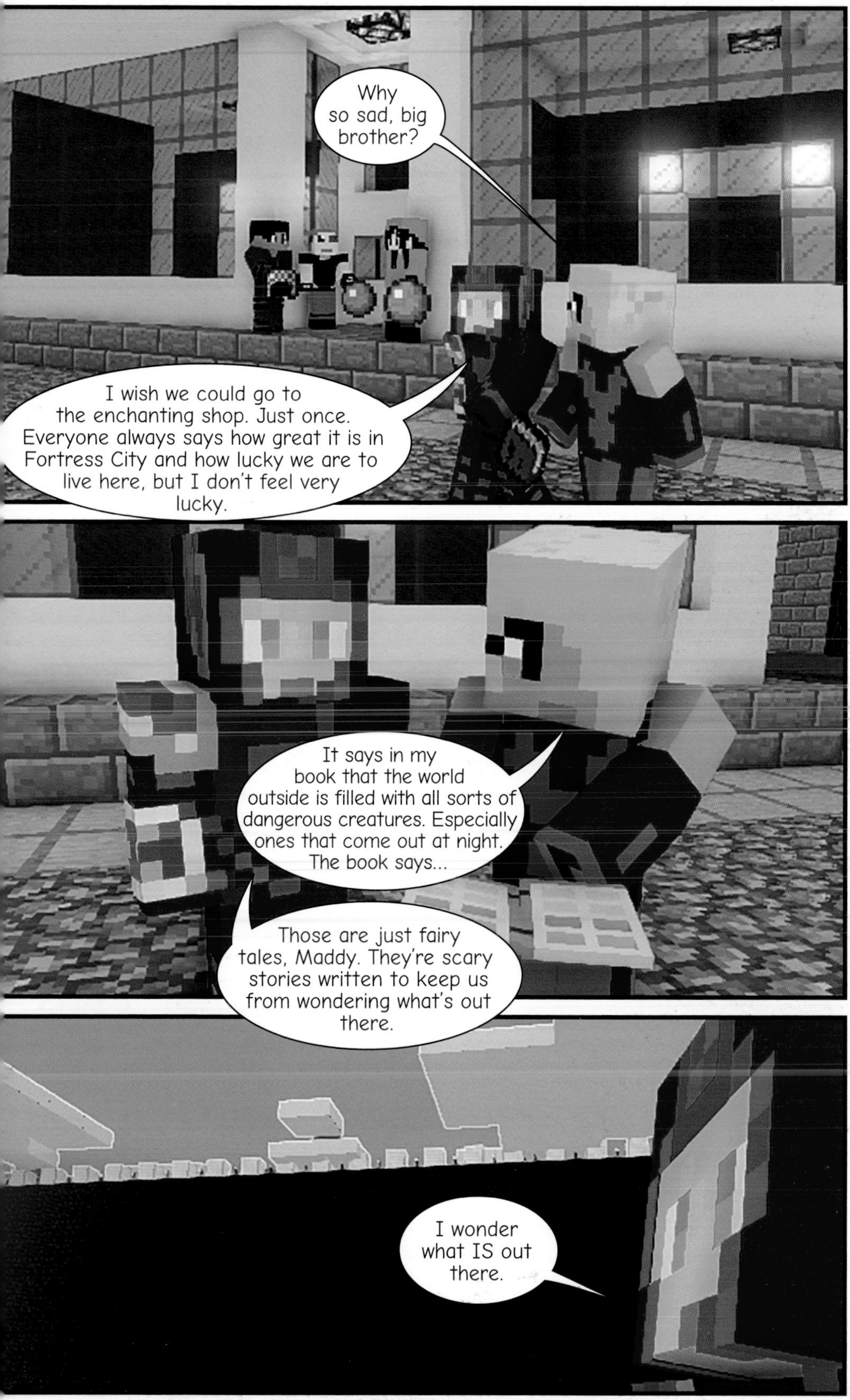
Why so sad, big brother?
I wish we could go to the enchanting shop. Just once. Everyone always says how great it is in Fortress City and how lucky we are to live here, but I don't feel very lucky.
It says in my book that the world outside is filled with all sorts of dangerous creatures. Especially ones that come out at night. The book says...
Those are just fairy tales, Maddy. They're scary stories written to keep us from wondering what's out there.
I wonder what IS out there.

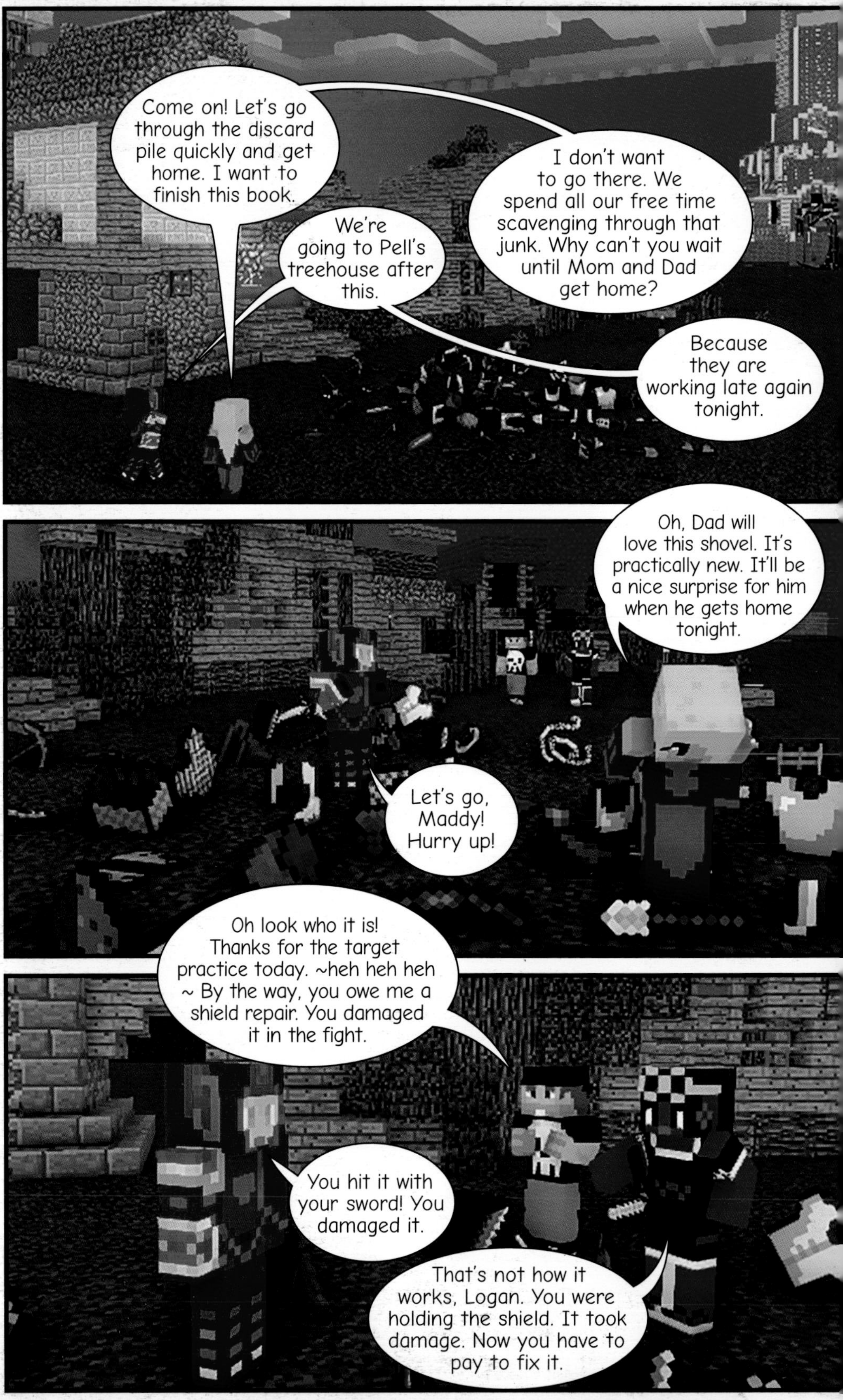
Come on! Let's go through the discard pile quickly and get home. I want to finish this book.
I don't want to go there. We spend all our free time scavenging through that junk. Why can't you wait until Mom and Dad get home?
We're going to Pell's treehouse after this.
Because they are working late again tonight.
Oh, Dad will love this shovel. It's practically new. It'll be a nice surprise for him when he gets home tonight.
Let's go, Maddy! Hurry up!
Oh look who it is! Thanks for the target practice today. ~heh heh heh ~ By the way, you owe me a shield repair. You damaged it in the fight.
You hit it with your sword! You damaged it.
That's not how it works, Logan. You were holding the shield. It took damage. Now you have to pay to fix it.

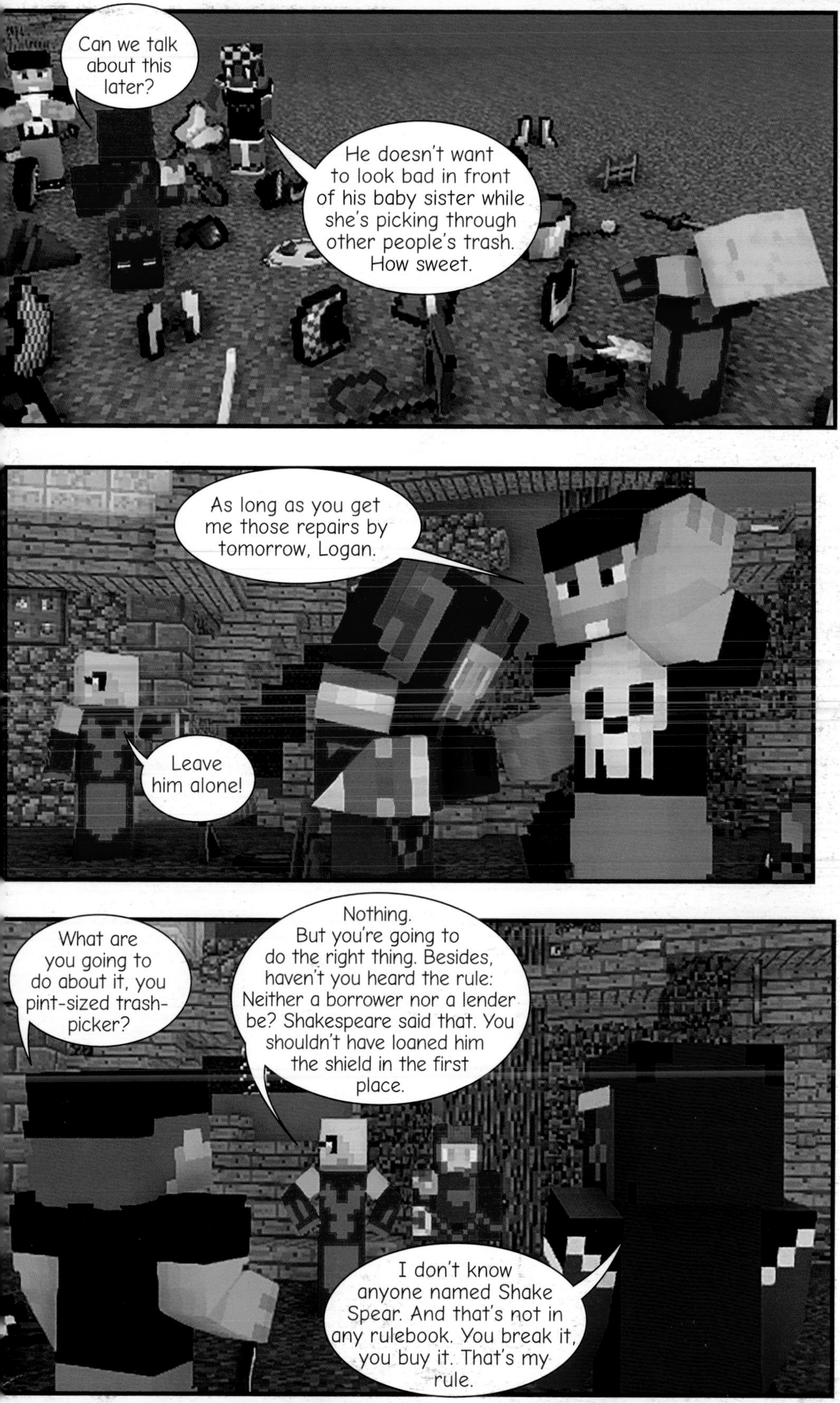
Can we talk about this later?
He doesn't want to look bad in front of his baby sister while she's picking through other people's trash. How sweet.
As long as you get me those repairs by tomorrow, Logan.
Leave him alone!
What are you going to do about it, you pint-sized trash-picker?
Nothing. But you're going to do the right thing. Besides, haven't you heard the rule: Neither a borrower nor a lender be? Shakespeare said that. You shouldn't have loaned him the shield in the first place.
I don't know anyone named Shake Spear. And that's not in any rulebook. You break it, you buy it. That's my rule.

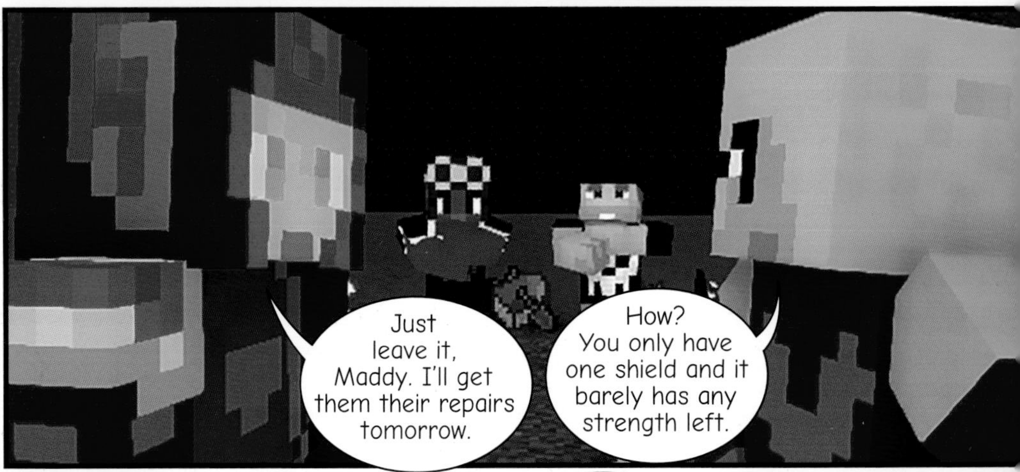
Just leave it, Maddy. I'll get them their repairs tomorrow.
How? You only have one shield and it barely has any strength left.

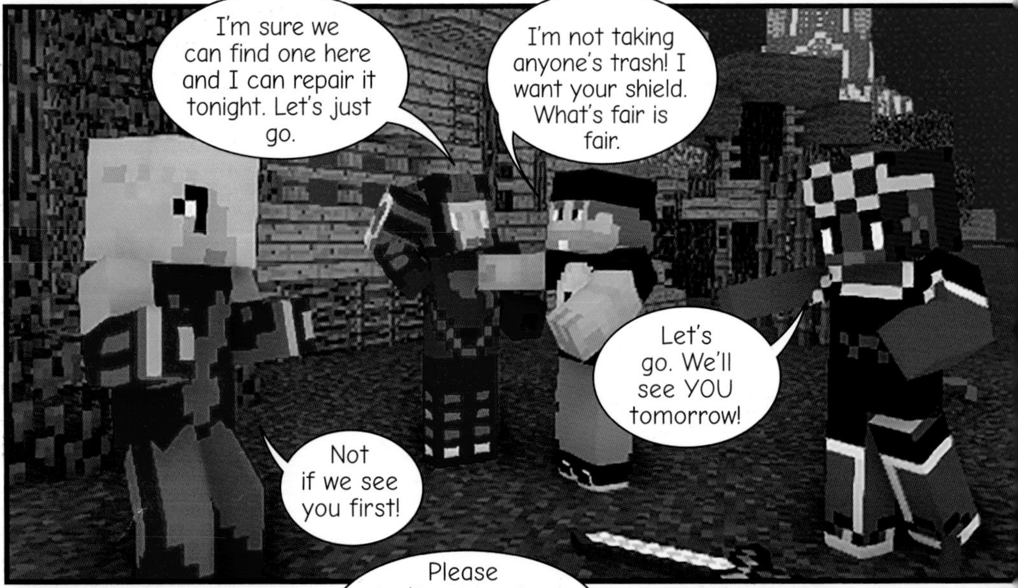
I'm sure we can find one here and I can repair it tonight. Let's just go.
I'm not taking anyone's trash! I want your shield. What's fair is fair.
Let's go. We'll see YOU tomorrow!
Not if we see you first!

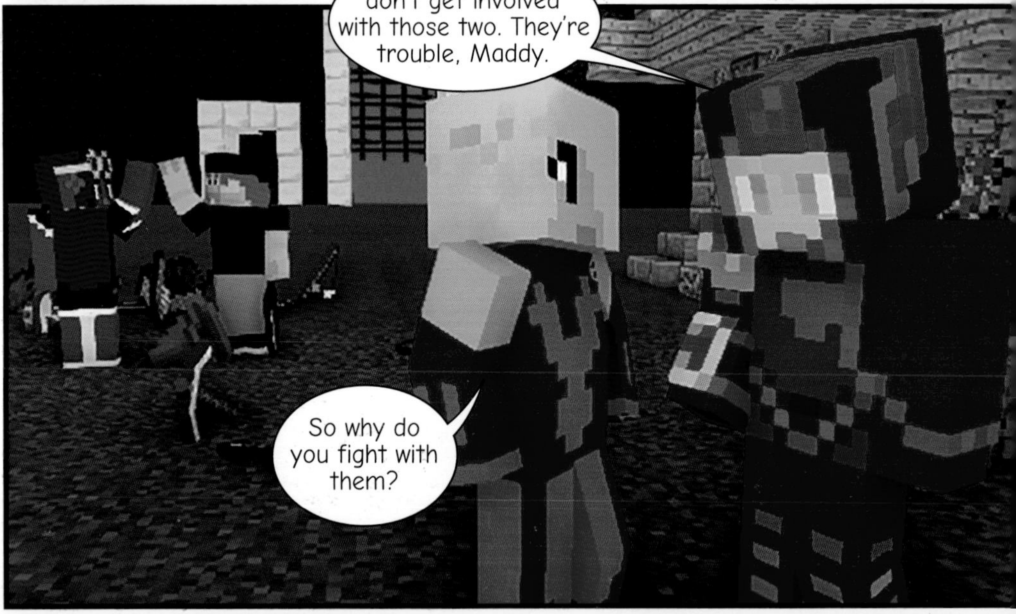
Please don't get involved with those two. They're trouble, Maddy.
So why do you fight with them?

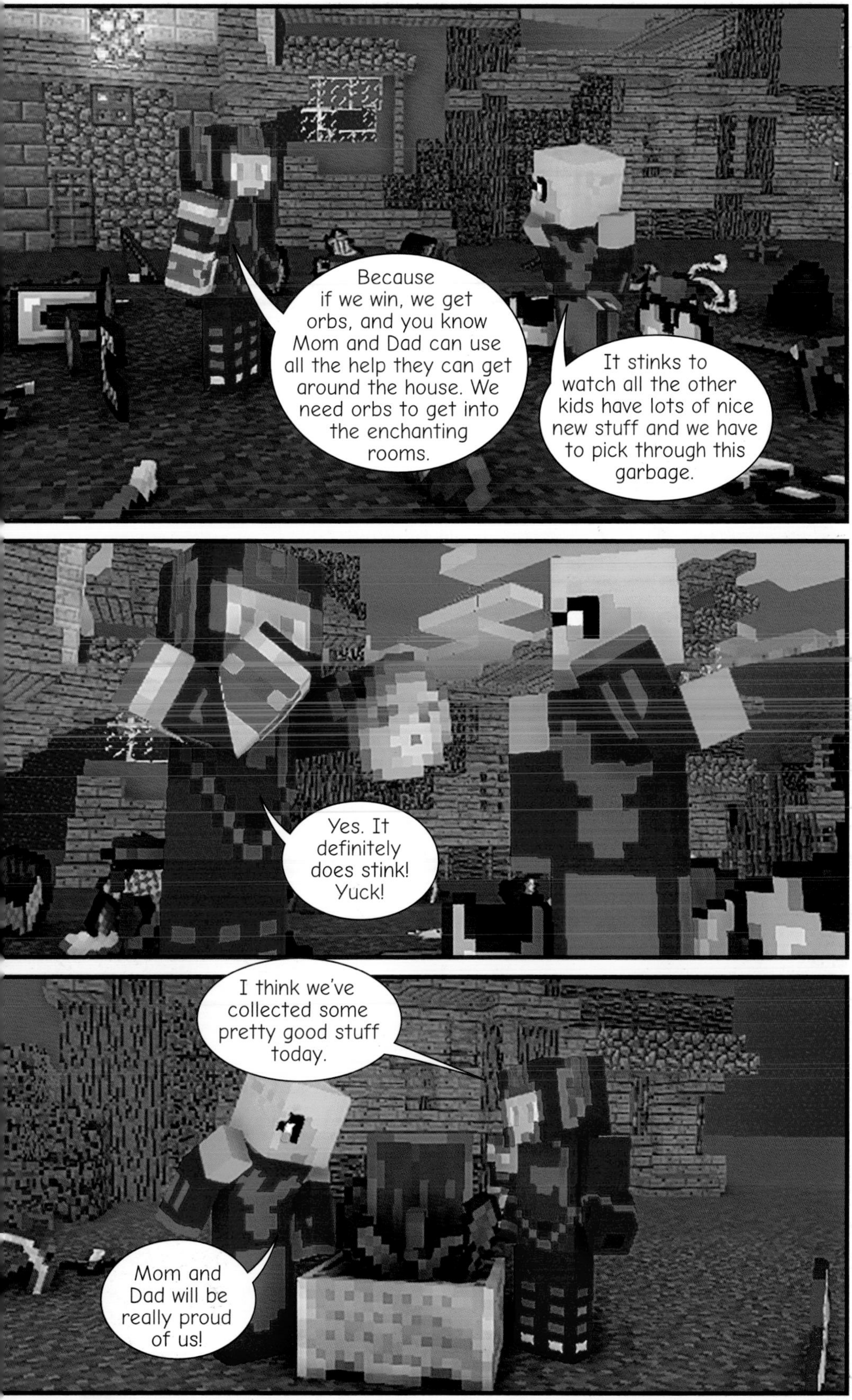
Because if we win, we get orbs, and you know Mom and Dad can use all the help they can get around the house. We need orbs to get into the enchanting rooms.
It stinks to watch all the other kids have lots of nice new stuff and we have to pick through this garbage.
Yes. It definitely does stink! Yuck!
I think we've collected some pretty good stuff today.
Mom and Dad will be really proud of us!

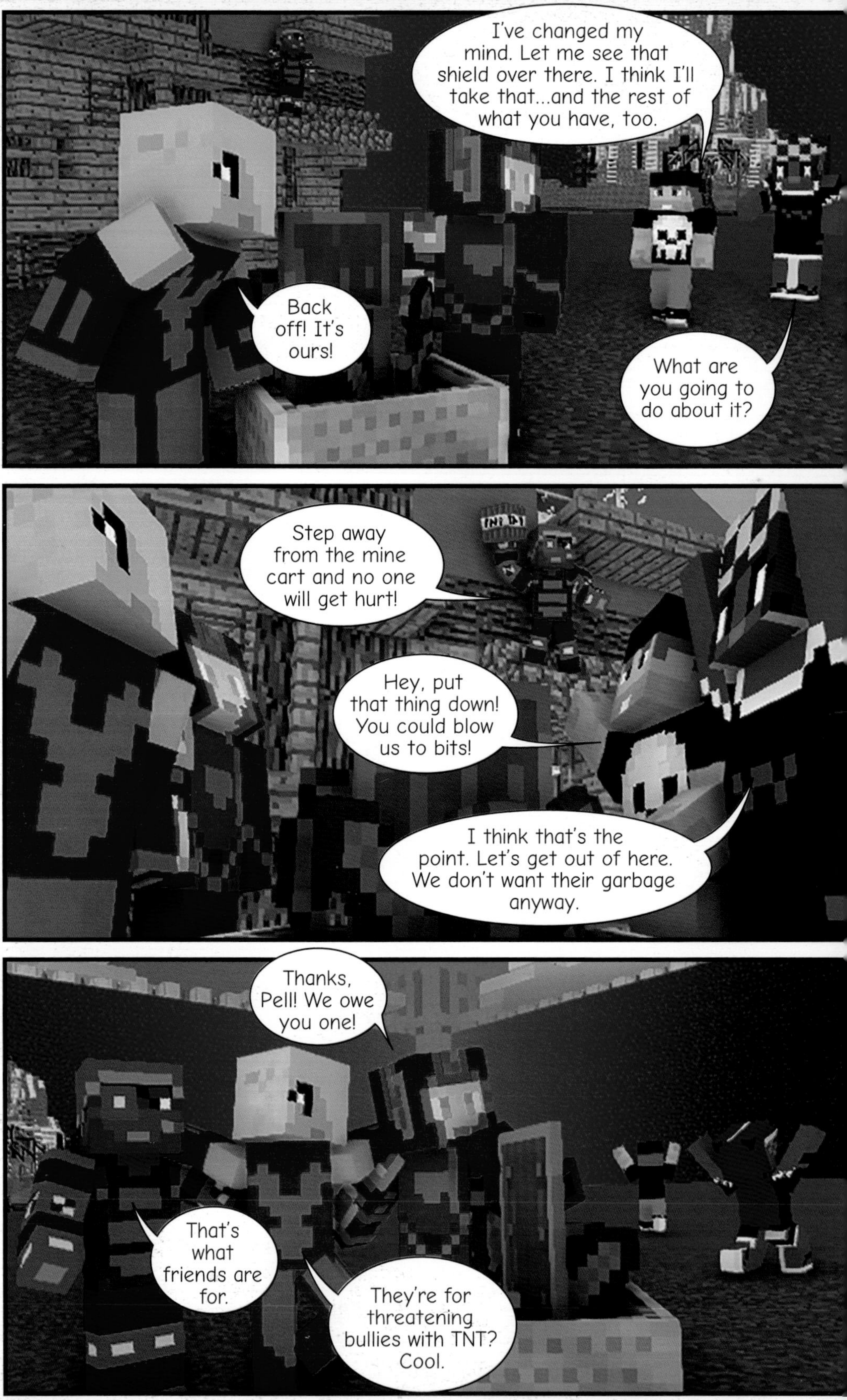
I've changed my mind. Let me see that shield over there. I think I'll take that...and the rest of what you have, too.
Back off! It's ours!
What are you going to do about it?
Step away from the mine cart and no one will get hurt!
Hey, put that thing down! You could blow us to bits!
I think that's the point. Let's get out of here. We don't want their garbage anyway.
Thanks, Pell! We owe you one!
That's what friends are for.
They're for threatening bullies with TNT? Cool.

CHAPTER 2

TEN THINGS WE HATE ABOUT FORTRESS CITY

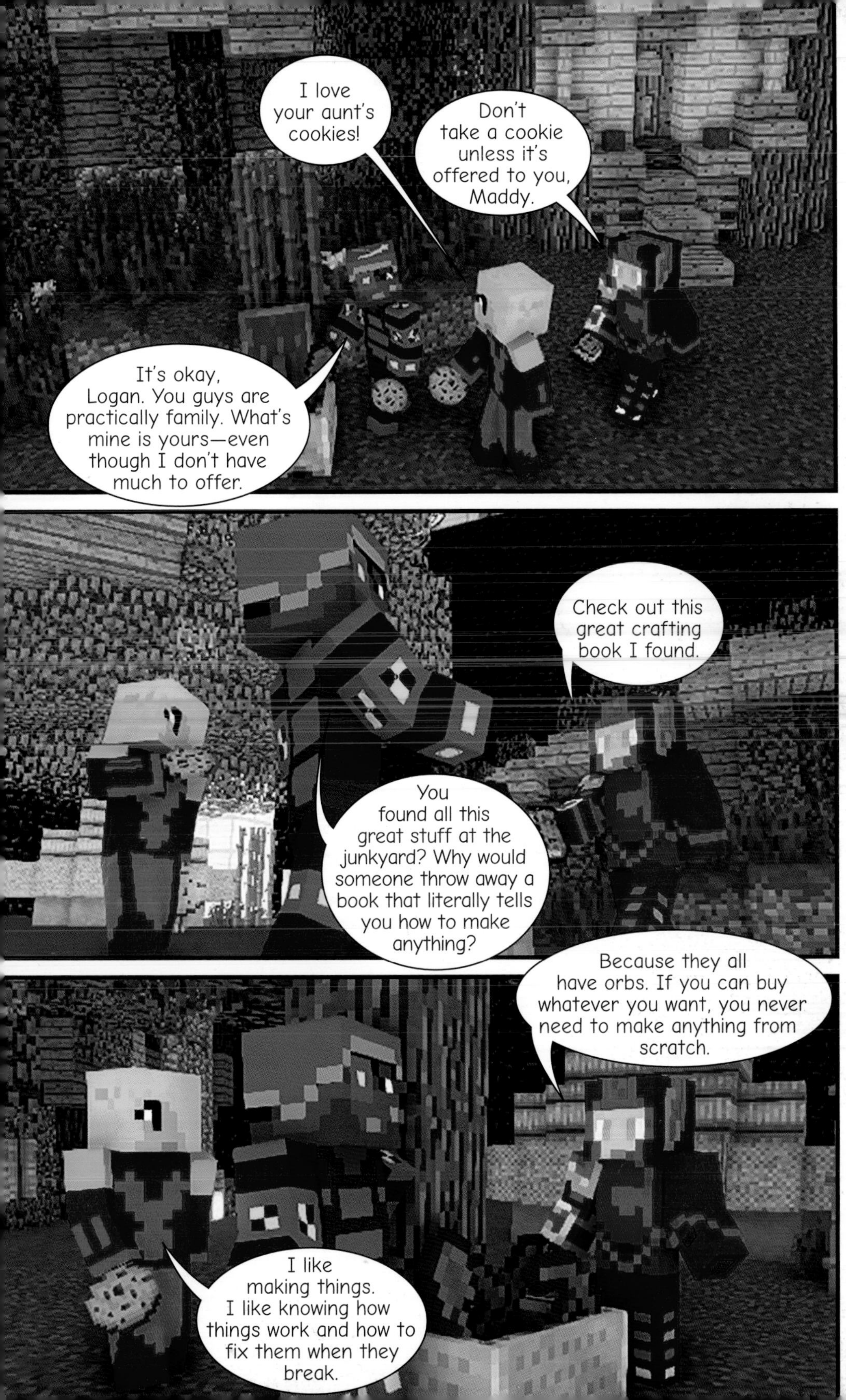
I love your aunt's cookies!
Don't take a cookie unless it's offered to you, Maddy.
It's okay, Logan. You guys are practically family. What's mine is yours—even though I don't have much to offer.
Check out this great crafting book I found.
You found all this great stuff at the junkyard? Why would someone throw away a book that literally tells you how to make anything?
Because they all have orbs. If you can buy whatever you want, you never need to make anything from scratch.
I like making things. I like knowing how things work and how to fix them when they break.

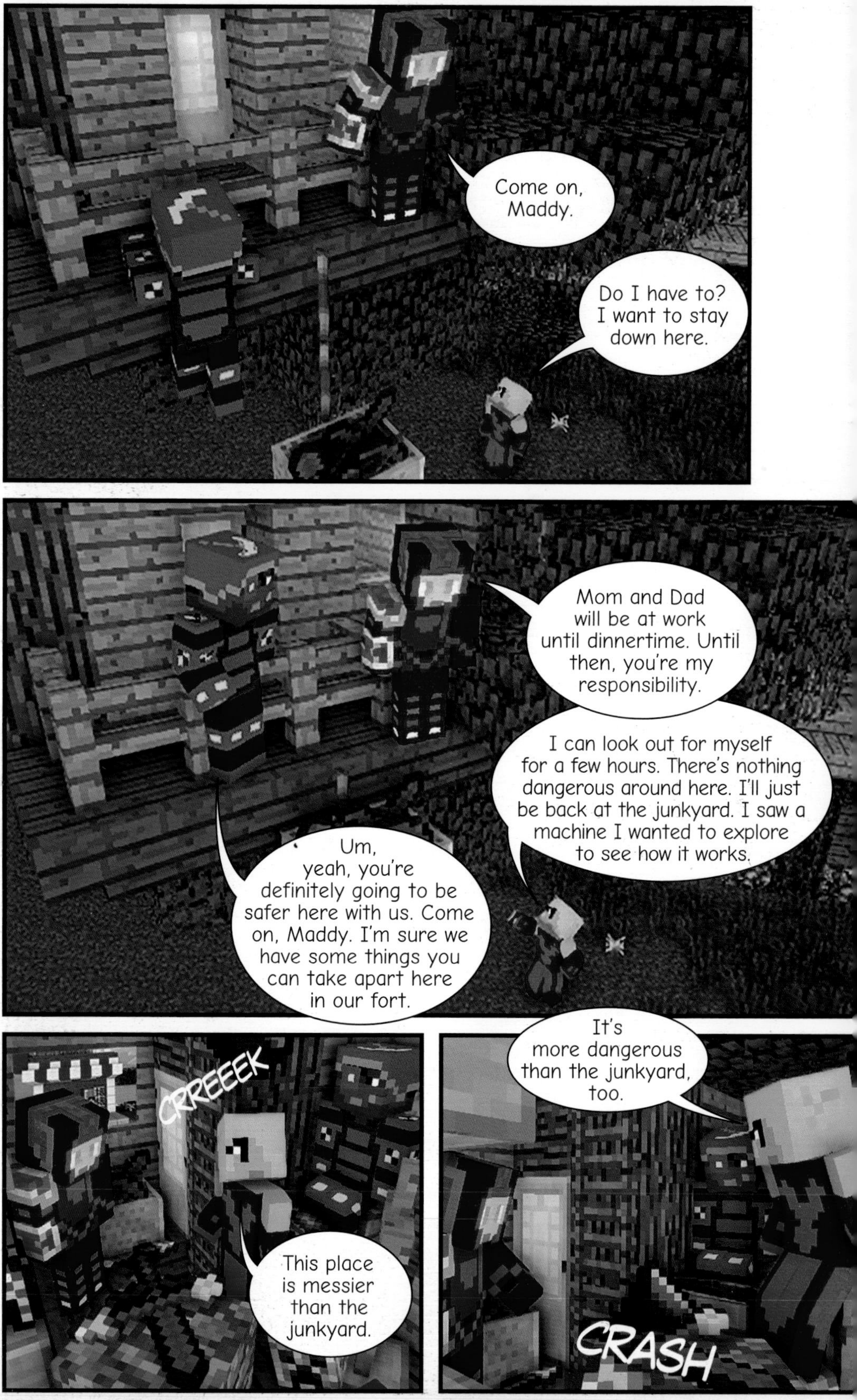
Come on, Maddy.
Do I have to? I want to stay down here.
Mom and Dad will be at work until dinnertime. Until then, you're my responsibility.
I can look out for myself for a few hours. There's nothing dangerous around here. I'll just be back at the junkyard. I saw a machine I wanted to explore to see how it works.
Um, yeah, you're definitely going to be safer here with us. Come on, Maddy. I'm sure we have some things you can take apart here in our fort.
CRREEEK
This place is messier than the junkyard.
It's more dangerous than the junkyard, too.
CRASH

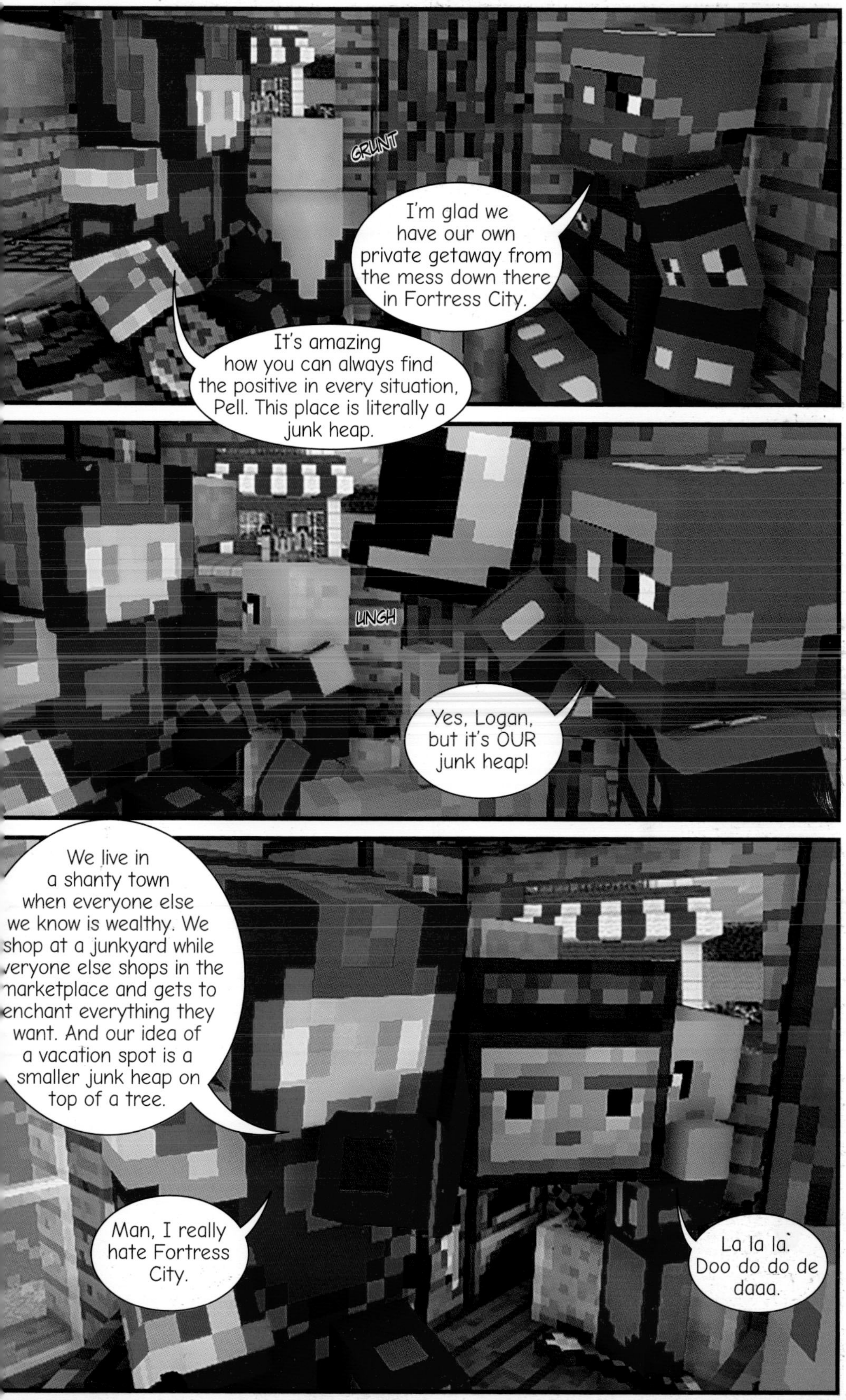
GRUNT
I'm glad we have our own private getaway from the mess down there in Fortress City.
It's amazing how you can always find the positive in every situation, Pell. This place is literally a junk heap.
UNGH
Yes, Logan, but it's OUR junk heap!
We live in a shanty town when everyone else we know is wealthy. We shop at a junkyard while everyone else shops in the marketplace and gets to enchant everything they want. And our idea of a vacation spot is a smaller junk heap on top of a tree.
Man, I really hate Fortress City.
La la la. Doo do do de daaa.

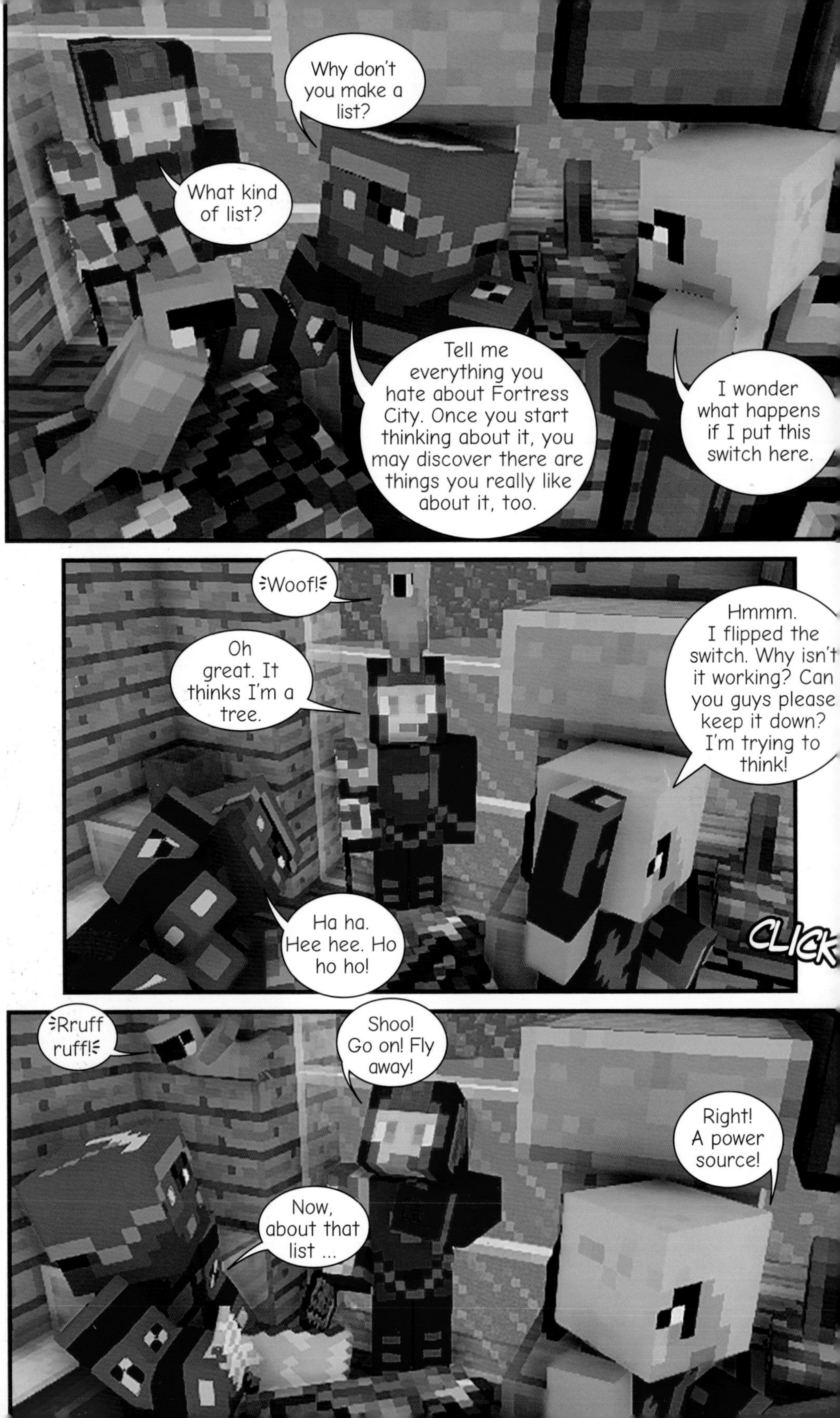
Why don't you make a list?
What kind of list?
Tell me everything you hate about Fortress City. Once you start thinking about it, you may discover there are things you really like about it, too.
I wonder what happens if I put this switch here.
Woof!
Oh great. It thinks I'm a tree.
Hmmm. I flipped the switch. Why isn't it working? Can you guys please keep it down? I'm trying to think!
Ha ha. Hee hee. Ho ho ho!
CLICK
Rruff ruff!
Shoo! Go on! Fly away!
Right! A power source!
Now, about that list ...

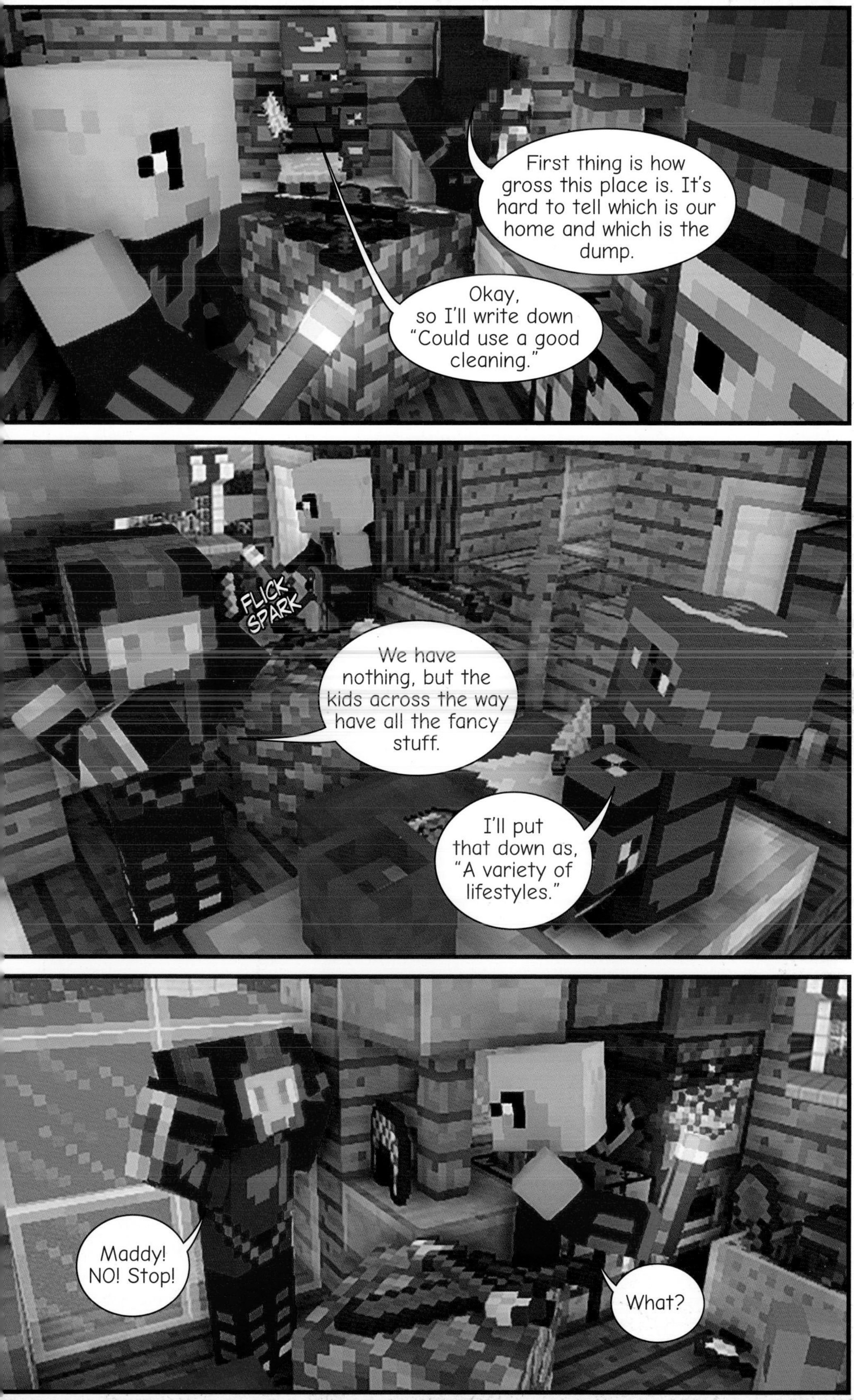
First thing is how gross this place is. It's hard to tell which is our home and which is the dump.
Okay, so I'll write down "Could use a good cleaning."
FLICK SPARK
We have nothing, but the kids across the way have all the fancy stuff.
I'll put that down as, "A variety of lifestyles."
Maddy! NO! Stop!
What?

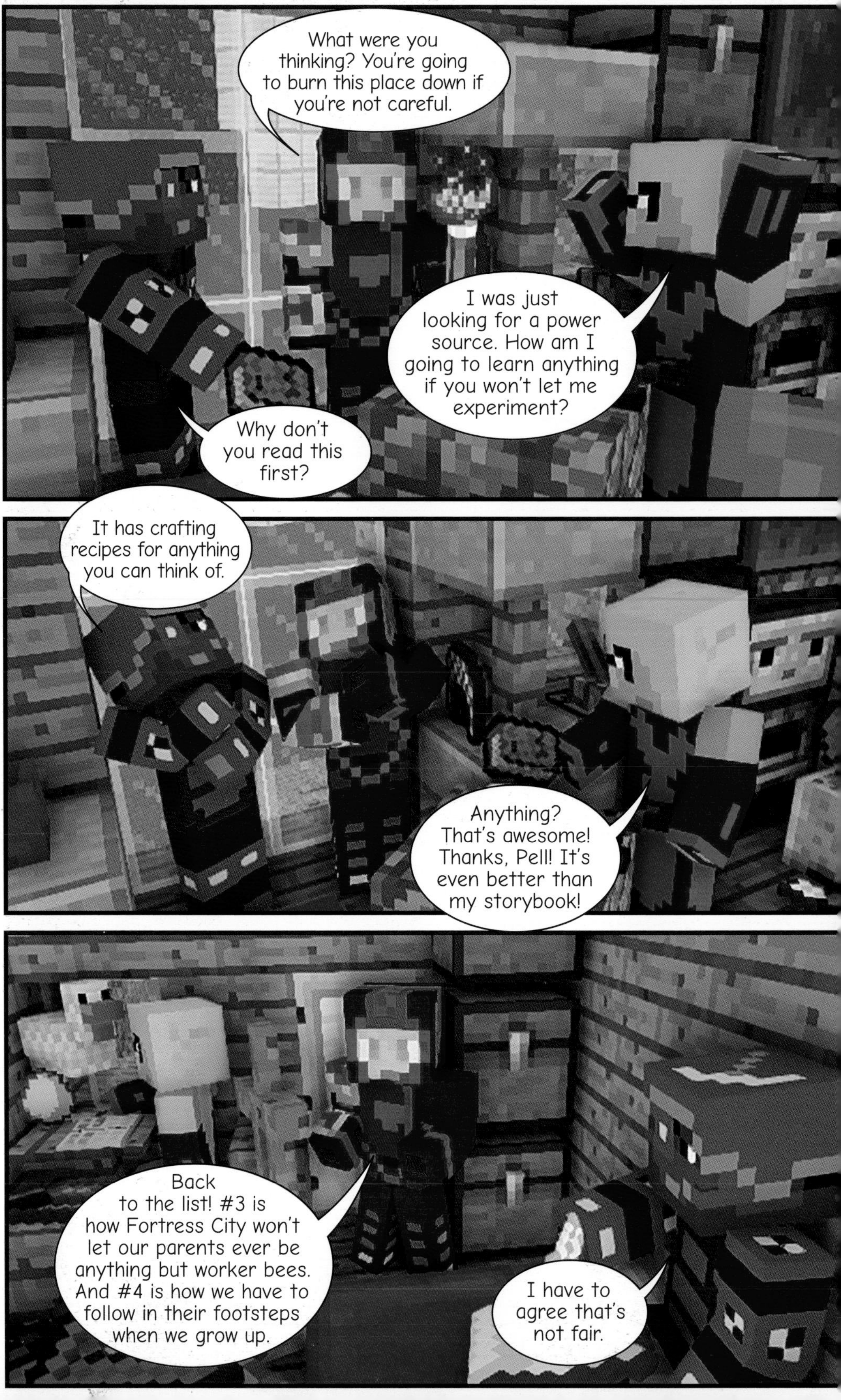
What were you thinking? You're going to burn this place down if you're not careful.
I was just looking for a power source. How am I going to learn anything if you won't let me experiment?
Why don't you read this first?
It has crafting recipes for anything you can think of.
Anything? That's awesome! Thanks, Pell! It's even better than my storybook!
Back to the list! #3 is how Fortress City won't let our parents ever be anything but worker bees. And #4 is how we have to follow in their footsteps when we grow up.
I have to agree that's not fair.

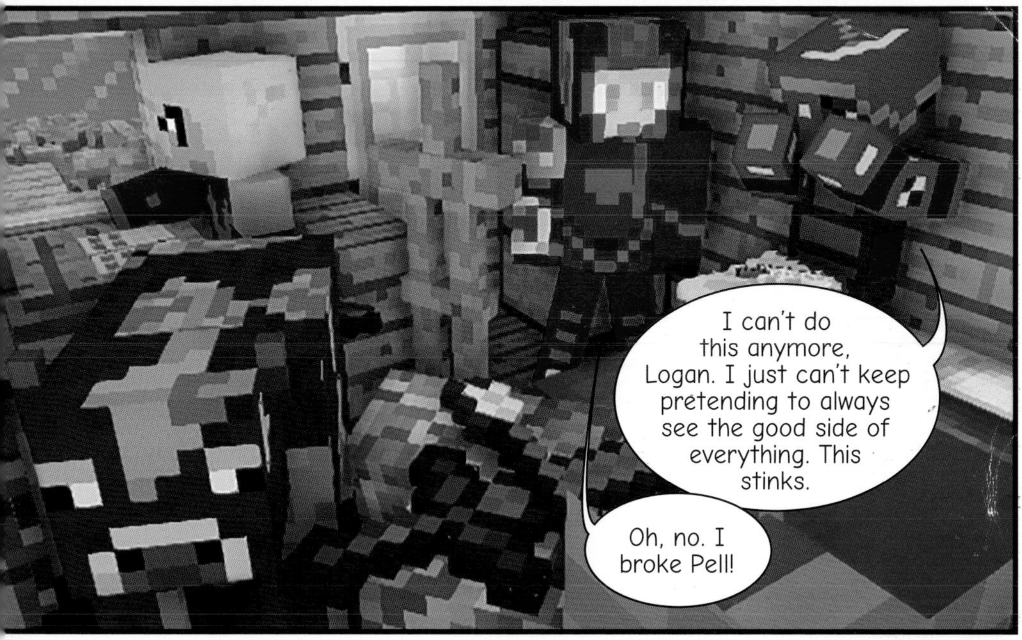
I can't do this anymore, Logan. I just can't keep pretending to always see the good side of everything. This stinks.
Oh, no. I broke Pell!

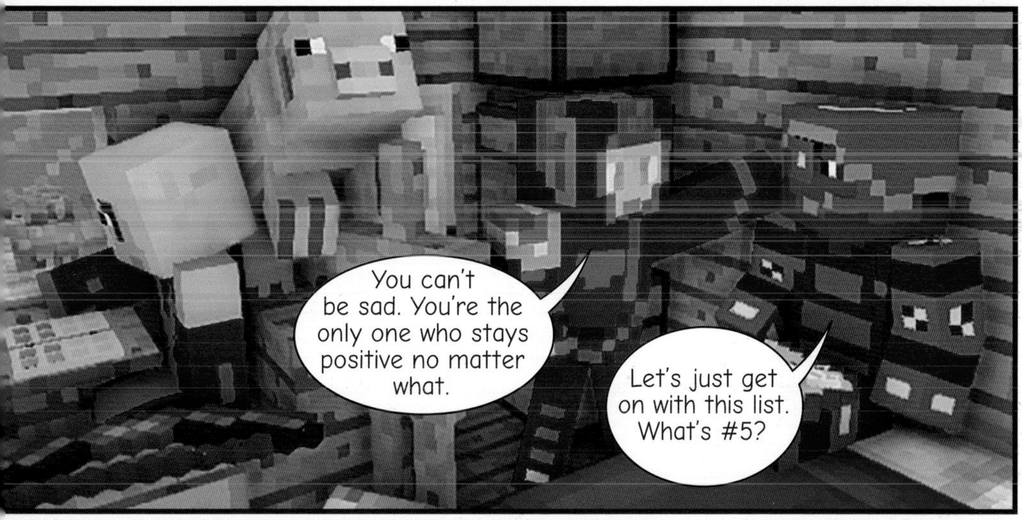
You can't be sad. You're the only one who stays positive no matter what.
Let's just get on with this list. What's #5?

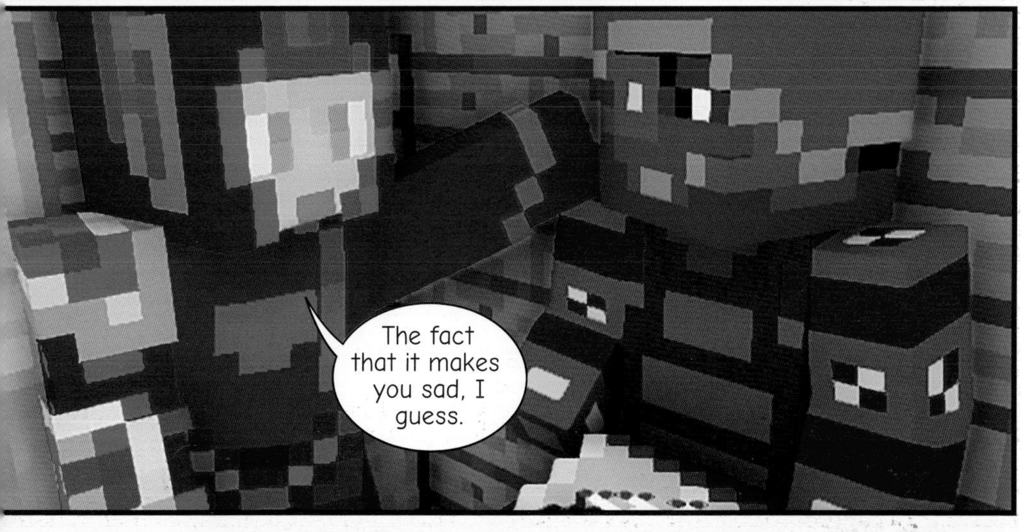
The fact that it makes you sad, I guess.

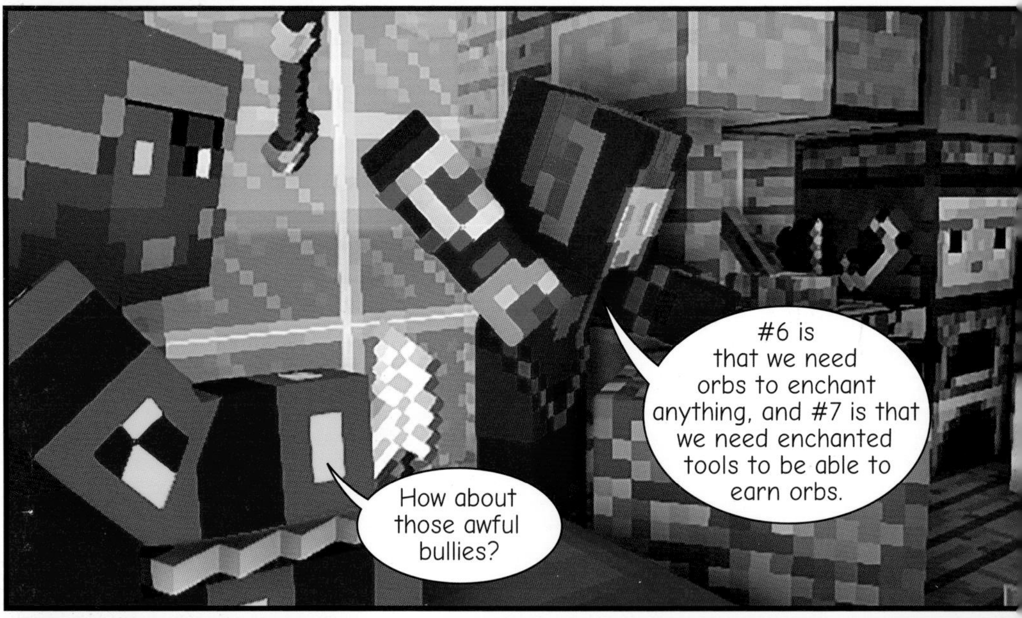
#6 is that we need orbs to enchant anything, and #7 is that we need enchanted tools to be able to earn orbs.
How about those awful bullies?

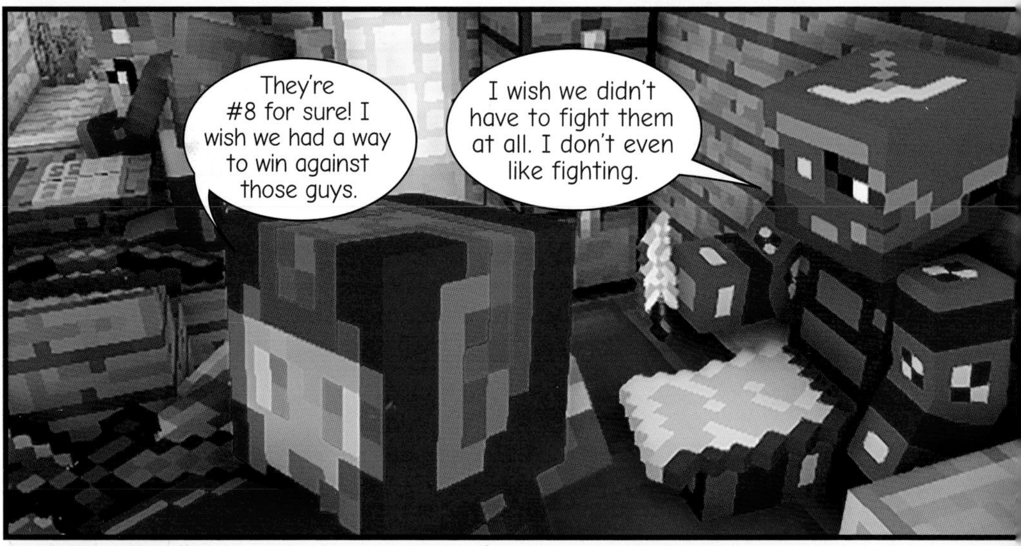
They're #8 for sure! I wish we had a way to win against those guys.
I wish we didn't have to fight them at all. I don't even like fighting.

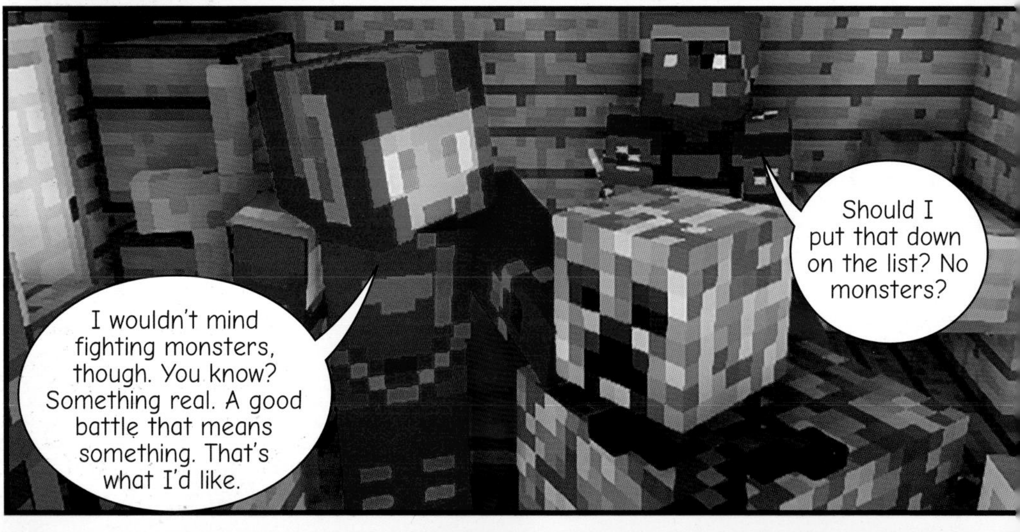
Should I put that down on the list? No monsters?
I wouldn't mind fighting monsters, though. You know? Something real. A good battle that means something. That's what I'd like.

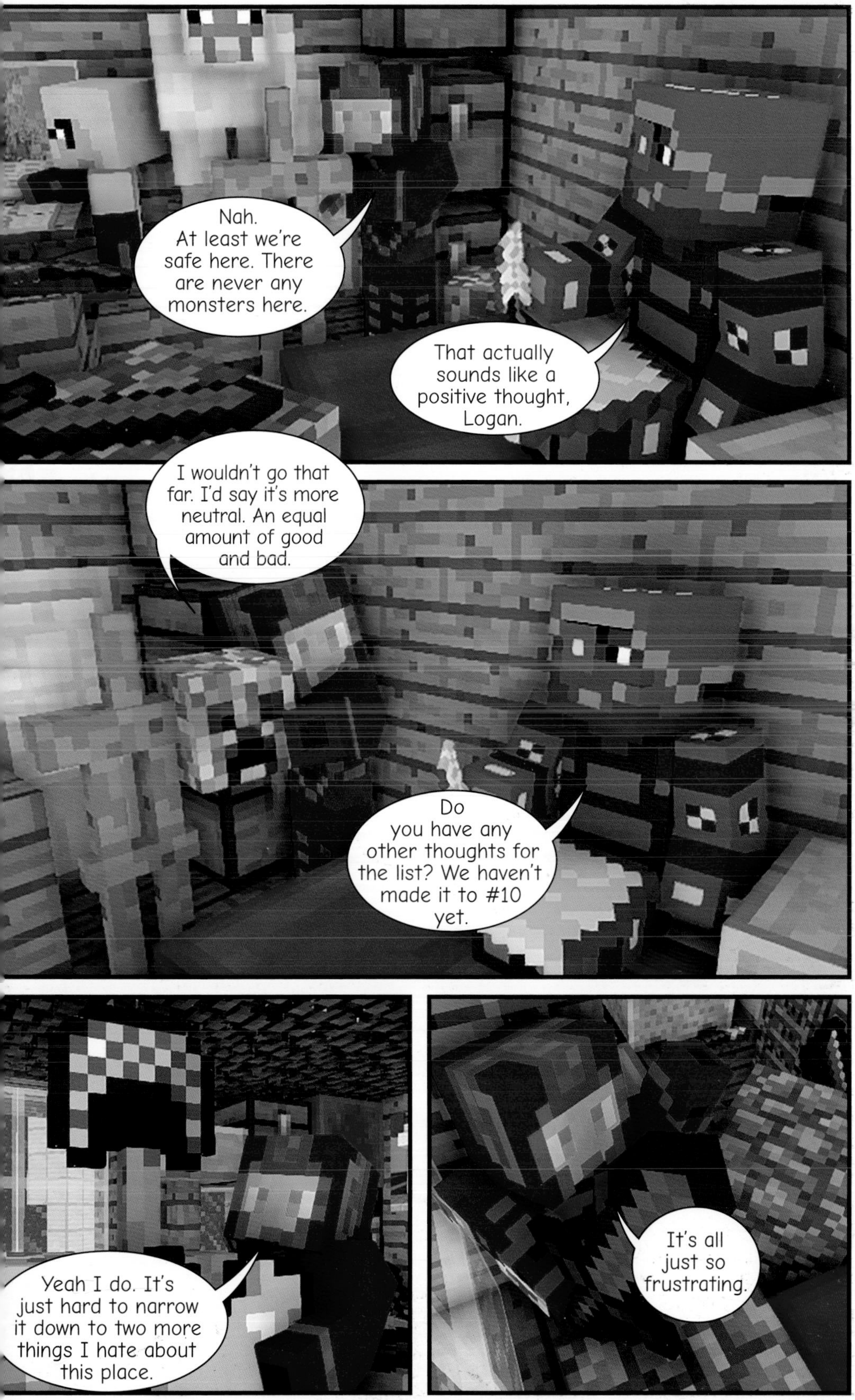
Nah. At least we're safe here. There are never any monsters here.
That actually sounds like a positive thought, Logan.
I wouldn't go that far. I'd say it's more neutral. An equal amount of good and bad.
Do you have any other thoughts for the list? We haven't made it to #10 yet.
Yeah I do. It's just hard to narrow it down to two more things I hate about this place.
It's all just so frustrating.

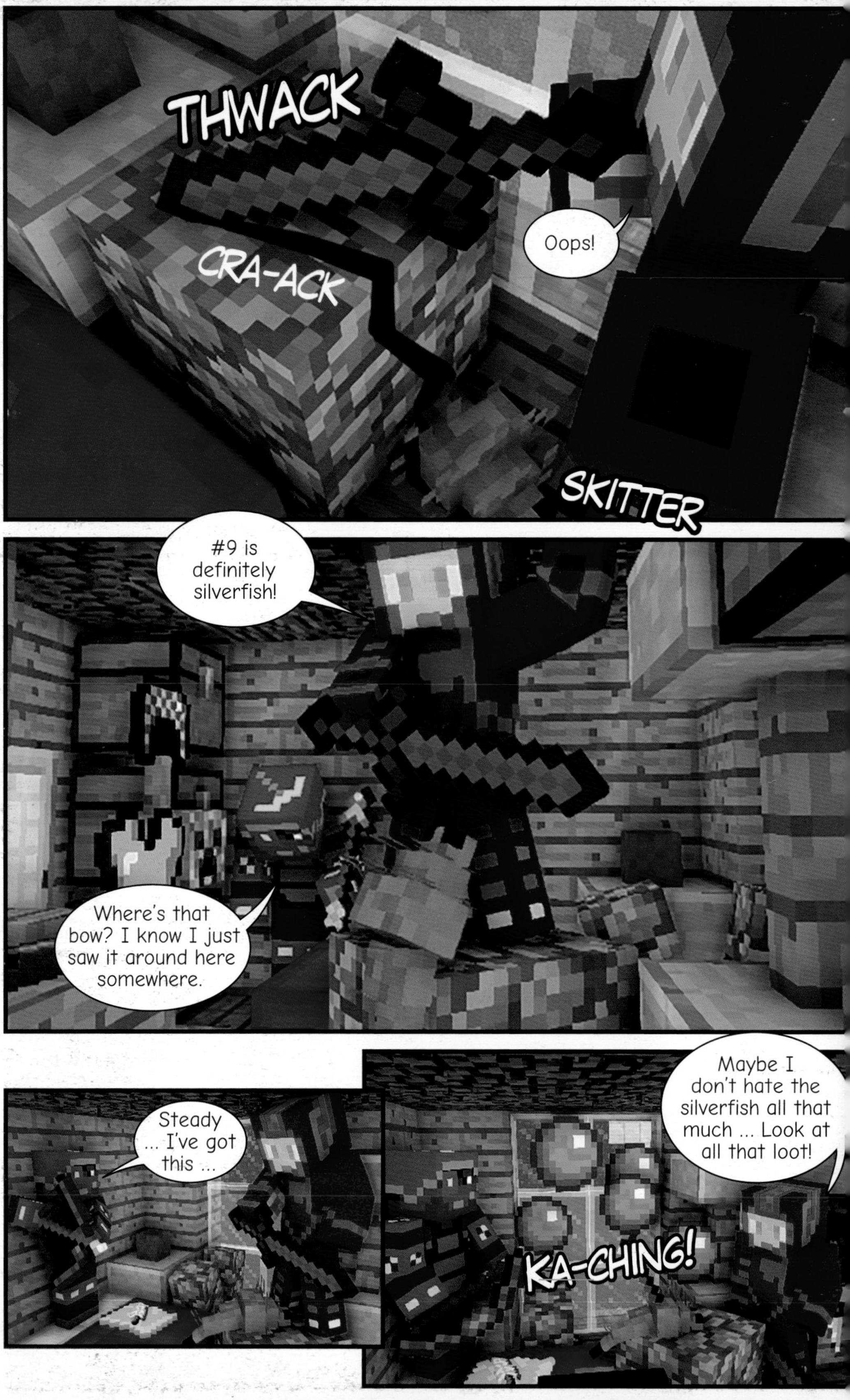
THWACK
CRA-ACK
Oops!
SKITTER
#9 is definitely silverfish!
Where's that bow? I know I just saw it around here somewhere.
Steady ... I've got this ...
Maybe I don't hate the silverfish all that much ... Look at all that loot!
KA-CHING!

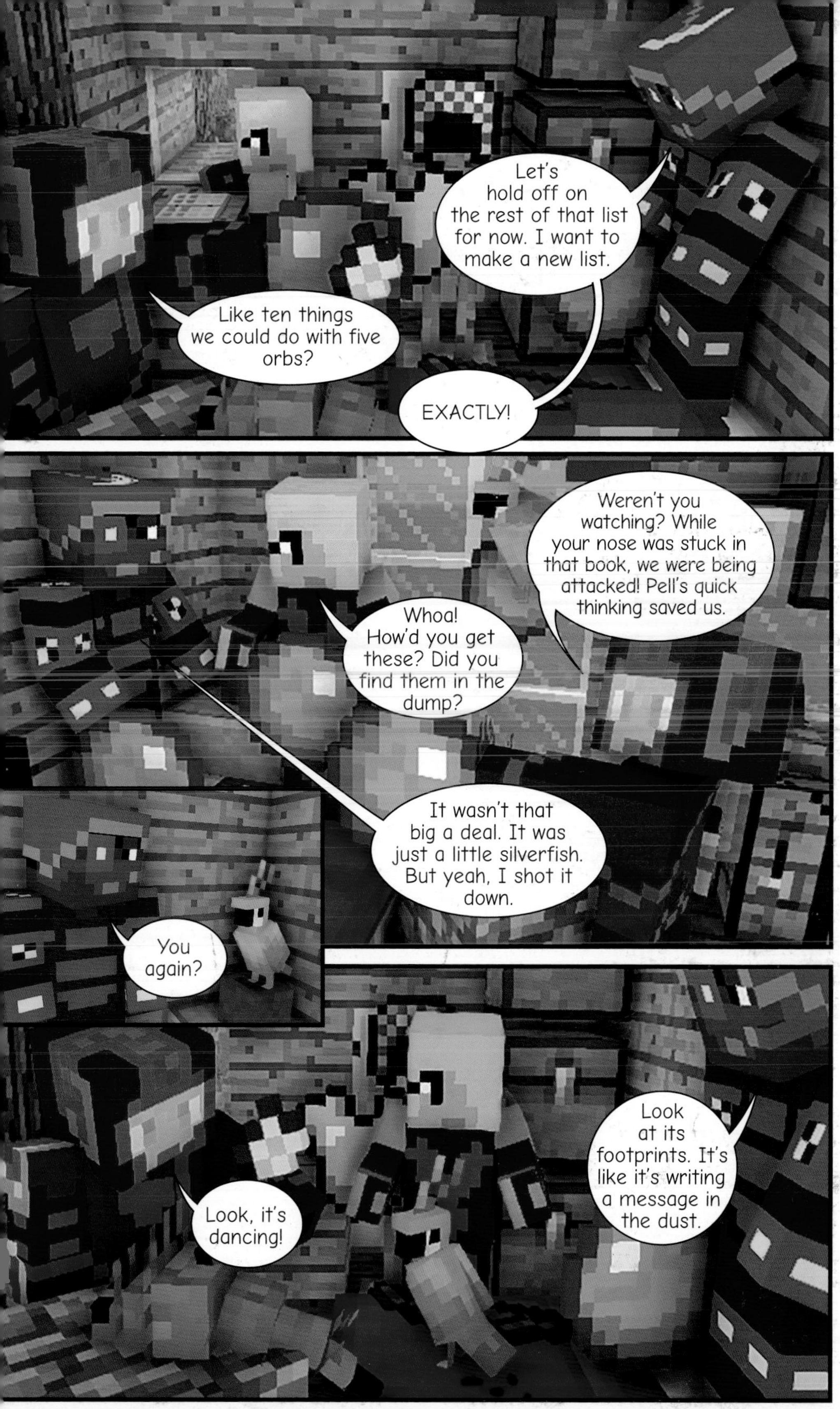
Let's hold off on the rest of that list for now. I want to make a new list.
Like ten things we could do with five orbs?
EXACTLY!
Whoa! How'd you get these? Did you find them in the dump?
Weren't you watching? While your nose was stuck in that book, we were being attacked! Pell's quick thinking saved us.
It wasn't that big a deal. It was just a little silverfish. But yeah, I shot it down.
You again?
Look, it's dancing!
Look at its footprints. It's like it's writing a message in the dust.

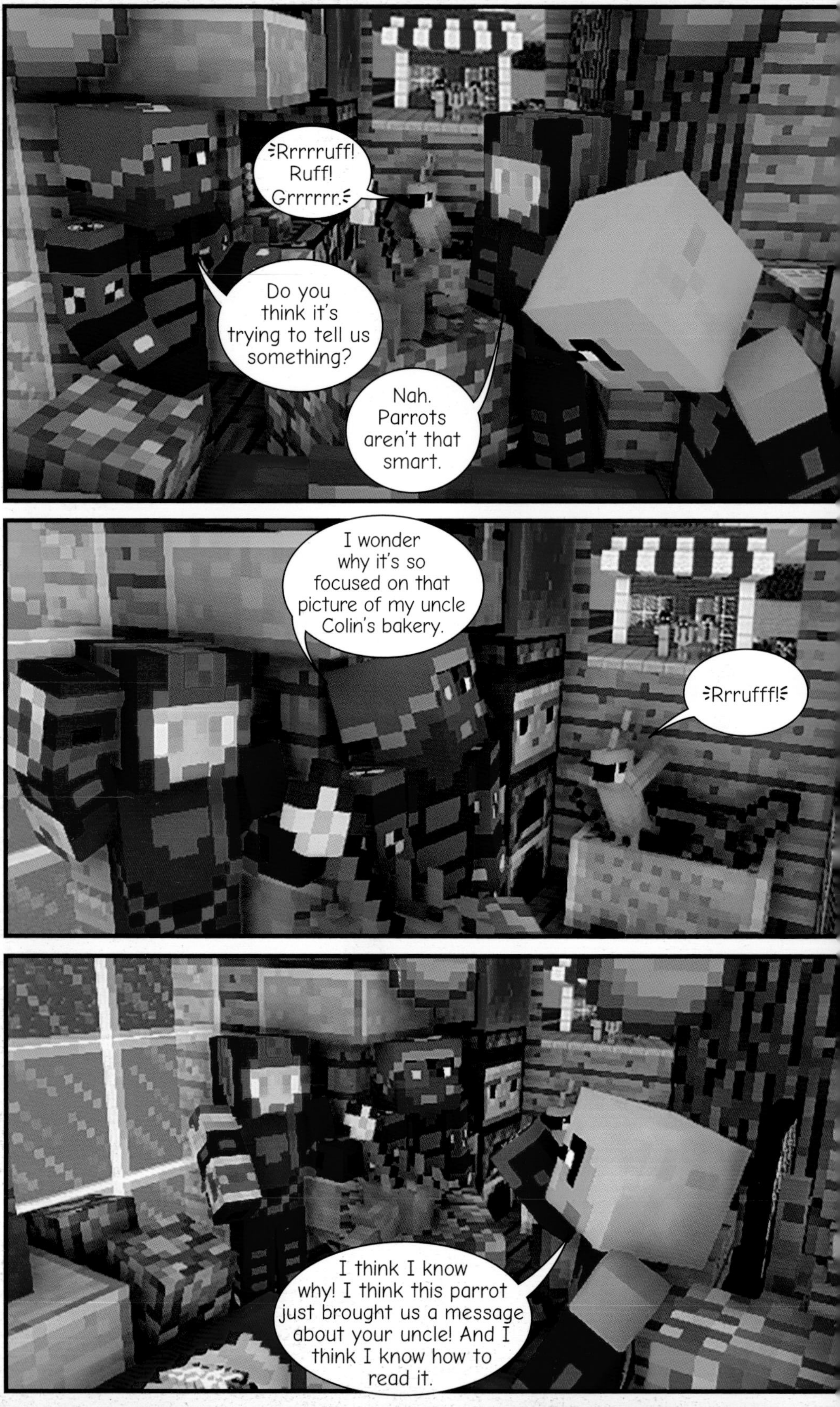
Rrrrruff! Ruff! Grrrrrr.
Do you think it's trying to tell us something?
Nah. Parrots aren't that smart.
I wonder why it's so focused on that picture of my uncle Colin's bakery.
Rrrufff!
I think I know why! I think this parrot just brought us a message about your uncle! And I think I know how to read it.

CHAPTER 3

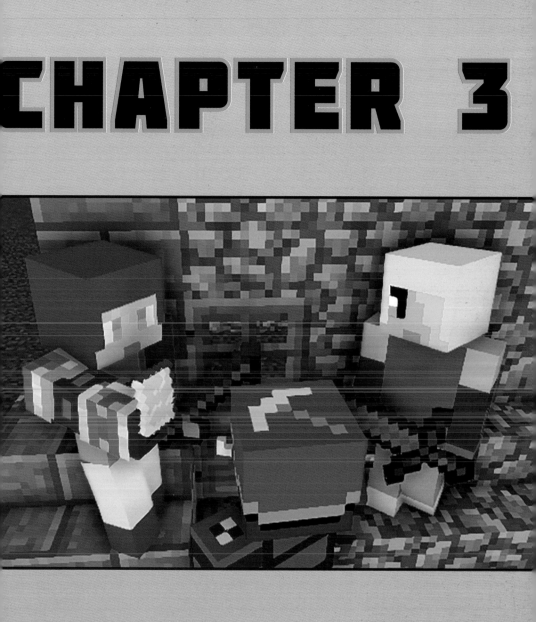

THE LETTER

It looks like coordinates for an address. 119.8—that's 119.8 degrees East. 67—that's how high it is, so it would be on the second floor or on a hill somewhere. And negative 95.599, which is 95.599 degrees north.
That doesn't help if we don't know where we are now. Or what it's the address for.
Here's a map of our town with coordinates. We just have to follow it to find the location.
What will we find when we get there? How will we know it's safe?
It depends on how much your trust your uncle Colin, Pell.
Whaaaat?
I think he's the one who sent the bird.
In that case, we'd better go check it out!

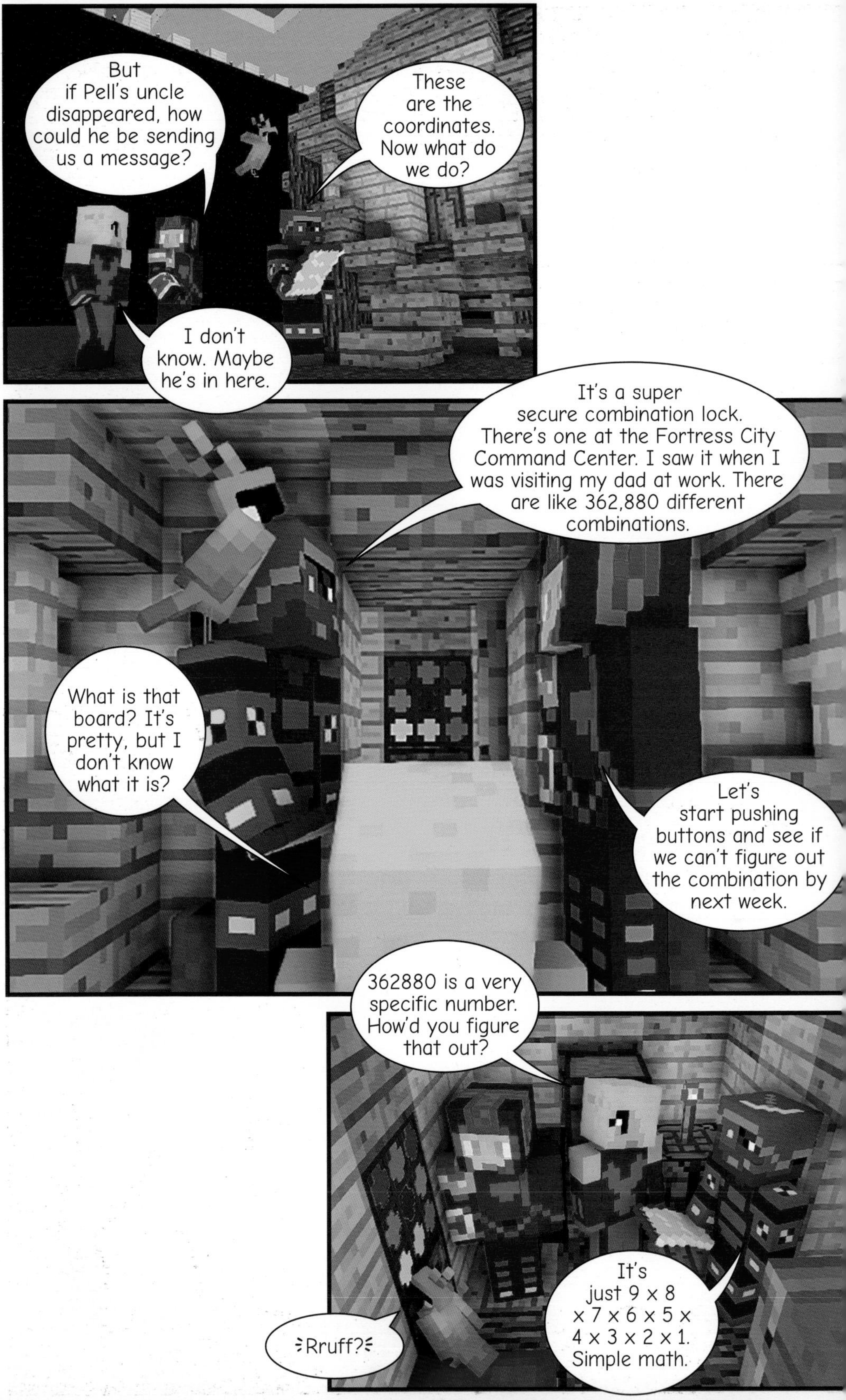
But if Pell's uncle disappeared, how could he be sending us a message?
These are the coordinates. Now what do we do?
I don't know. Maybe he's in here.
What is that board? It's pretty, but I don't know what it is?
It's a super secure combination lock. There's one at the Fortress City Command Center. I saw it when I was visiting my dad at work. There are like 362,880 different combinations.
Let's start pushing buttons and see if we can't figure out the combination by next week.
362880 is a very specific number. How'd you figure that out?
It's just 9 × 8 × 7 × 6 × 5 × 4 × 3 × 2 × 1. Simple math.
Rruff?

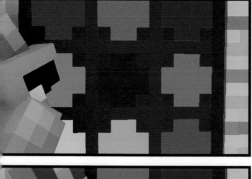
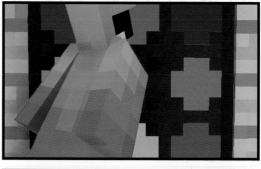
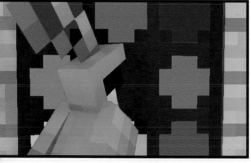
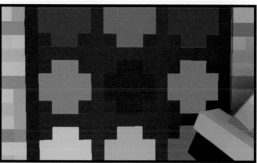

CLICK!

Dear Pell, Logan, and Maddy,

If you are reading this, then either all is well and I can't wait to
tell you about my adventure, or all has gone horribly wrong and I
need rescuing. Either way, I hope you will join me. Your parents
never told you this, but it's about time you knew: your destiny is
not here inside these walls. I cannot say more in case this message
falls into the wrong hands.

I left Fortress City because, as you know, it is a horrible place
for people like us. I made some friends who agree. They have
left and started a new city that promises to be better for everyone
and I have joined them. I believe I can do a lot more for the world from
outside Fortress City. I am certain you can, too.

I have written down instructions on how you can leave without getting
caught. It will be dangerous, but knowing you and your friends, I think
it will also be a fun and exciting adventure! You can tell your parents,
of course, but please do not tell anyone outside of our family. My safety
depends on complete secrecy.

I hope to see you very soon. Good luck and stay safe!

Uncle Colin

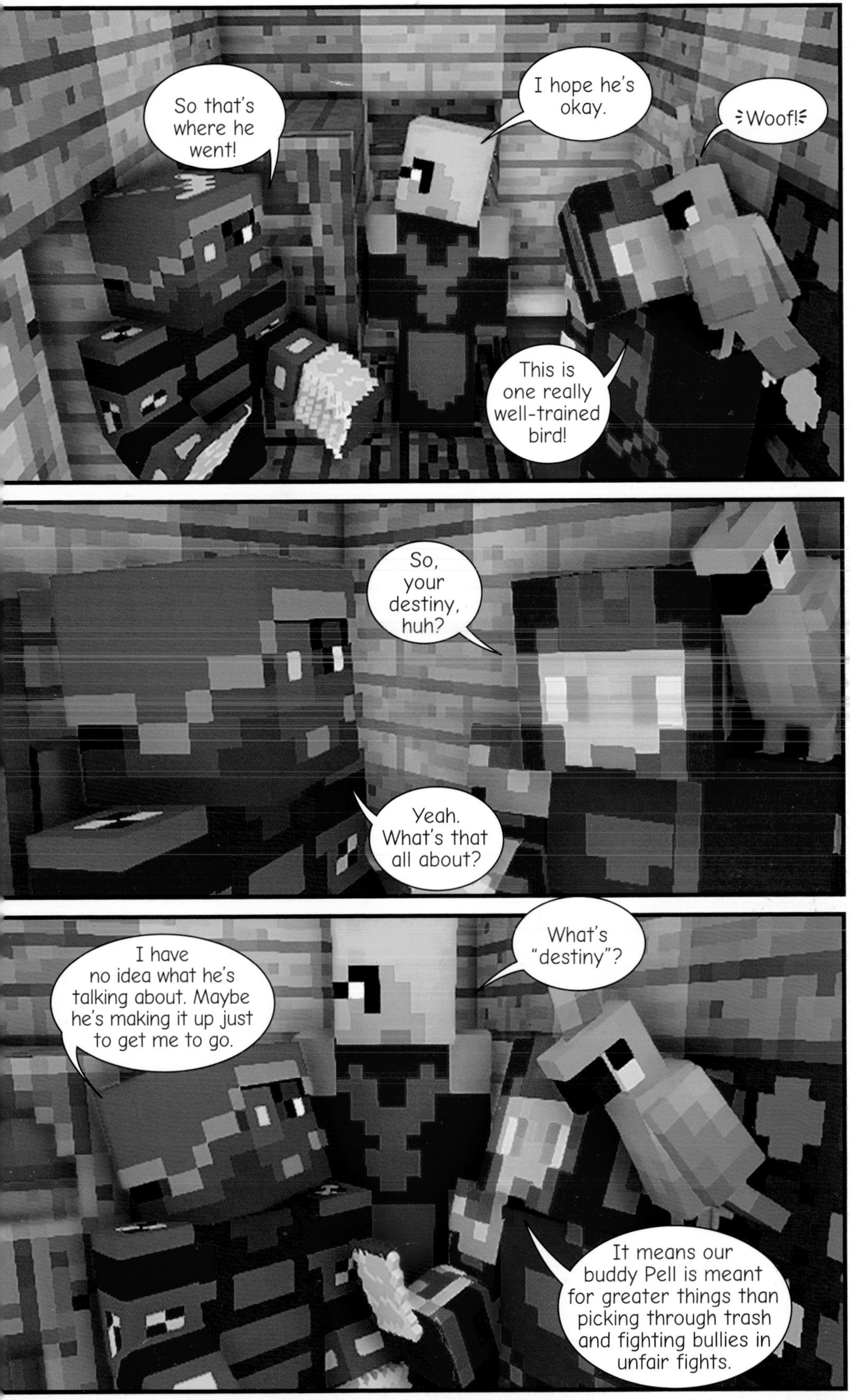
So that's where he went!
I hope he's okay.
Woof!
This is one really well-trained bird!
So, your destiny, huh?
Yeah. What's that all about?
I have no idea what he's talking about. Maybe he's making it up just to get me to go.
What's "destiny"?
It means our buddy Pell is meant for greater things than picking through trash and fighting bullies in unfair fights.

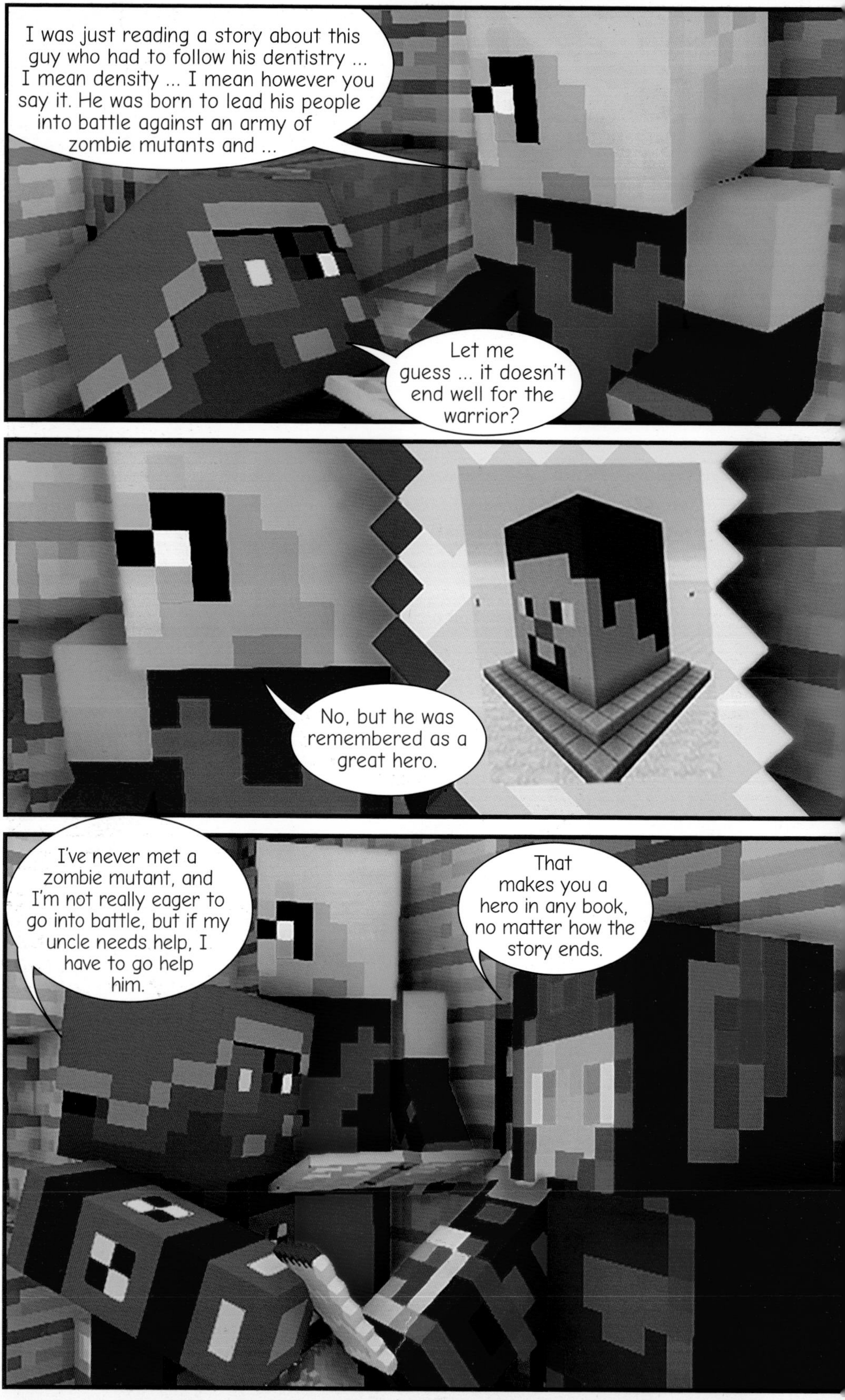
I was just reading a story about this guy who had to follow his dentistry ... I mean density ... I mean however you say it. He was born to lead his people into battle against an army of zombie mutants and ...
Let me guess ... it doesn't end well for the warrior?
No, but he was remembered as a great hero.
I've never met a zombie mutant, and I'm not really eager to go into battle, but if my uncle needs help, I have to go help him.
That makes you a hero in any book, no matter how the story ends.

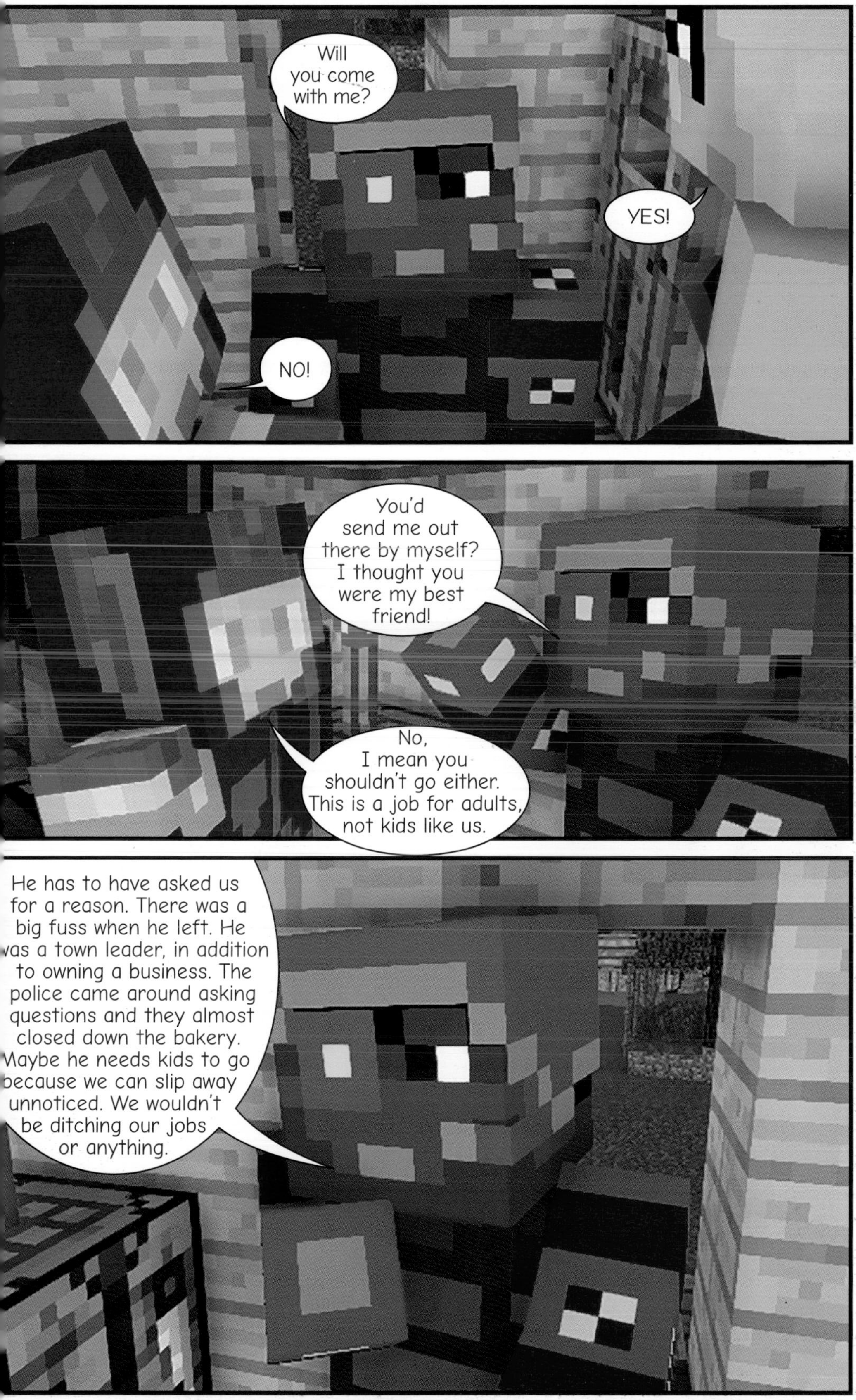
Will you come with me?
YES!
NO!
You'd send me out there by myself? I thought you were my best friend!
No, I mean you shouldn't go either. This is a job for adults, not kids like us.
He has to have asked us for a reason. There was a big fuss when he left. He was a town leader, in addition to owning a business. The police came around asking questions and they almost closed down the bakery. Maybe he needs kids to go because we can slip away unnoticed. We wouldn't be ditching our jobs or anything.

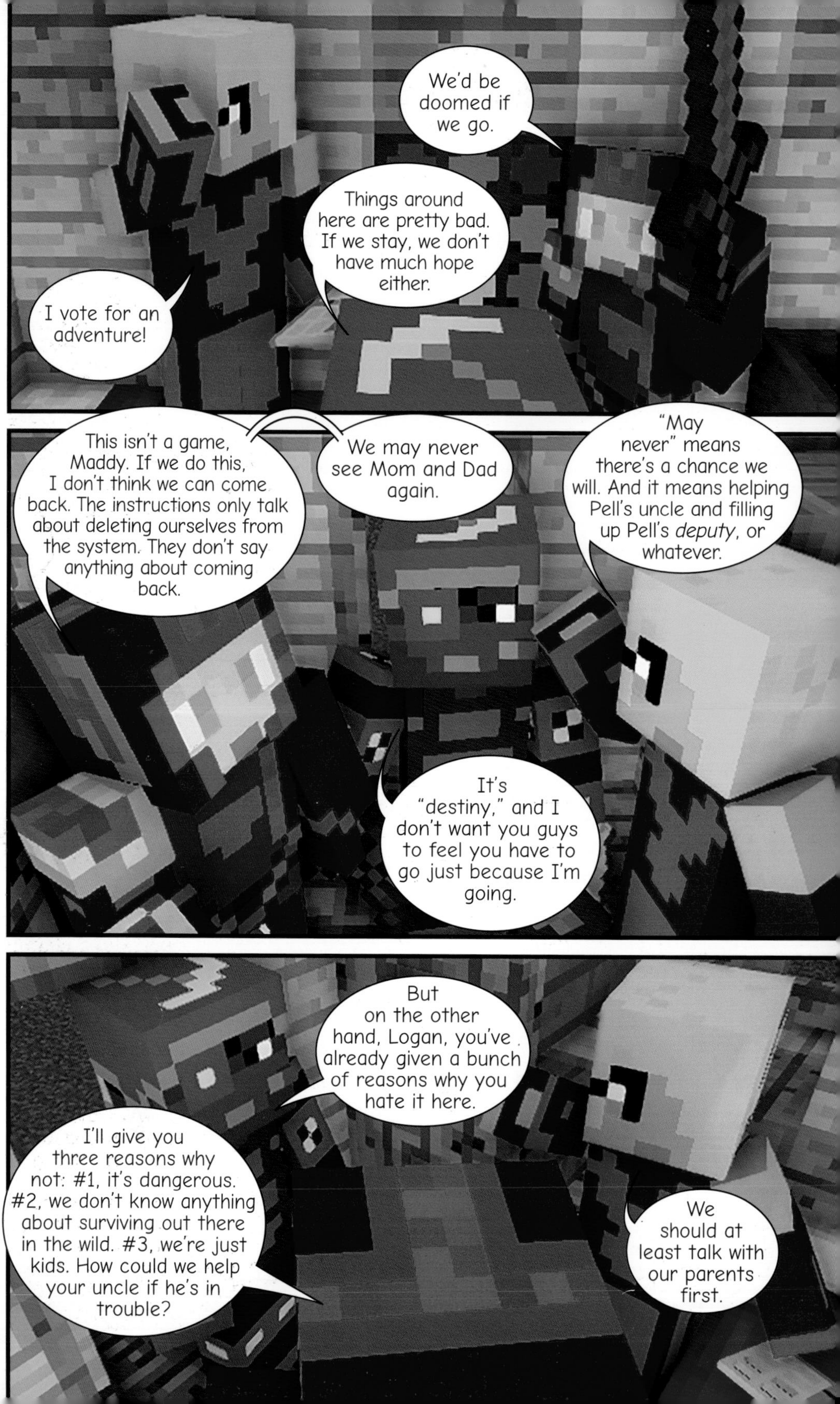
We'd be doomed if we go.
Things around here are pretty bad. If we stay, we don't have much hope either.
I vote for an adventure!
This isn't a game, Maddy. If we do this, I don't think we can come back. The instructions only talk about deleting ourselves from the system. They don't say anything about coming back.
We may never see Mom and Dad again.
"May never" means there's a chance we will. And it means helping Pell's uncle and filling up Pell's *deputy*, or whatever.
It's "destiny," and I don't want you guys to feel you have to go just because I'm going.
But on the other hand, Logan, you've already given a bunch of reasons why you hate it here.
I'll give you three reasons why not: #1, it's dangerous. #2, we don't know anything about surviving out there in the wild. #3, we're just kids. How could we help your uncle if he's in trouble?
We should at least talk with our parents first.

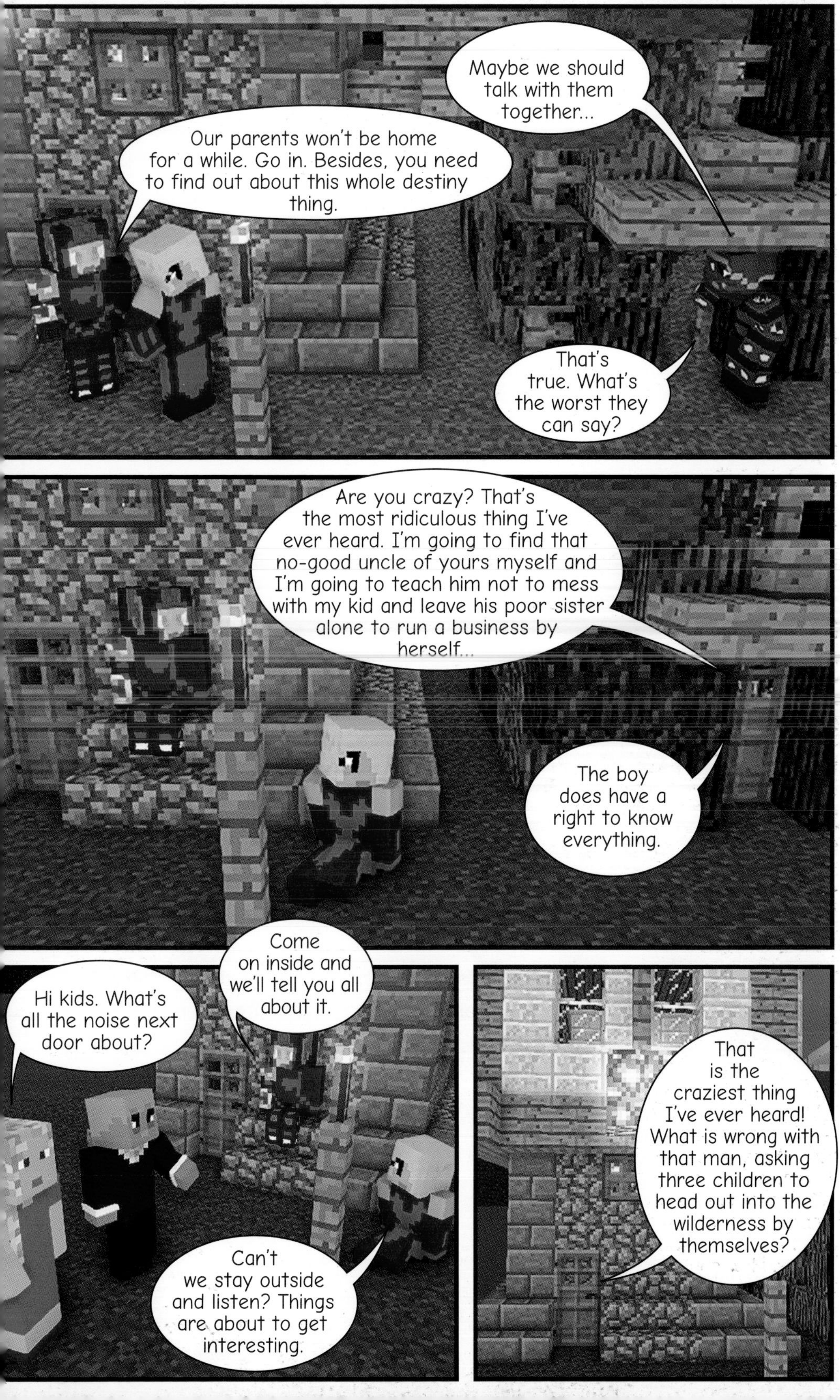
Our parents won't be home for a while. Go in. Besides, you need to find out about this whole destiny thing.
Maybe we should talk with them together...
That's true. What's the worst they can say?
Are you crazy? That's the most ridiculous thing I've ever heard. I'm going to find that no-good uncle of yours myself and I'm going to teach him not to mess with my kid and leave his poor sister alone to run a business by herself...
The boy does have a right to know everything.
Hi kids. What's all the noise next door about?
Come on inside and we'll tell you all about it.
Can't we stay outside and listen? Things are about to get interesting.
That is the craziest thing I've ever heard! What is wrong with that man, asking three children to head out into the wilderness by themselves?

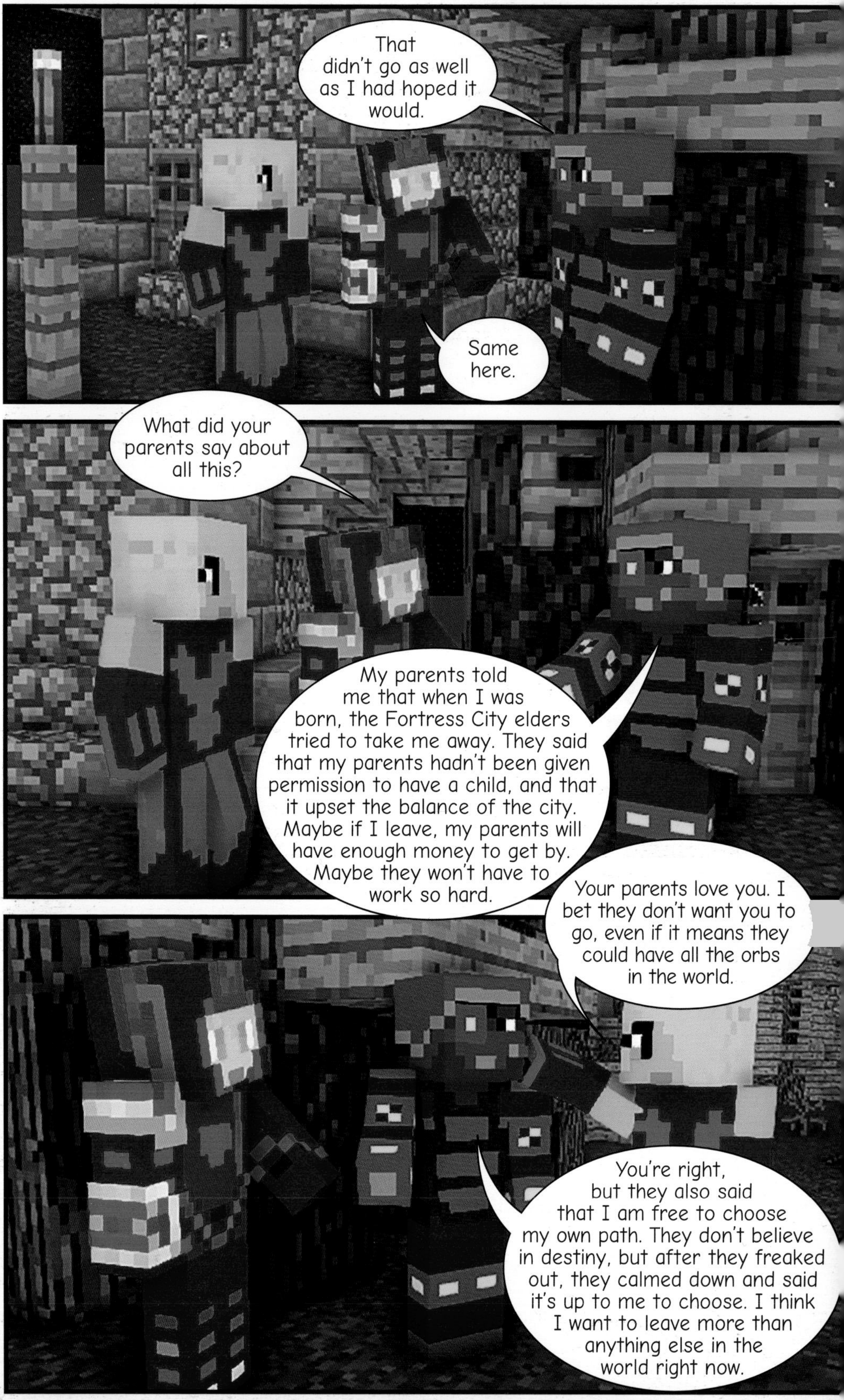
That didn't go as well as I had hoped it would.
Same here.
What did your parents say about all this?
My parents told me that when I was born, the Fortress City elders tried to take me away. They said that my parents hadn't been given permission to have a child, and that it upset the balance of the city. Maybe if I leave, my parents will have enough money to get by. Maybe they won't have to work so hard.
Your parents love you. I bet they don't want you to go, even if it means they could have all the orbs in the world.
You're right, but they also said that I am free to choose my own path. They don't believe in destiny, but after they freaked out, they calmed down and said it's up to me to choose. I think I want to leave more than anything else in the world right now.

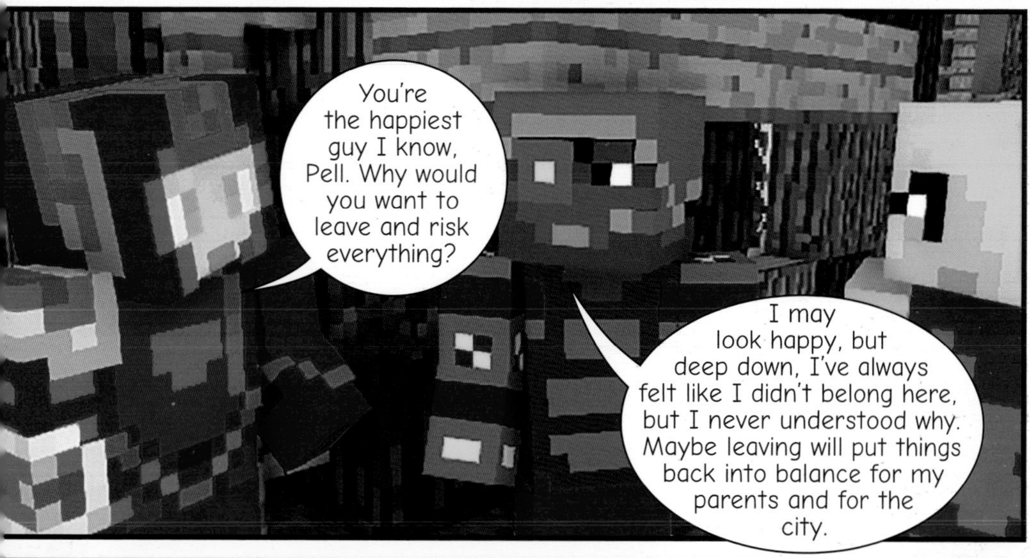

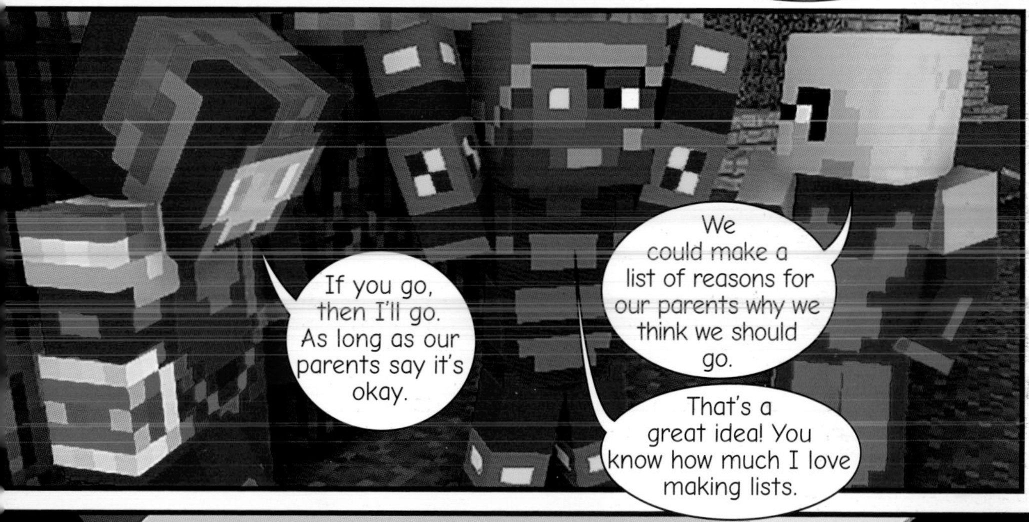

Reasons we should go

1. Help Uncle Colin if he's in trouble
2. Escape from bullies
3. Have an adventure
4. Learn about the world
5. Find a better life outside the walls of Fortress City
6. Fulfill Pell's destiny

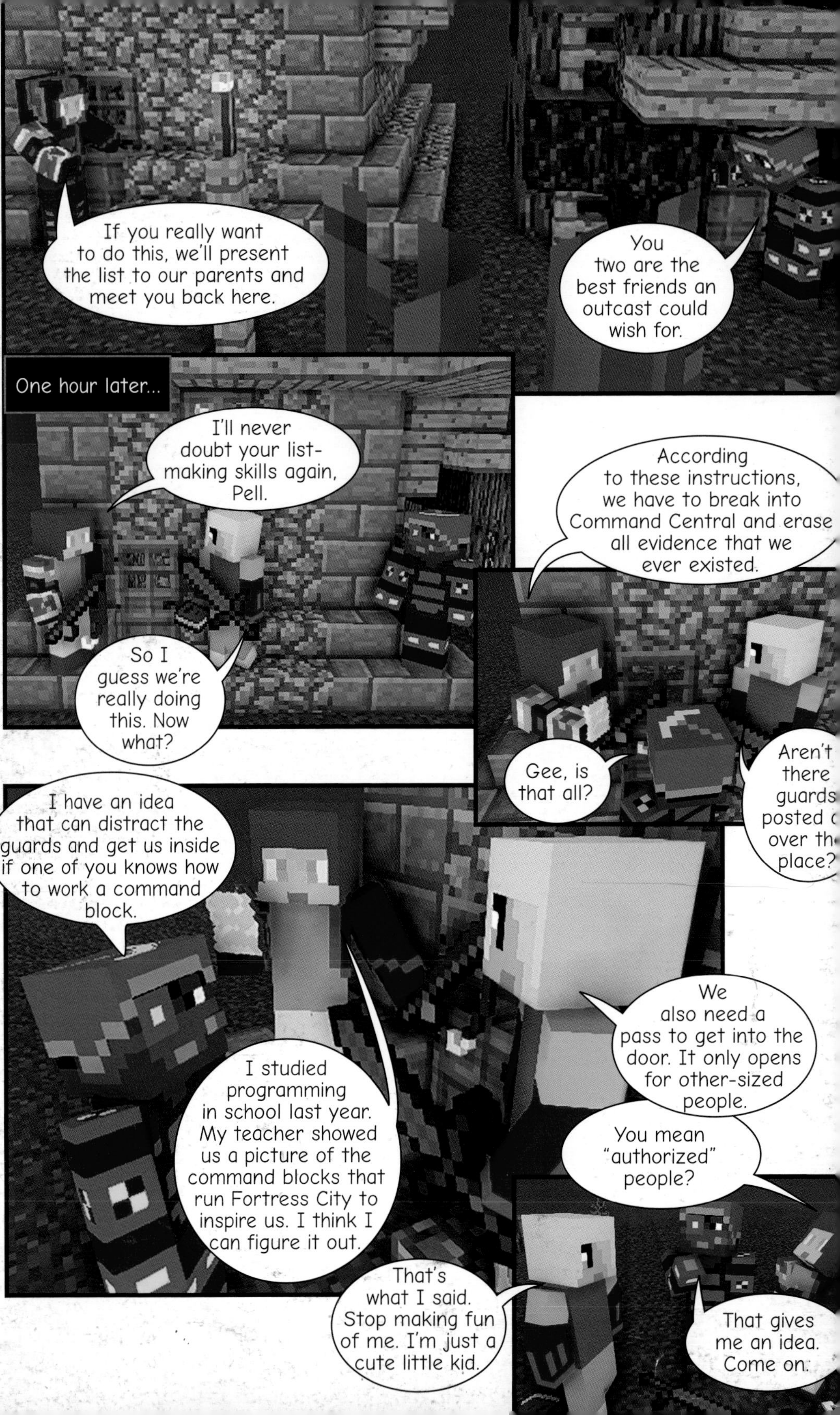
If you really want to do this, we'll present the list to our parents and meet you back here.
You two are the best friends an outcast could wish for.
One hour later...
I'll never doubt your list-making skills again, Pell.
So I guess we're really doing this. Now what?
According to these instructions, we have to break into Command Central and erase all evidence that we ever existed.
Gee, is that all?
Aren't there guards posted over th place?
I have an idea that can distract the guards and get us inside if one of you knows how to work a command block.
I studied programming in school last year. My teacher showed us a picture of the command blocks that run Fortress City to inspire us. I think I can figure it out.
We also need a pass to get into the door. It only opens for other-sized people.
You mean "authorized" people?
That's what I said. Stop making fun of me. I'm just a cute little kid.
That gives me an idea. Come on.

CHAPTER 4

DELETE
HISTORY

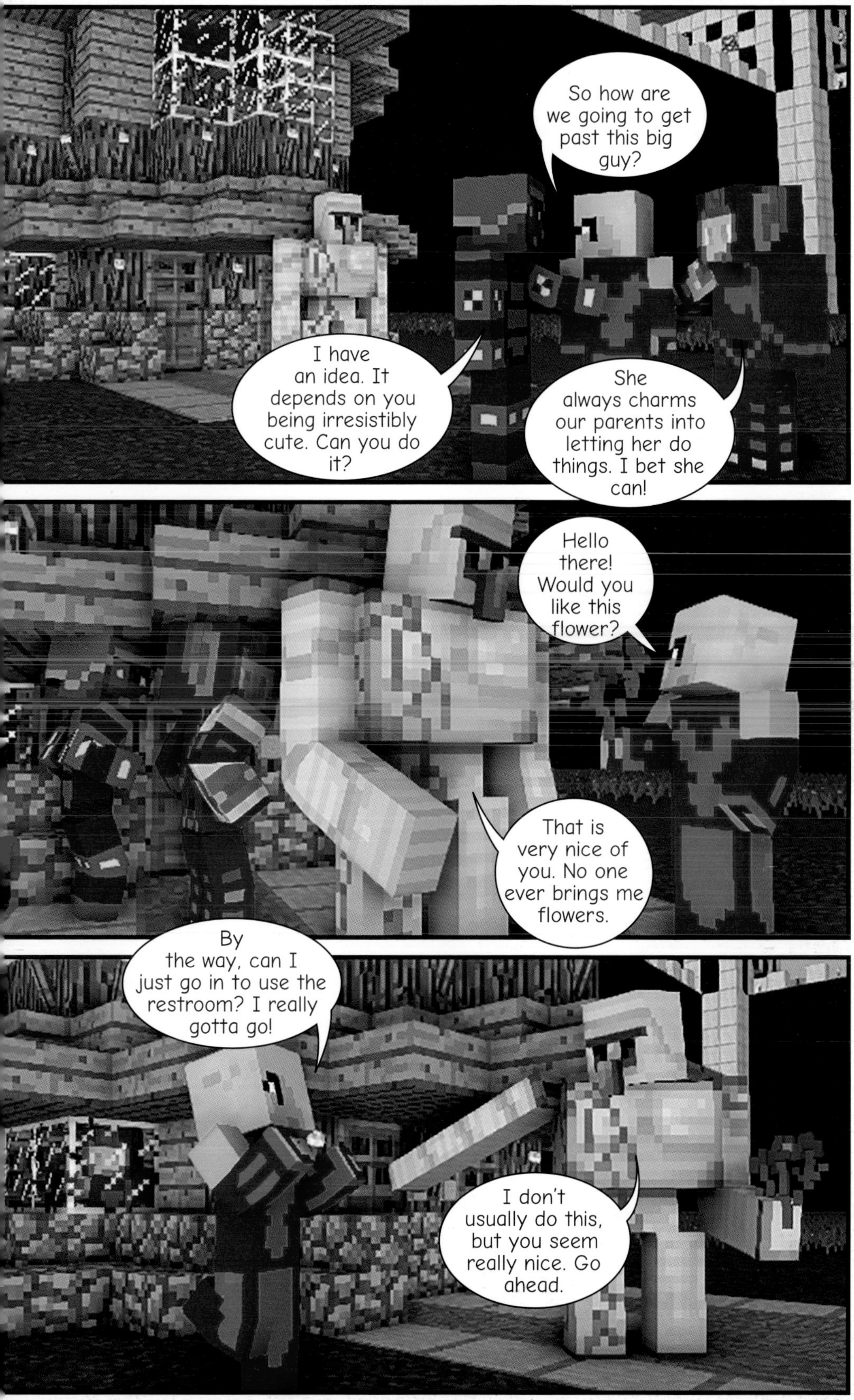
So how are we going to get past this big guy?
I have an idea. It depends on you being irresistibly cute. Can you do it?
She always charms our parents into letting her do things. I bet she can!
Hello there! Would you like this flower?
That is very nice of you. No one ever brings me flowers.
By the way, can I just go in to use the restroom? I really gotta go!
I don't usually do this, but you seem really nice. Go ahead.

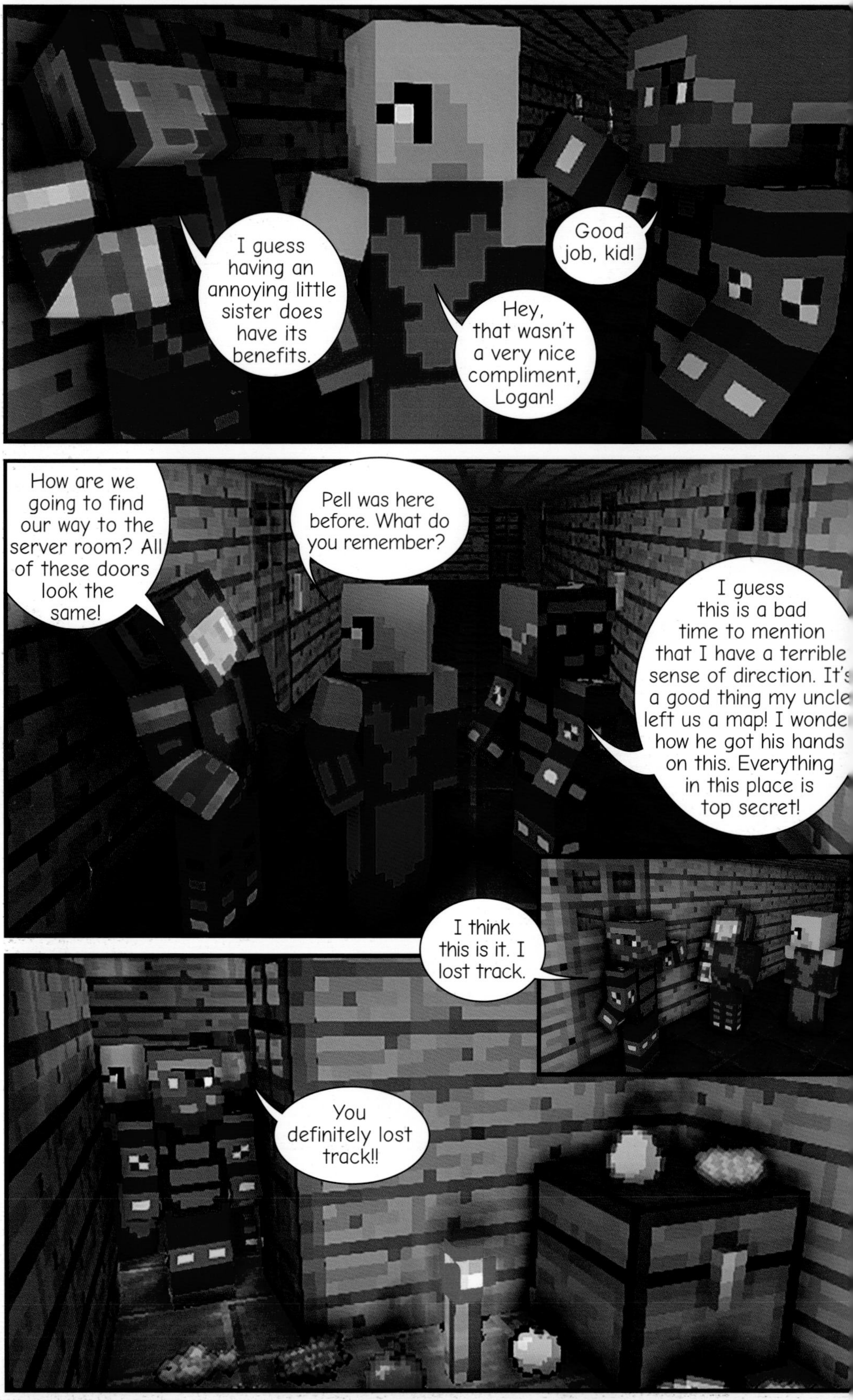
I guess having an annoying little sister does have its benefits.
Hey, that wasn't a very nice compliment, Logan!
Good job, kid!
How are we going to find our way to the server room? All of these doors look the same!
Pell was here before. What do you remember?
I guess this is a bad time to mention that I have a terrible sense of direction. It's a good thing my uncle left us a map! I wonde how he got his hands on this. Everything in this place is top secret!
I think this is it. I lost track.
You definitely lost track!!

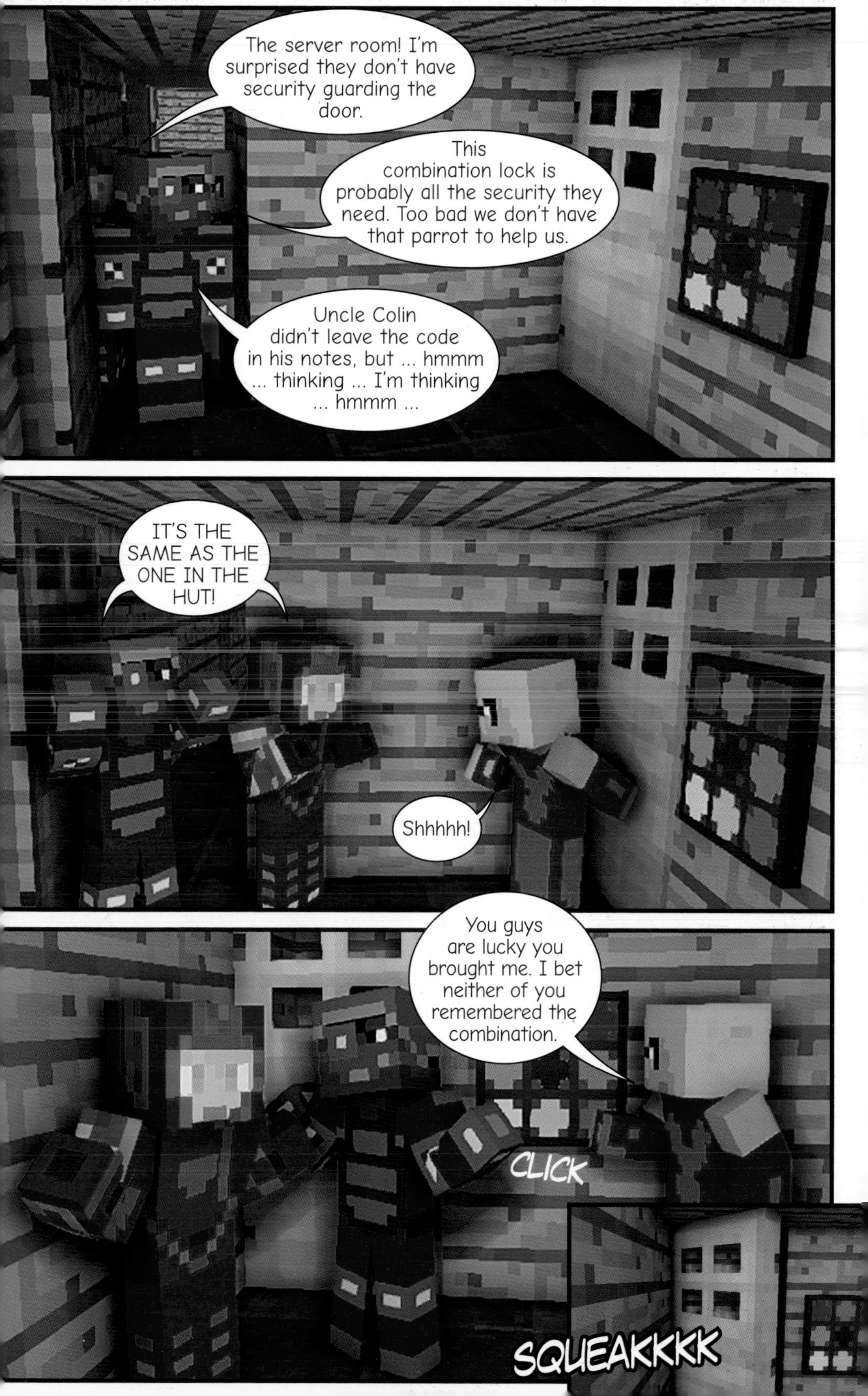
The server room! I'm surprised they don't have security guarding the door.
This combination lock is probably all the security they need. Too bad we don't have that parrot to help us.
Uncle Colin didn't leave the code in his notes, but ... hmmm ... thinking ... I'm thinking ... hmmm ...
IT'S THE SAME AS THE ONE IN THE HUT!
Shhhhh!
You guys are lucky you brought me. I bet neither of you remembered the combination.
CLICK
SQUEAKKKK

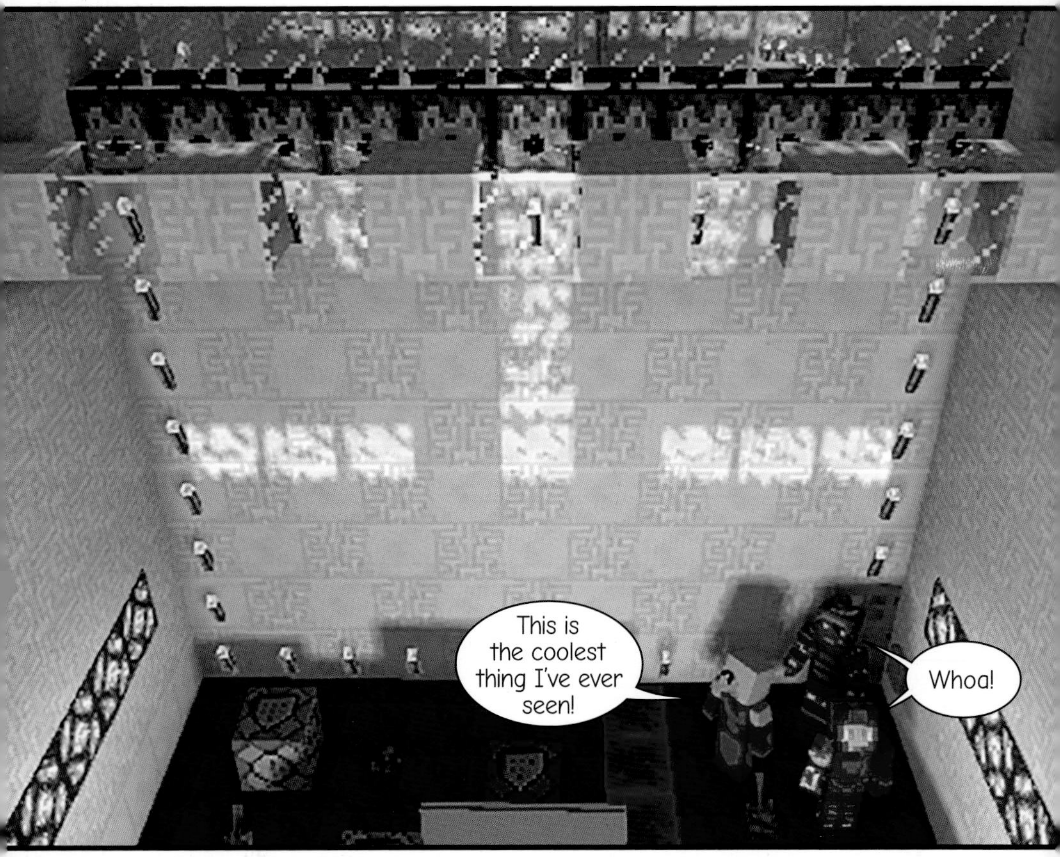
This is the coolest thing I've ever seen!
Whoa!

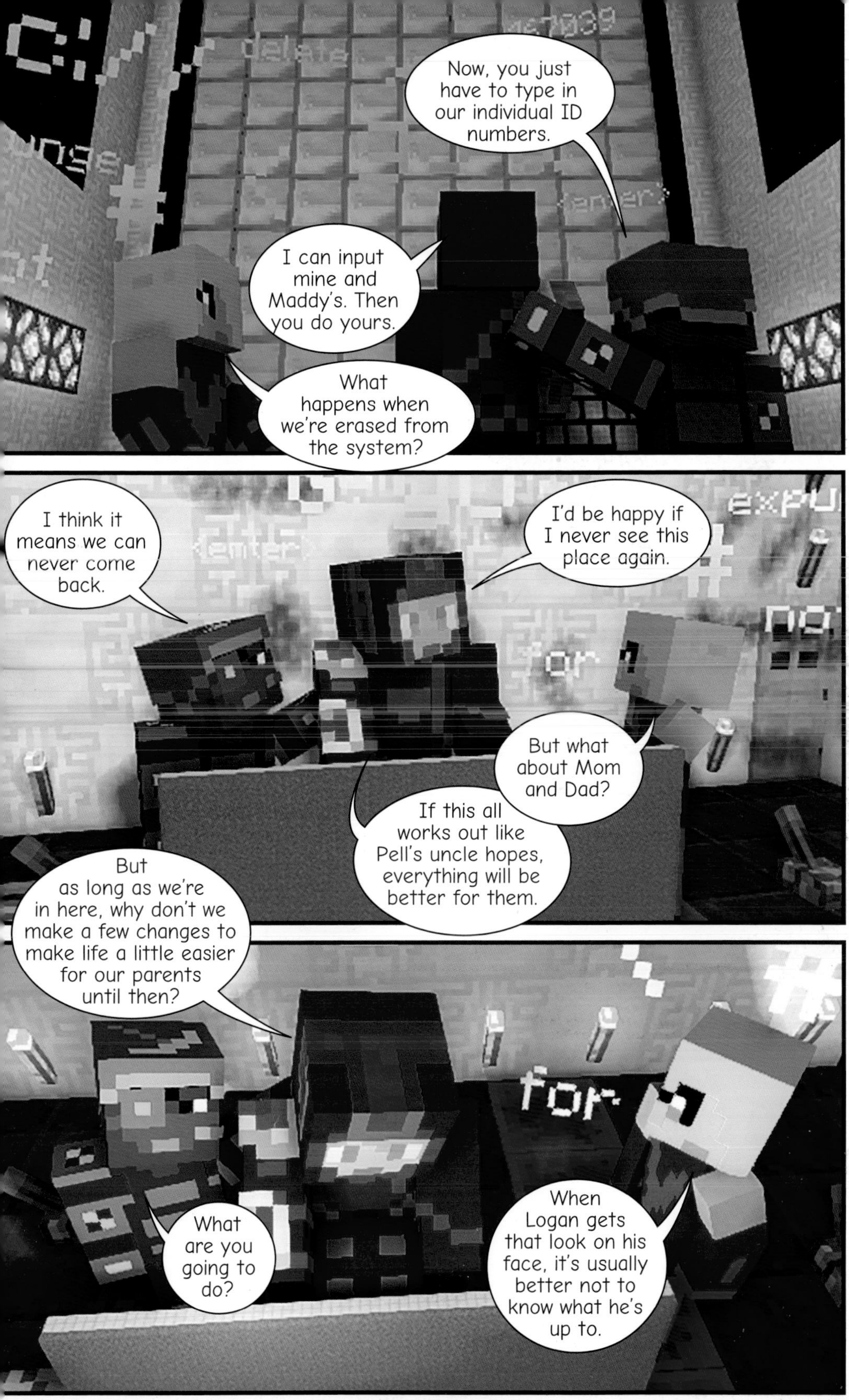
Now, you just have to type in our individual ID numbers.
I can input mine and Maddy's. Then you do yours.
What happens when we're erased from the system?
I think it means we can never come back.
I'd be happy if I never see this place again.
But what about Mom and Dad?
If this all works out like Pell's uncle hopes, everything will be better for them.
But as long as we're in here, why don't we make a few changes to make life a little easier for our parents until then?
What are you going to do?
When Logan gets that look on his face, it's usually better not to know what he's up to.

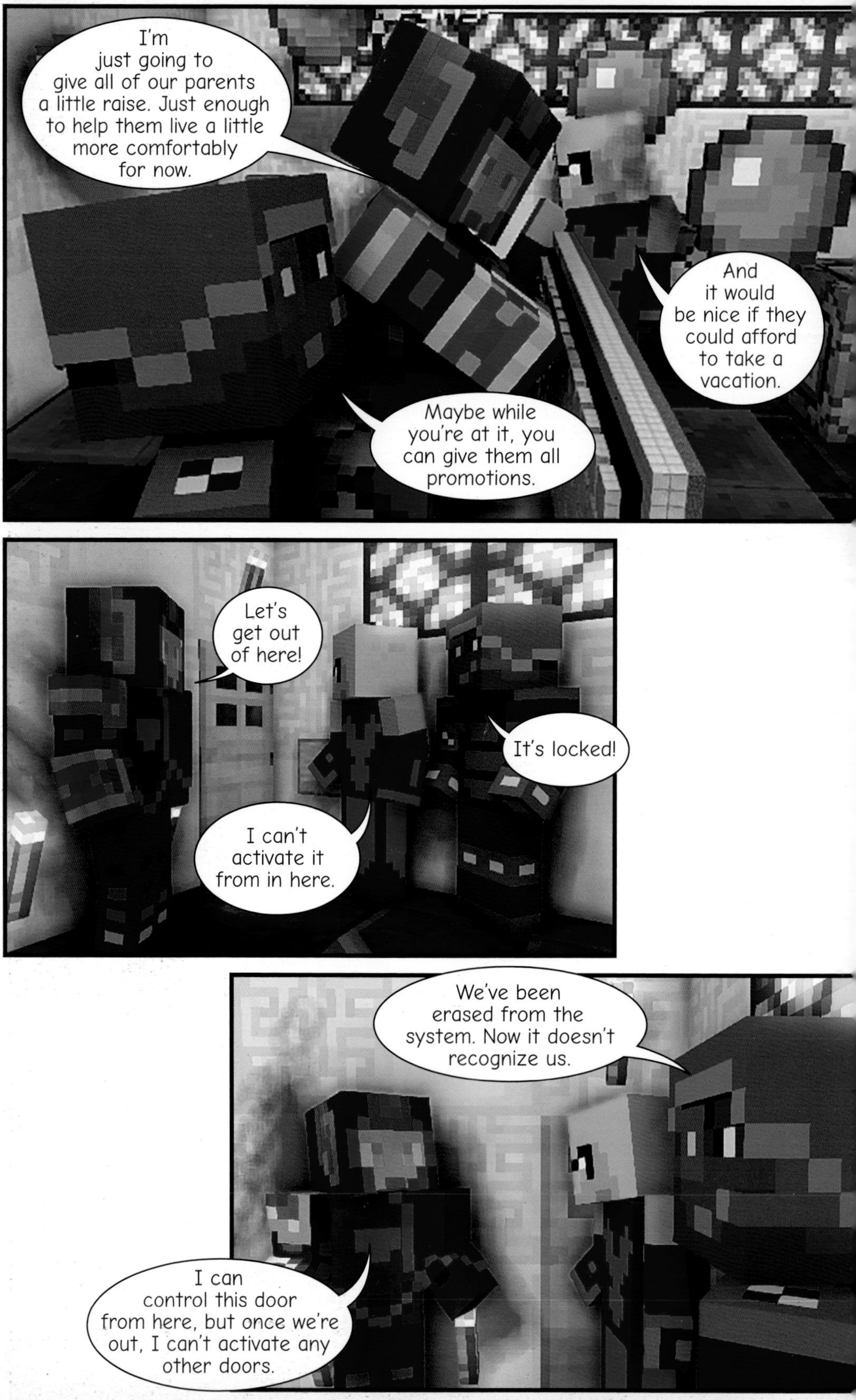
I'm just going to give all of our parents a little raise. Just enough to help them live a little more comfortably for now.
And it would be nice if they could afford to take a vacation.
Maybe while you're at it, you can give them all promotions.
Let's get out of here!
It's locked!
I can't activate it from in here.
We've been erased from the system. Now it doesn't recognize us.
I can control this door from here, but once we're out, I can't activate any other doors.

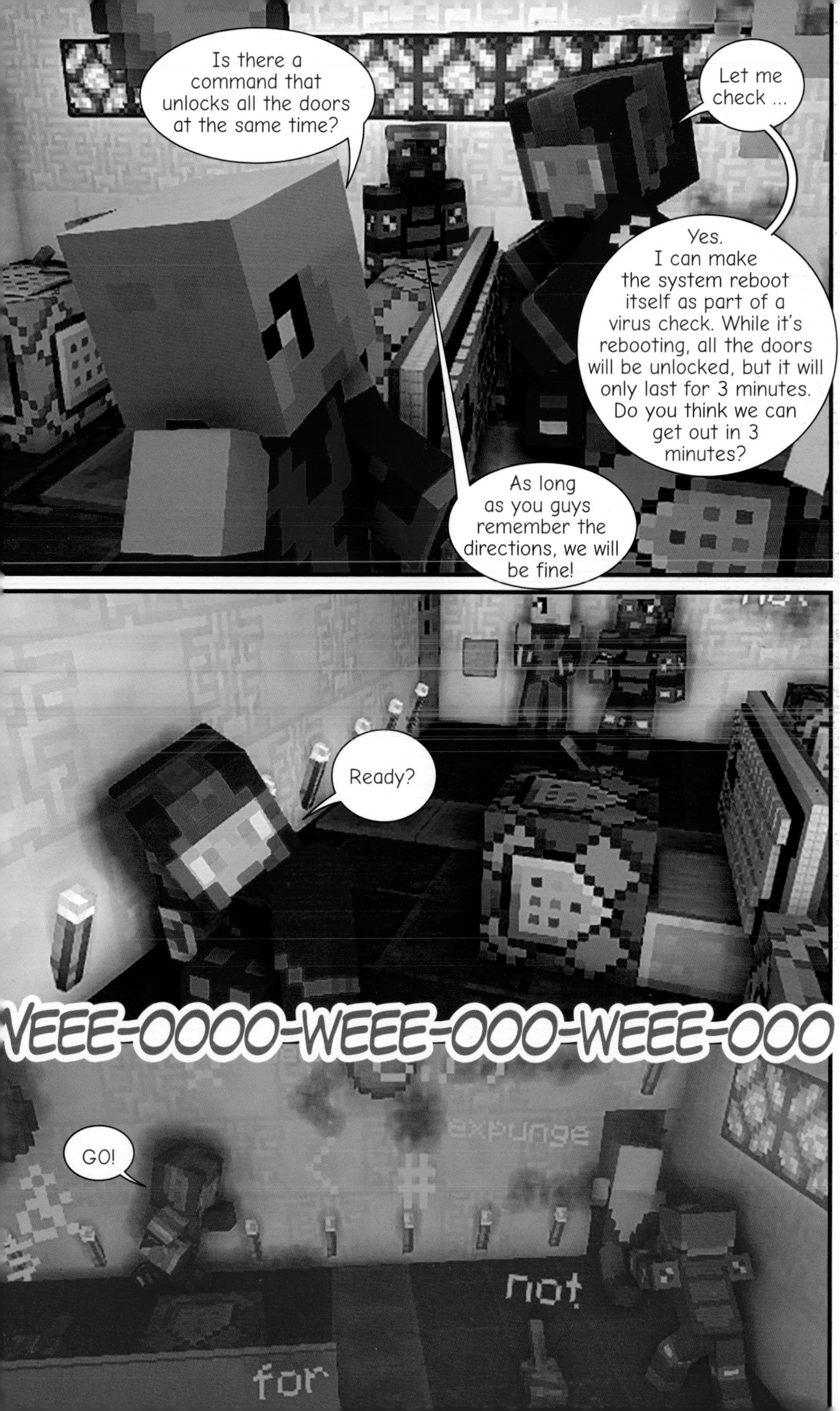
Is there a command that unlocks all the doors at the same time?
Let me check ...
Yes. I can make the system reboot itself as part of a virus check. While it's rebooting, all the doors will be unlocked, but it will only last for 3 minutes. Do you think we can get out in 3 minutes?
As long as you guys remember the directions, we will be fine!
Ready?
VEEE-OOOO-WEEE-OOO-WEEE-OOO
GO!
expunge
not
for

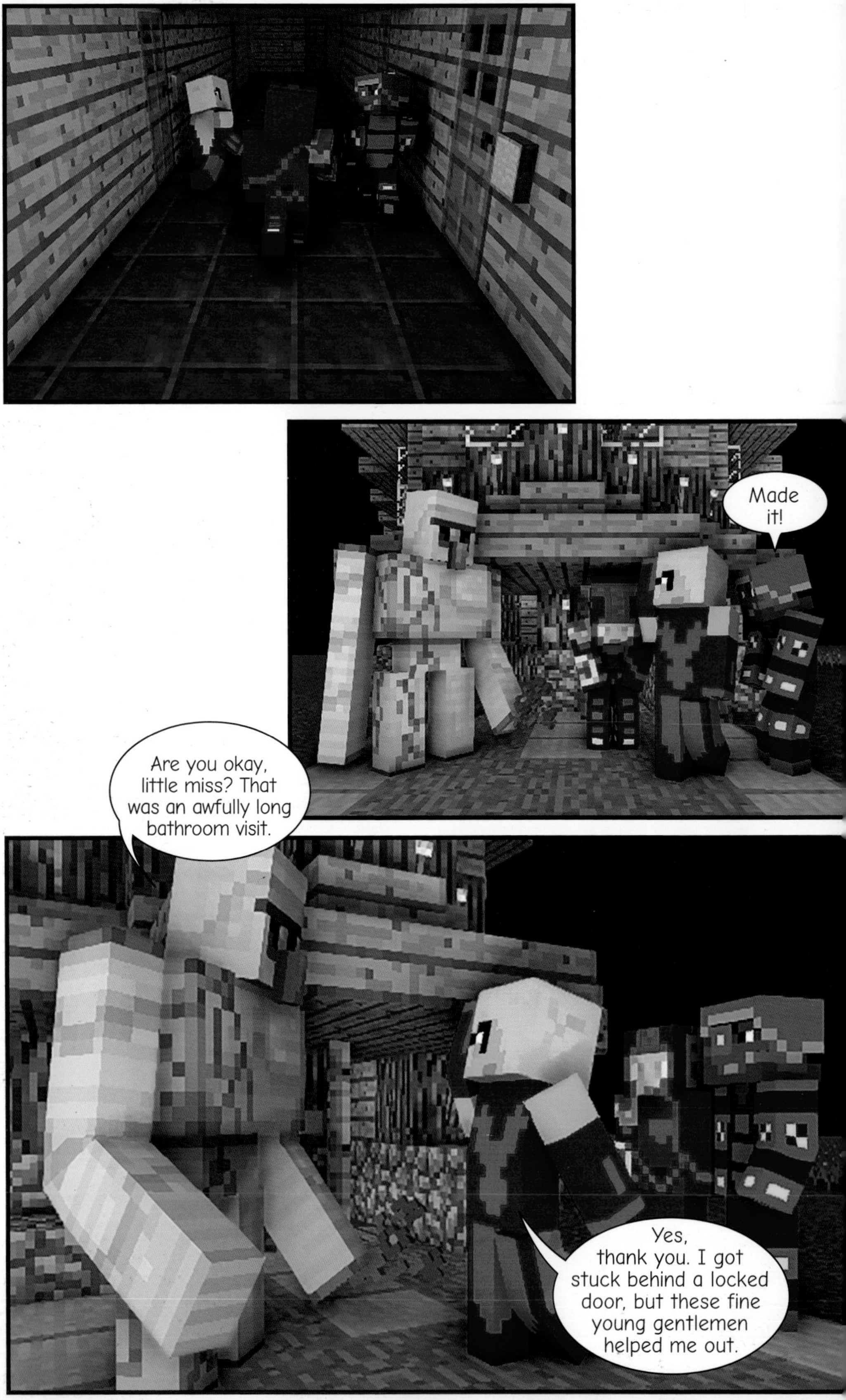
Made it!
Are you okay, little miss? That was an awfully long bathroom visit.
Yes, thank you. I got stuck behind a locked door, but these fine young gentlemen helped me out.

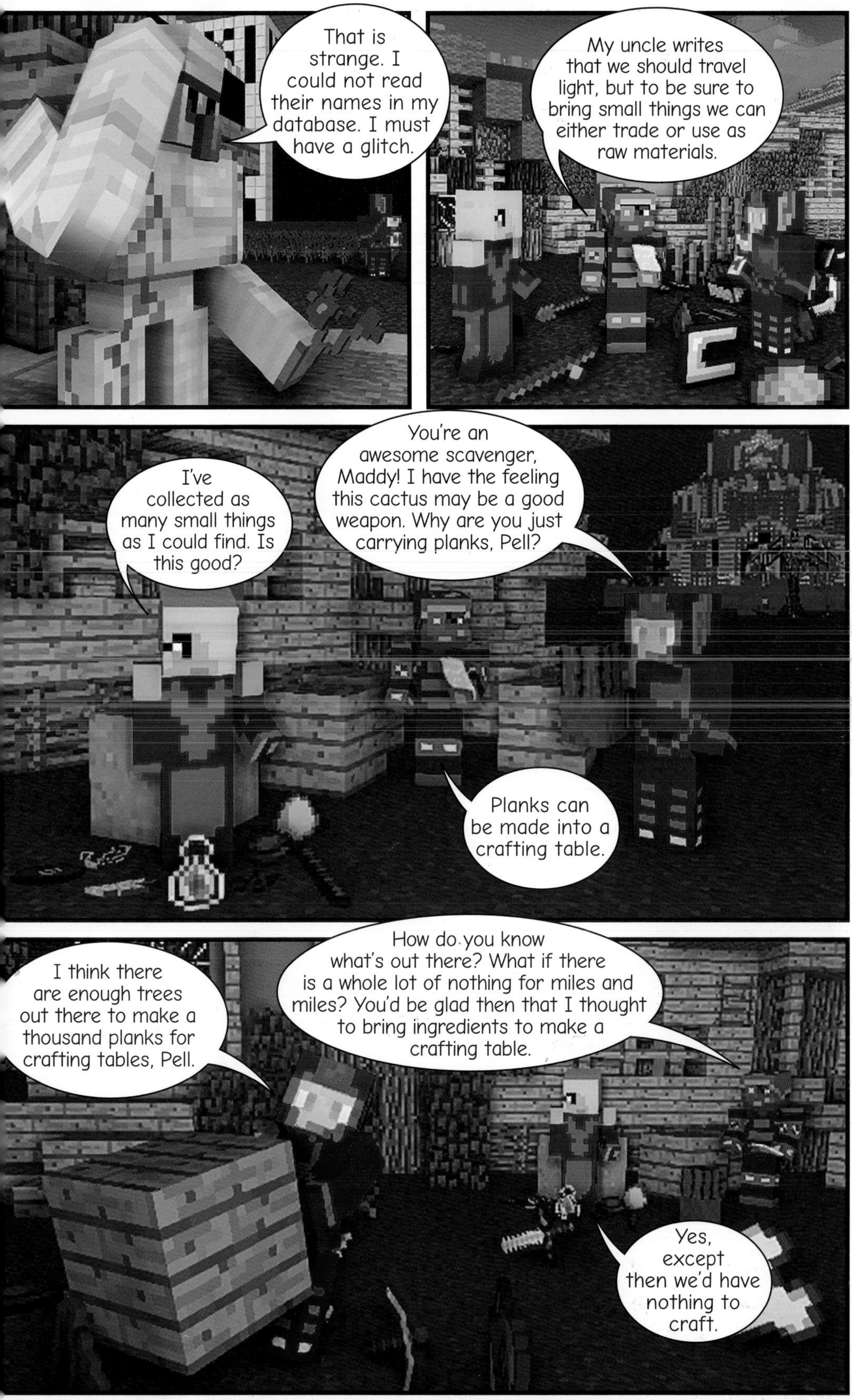

That is strange. I could not read their names in my database. I must have a glitch.
My uncle writes that we should travel light, but to be sure to bring small things we can either trade or use as raw materials.
I've collected as many small things as I could find. Is this good?
You're an awesome scavenger, Maddy! I have the feeling this cactus may be a good weapon. Why are you just carrying planks, Pell?
Planks can be made into a crafting table.
I think there are enough trees out there to make a thousand planks for crafting tables, Pell.
How do you know what's out there? What if there is a whole lot of nothing for miles and miles? You'd be glad then that I thought to bring ingredients to make a crafting table.
Yes, except then we'd have nothing to craft.

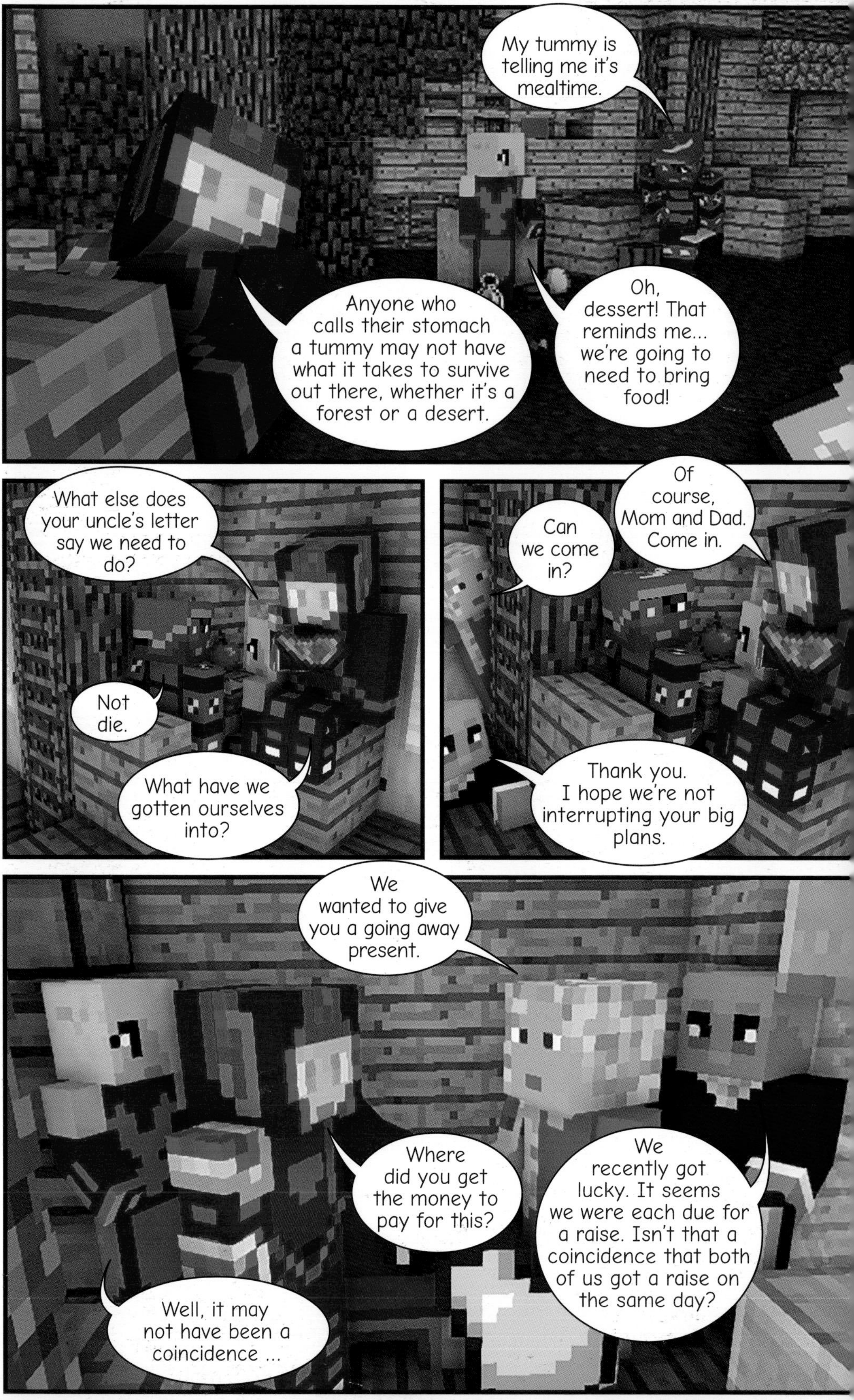

My tummy is telling me it's mealtime.
Anyone who calls their stomach a tummy may not have what it takes to survive out there, whether it's a forest or a desert.
Oh, dessert! That reminds me... we're going to need to bring food!
What else does your uncle's letter say we need to do?
Not die.
What have we gotten ourselves into?
Can we come in?
Of course, Mom and Dad. Come in.
Thank you. I hope we're not interrupting your big plans.
We wanted to give you a going away present.
Where did you get the money to pay for this?
We recently got lucky. It seems we were each due for a raise. Isn't that a coincidence that both of us got a raise on the same day?
Well, it may not have been a coincidence ...

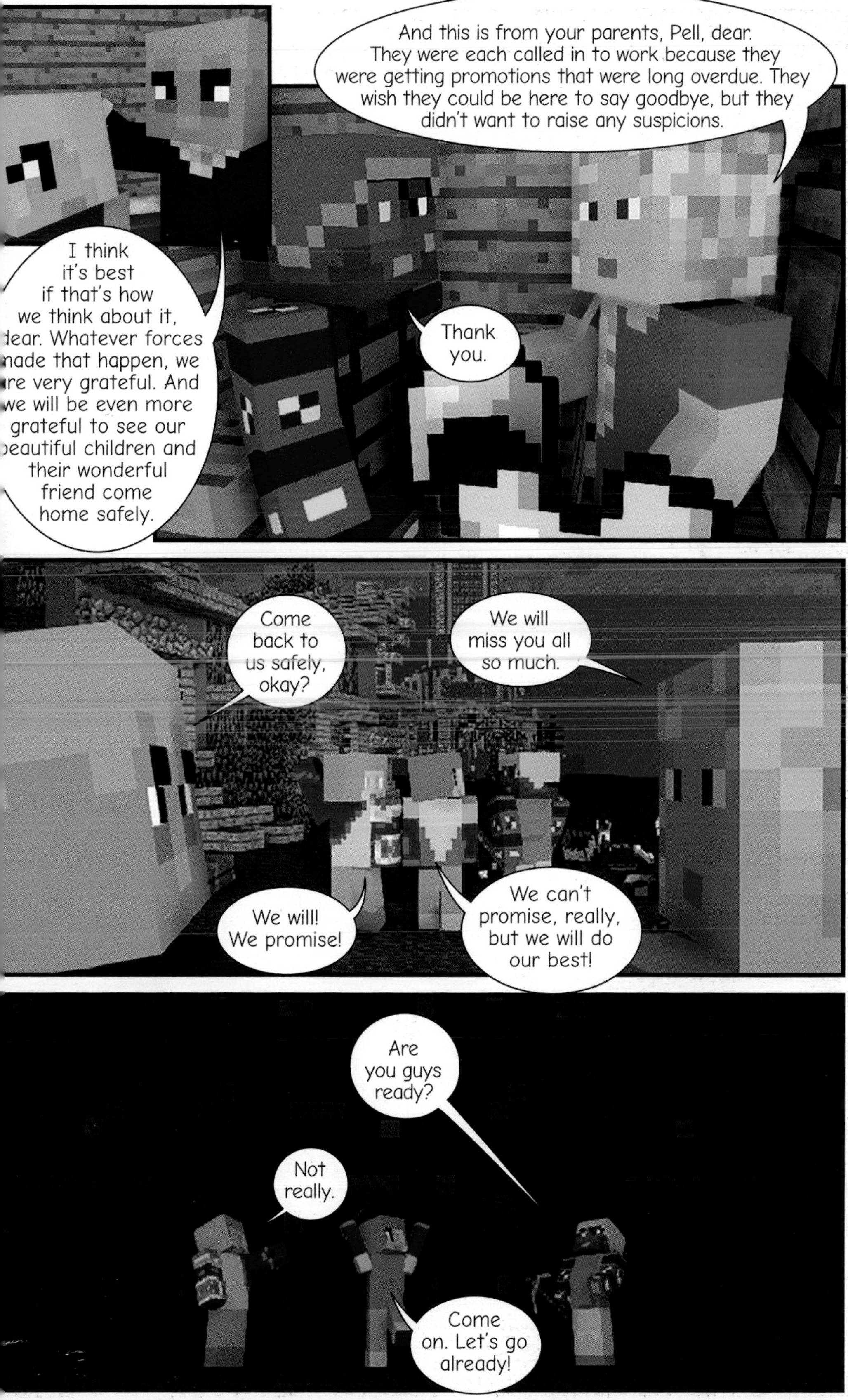
And this is from your parents, Pell, dear. They were each called in to work because they were getting promotions that were long overdue. They wish they could be here to say goodbye, but they didn't want to raise any suspicions.
I think it's best if that's how we think about it, ear. Whatever forces nade that happen, we re very grateful. And we will be even more grateful to see our eautiful children and their wonderful friend come home safely.
Thank you.
Come back to us safely, okay?
We will miss you all so much.
We will! We promise!
We can't promise, really, but we will do our best!
Are you guys ready?
Not really.
Come on. Let's go already!

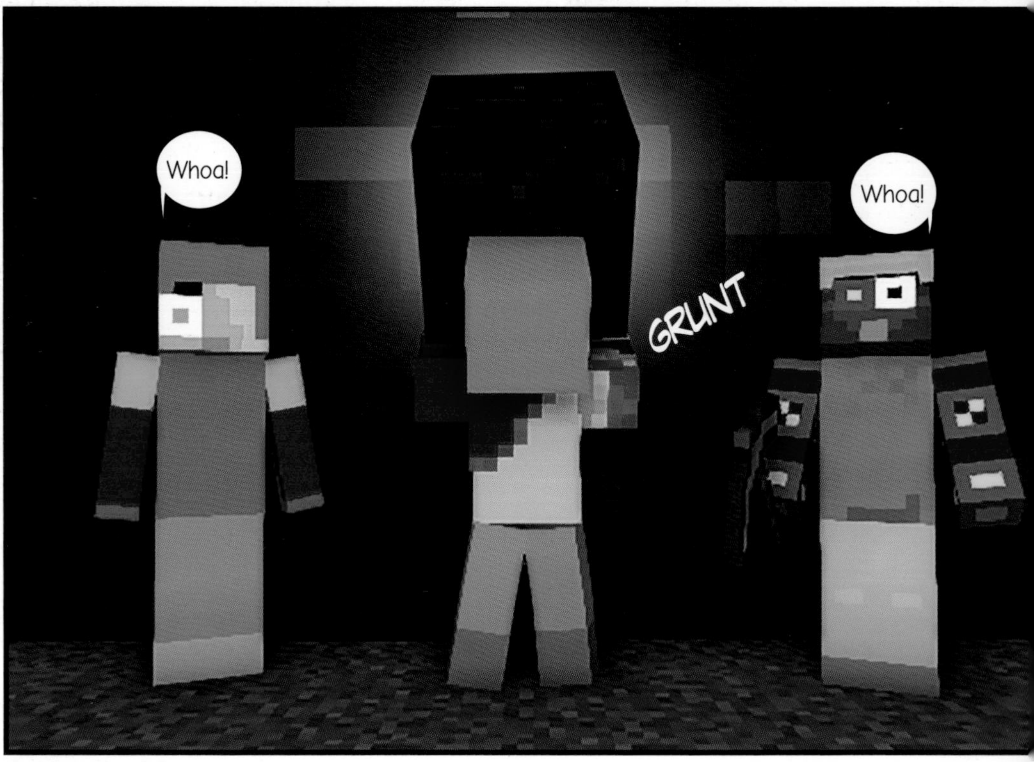
Whoa!
Whoa!
GRUNT

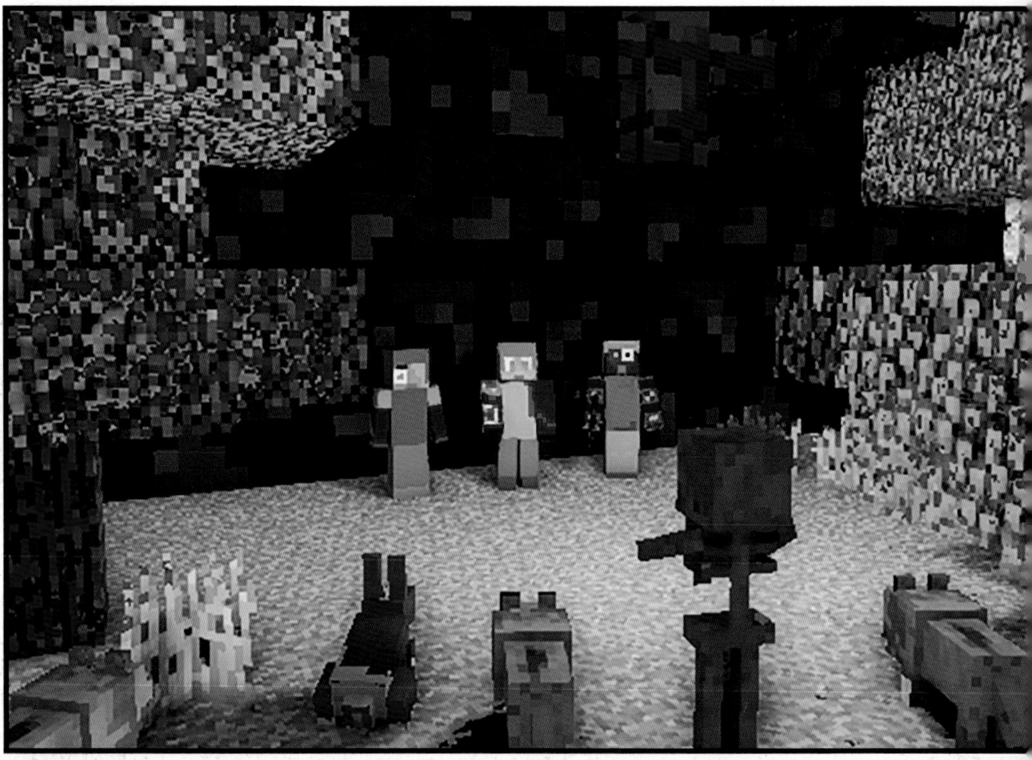

CHAPTER 5

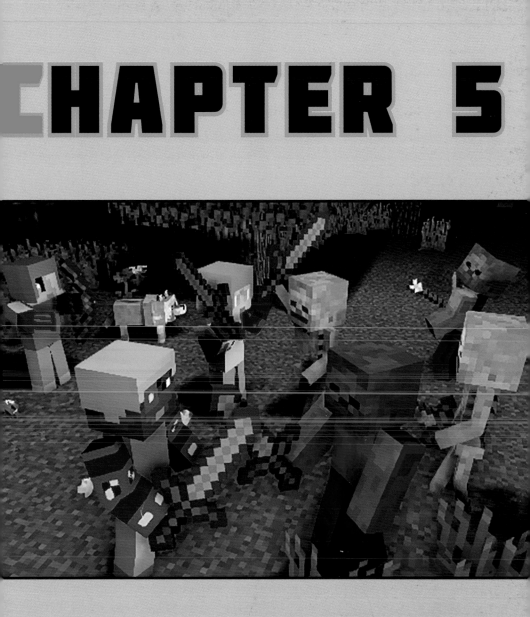

MONSTERS

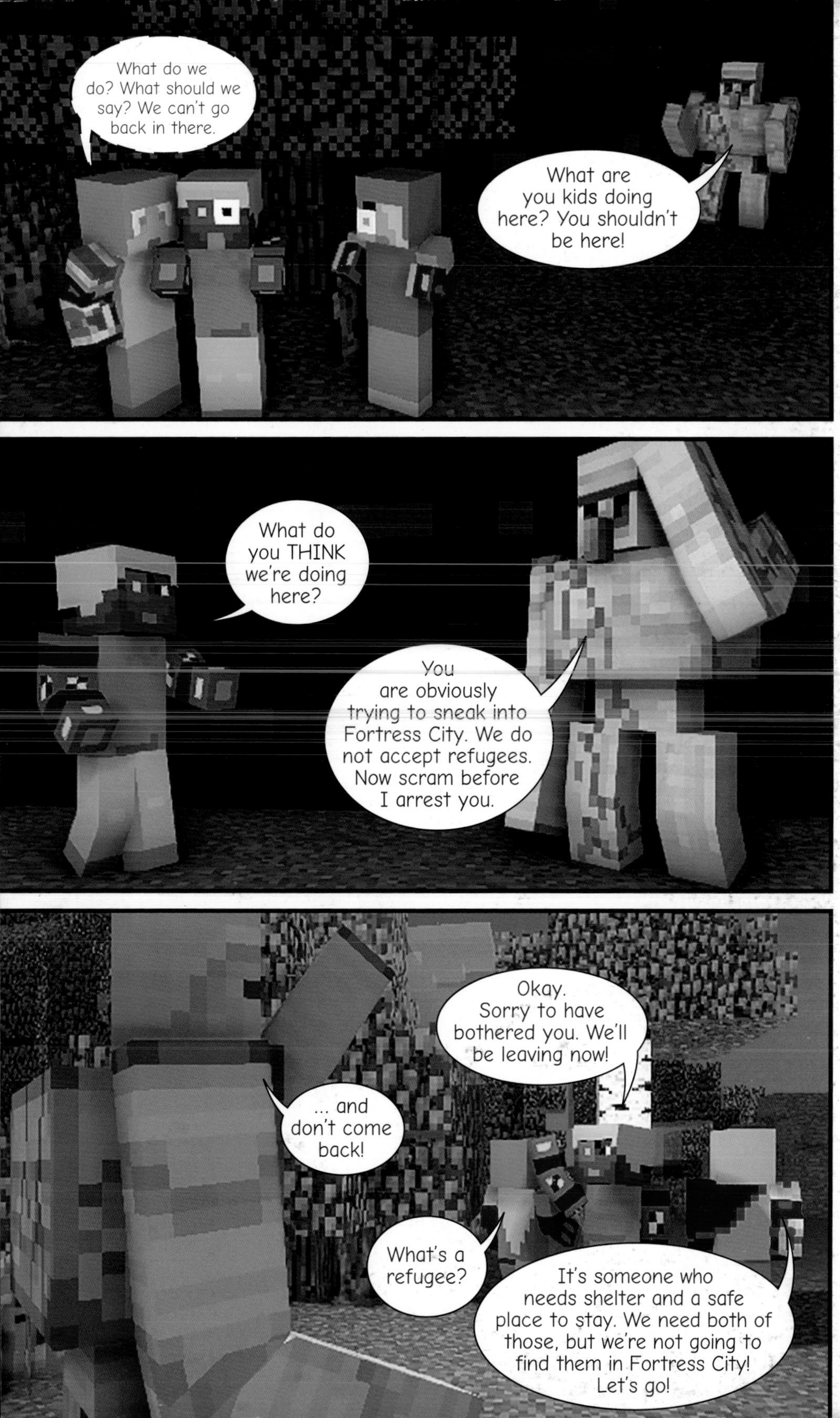
What do we do? What should we say? We can't go back in there.
What are you kids doing here? You shouldn't be here!
What do you THINK we're doing here?
You are obviously trying to sneak into Fortress City. We do not accept refugees. Now scram before I arrest you.
Okay. Sorry to have bothered you. We'll be leaving now!
... and don't come back!
What's a refugee?
It's someone who needs shelter and a safe place to stay. We need both of those, but we're not going to find them in Fortress City! Let's go!

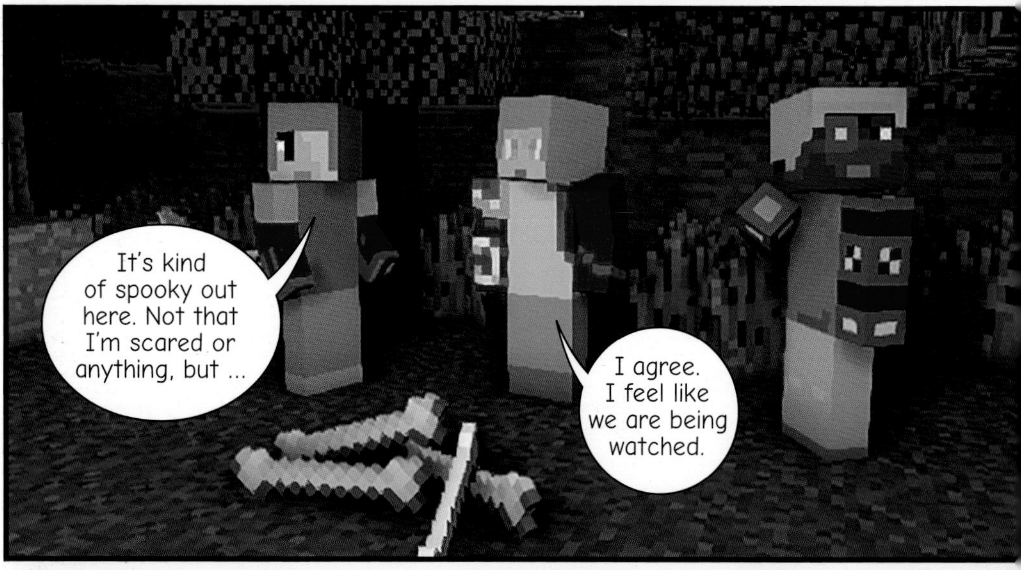
It's kind of spooky out here. Not that I'm scared or anything, but ...
I agree. I feel like we are being watched.

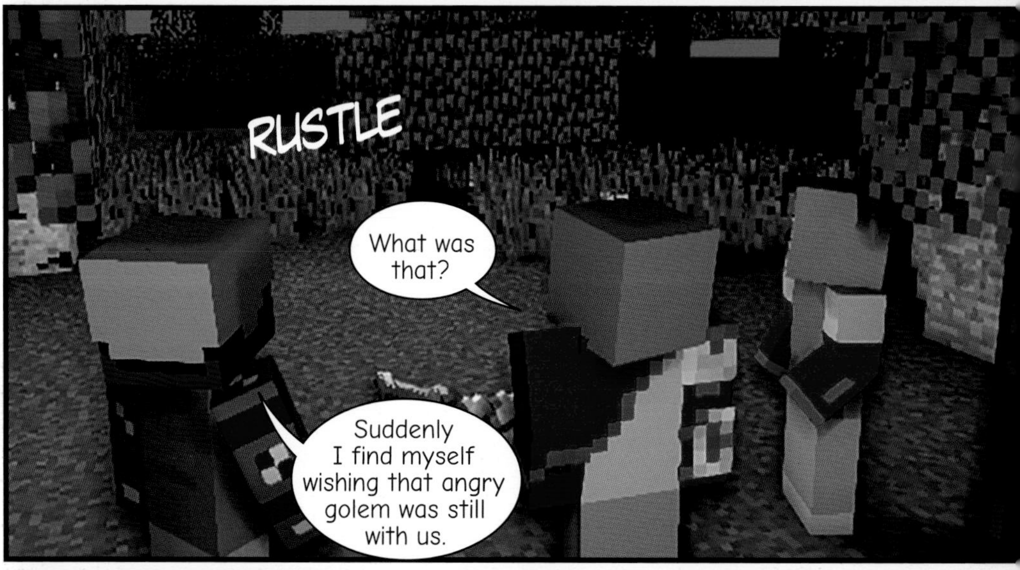
RUSTLE
What was that?
Suddenly I find myself wishing that angry golem was still with us.

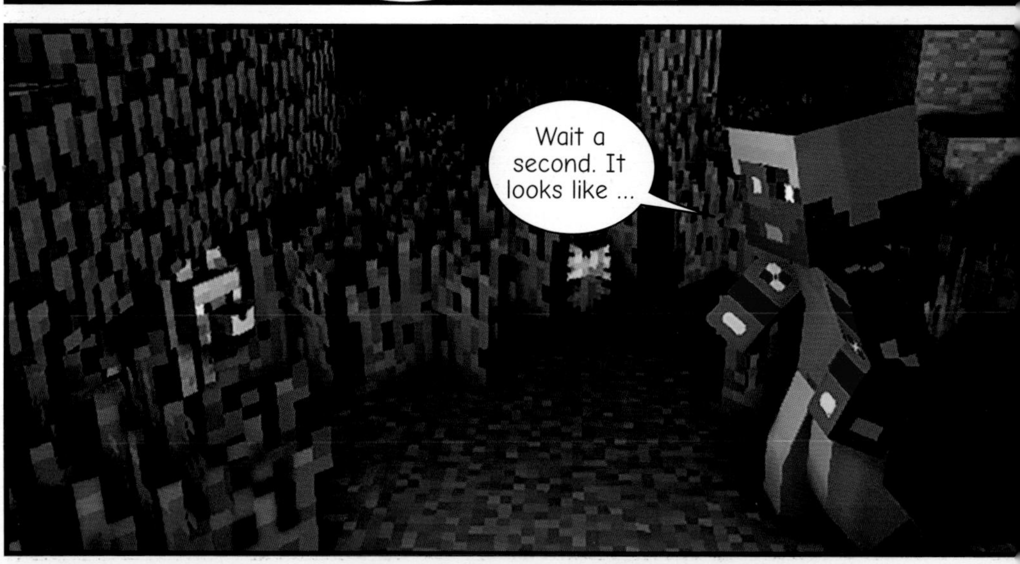
Wait a second. It looks like ...

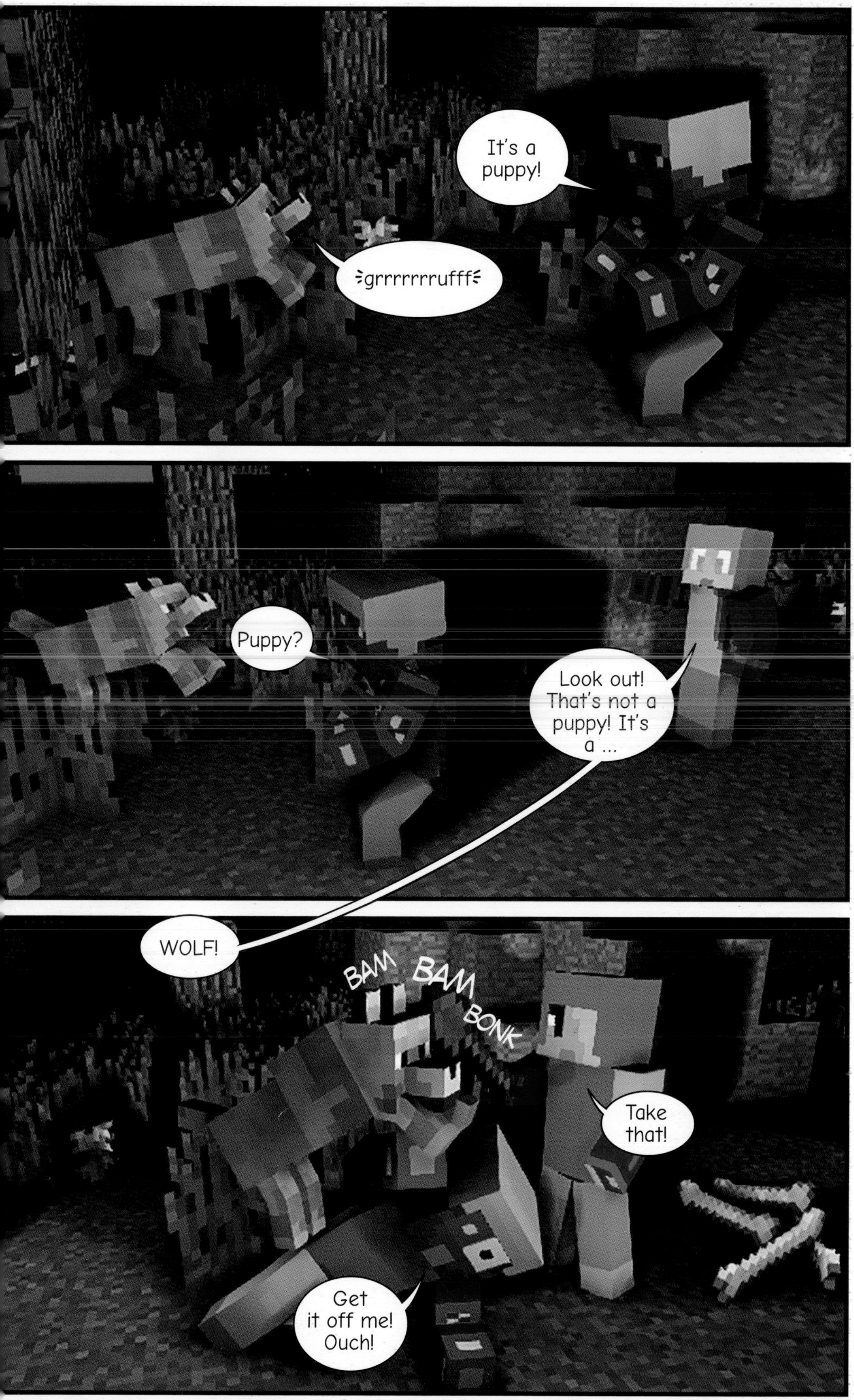
It's a puppy!
grrrrrrrufff
Puppy?
Look out! That's not a puppy! It's a ...
WOLF!
BAM
BAM
BONK
Take that!
Get it off me! Ouch!

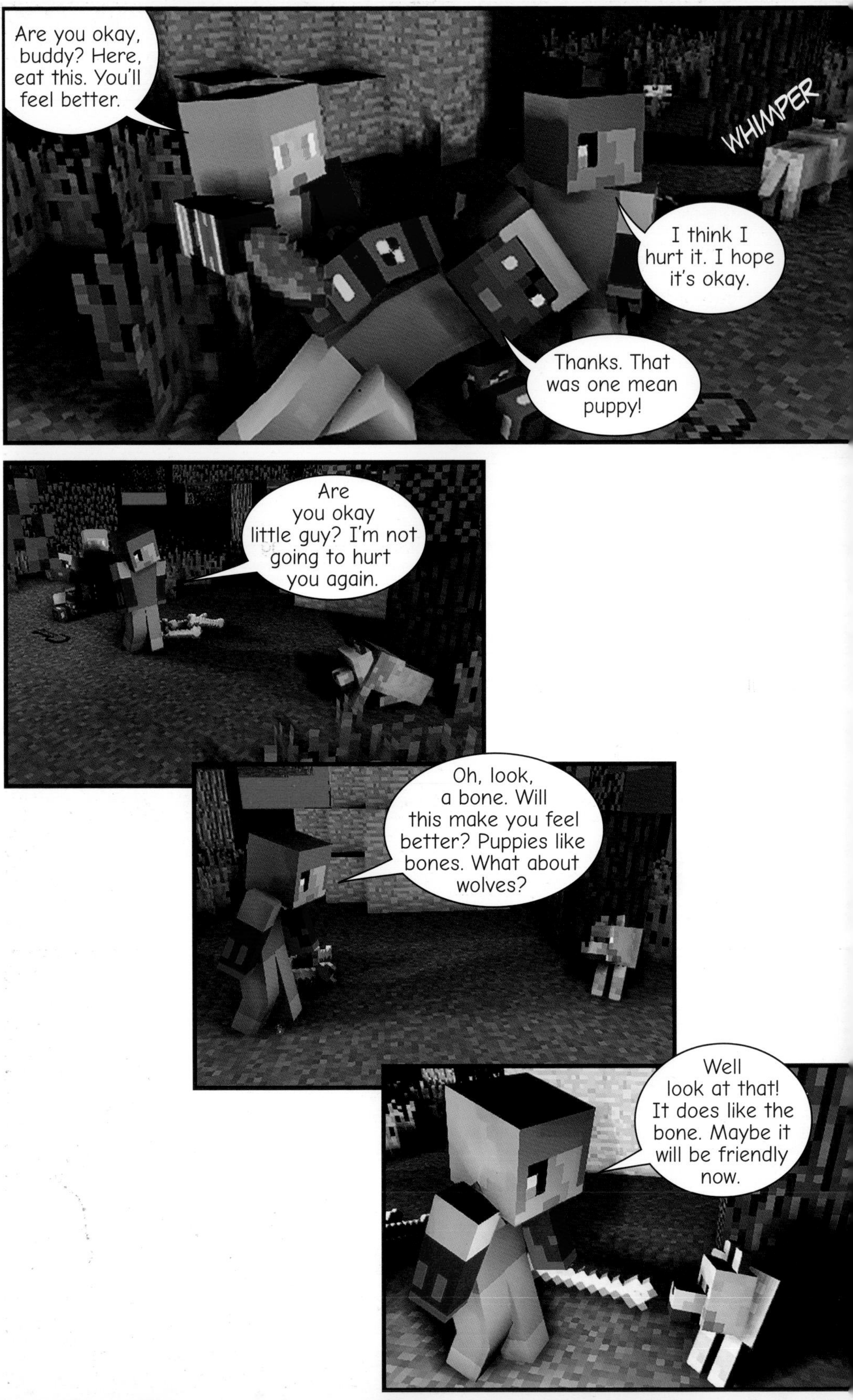

Are you okay, buddy? Here, eat this. You'll feel better.
WHIMPER
I think I hurt it. I hope it's okay.
Thanks. That was one mean puppy!
Are you okay little guy? I'm not going to hurt you again.
Oh, look, a bone. Will this make you feel better? Puppies like bones. What about wolves?
Well look at that! It does like the bone. Maybe it will be friendly now.

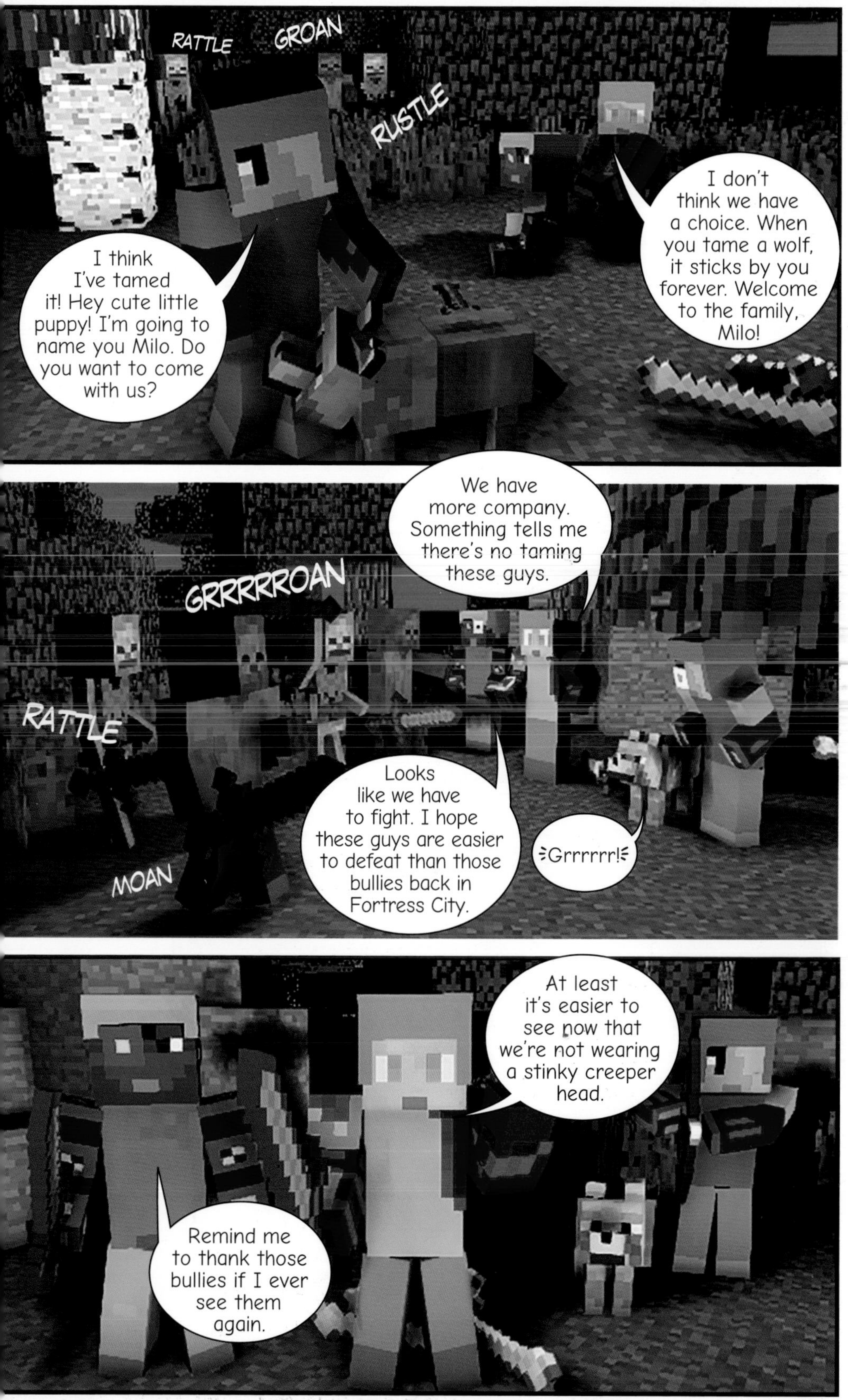
RATTLE
GROAN
RUSTLE
I think I've tamed it! Hey cute little puppy! I'm going to name you Milo. Do you want to come with us?
I don't think we have a choice. When you tame a wolf, it sticks by you forever. Welcome to the family, Milo!
GRRRRROAN
We have more company. Something tells me there's no taming these guys.
RATTLE
Looks like we have to fight. I hope these guys are easier to defeat than those bullies back in Fortress City.
Grrrrrr!
MOAN
At least it's easier to see now that we're not wearing a stinky creeper head.
Remind me to thank those bullies if I ever see them again.

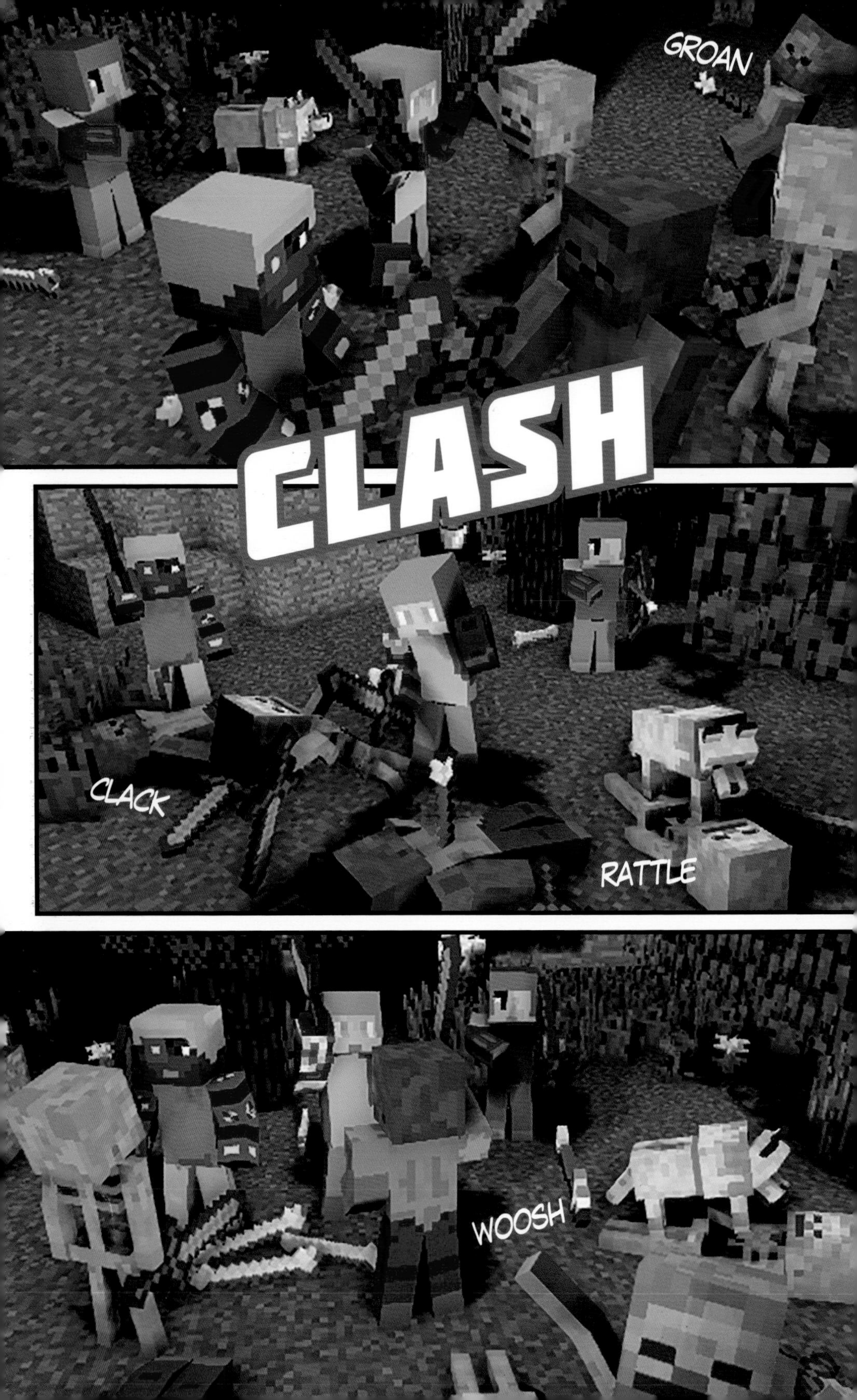
GROAN
CLASH
CLACK
RATTLE
WOOSH

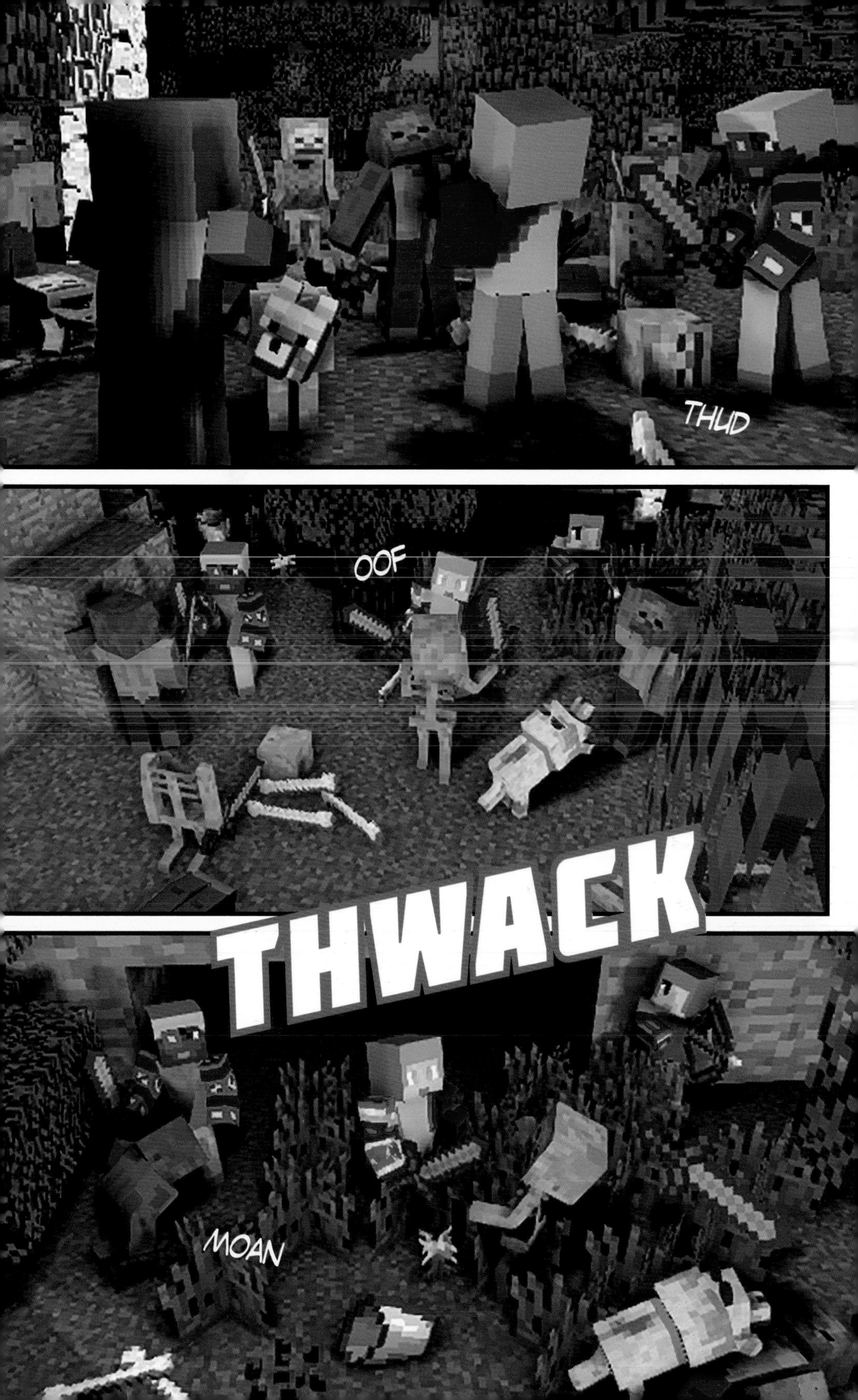
THUD
OOF
THWACK
MOAN

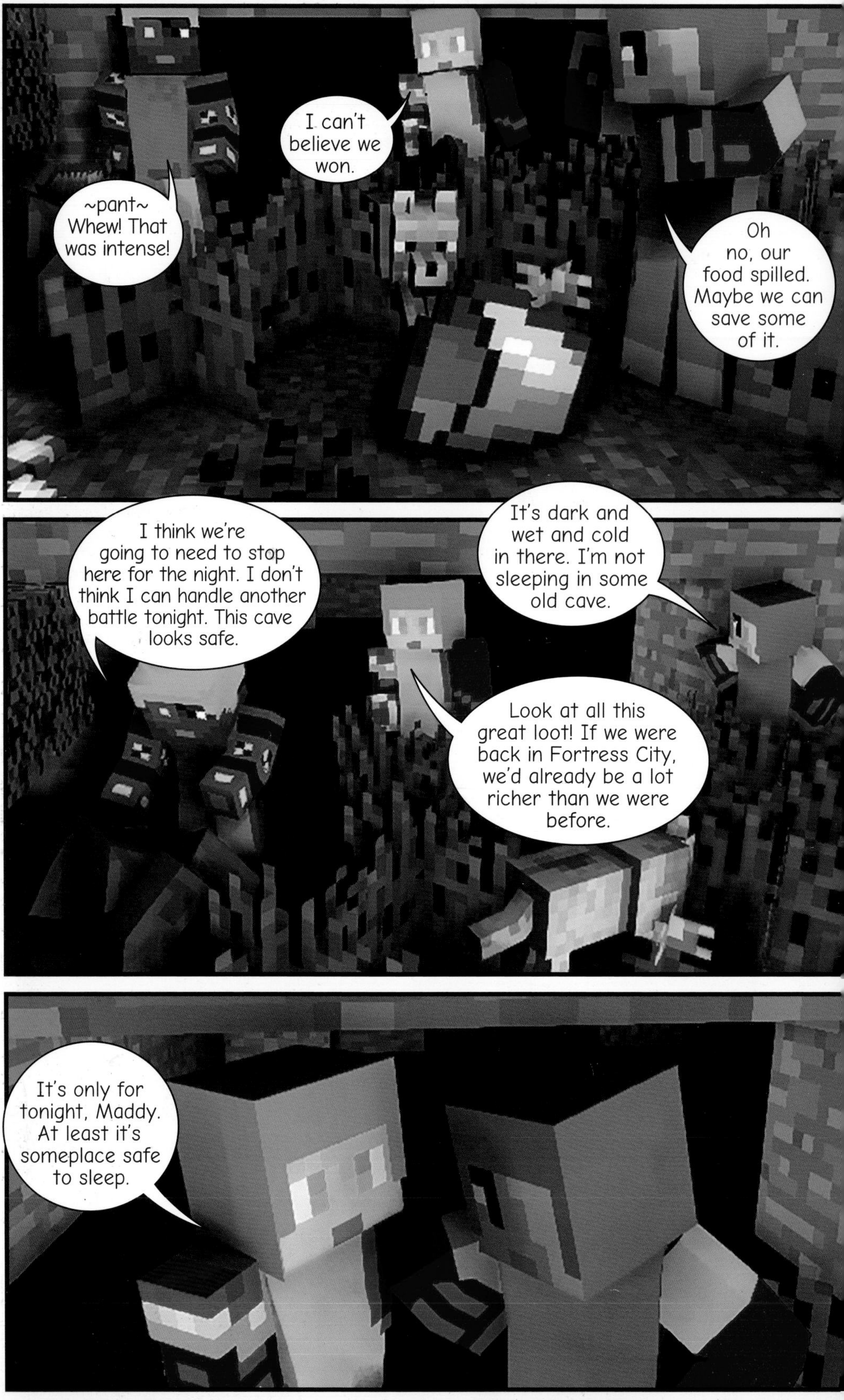
~pant~ Whew! That was intense!
I can't believe we won.
Oh no, our food spilled. Maybe we can save some of it.
I think we're going to need to stop here for the night. I don't think I can handle another battle tonight. This cave looks safe.
It's dark and wet and cold in there. I'm not sleeping in some old cave.
Look at all this great loot! If we were back in Fortress City, we'd already be a lot richer than we were before.
It's only for tonight, Maddy. At least it's someplace safe to sleep.

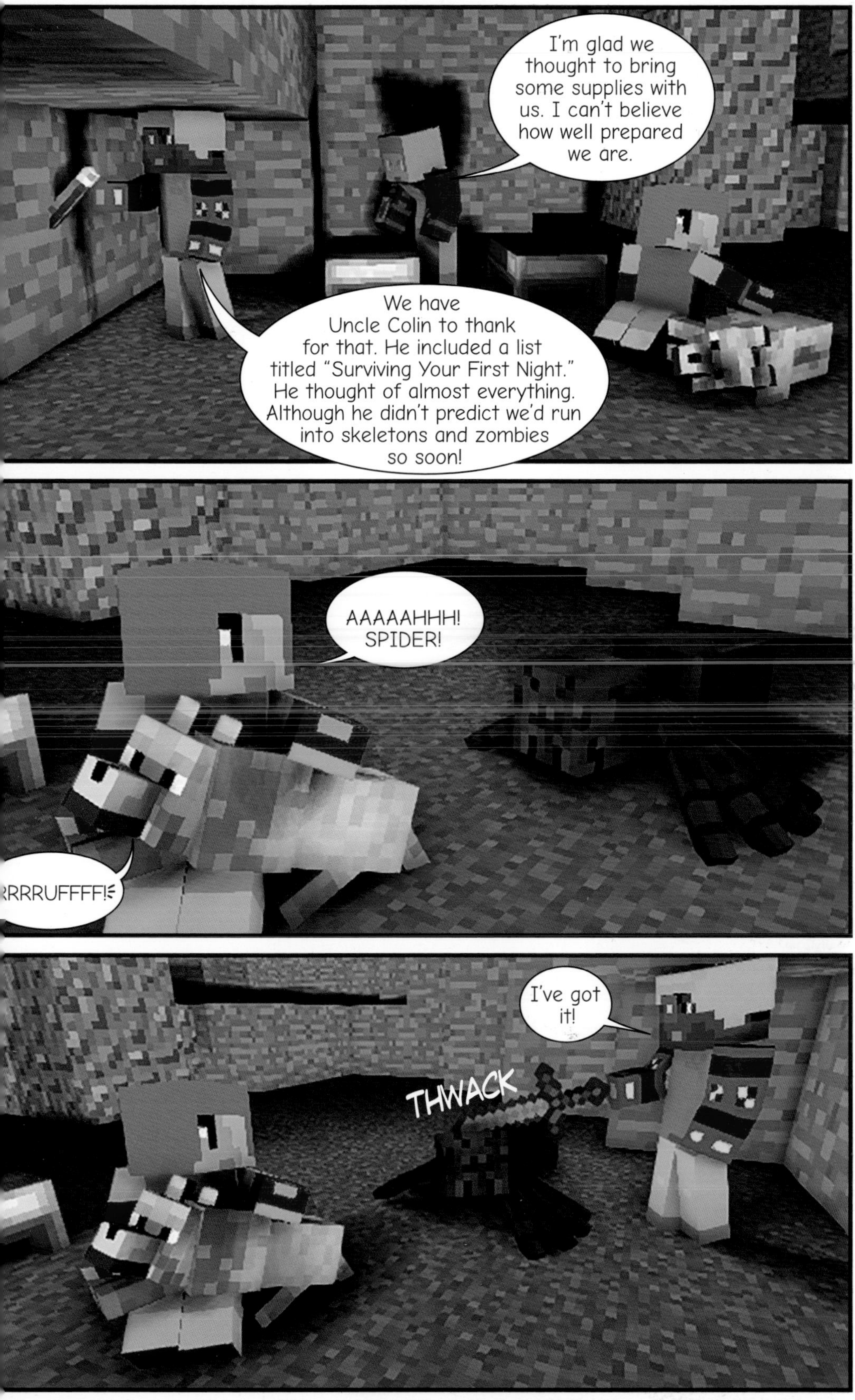
I'm glad we thought to bring some supplies with us. I can't believe how well prepared we are.
We have Uncle Colin to thank for that. He included a list titled "Surviving Your First Night." He thought of almost everything. Although he didn't predict we'd run into skeletons and zombies so soon!
AAAAAHHH! SPIDER!
RRRUFFFFF!
I've got it!
THWACK

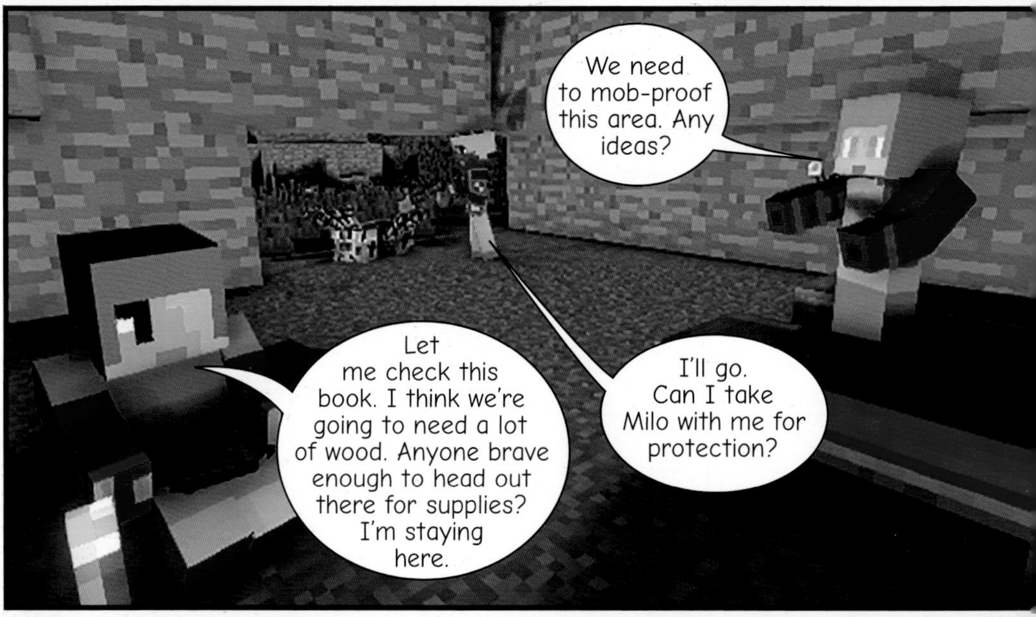
We need to mob-proof this area. Any ideas?
Let me check this book. I think we're going to need a lot of wood. Anyone brave enough to head out there for supplies? I'm staying here.
I'll go. Can I take Milo with me for protection?

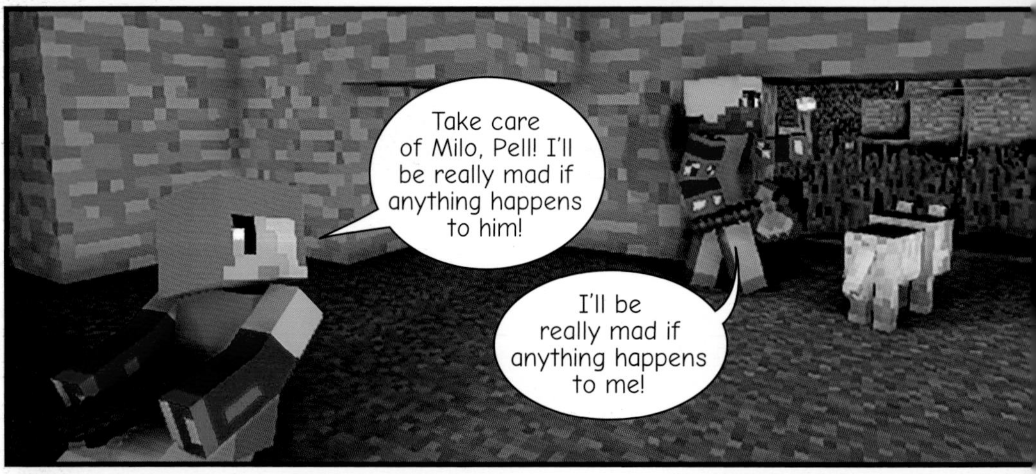
Take care of Milo, Pell! I'll be really mad if anything happens to him!
I'll be really mad if anything happens to me!

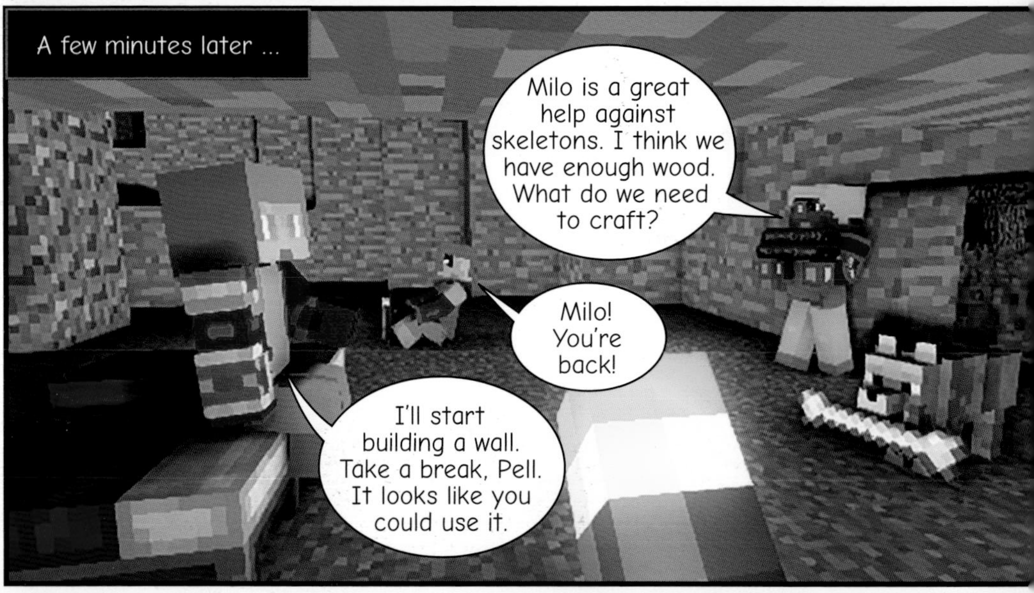
A few minutes later ...
Milo is a great help against skeletons. I think we have enough wood. What do we need to craft?
Milo! You're back!
I'll start building a wall. Take a break, Pell. It looks like you could use it.

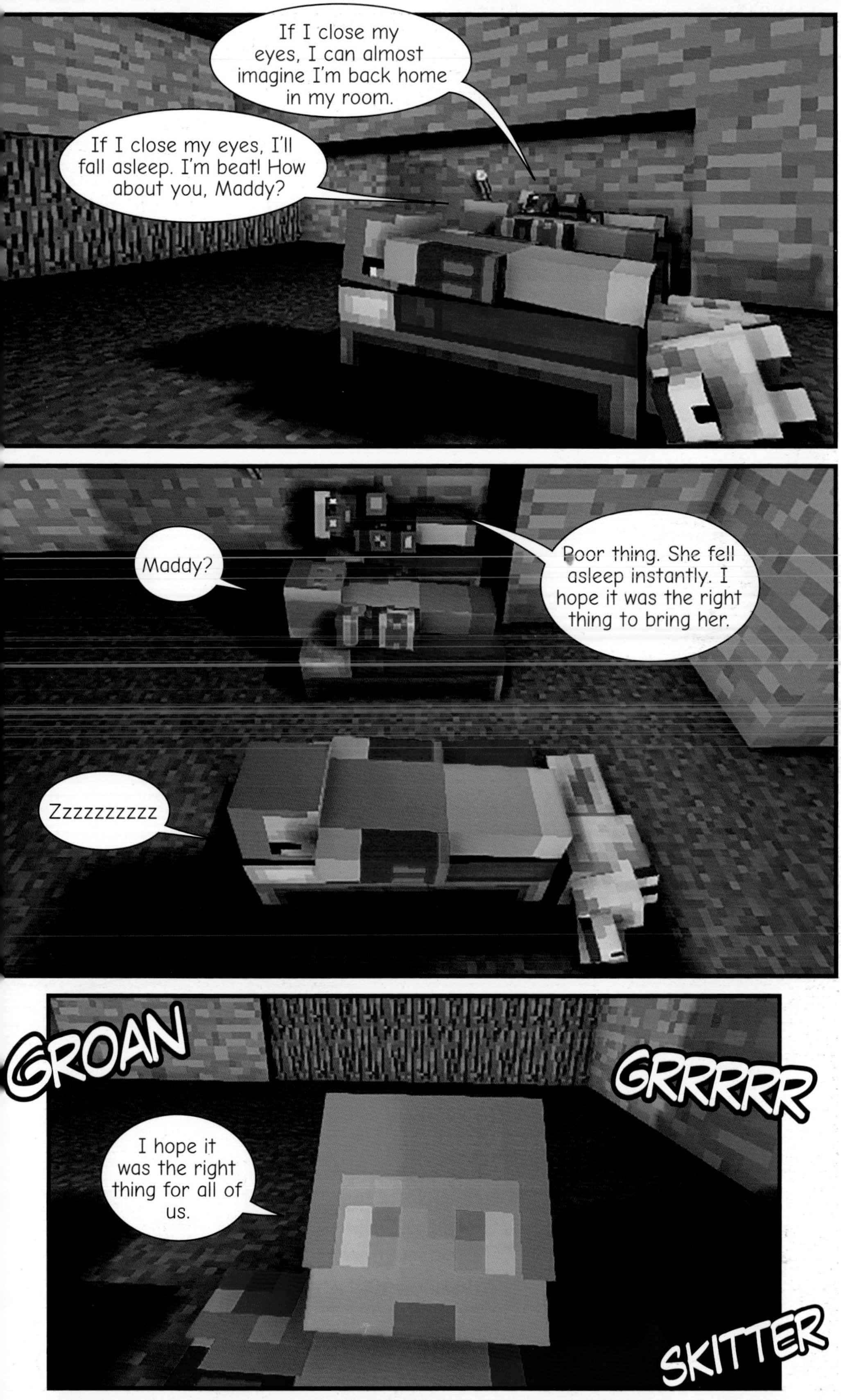

If I close my eyes, I can almost imagine I'm back home in my room.
If I close my eyes, I'll fall asleep. I'm beat! How about you, Maddy?
Maddy?
Poor thing. She fell asleep instantly. I hope it was the right thing to bring her.
Zzzzzzzzzz
GROAN
GRRRRR
I hope it was the right thing for all of us.
SKITTER

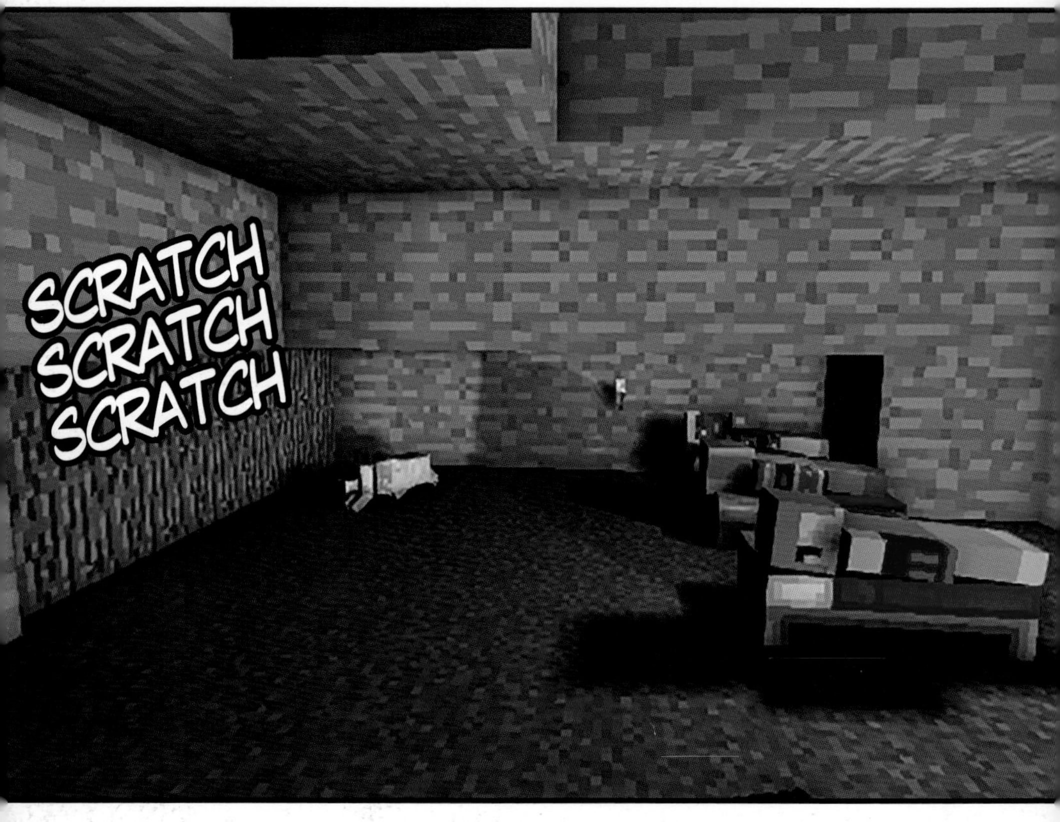
SCRATCH
SCRATCH
SCRATCH

CHAPTER 6

A BEAUTIFUL
MORNING

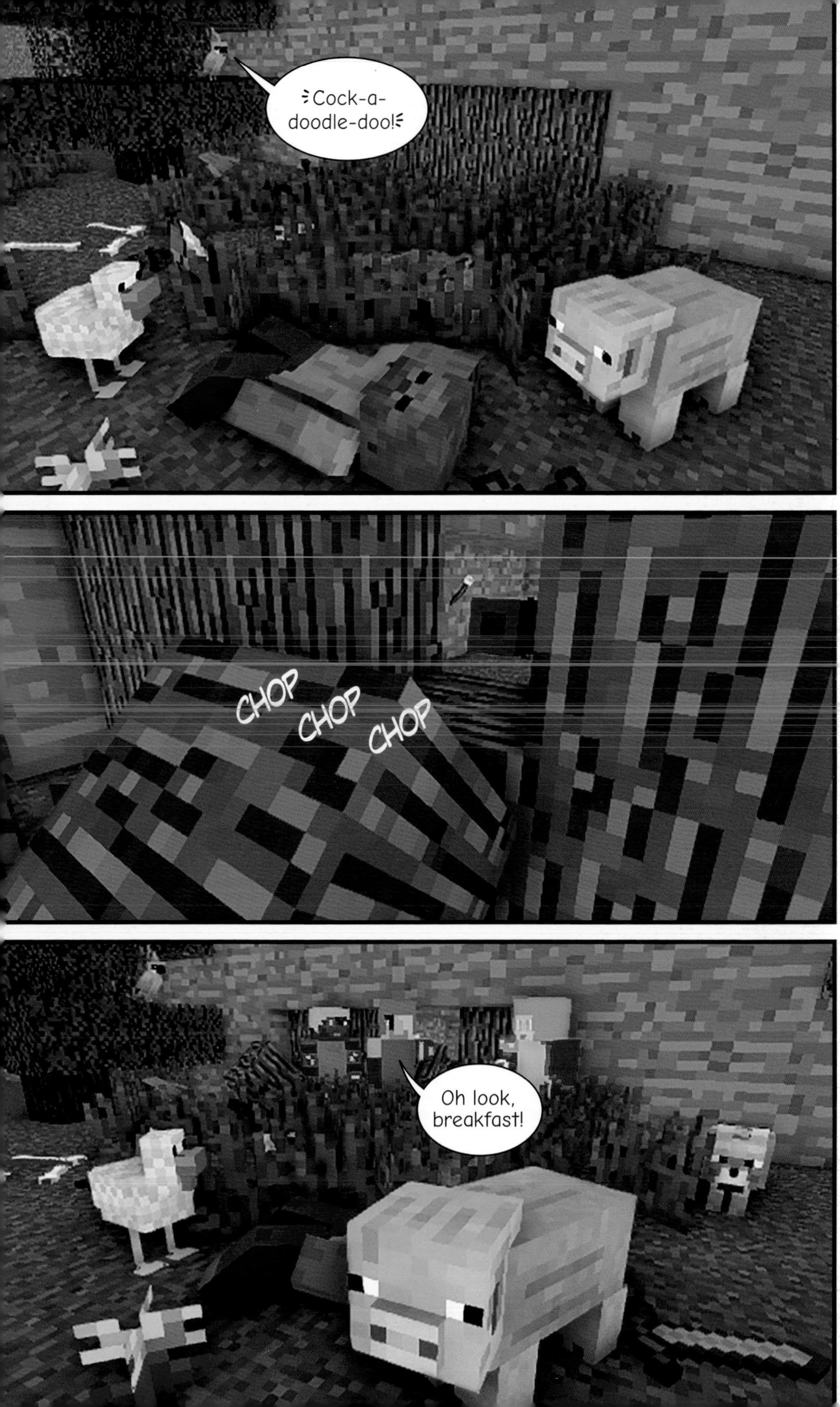
Cock-a-doodle-doo!
CHOP
CHOP
CHOP
Oh look, breakfast!

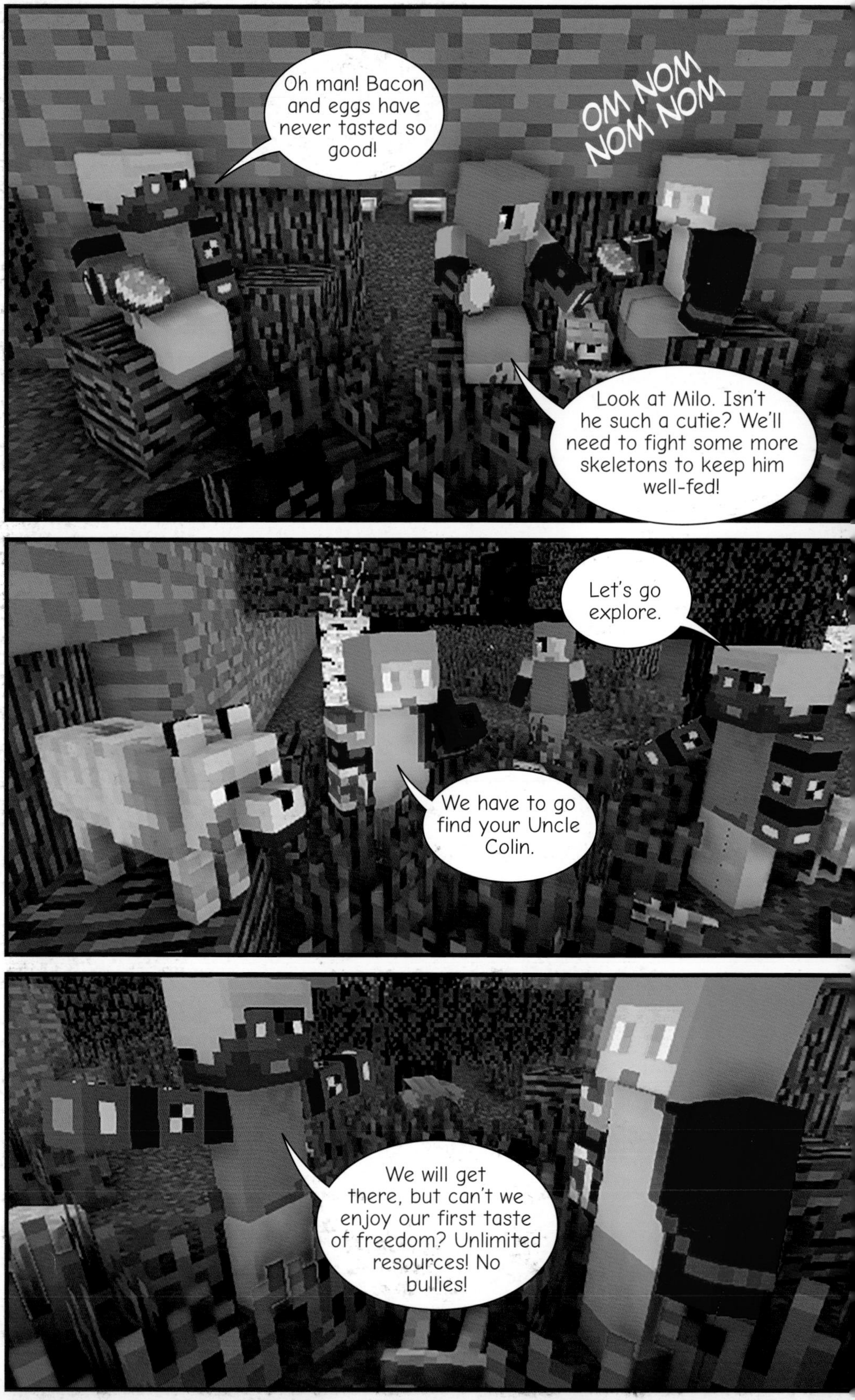

Oh man! Bacon and eggs have never tasted so good!
OM NOM NOM NOM
Look at Milo. Isn't he such a cutie? We'll need to fight some more skeletons to keep him well-fed!
Let's go explore.
We have to go find your Uncle Colin.
We will get there, but can't we enjoy our first taste of freedom? Unlimited resources! No bullies!

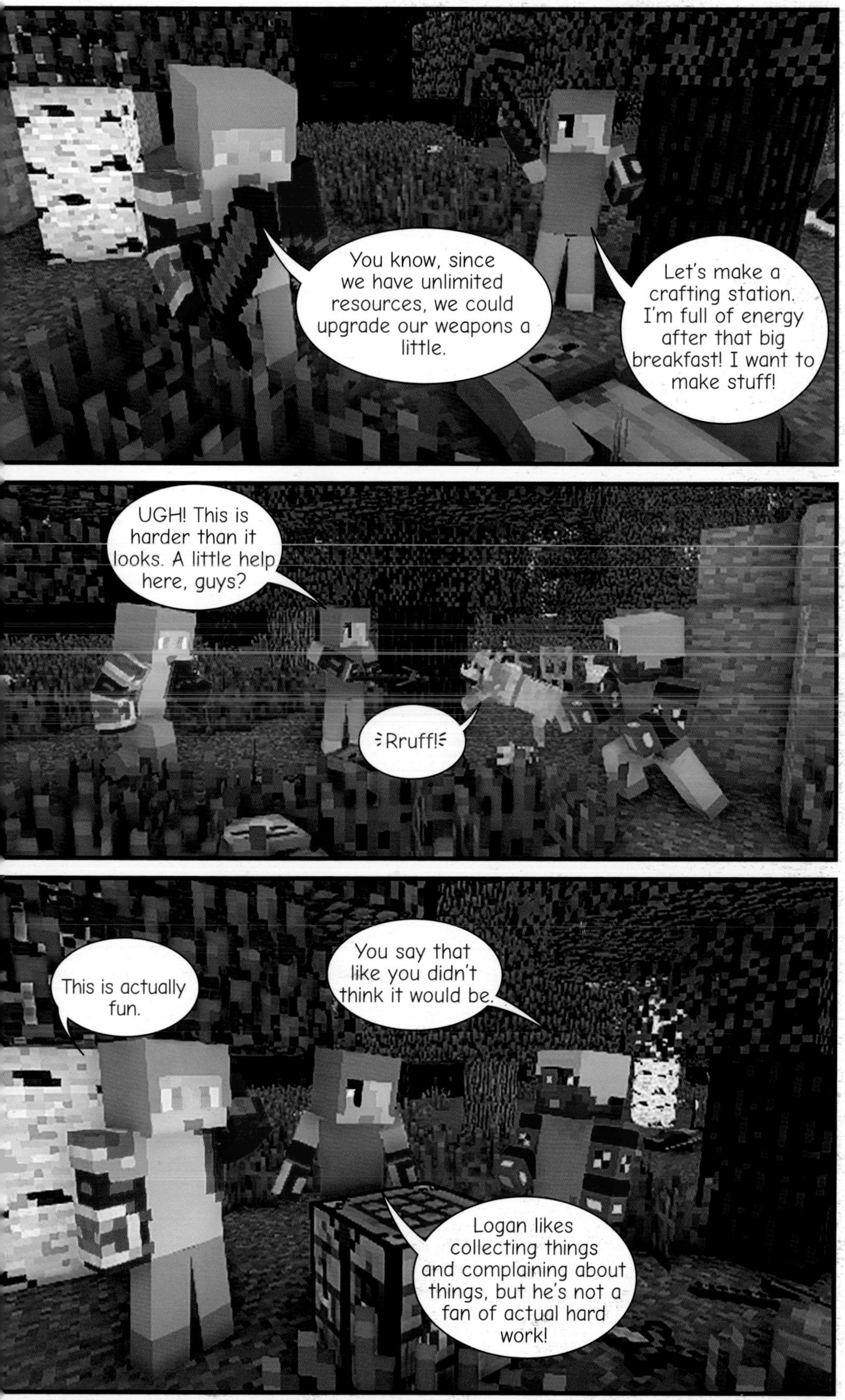
You know, since we have unlimited resources, we could upgrade our weapons a little.
Let's make a crafting station. I'm full of energy after that big breakfast! I want to make stuff!
UGH! This is harder than it looks. A little help here, guys?
Rruff!
This is actually fun.
You say that like you didn't think it would be.
Logan likes collecting things and complaining about things, but he's not a fan of actual hard work!

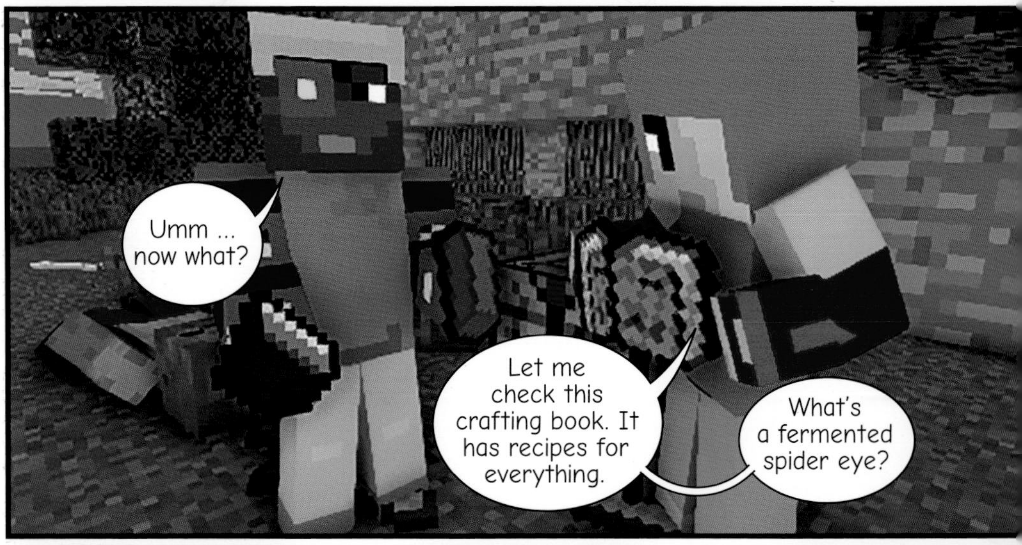
Umm ... now what?
Let me check this crafting book. It has recipes for everything.
What's a fermented spider eye?

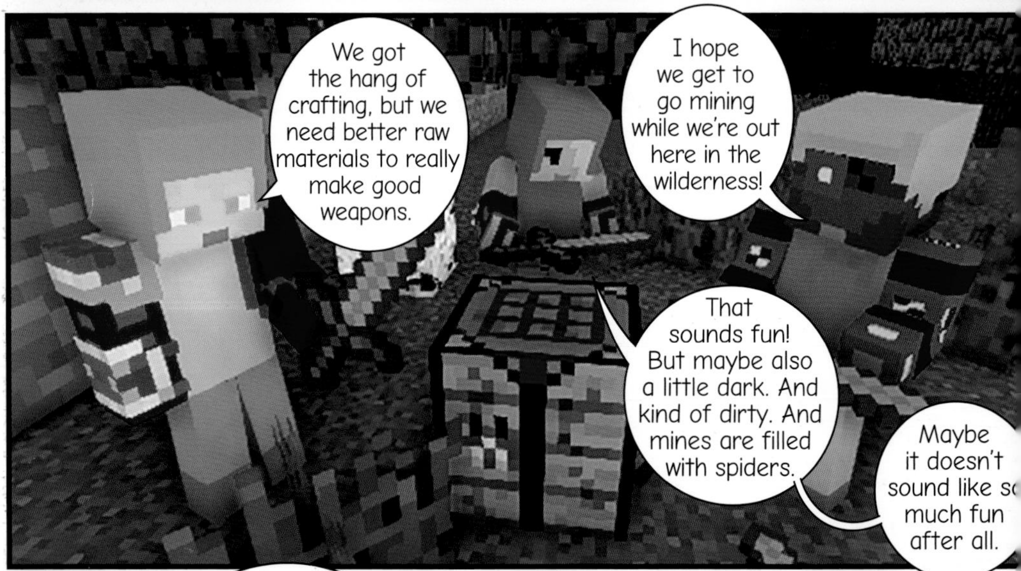
We got the hang of crafting, but we need better raw materials to really make good weapons.
I hope we get to go mining while we're out here in the wilderness!
That sounds fun! But maybe also a little dark. And kind of dirty. And mines are filled with spiders.

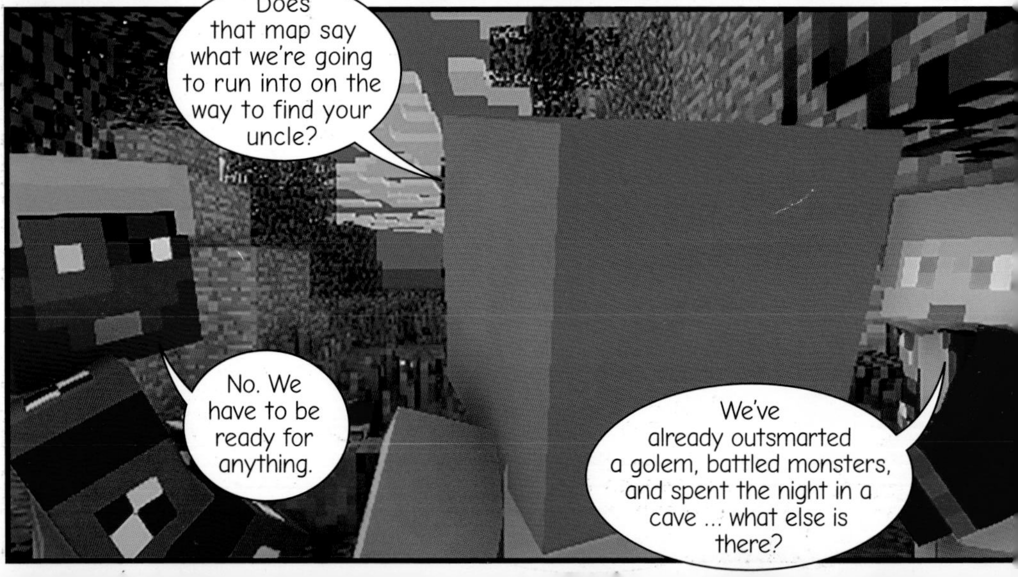
Does that map say what we're going to run into on the way to find your uncle?
No. We have to be ready for anything.
We've already outsmarted a golem, battled monsters, and spent the night in a cave ... what else is there?

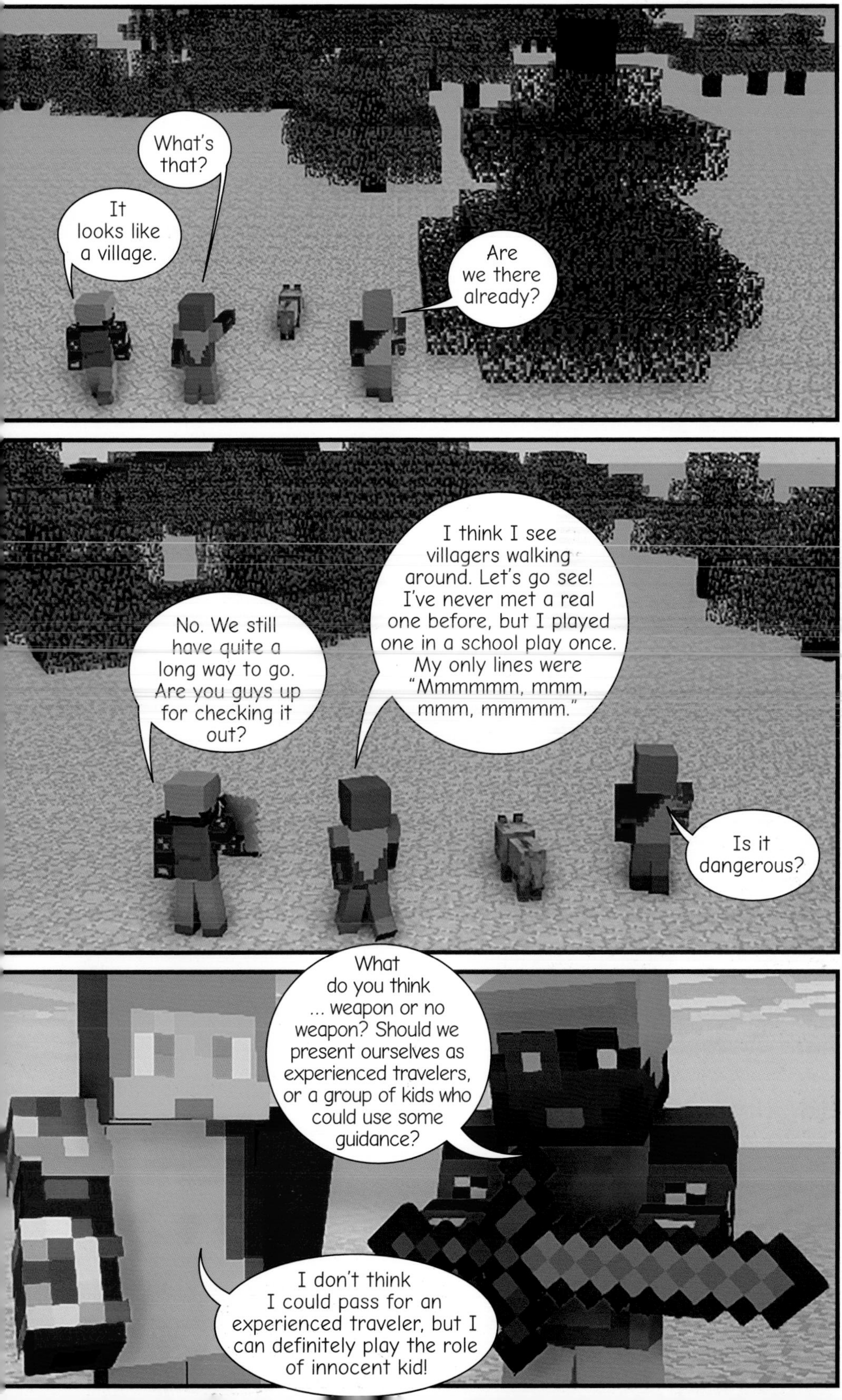
What's that?
It looks like a village.
Are we there already?
No. We still have quite a long way to go. Are you guys up for checking it out?
I think I see villagers walking around. Let's go see! I've never met a real one before, but I played one in a school play once. My only lines were "Mmmmmm, mmm, mmm, mmmmm."
Is it dangerous?
What do you think ... weapon or no weapon? Should we present ourselves as experienced travelers, or a group of kids who could use some guidance?
I don't think I could pass for an experienced traveler, but I can definitely play the role of innocent kid!

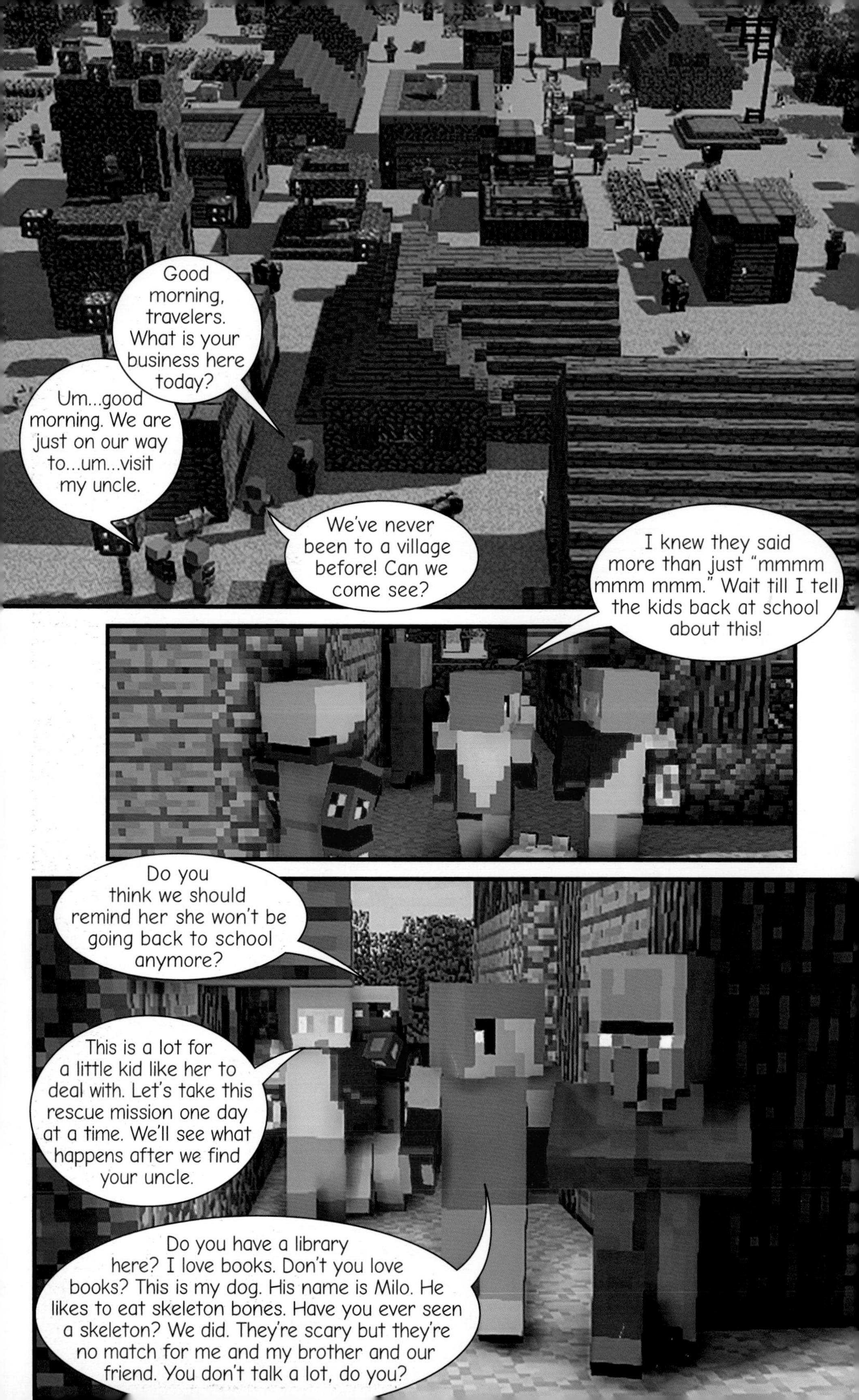
Good morning, travelers. What is your business here today?
Um...good morning. We are just on our way to...um...visit my uncle.
We've never been to a village before! Can we come see?
I knew they said more than just "mmmm mmm mmm." Wait till I tell the kids back at school about this!
Do you think we should remind her she won't be going back to school anymore?
This is a lot for a little kid like her to deal with. Let's take this rescue mission one day at a time. We'll see what happens after we find your uncle.
Do you have a library here? I love books. Don't you love books? This is my dog. His name is Milo. He likes to eat skeleton bones. Have you ever seen a skeleton? We did. They're scary but they're no match for me and my brother and our friend. You don't talk a lot, do you?

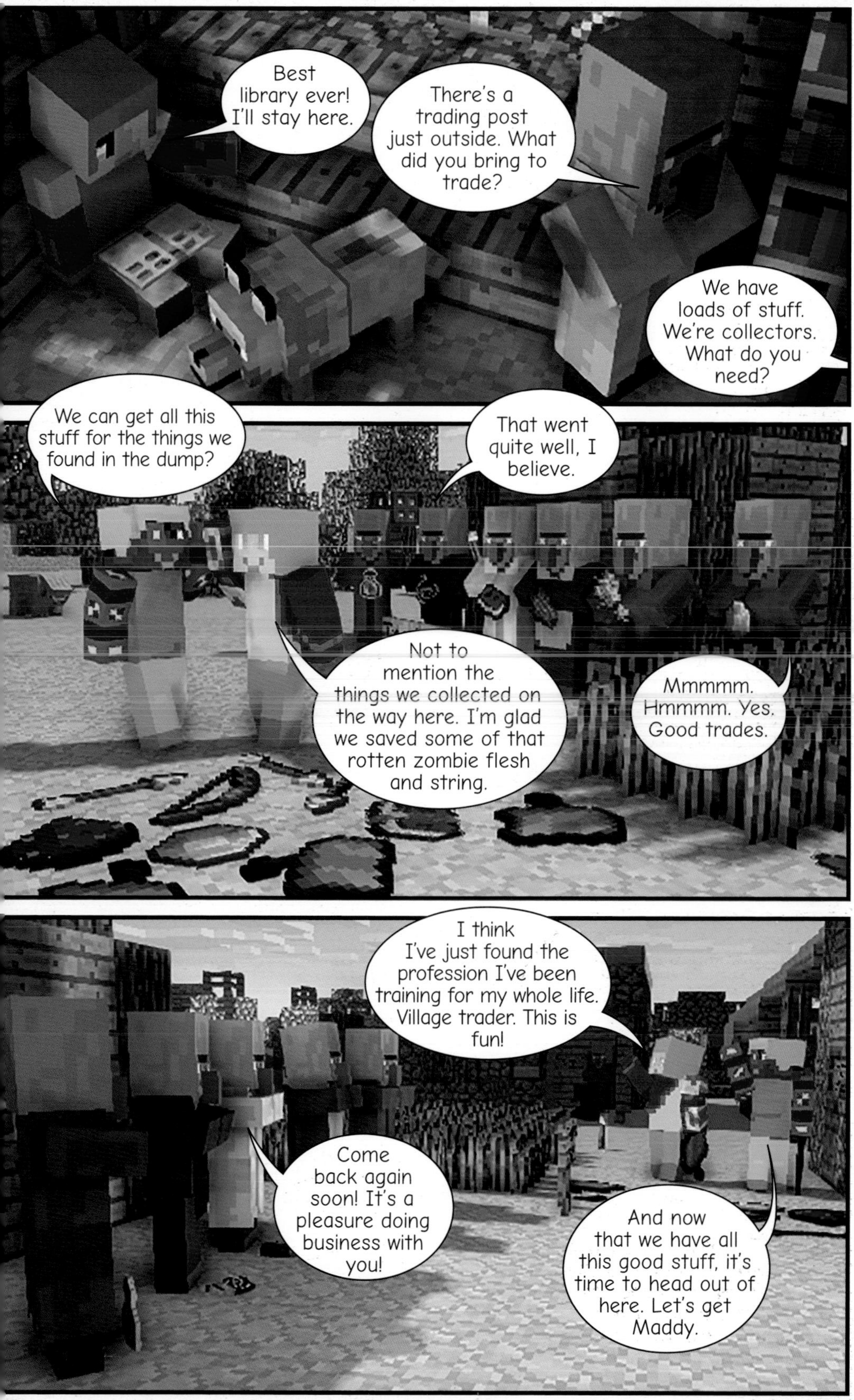

Best library ever! I'll stay here.
There's a trading post just outside. What did you bring to trade?
We have loads of stuff. We're collectors. What do you need?
We can get all this stuff for the things we found in the dump?
That went quite well, I believe.
Not to mention the things we collected on the way here. I'm glad we saved some of that rotten zombie flesh and string.
Mmmmm. Hmmmm. Yes. Good trades.
I think I've just found the profession I've been training for my whole life. Village trader. This is fun!
Come back again soon! It's a pleasure doing business with you!
And now that we have all this good stuff, it's time to head out of here. Let's get Maddy.

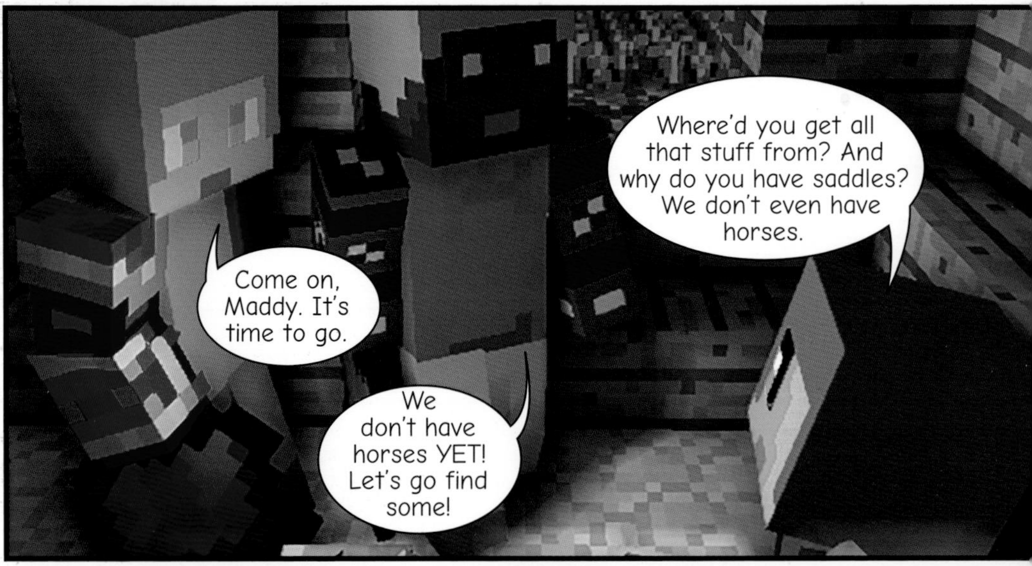
Come on, Maddy. It's time to go.
Where'd you get all that stuff from? And why do you have saddles? We don't even have horses.
We don't have horses YET! Let's go find some!

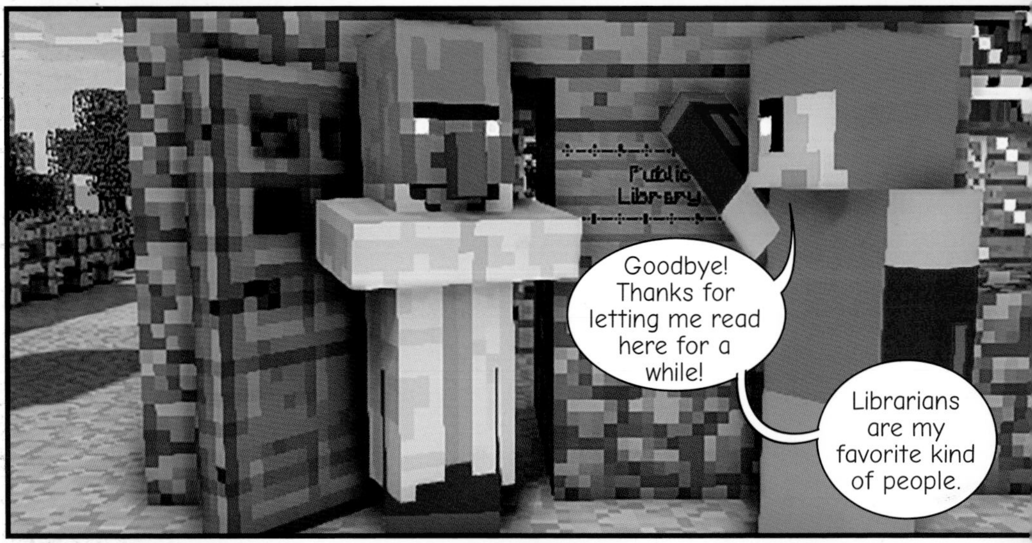
Public Library
Goodbye! Thanks for letting me read here for a while!
Librarians are my favorite kind of people.

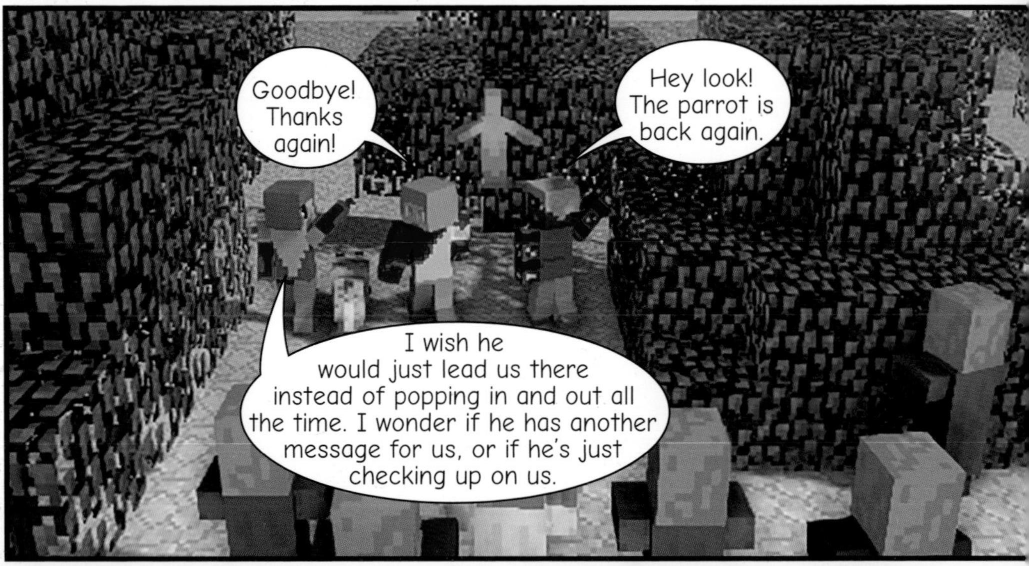
Goodbye! Thanks again!
Hey look! The parrot is back again.
I wish he would just lead us there instead of popping in and out all the time. I wonder if he has another message for us, or if he's just checking up on us.

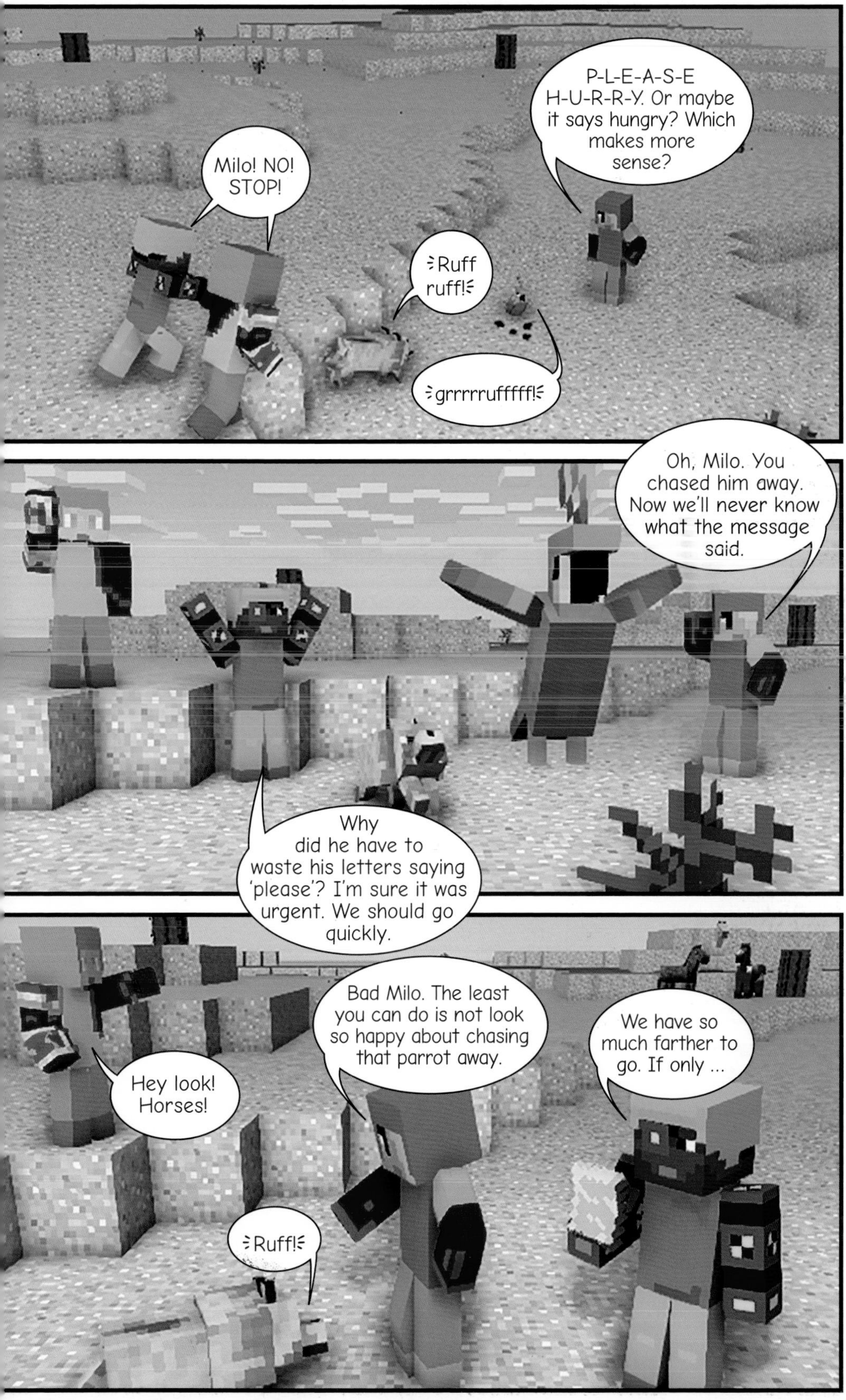
Milo! NO! STOP!
P-L-E-A-S-E H-U-R-R-Y. Or maybe it says hungry? Which makes more sense?
Ruff ruff!
grrrrrufffff!
Oh, Milo. You chased him away. Now we'll never know what the message said.
Why did he have to waste his letters saying 'please'? I'm sure it was urgent. We should go quickly.
Hey look! Horses!
Bad Milo. The least you can do is not look so happy about chasing that parrot away.
We have so much farther to go. If only ...
Ruff!

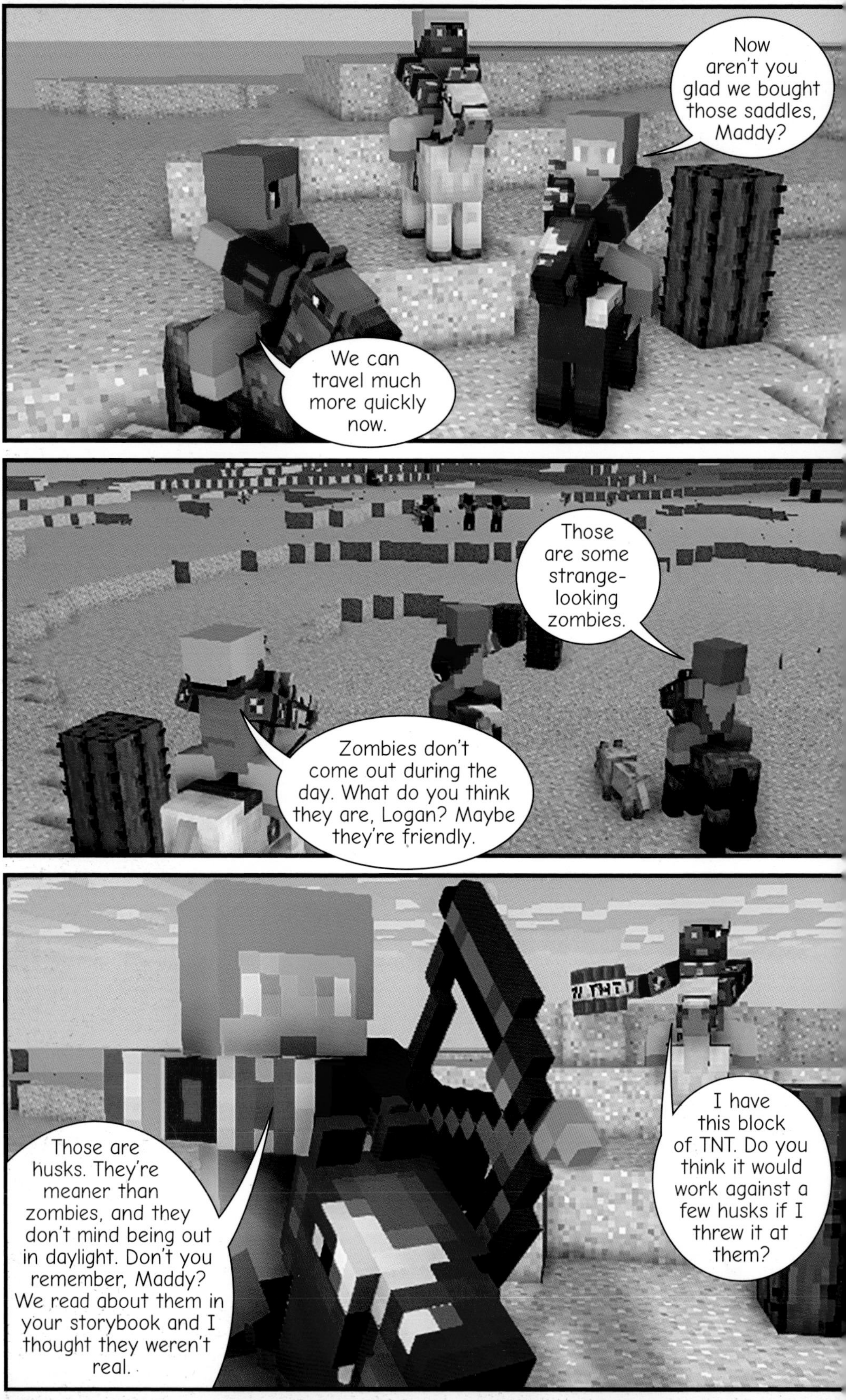
Now aren't you glad we bought those saddles, Maddy?
We can travel much more quickly now.
Those are some strange-looking zombies.
Zombies don't come out during the day. What do you think they are, Logan? Maybe they're friendly.
Those are husks. They're meaner than zombies, and they don't mind being out in daylight. Don't you remember, Maddy? We read about them in your storybook and I thought they weren't real.
I have this block of TNT. Do you think it would work against a few husks if I threw it at them?

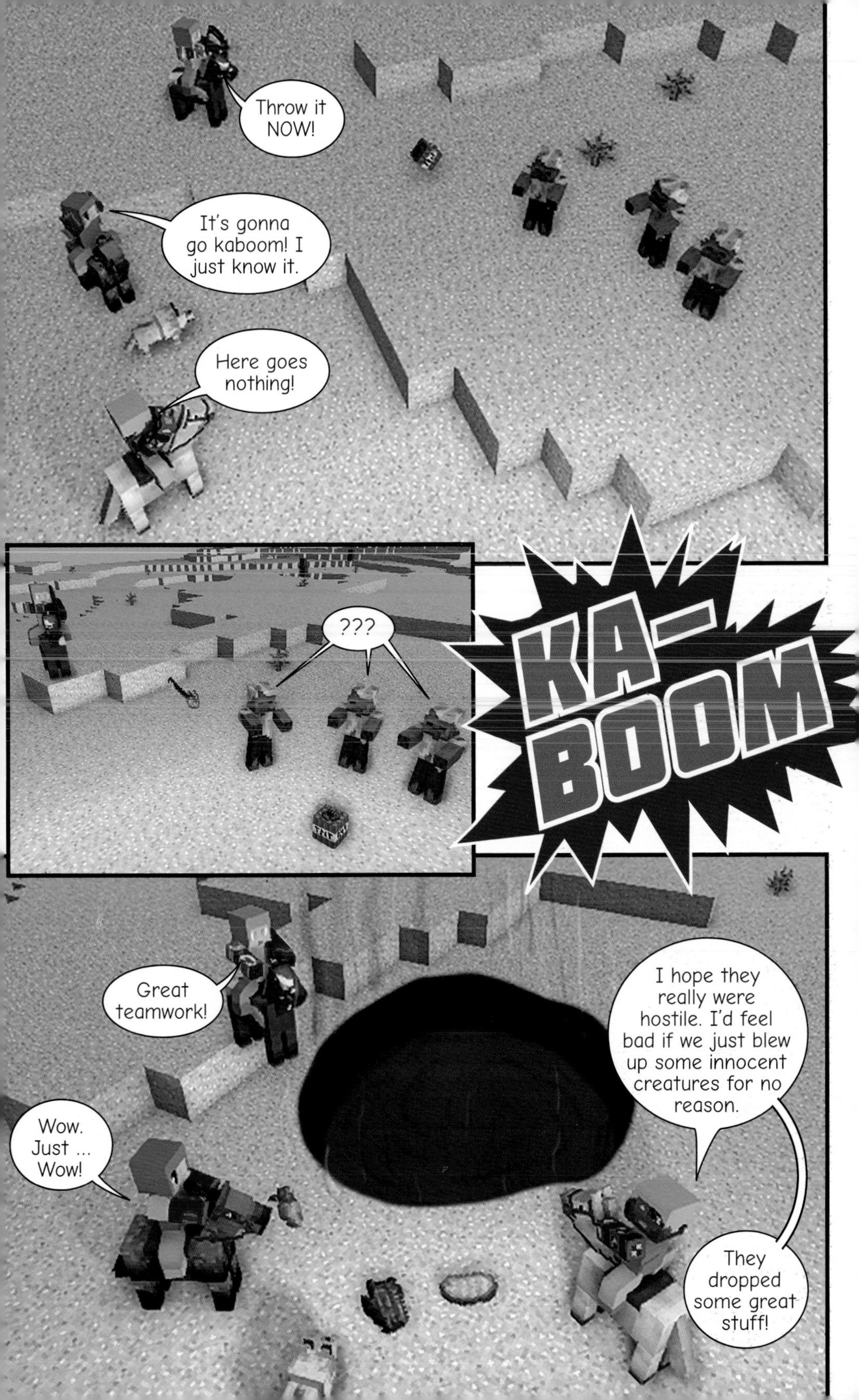
Throw it NOW!
It's gonna go kaboom! I just know it.
Here goes nothing!
???
KA-BOOM
Great teamwork!
I hope they really were hostile. I'd feel bad if we just blew up some innocent creatures for no reason.
Wow. Just ... Wow!
They dropped some great stuff!

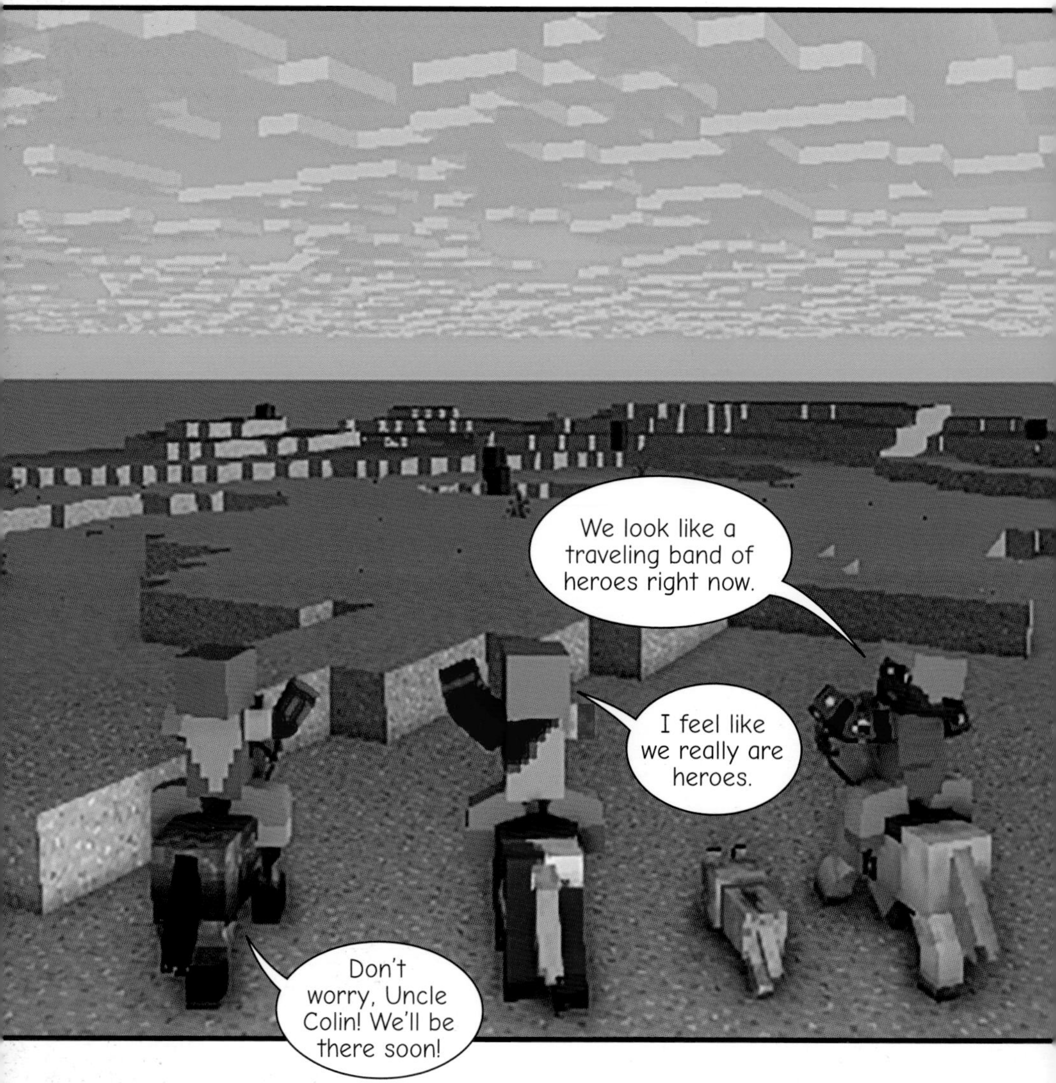
We look like a traveling band of heroes right now.
I feel like we really are heroes.
Don't worry, Uncle Colin! We'll be there soon!

CHAPTER 7

LIGHTNING STRIKES

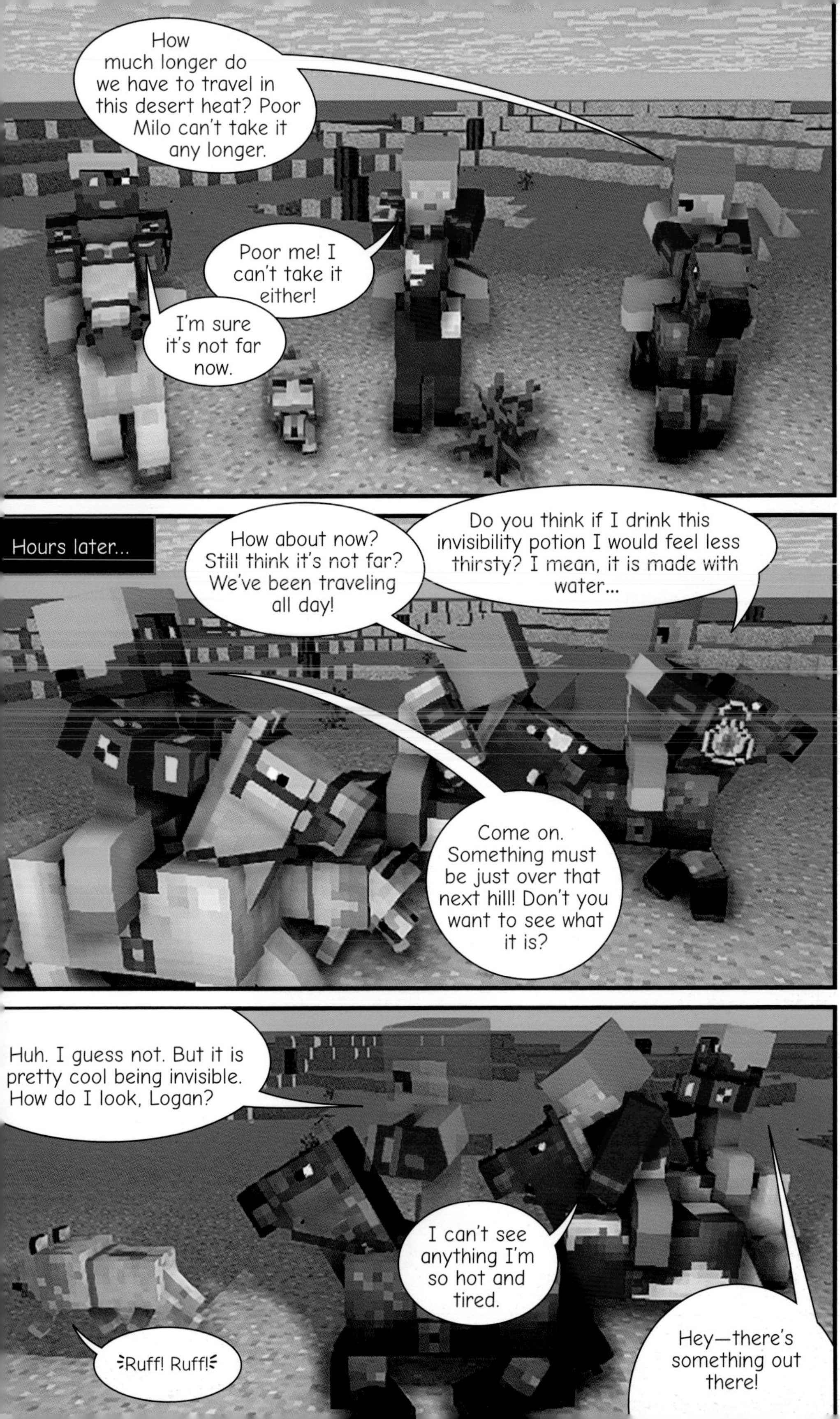
How much longer do we have to travel in this desert heat? Poor Milo can't take it any longer.
Poor me! I can't take it either!
I'm sure it's not far now.
Hours later...
How about now? Still think it's not far? We've been traveling all day!
Do you think if I drink this invisibility potion I would feel less thirsty? I mean, it is made with water...
Come on. Something must be just over that next hill! Don't you want to see what it is?
Huh. I guess not. But it is pretty cool being invisible. How do I look, Logan?
I can't see anything I'm so hot and tired.
Ruff! Ruff!
Hey—there's something out there!

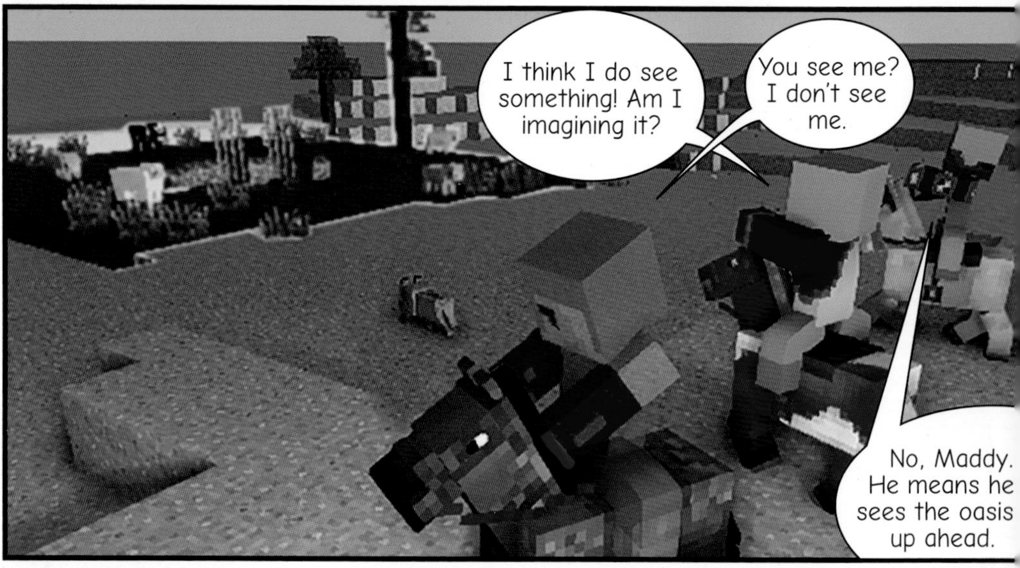
I think I do see something! Am I imagining it?
You see me? I don't see me.
No, Maddy. He means he sees the oasis up ahead.

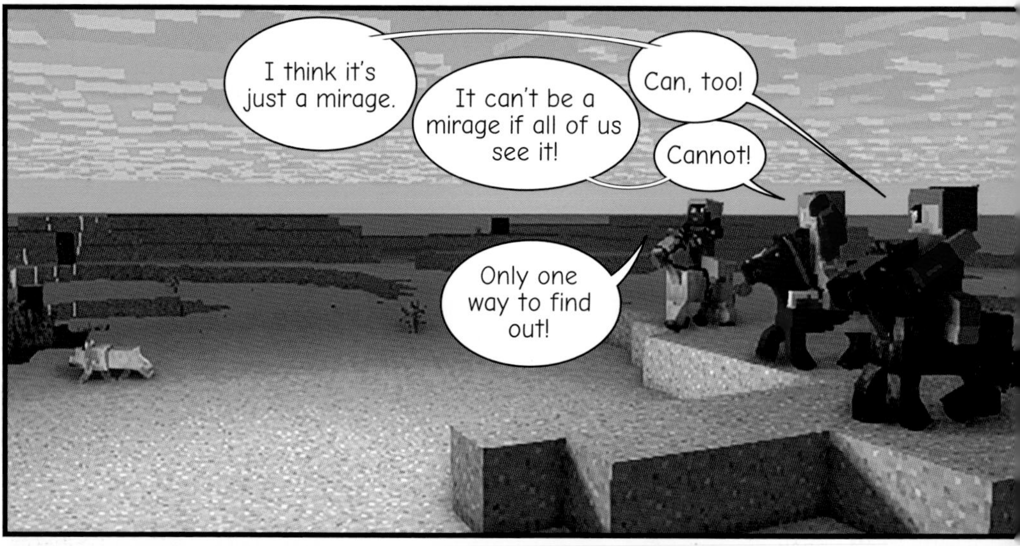
I think it's just a mirage.
It can't be a mirage if all of us see it!
Can, too!
Cannot!
Only one way to find out!

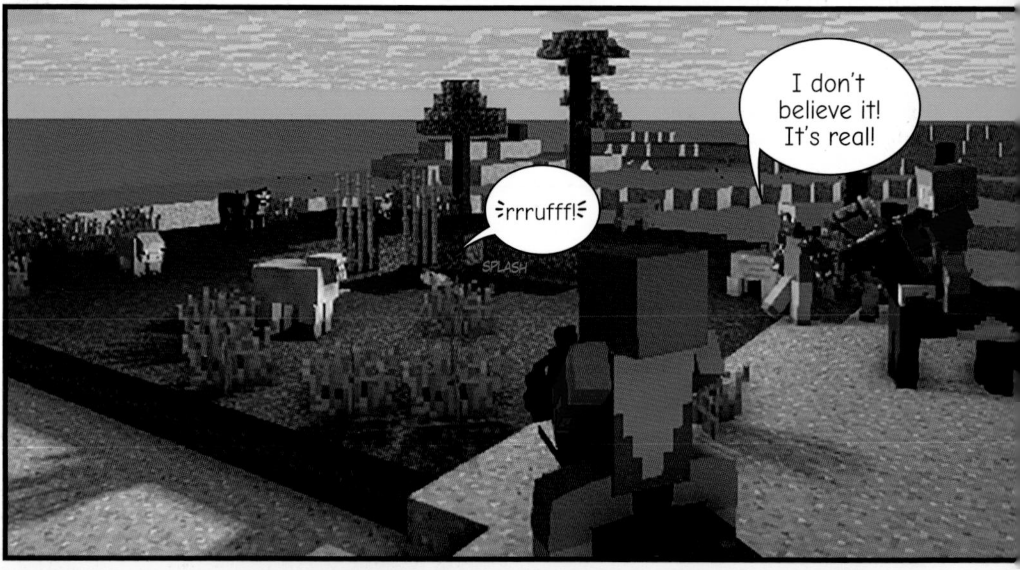
I don't believe it! It's real!
rrrufff!
SPLASH

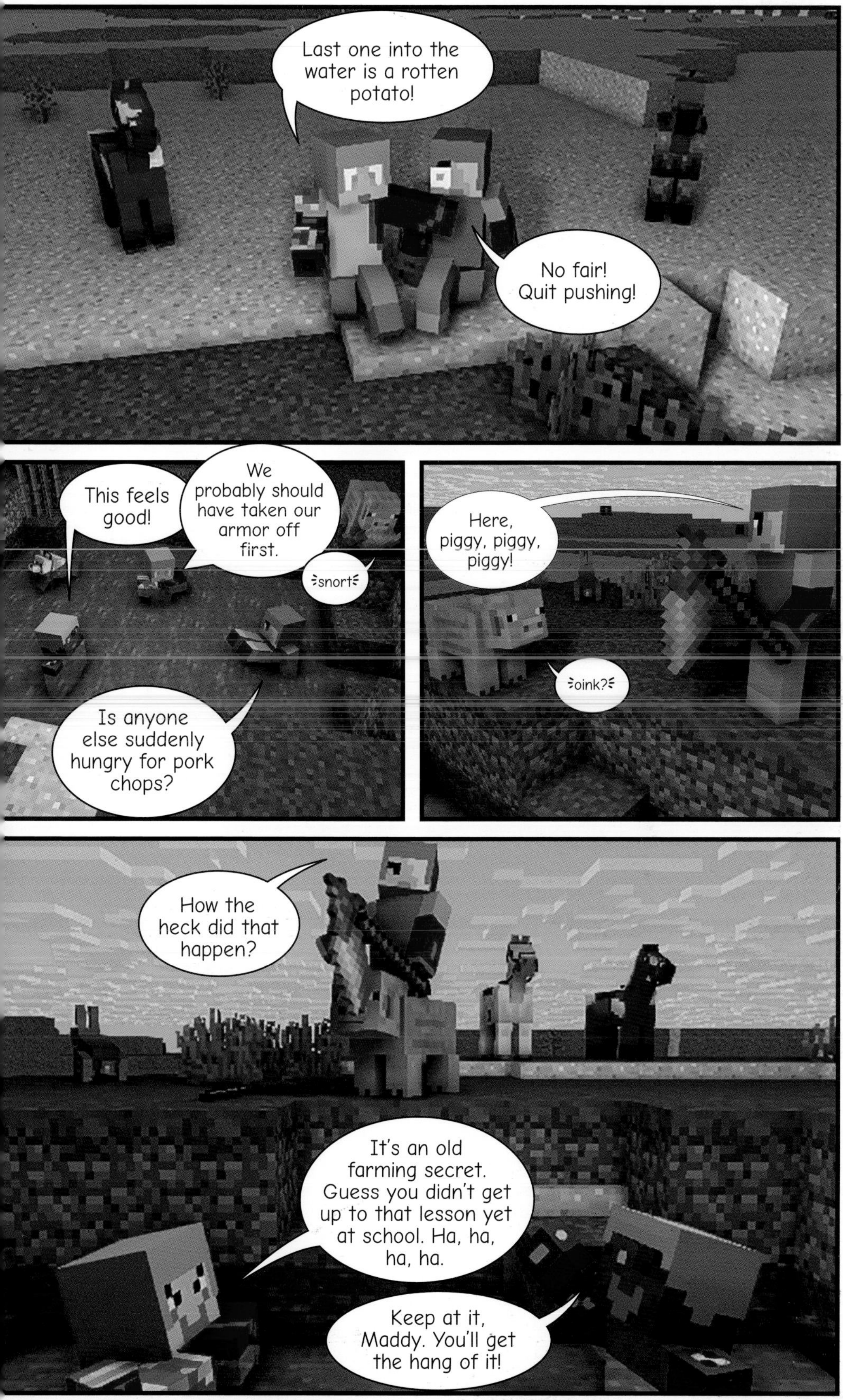
Last one into the water is a rotten potato!
No fair! Quit pushing!
This feels good!
We probably should have taken our armor off first.
snort
Is anyone else suddenly hungry for pork chops?
Here, piggy, piggy, piggy!
oink?
How the heck did that happen?
It's an old farming secret. Guess you didn't get up to that lesson yet at school. Ha, ha, ha, ha.
Keep at it, Maddy. You'll get the hang of it!

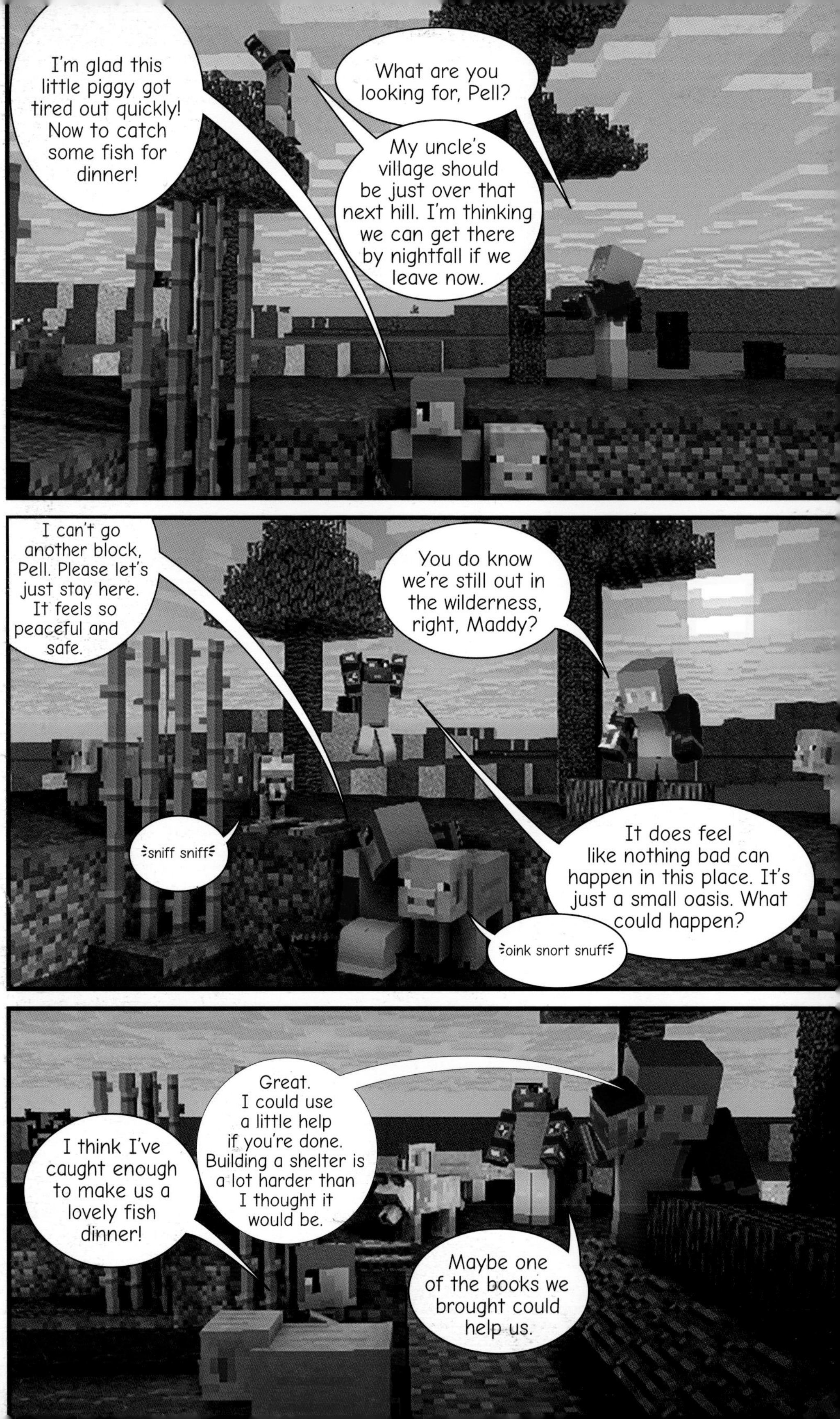
I'm glad this little piggy got tired out quickly! Now to catch some fish for dinner!
What are you looking for, Pell?
My uncle's village should be just over that next hill. I'm thinking we can get there by nightfall if we leave now.
I can't go another block, Pell. Please let's just stay here. It feels so peaceful and safe.
You do know we're still out in the wilderness, right, Maddy?
sniff sniff
It does feel like nothing bad can happen in this place. It's just a small oasis. What could happen?
oink snort snuff
I think I've caught enough to make us a lovely fish dinner!
Great. I could use a little help if you're done. Building a shelter is a lot harder than I thought it would be.
Maybe one of the books we brought could help us.

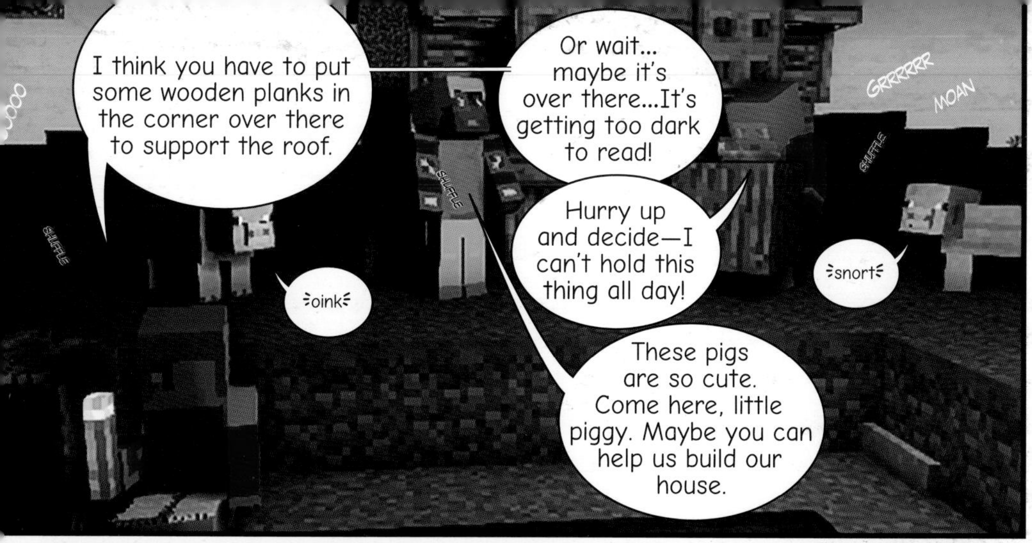
I think you have to put some wooden planks in the corner over there to support the roof.
Or wait... maybe it's over there...It's getting too dark to read!
Hurry up and decide—I can't hold this thing all day!
These pigs are so cute. Come here, little piggy. Maybe you can help us build our house.
GRRRRRR
MOAN
SHUFFLE
SHUFFLE
SHUFFLE
oink
snort

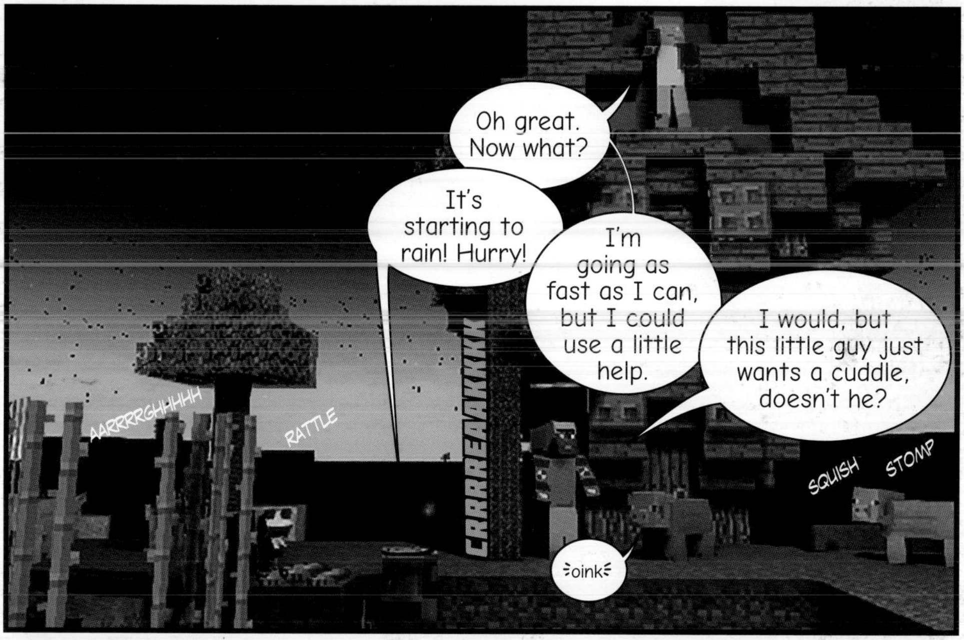
Oh great. Now what?
It's starting to rain! Hurry!
I'm going as fast as I can, but I could use a little help.
I would, but this little guy just wants a cuddle, doesn't he?
AARRRRGHHHHH
RATTLE
CRRRREAAKKKK
SQUISH
STOMP
oink

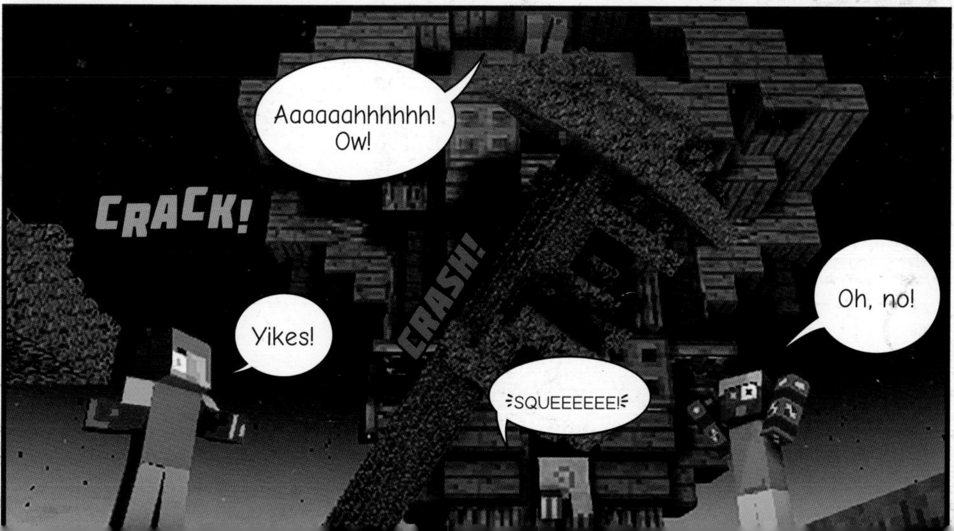
Aaaaaahhhhhh! Ow!
CRACK!
CRASH!
Yikes!
Oh, no!
SQUEEEEEE!

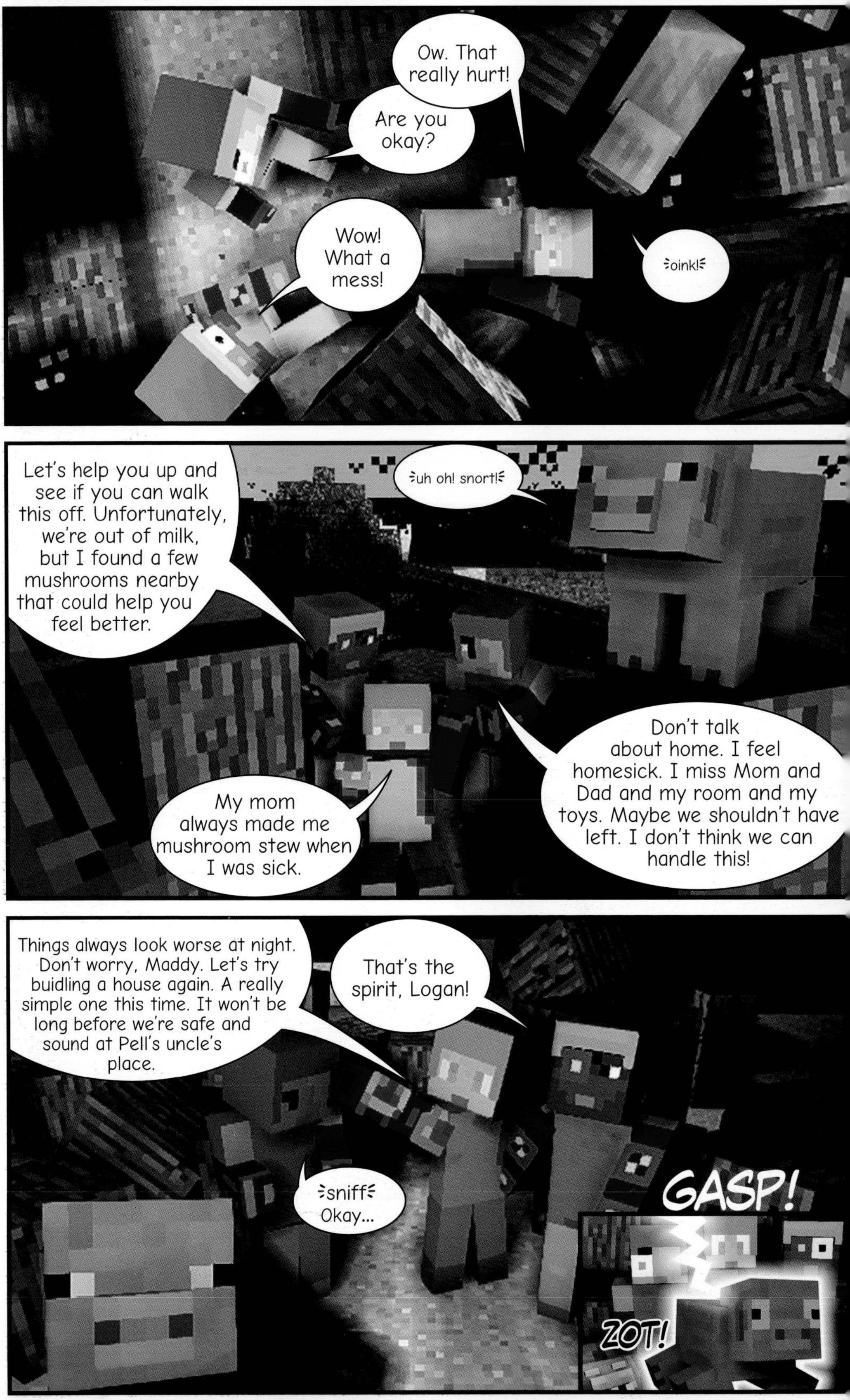
Ow. That really hurt!
Are you okay?
Wow! What a mess!
oink!
Let's help you up and see if you can walk this off. Unfortunately, we're out of milk, but I found a few mushrooms nearby that could help you feel better.
uh oh! snort!
My mom always made me mushroom stew when I was sick.
Don't talk about home. I feel homesick. I miss Mom and Dad and my room and my toys. Maybe we shouldn't have left. I don't think we can handle this!
Things always look worse at night. Don't worry, Maddy. Let's try buidling a house again. A really simple one this time. It won't be long before we're safe and sound at Pell's uncle's place.
That's the spirit, Logan!
sniff Okay...
GASP!
ZOT!

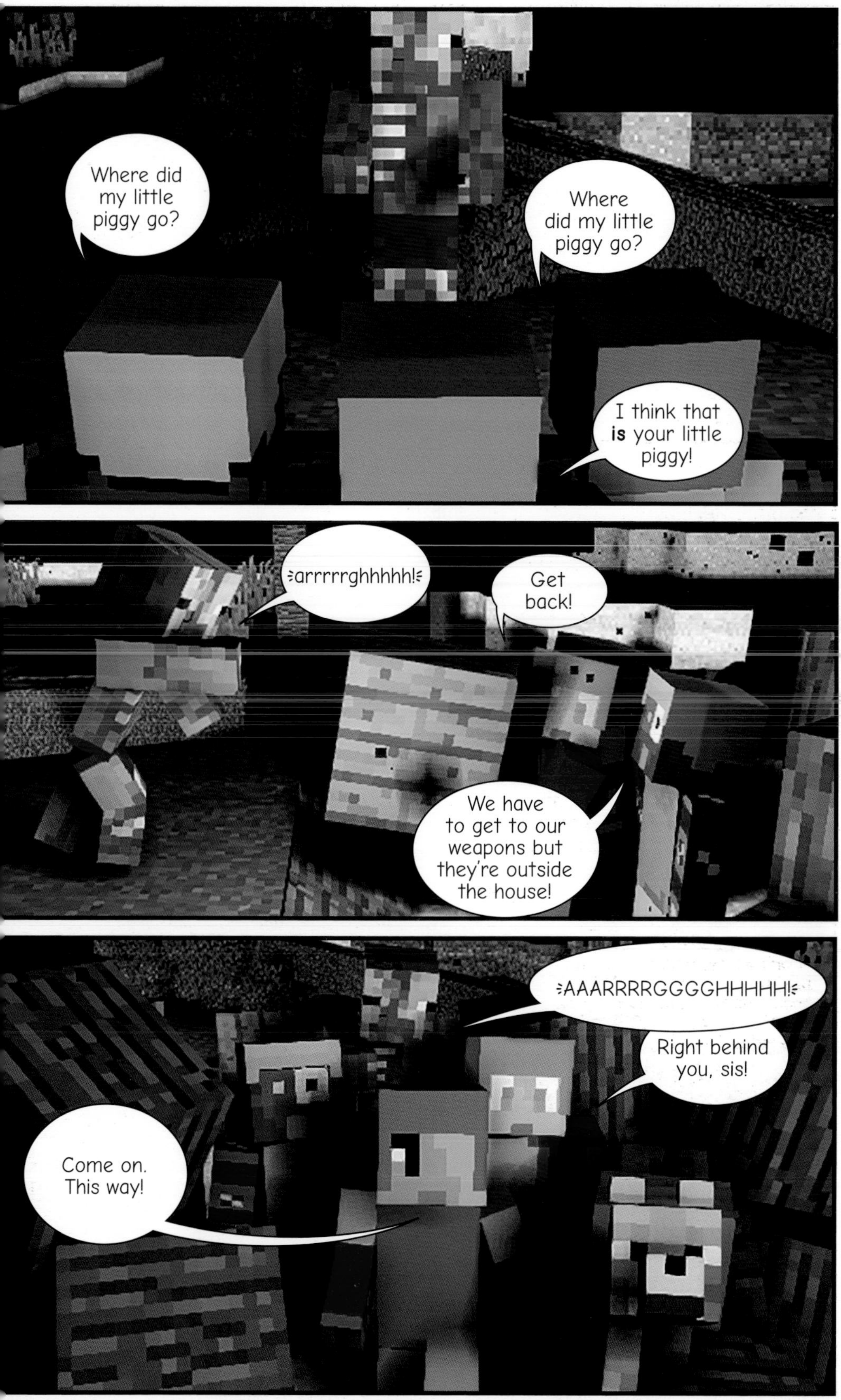
Where did my little piggy go?
Where did my little piggy go?
I think that **is** your little piggy!
arrrrrghhhhh!
Get back!
We have to get to our weapons but they're outside the house!
AAARRRRGGGGHHHHH!
Right behind you, sis!
Come on. This way!

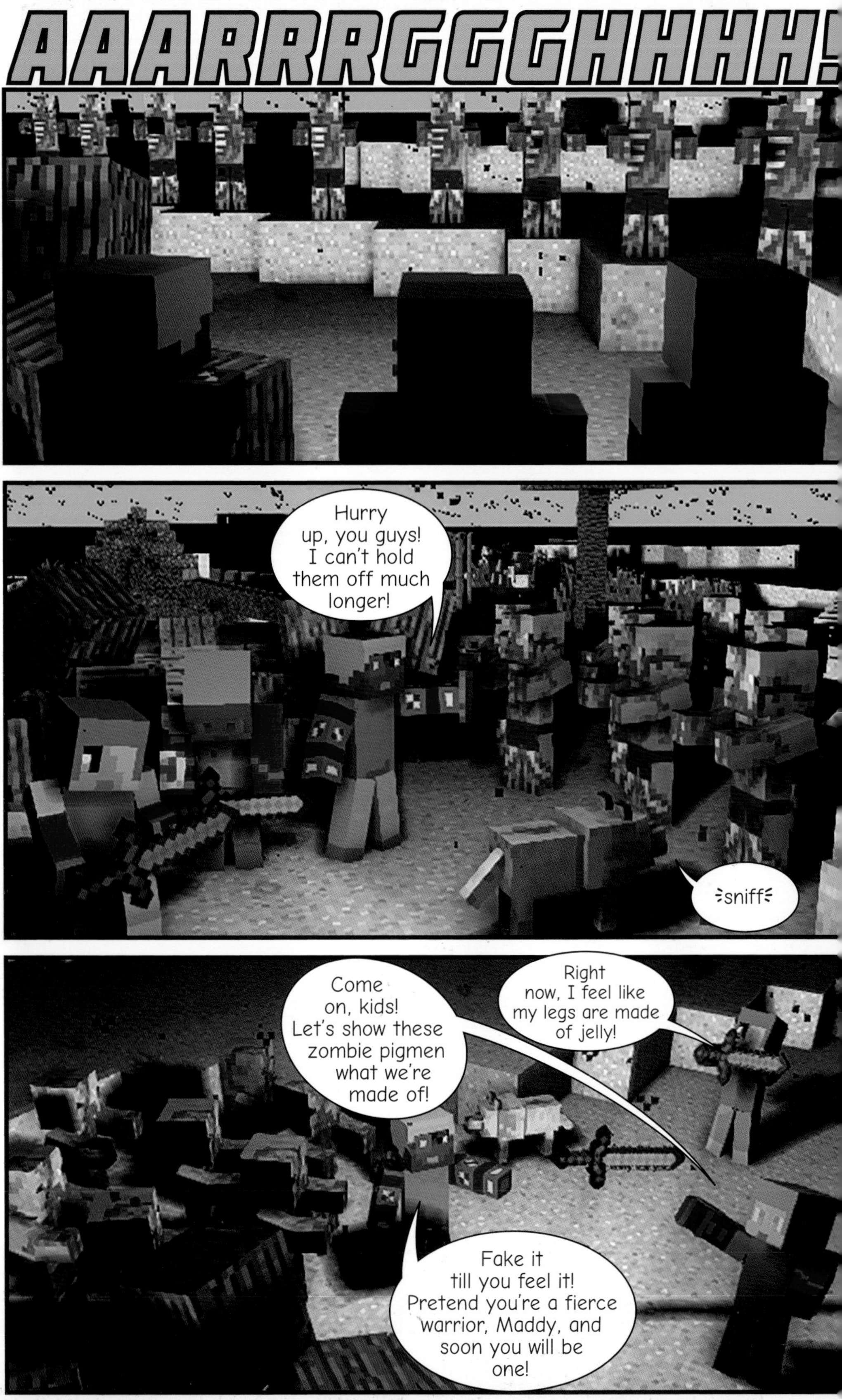
AAARRRGGGHHHH!
Hurry up, you guys! I can't hold them off much longer!
sniff
Come on, kids! Let's show these zombie pigmen what we're made of!
Right now, I feel like my legs are made of jelly!
Fake it till you feel it! Pretend you're a fierce warrior, Maddy, and soon you will be one!

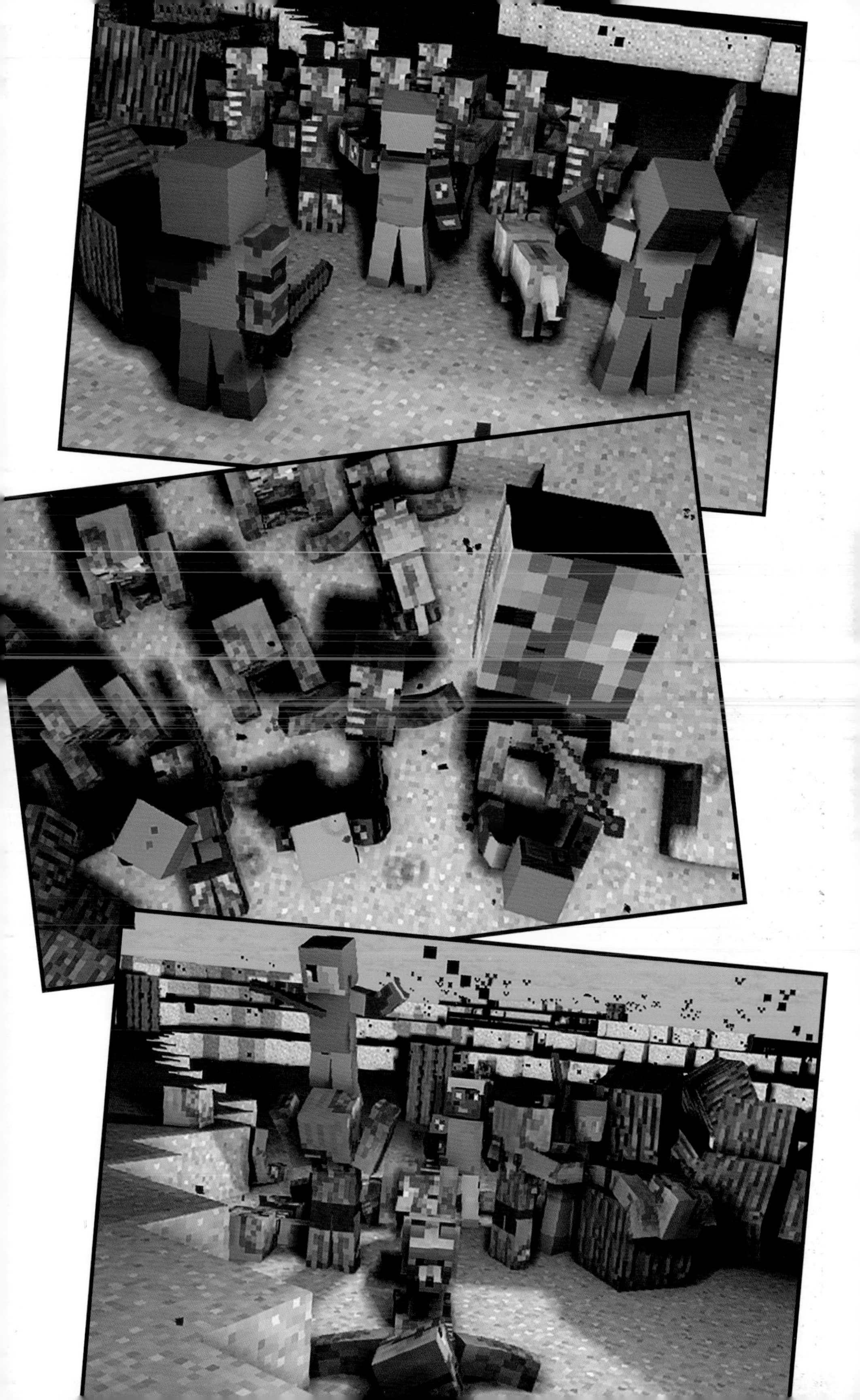

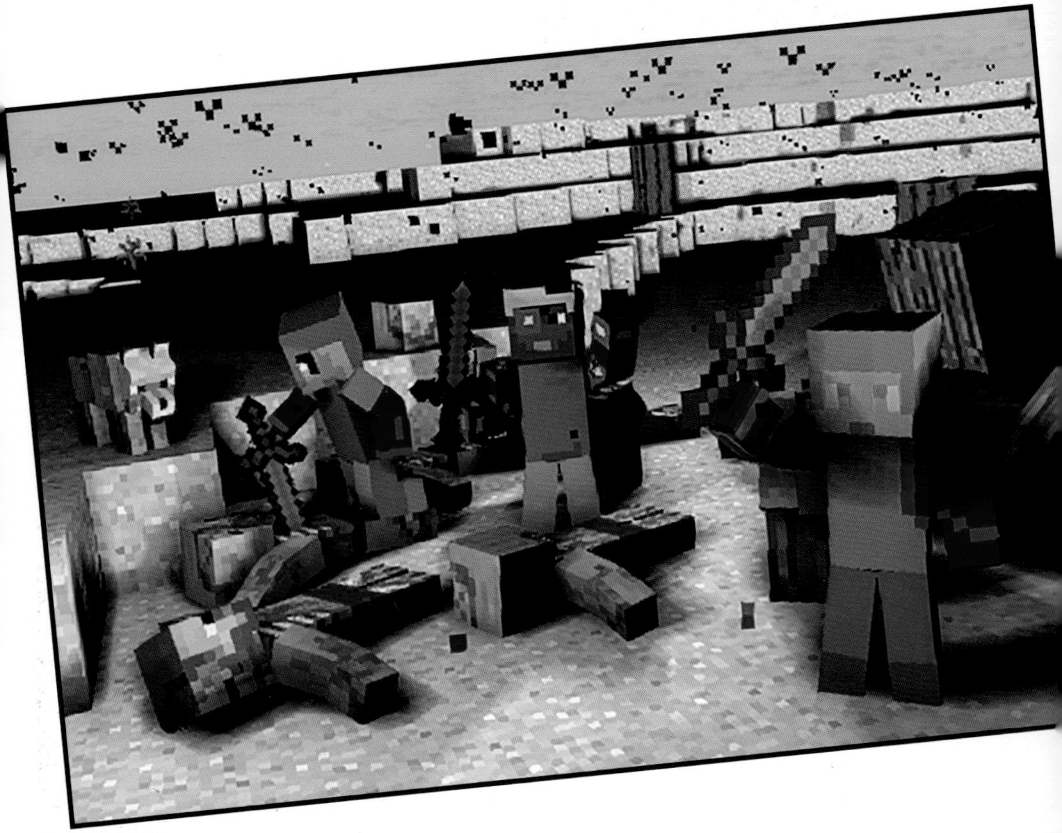

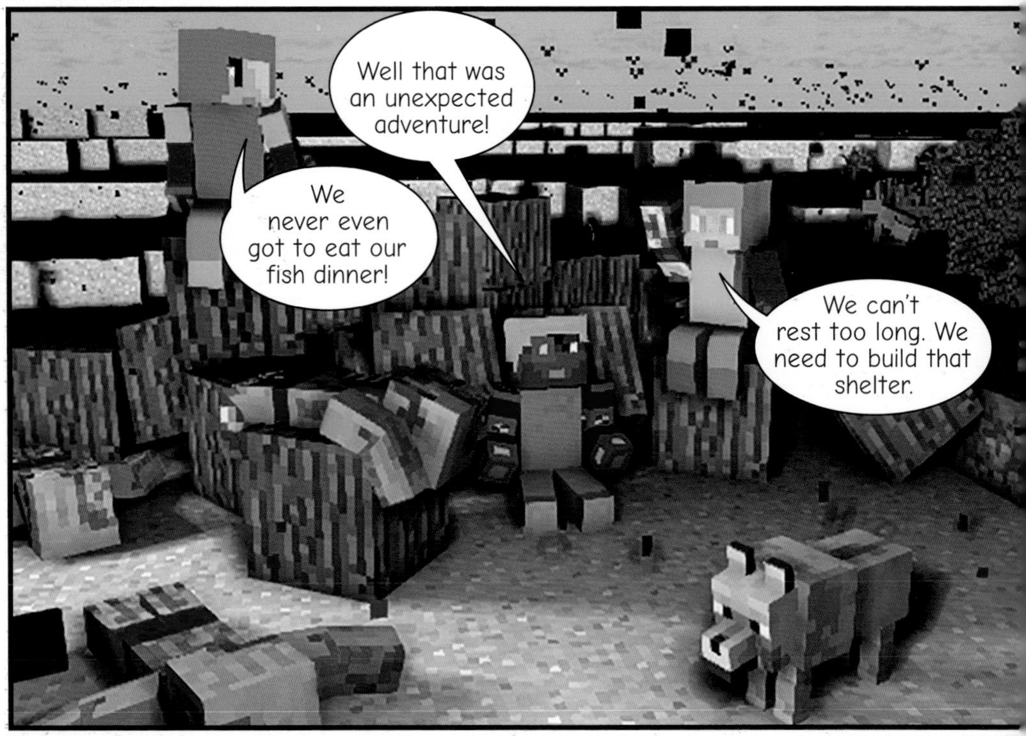
We never even got to eat our fish dinner!
Well that was an unexpected adventure!
We can't rest too long. We need to build that shelter.

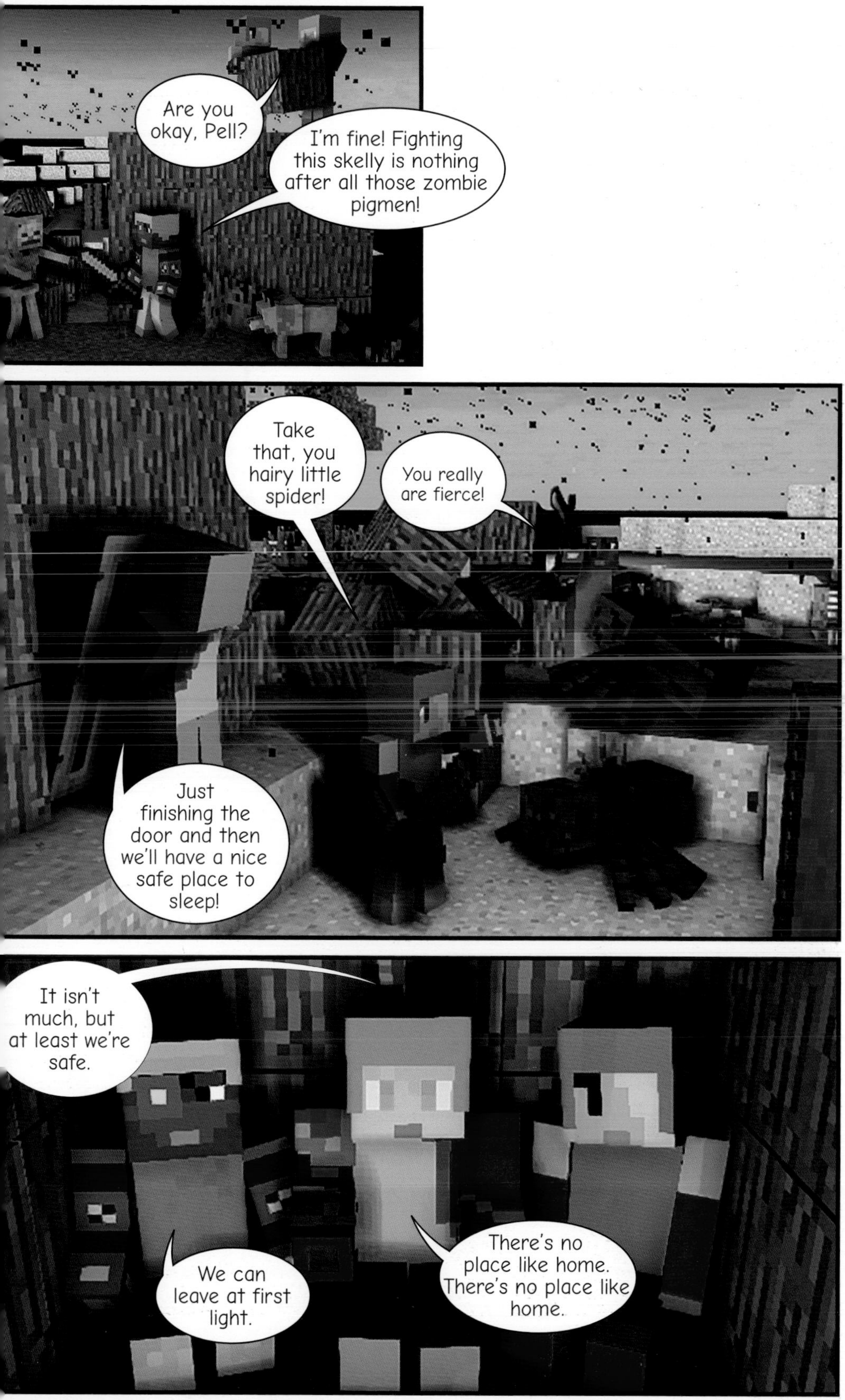

Are you okay, Pell?
I'm fine! Fighting this skelly is nothing after all those zombie pigmen!
Take that, you hairy little spider!
You really are fierce!
Just finishing the door and then we'll have a nice safe place to sleep!
It isn't much, but at least we're safe.
We can leave at first light.
There's no place like home. There's no place like home.

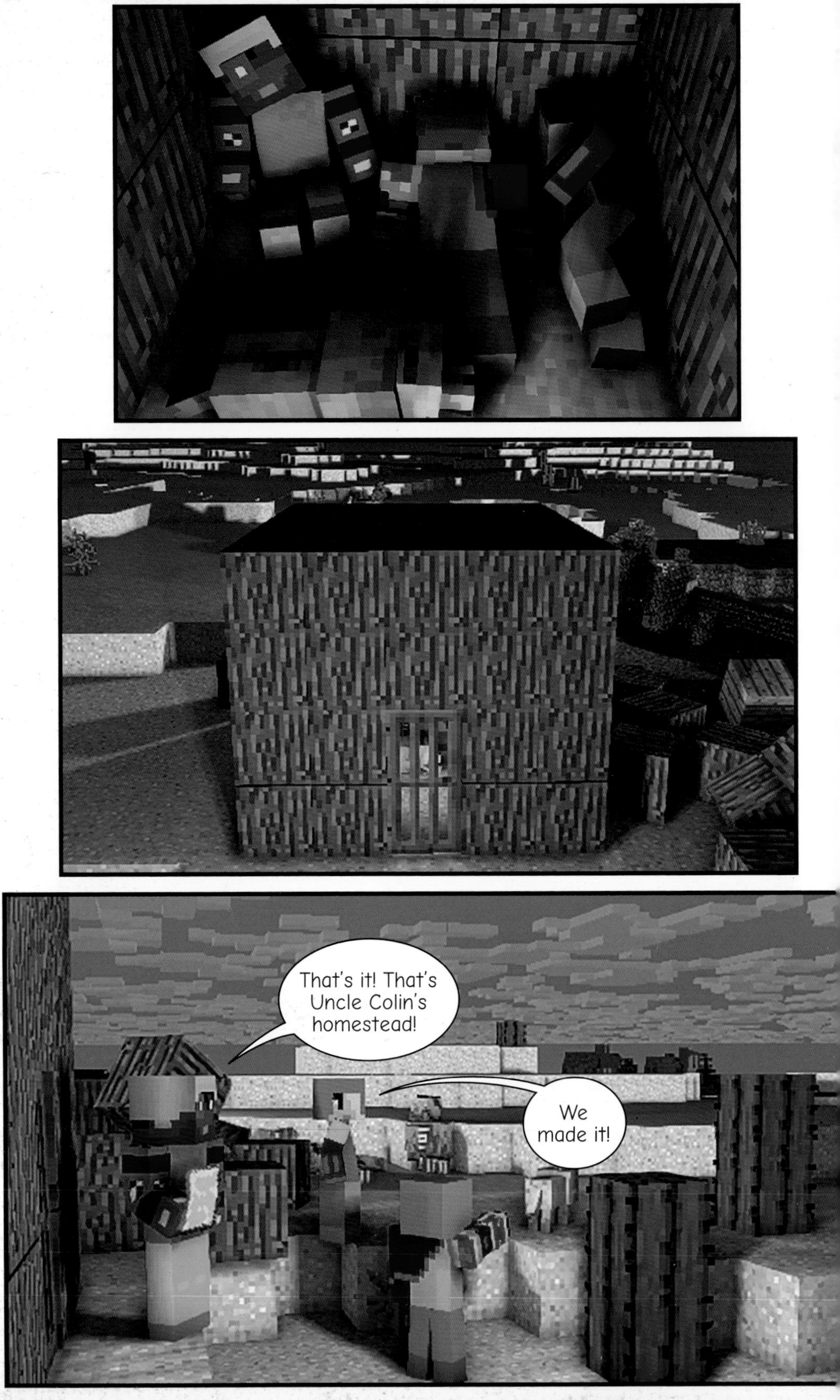
That's it! That's Uncle Colin's homestead!
We made it!

CHAPTER 8

BROKEN HOMESTEAD

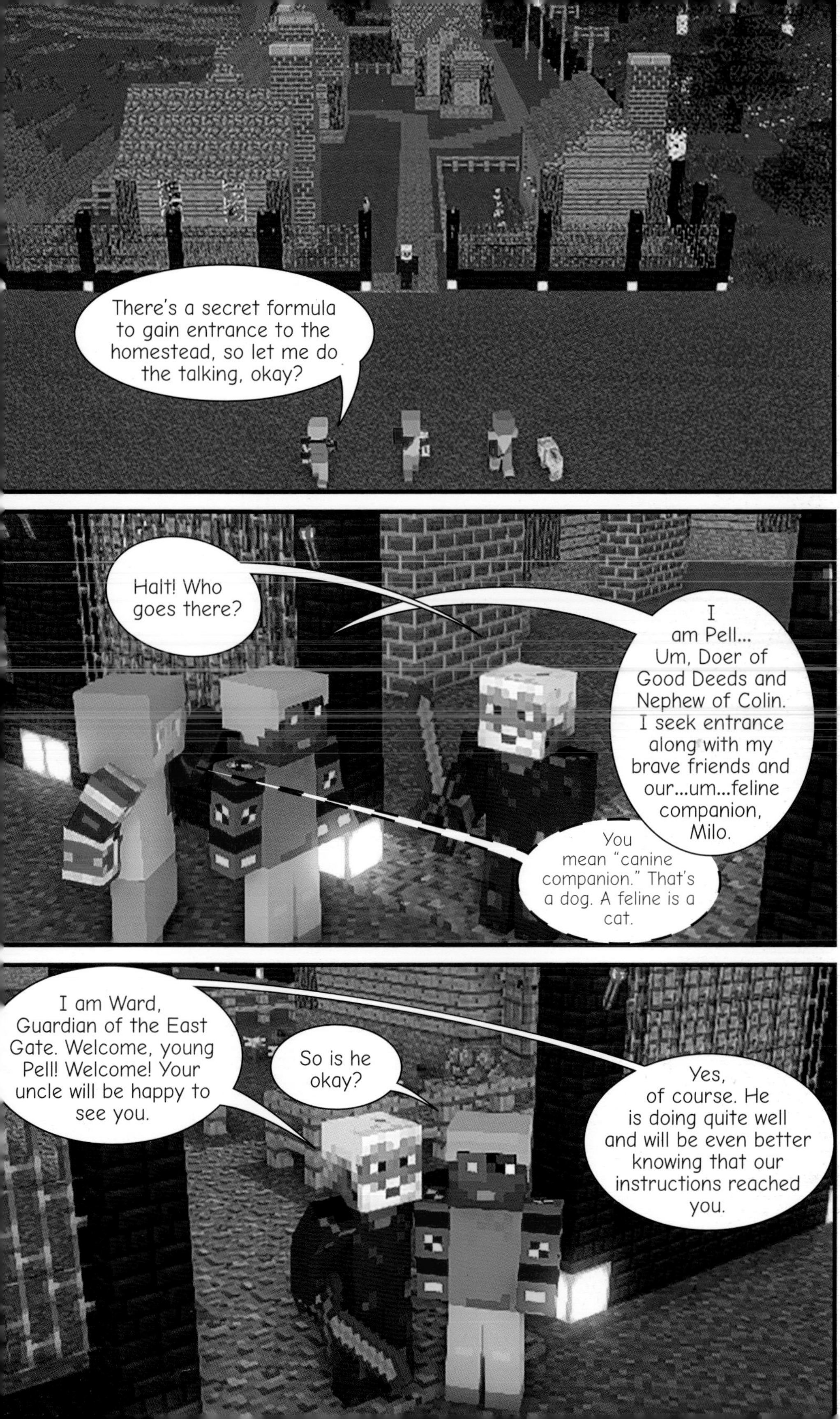

There's a secret formula to gain entrance to the homestead, so let me do the talking, okay?
Halt! Who goes there?
I am Pell... Um, Doer of Good Deeds and Nephew of Colin. I seek entrance along with my brave friends and our...um...feline companion, Milo.
You mean "canine companion." That's a dog. A feline is a cat.
I am Ward, Guardian of the East Gate. Welcome, young Pell! Welcome! Your uncle will be happy to see you.
So is he okay?
Yes, of course. He is doing quite well and will be even better knowing that our instructions reached you.

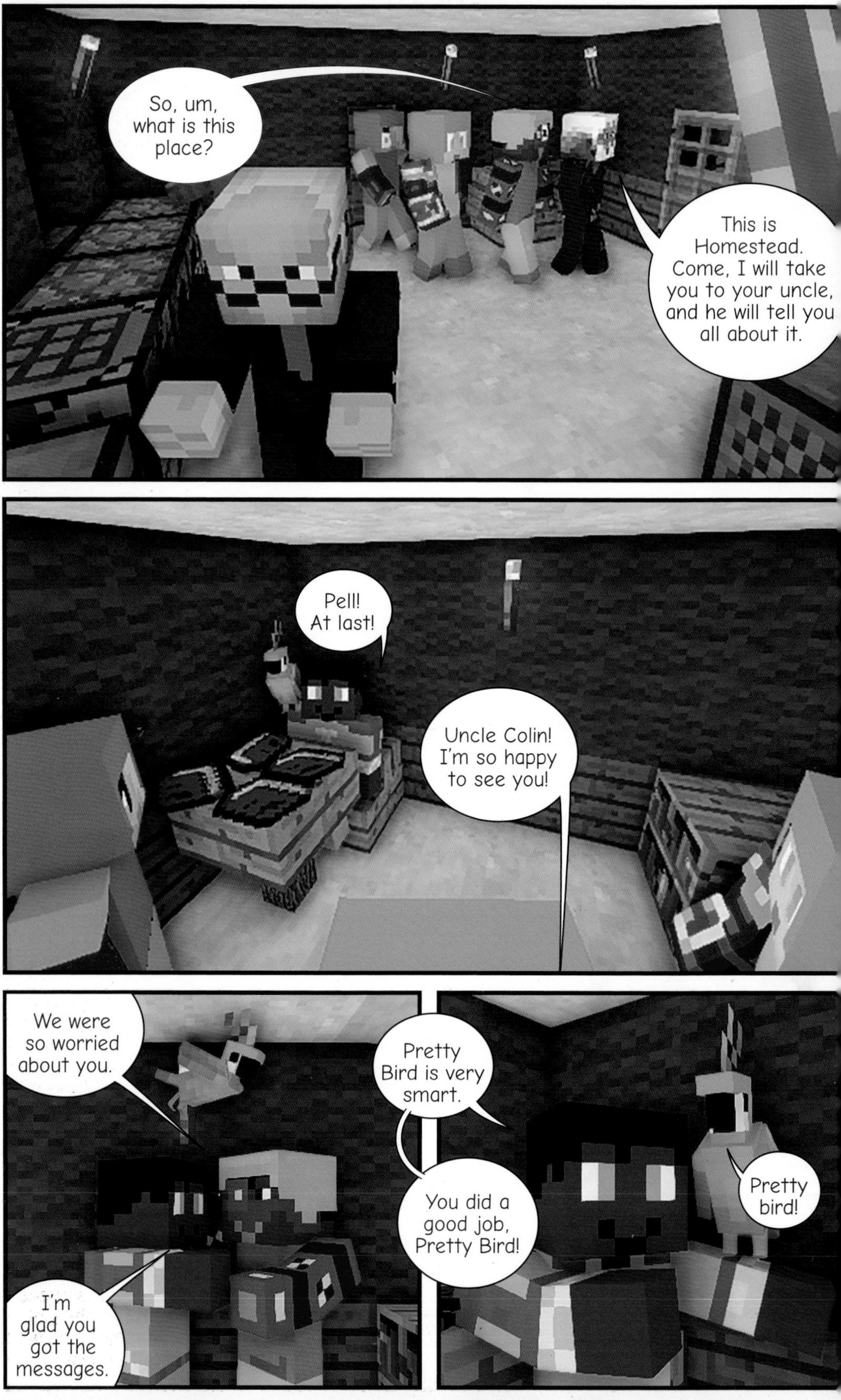
So, um, what is this place?
This is Homestead. Come, I will take you to your uncle, and he will tell you all about it.
Pell! At last!
Uncle Colin! I'm so happy to see you!
We were so worried about you.
I'm glad you got the messages.
Pretty Bird is very smart.
You did a good job, Pretty Bird!
Pretty bird!

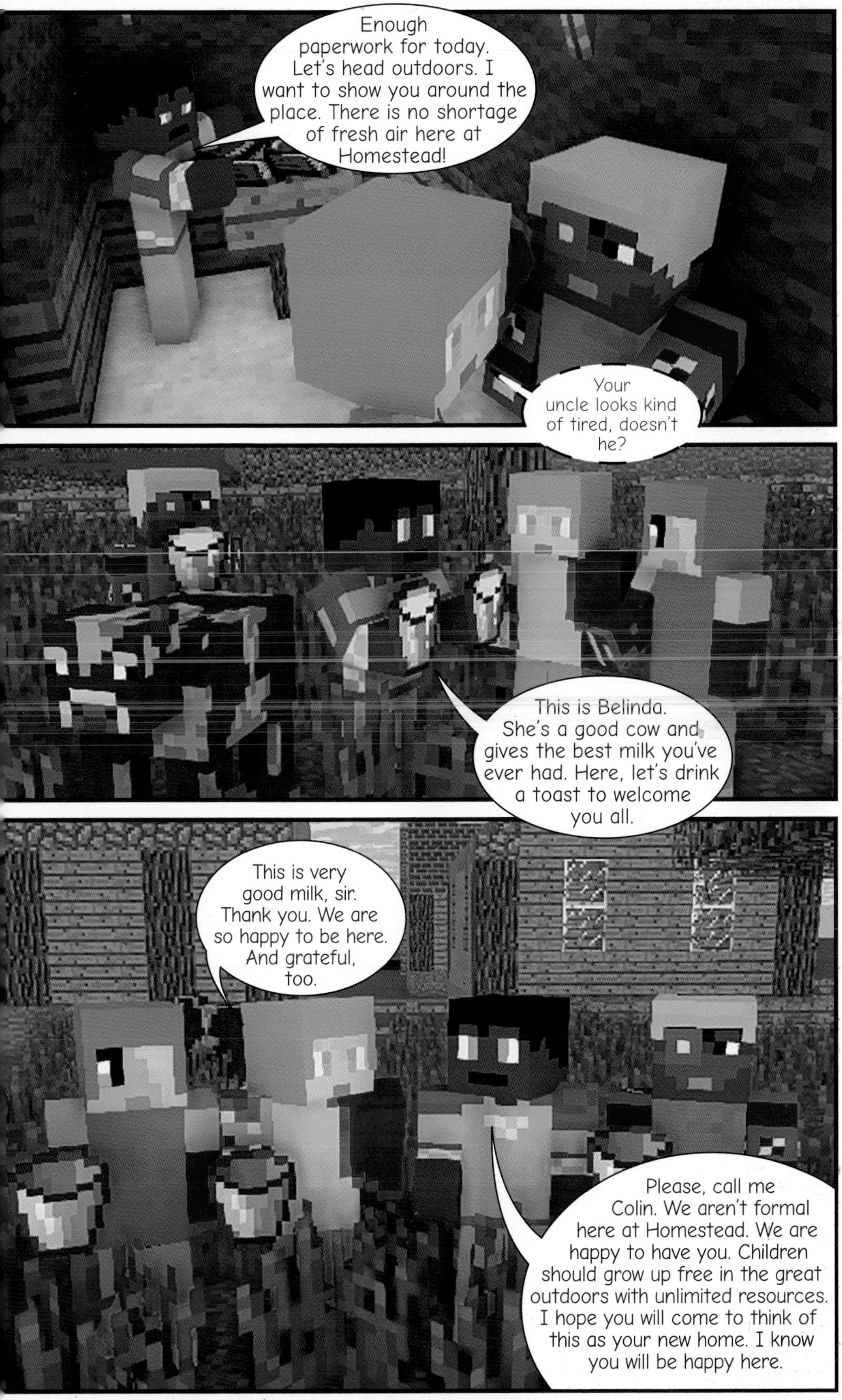
Enough paperwork for today. Let's head outdoors. I want to show you around the place. There is no shortage of fresh air here at Homestead!
Your uncle looks kind of tired, doesn't he?
This is Belinda. She's a good cow and gives the best milk you've ever had. Here, let's drink a toast to welcome you all.
This is very good milk, sir. Thank you. We are so happy to be here. And grateful, too.
Please, call me Colin. We aren't formal here at Homestead. We are happy to have you. Children should grow up free in the great outdoors with unlimited resources. I hope you will come to think of this as your new home. I know you will be happy here.

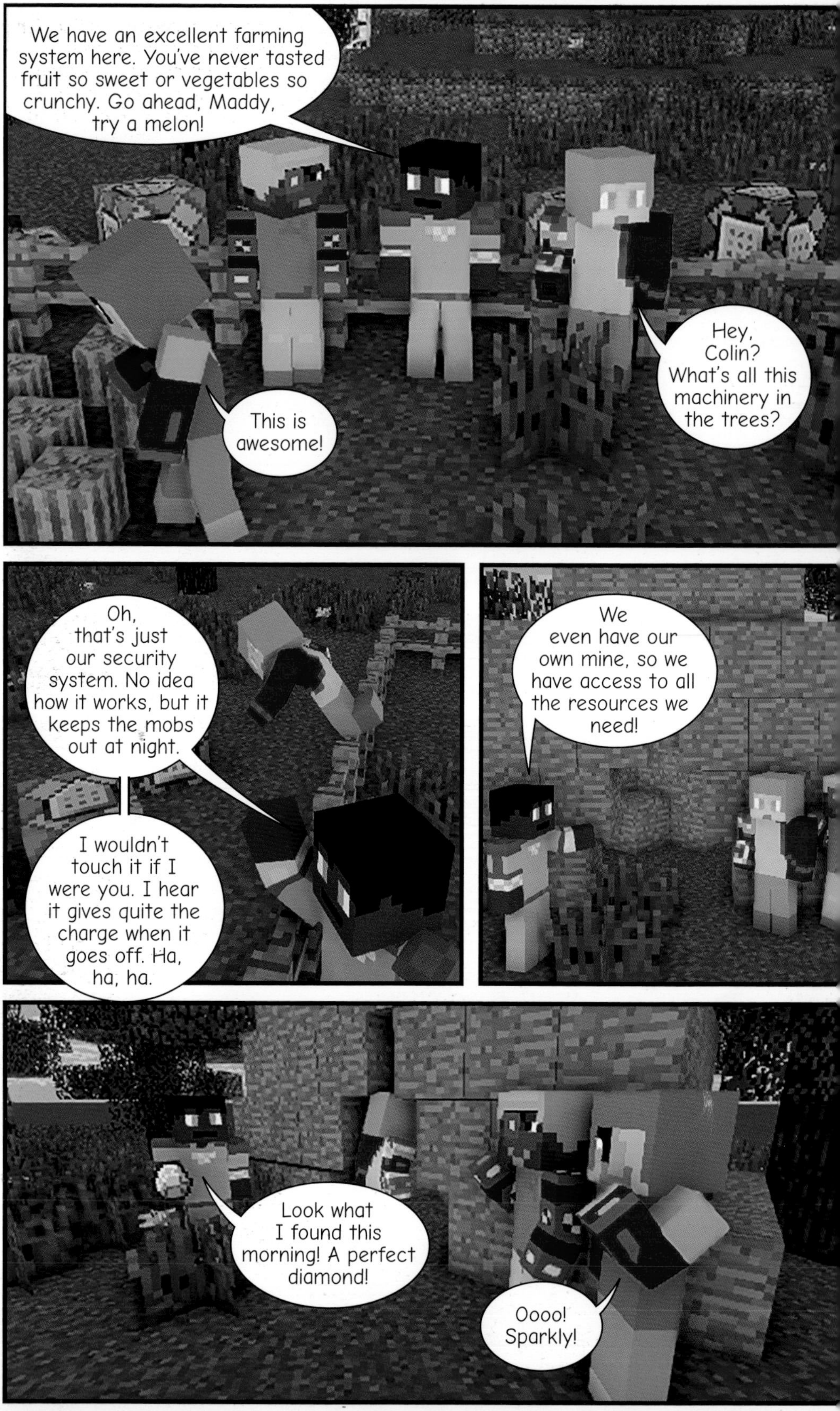
We have an excellent farming system here. You've never tasted fruit so sweet or vegetables so crunchy. Go ahead, Maddy, try a melon!
This is awesome!
Hey, Colin? What's all this machinery in the trees?
Oh, that's just our security system. No idea how it works, but it keeps the mobs out at night.
I wouldn't touch it if I were you. I hear it gives quite the charge when it goes off. Ha, ha, ha.
We even have our own mine, so we have access to all the resources we need!
Look what I found this morning! A perfect diamond!
Oooo! Sparkly!

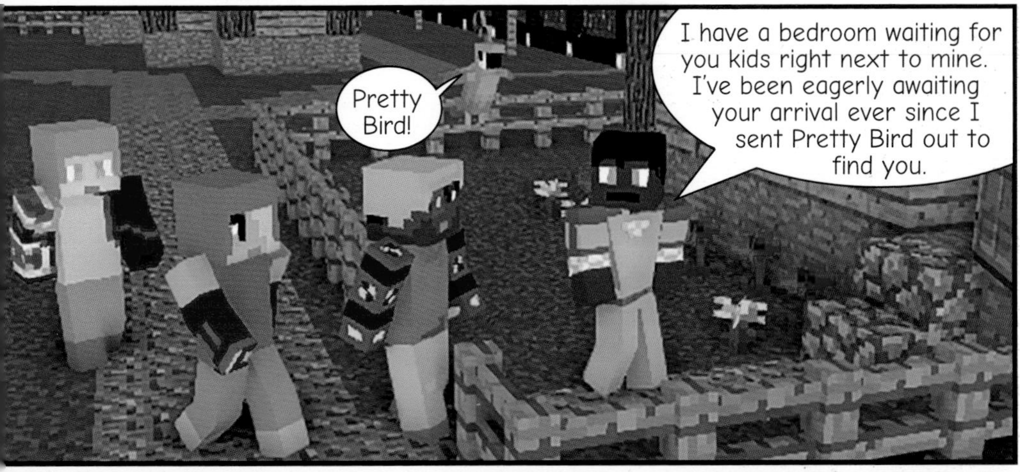
Pretty Bird!
I have a bedroom waiting for you kids right next to mine. I've been eagerly awaiting your arrival ever since I sent Pretty Bird out to find you.

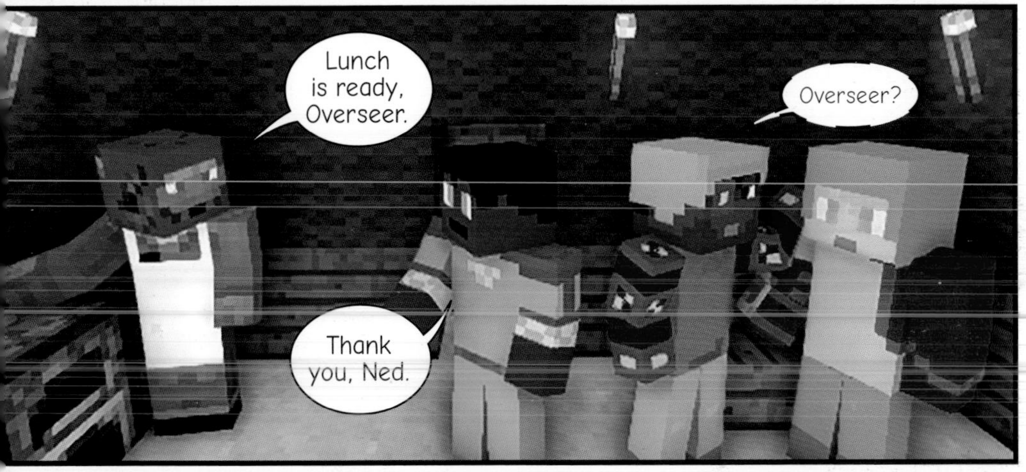
Lunch is ready, Overseer.
Overseer?
Thank you, Ned.

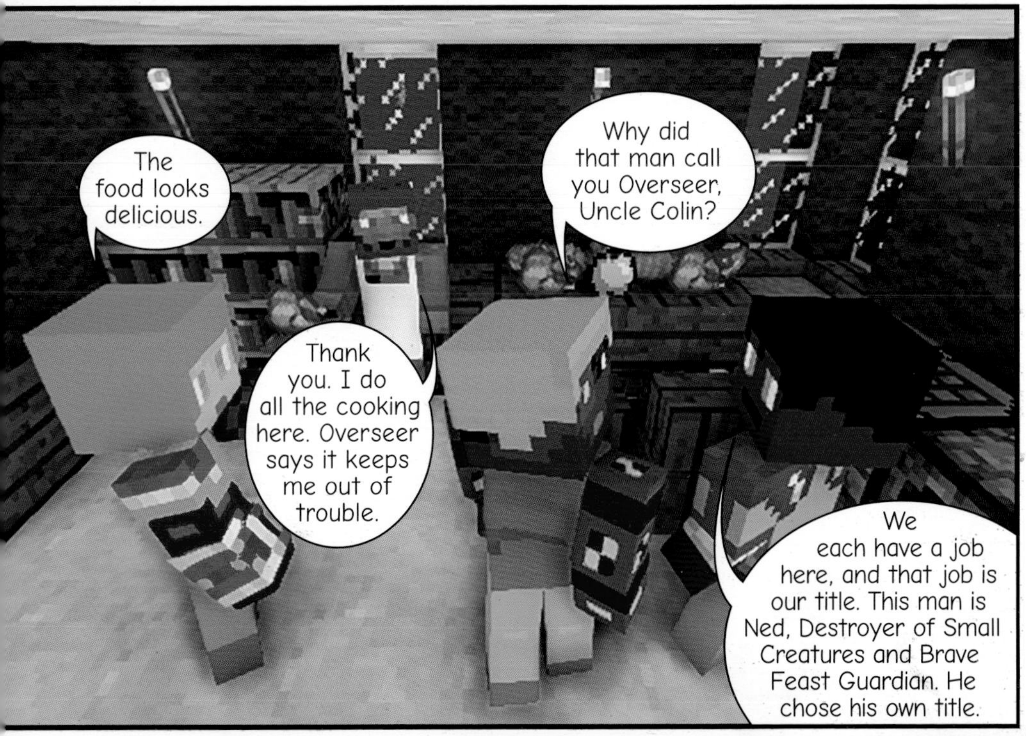
The food looks delicious.
Thank you. I do all the cooking here. Overseer says it keeps me out of trouble.
Why did that man call you Overseer, Uncle Colin?
We each have a job here, and that job is our title. This man is Ned, Destroyer of Small Creatures and Brave Feast Guardian. He chose his own title.

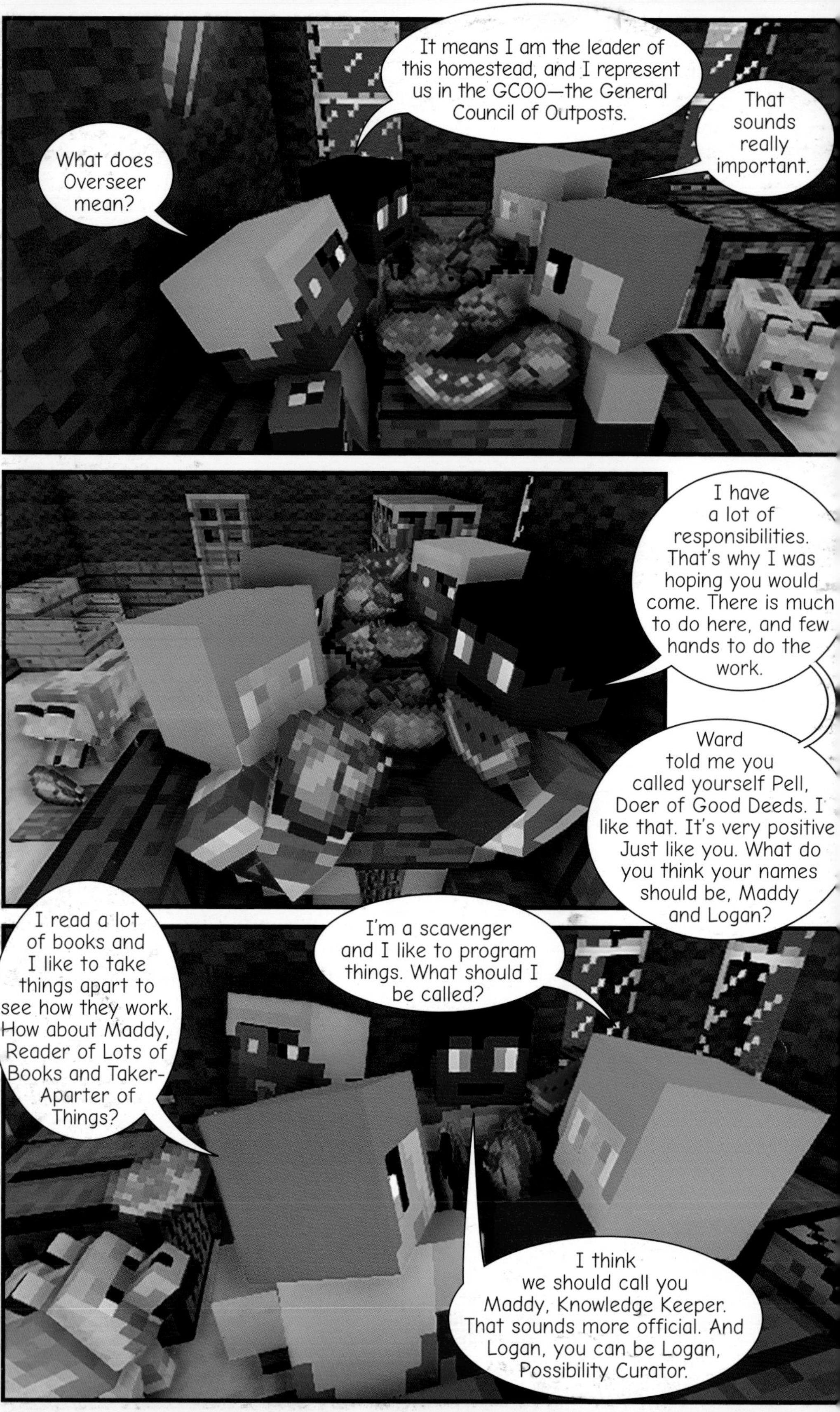
What does Overseer mean?
It means I am the leader of this homestead, and I represent us in the GCOO—the General Council of Outposts.
That sounds really important.
I have a lot of responsibilities. That's why I was hoping you would come. There is much to do here, and few hands to do the work.
Ward told me you called yourself Pell, Doer of Good Deeds. I like that. It's very positive Just like you. What do you think your names should be, Maddy and Logan?
I read a lot of books and I like to take things apart to see how they work. How about Maddy, Reader of Lots of Books and Taker-Aparter of Things?
I'm a scavenger and I like to program things. What should I be called?
I think we should call you Maddy, Knowledge Keeper. That sounds more official. And Logan, you can be Logan, Possibility Curator.

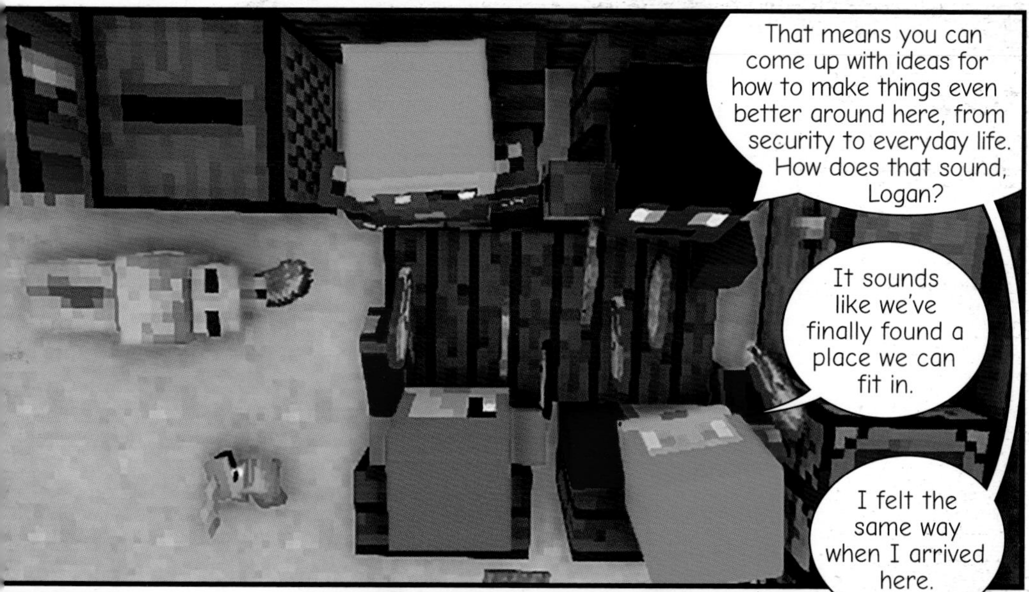
That means you can come up with ideas for how to make things even better around here, from security to everyday life. How does that sound, Logan?
It sounds like we've finally found a place we can fit in.
I felt the same way when I arrived here.

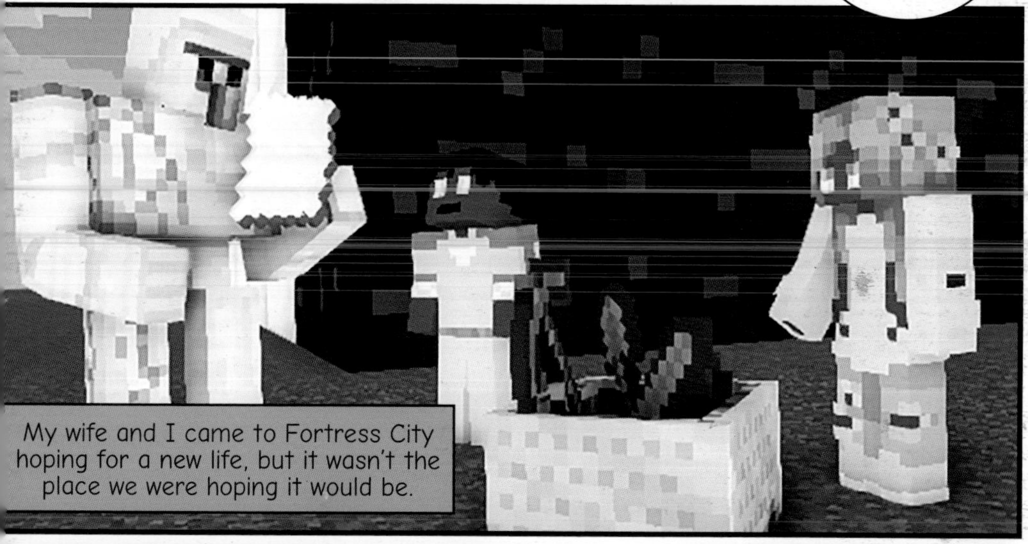
My wife and I came to Fortress City hoping for a new life, but it wasn't the place we were hoping it would be.

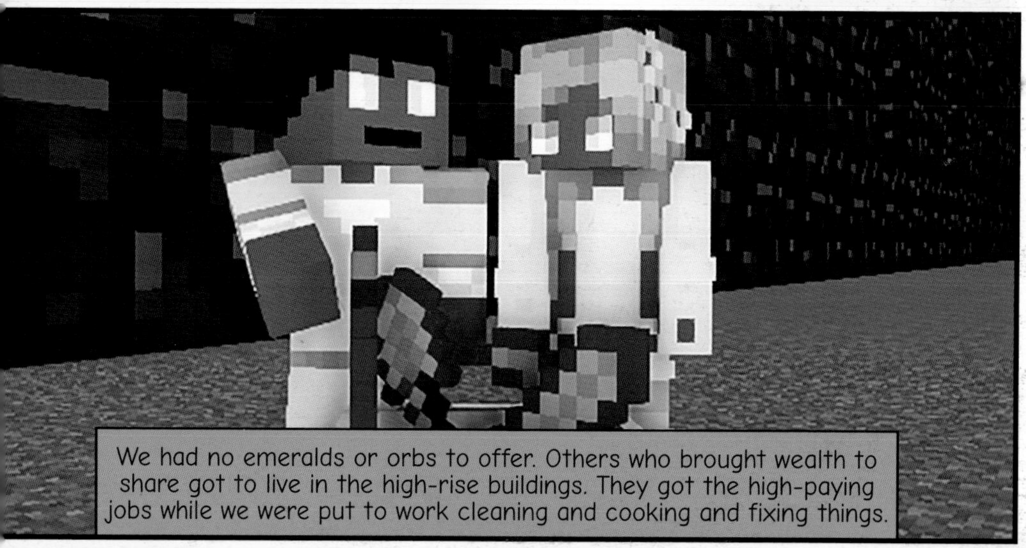
We had no emeralds or orbs to offer. Others who brought wealth to share got to live in the high-rise buildings. They got the high-paying jobs while we were put to work cleaning and cooking and fixing things.

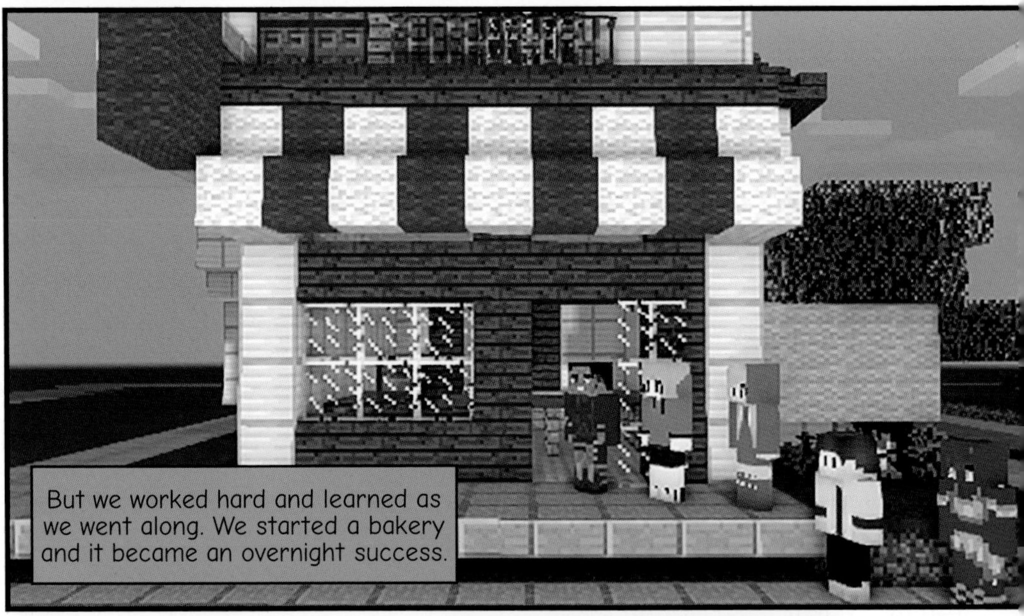
But we worked hard and learned as we went along. We started a bakery and it became an overnight success.

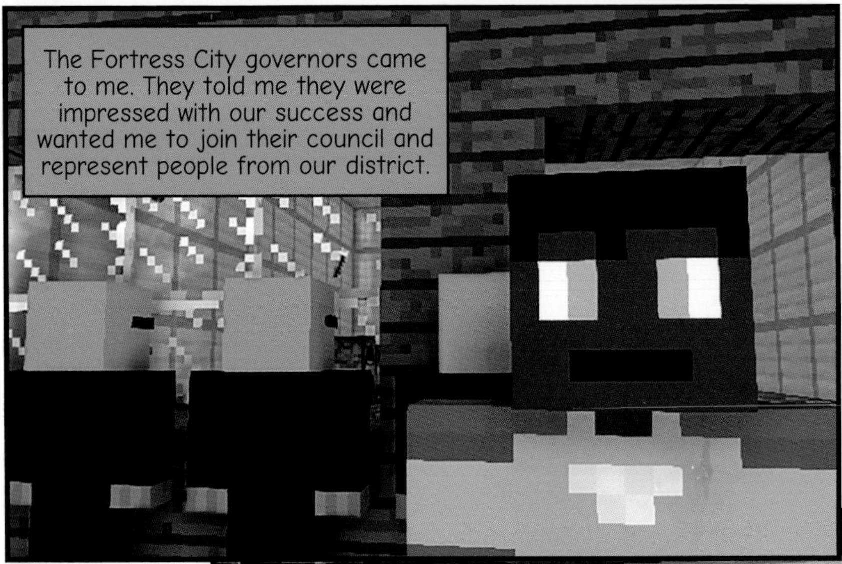
The Fortress City governors came to me. They told me they were impressed with our success and wanted me to join their council and represent people from our district.

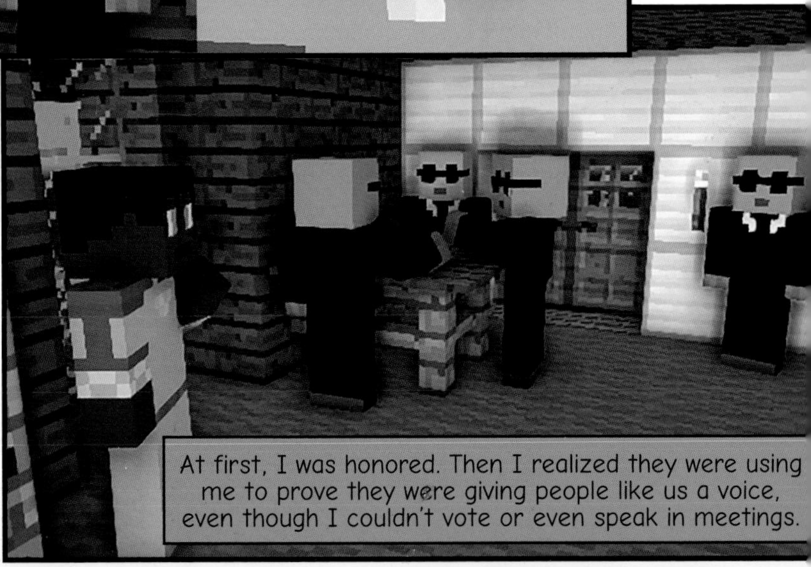
At first, I was honored. Then I realized they were using me to prove they were giving people like us a voice, even though I couldn't vote or even speak in meetings.

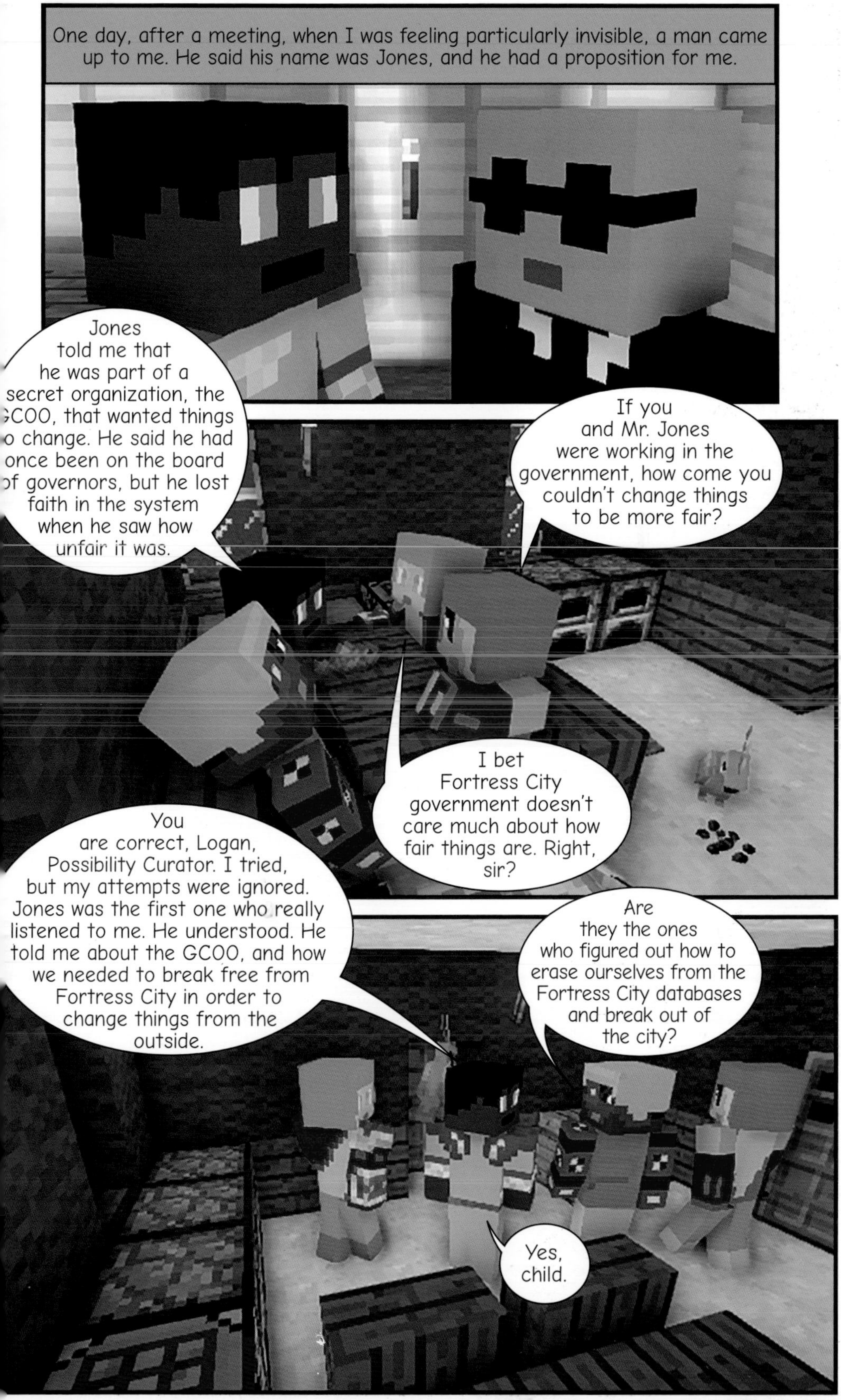
One day, after a meeting, when I was feeling particularly invisible, a man came up to me. He said his name was Jones, and he had a proposition for me.
Jones told me that he was part of a secret organization, the GCOO, that wanted things to change. He said he had once been on the board of governors, but he lost faith in the system when he saw how unfair it was.
If you and Mr. Jones were working in the government, how come you couldn't change things to be more fair?
I bet Fortress City government doesn't care much about how fair things are. Right, sir?
You are correct, Logan, Possibility Curator. I tried, but my attempts were ignored. Jones was the first one who really listened to me. He understood. He told me about the GCOO, and how we needed to break free from Fortress City in order to change things from the outside.
Are they the ones who figured out how to erase ourselves from the Fortress City databases and break out of the city?
Yes, child.

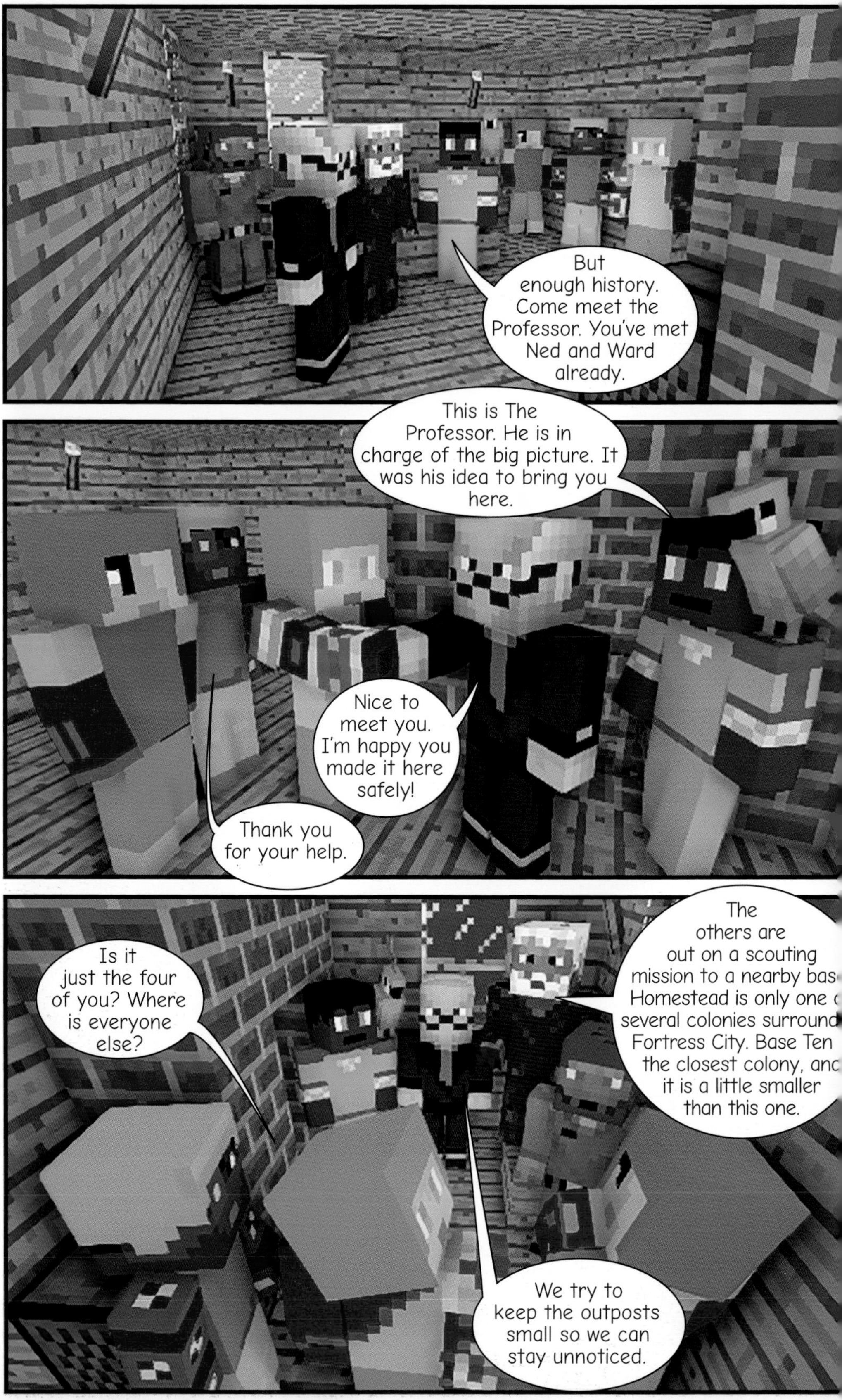
But enough history. Come meet the Professor. You've met Ned and Ward already.
This is The Professor. He is in charge of the big picture. It was his idea to bring you here.
Nice to meet you. I'm happy you made it here safely!
Thank you for your help.
Is it just the four of you? Where is everyone else?
The others are out on a scouting mission to a nearby bas
Homestead is only one
several colonies surround
Fortress City. Base Ten
the closest colony, an
it is a little smaller than this one.
We try to keep the outposts small so we can stay unnoticed.

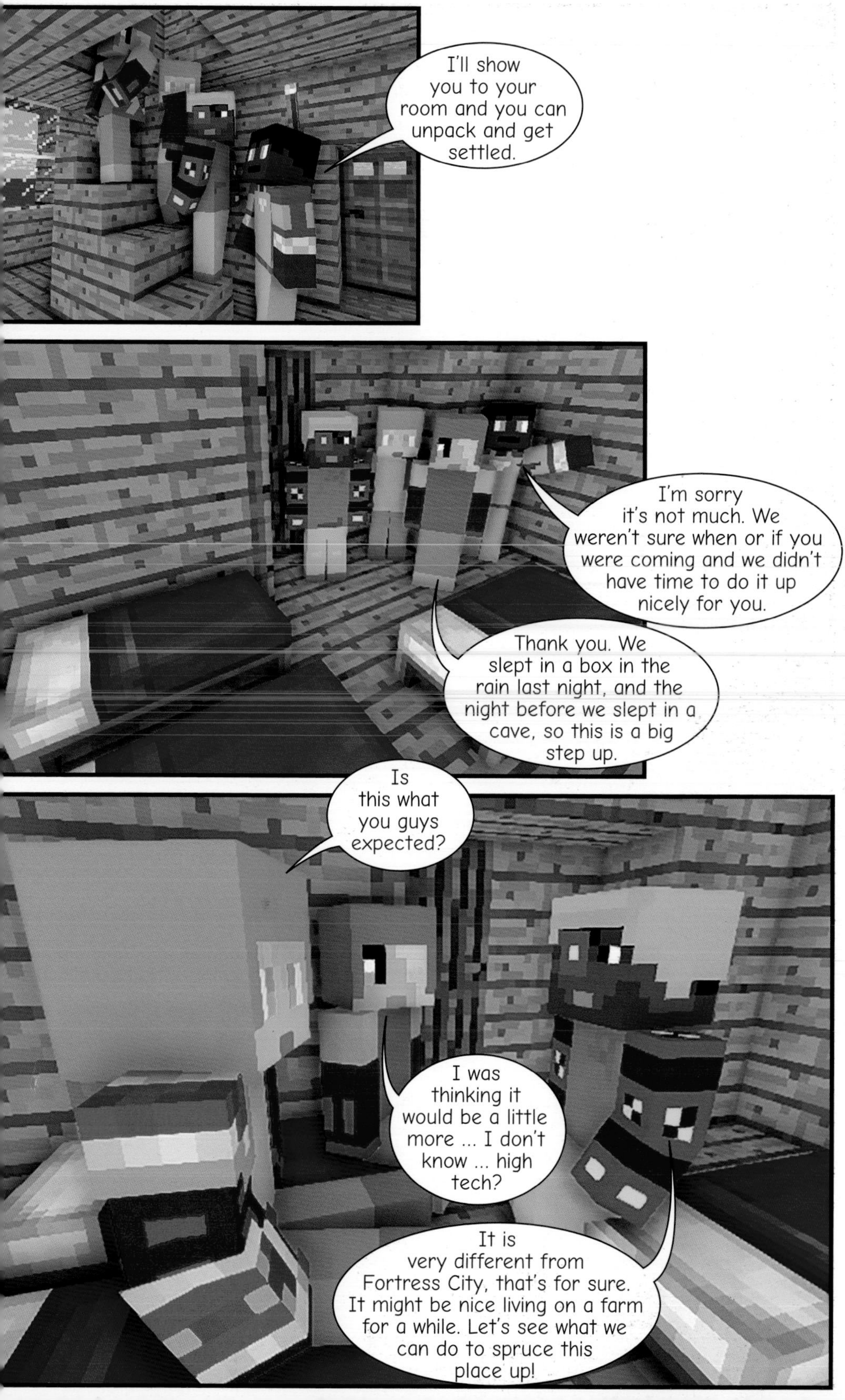
I'll show you to your room and you can unpack and get settled.
I'm sorry it's not much. We weren't sure when or if you were coming and we didn't have time to do it up nicely for you.
Thank you. We slept in a box in the rain last night, and the night before we slept in a cave, so this is a big step up.
Is this what you guys expected?
I was thinking it would be a little more ... I don't know ... high tech?
It is very different from Fortress City, that's for sure. It might be nice living on a farm for a while. Let's see what we can do to spruce this place up!

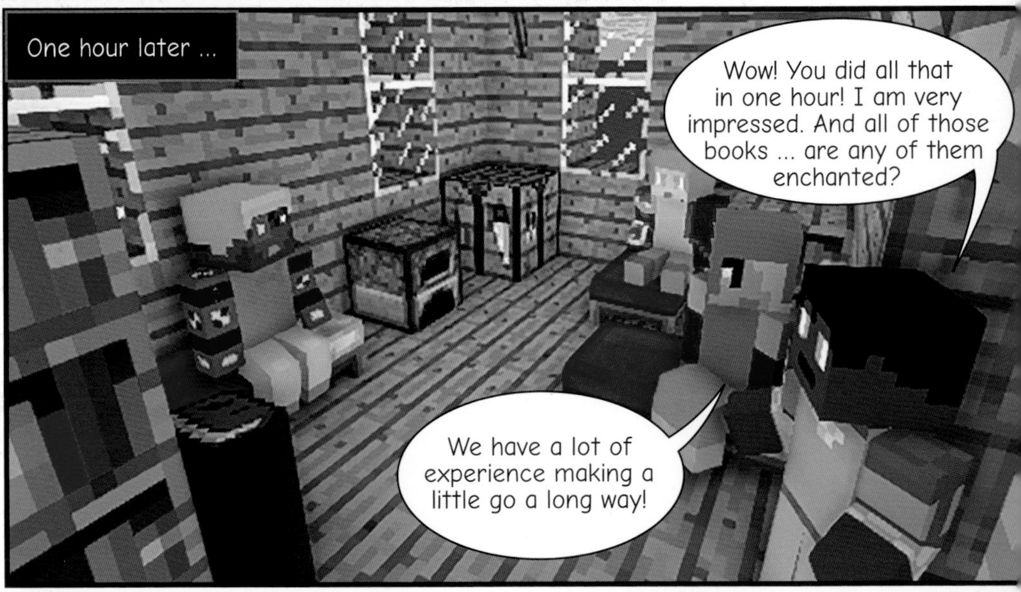
One hour later ...
Wow! You did all that in one hour! I am very impressed. And all of those books ... are any of them enchanted?
We have a lot of experience making a little go a long way!

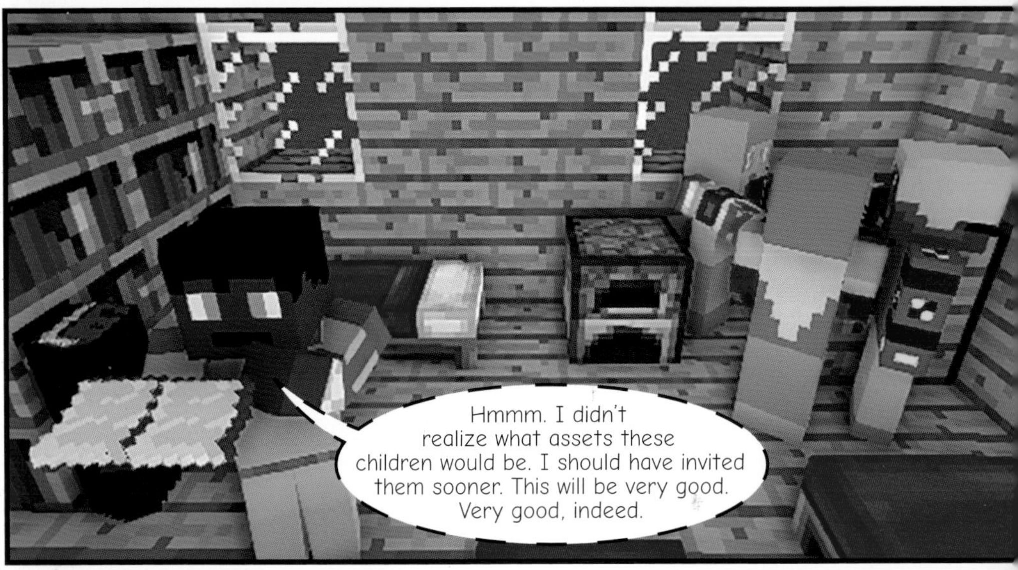
Hmmm. I didn't realize what assets these children would be. I should have invited them sooner. This will be very good. Very good, indeed.

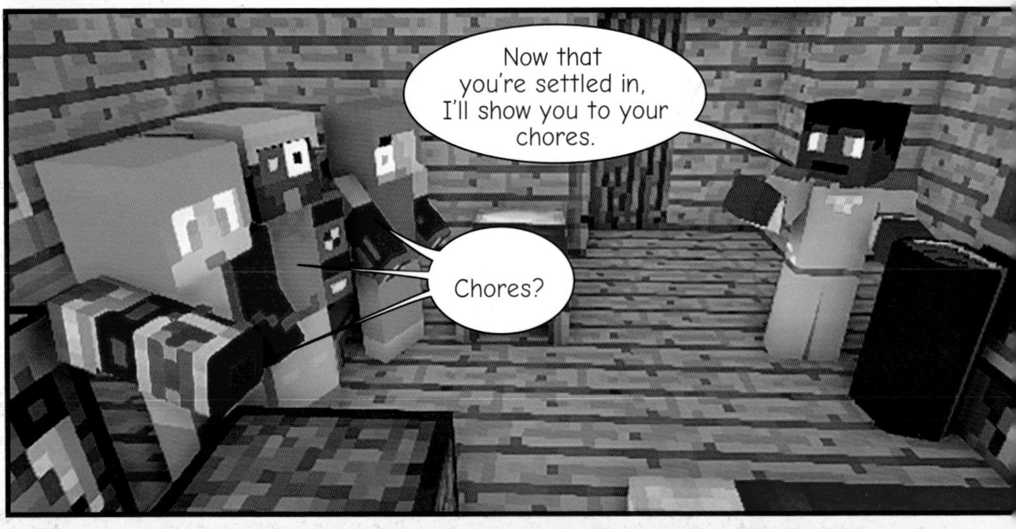
Now that you're settled in, I'll show you to your chores.
Chores?

CHAPTER 9

CHORES

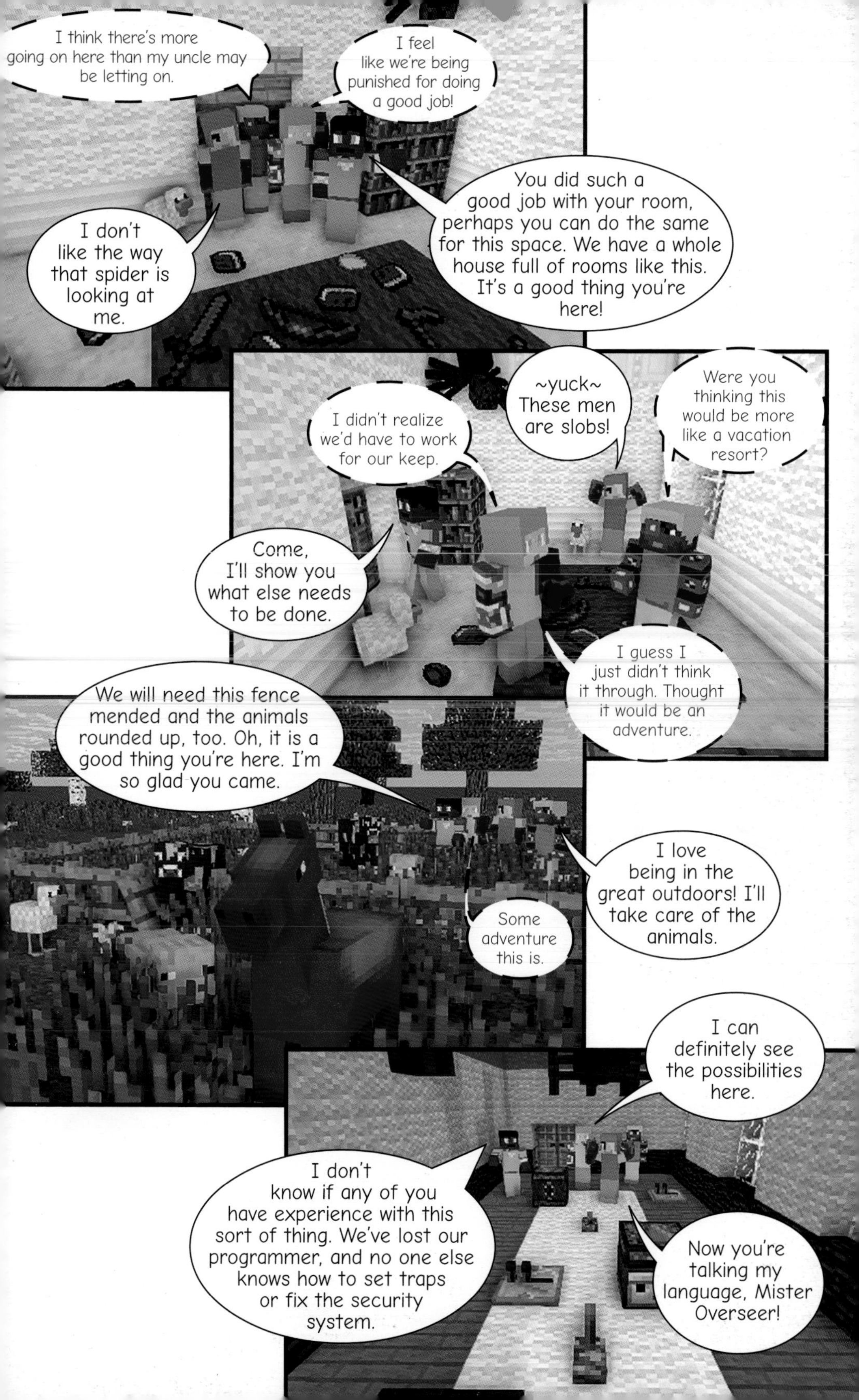
I think there's more going on here than my uncle may be letting on.
I feel like we're being punished for doing a good job!
You did such a good job with your room, perhaps you can do the same for this space. We have a whole house full of rooms like this. It's a good thing you're here!
I don't like the way that spider is looking at me.
I didn't realize we'd have to work for our keep.
~yuck~ These men are slobs!
Were you thinking this would be more like a vacation resort?
Come, I'll show you what else needs to be done.
I guess I just didn't think it through. Thought it would be an adventure.
We will need this fence mended and the animals rounded up, too. Oh, it is a good thing you're here. I'm so glad you came.
I love being in the great outdoors! I'll take care of the animals.
Some adventure this is.
I can definitely see the possibilities here.
I don't know if any of you have experience with this sort of thing. We've lost our programmer, and no one else knows how to set traps or fix the security system.
Now you're talking my language, Mister Overseer!

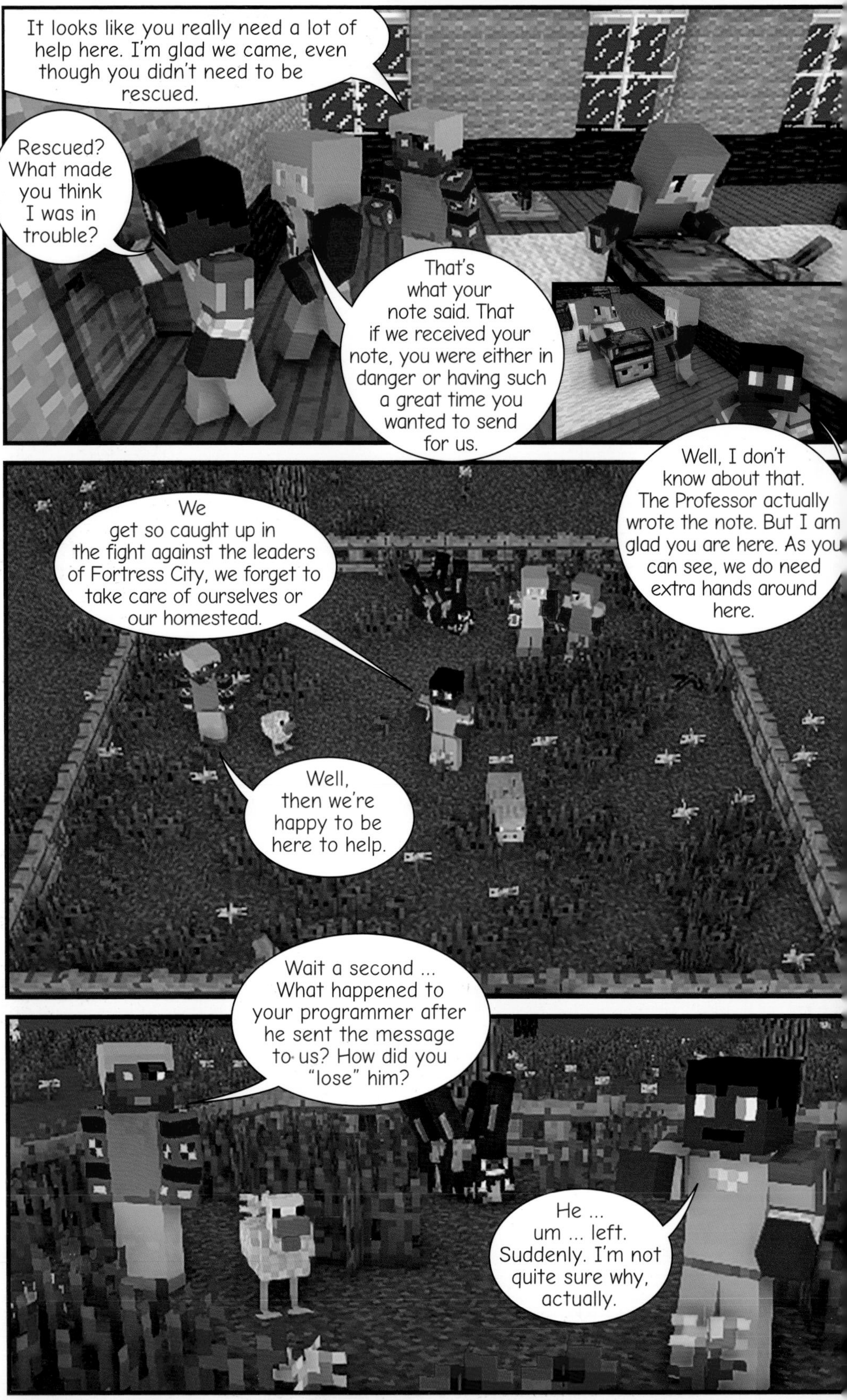
It looks like you really need a lot of help here. I'm glad we came, even though you didn't need to be rescued.
Rescued? What made you think I was in trouble?
That's what your note said. That if we received your note, you were either in danger or having such a great time you wanted to send for us.
Well, I don't know about that. The Professor actually wrote the note. But I am glad you are here. As you can see, we do need extra hands around here.
We get so caught up in the fight against the leaders of Fortress City, we forget to take care of ourselves or our homestead.
Well, then we're happy to be here to help.
Wait a second ... What happened to your programmer after he sent the message to us? How did you "lose" him?
He ... um ... left. Suddenly. I'm not quite sure why, actually.

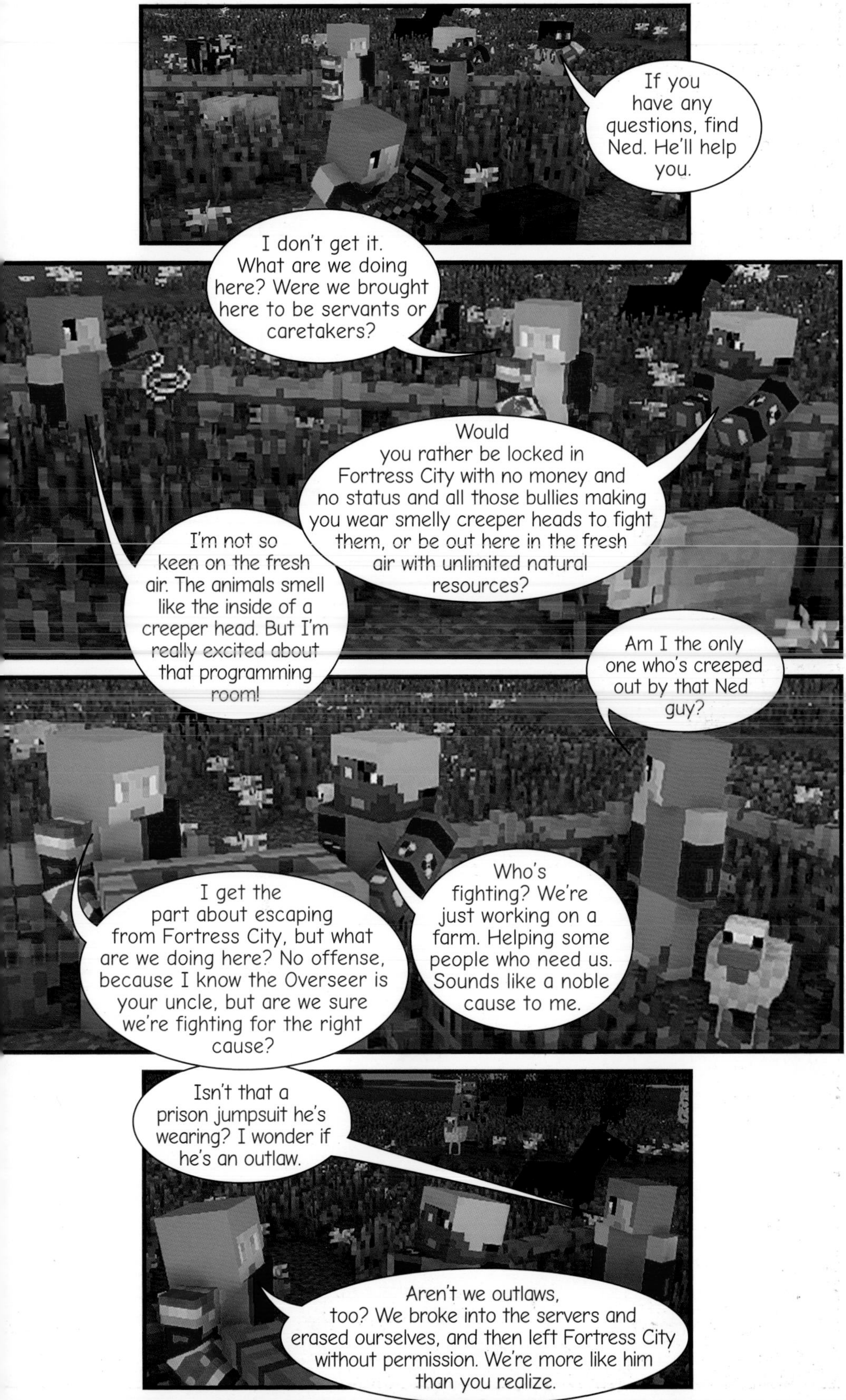
If you have any questions, find Ned. He'll help you.
I don't get it. What are we doing here? Were we brought here to be servants or caretakers?
Would you rather be locked in Fortress City with no money and no status and all those bullies making you wear smelly creeper heads to fight them, or be out here in the fresh air with unlimited natural resources?
I'm not so keen on the fresh air. The animals smell like the inside of a creeper head. But I'm really excited about that programming room!
Am I the only one who's creeped out by that Ned guy?
I get the part about escaping from Fortress City, but what are we doing here? No offense, because I know the Overseer is your uncle, but are we sure we're fighting for the right cause?
Who's fighting? We're just working on a farm. Helping some people who need us. Sounds like a noble cause to me.
Isn't that a prison jumpsuit he's wearing? I wonder if he's an outlaw.
Aren't we outlaws, too? We broke into the servers and erased ourselves, and then left Fortress City without permission. We're more like him than you realize.

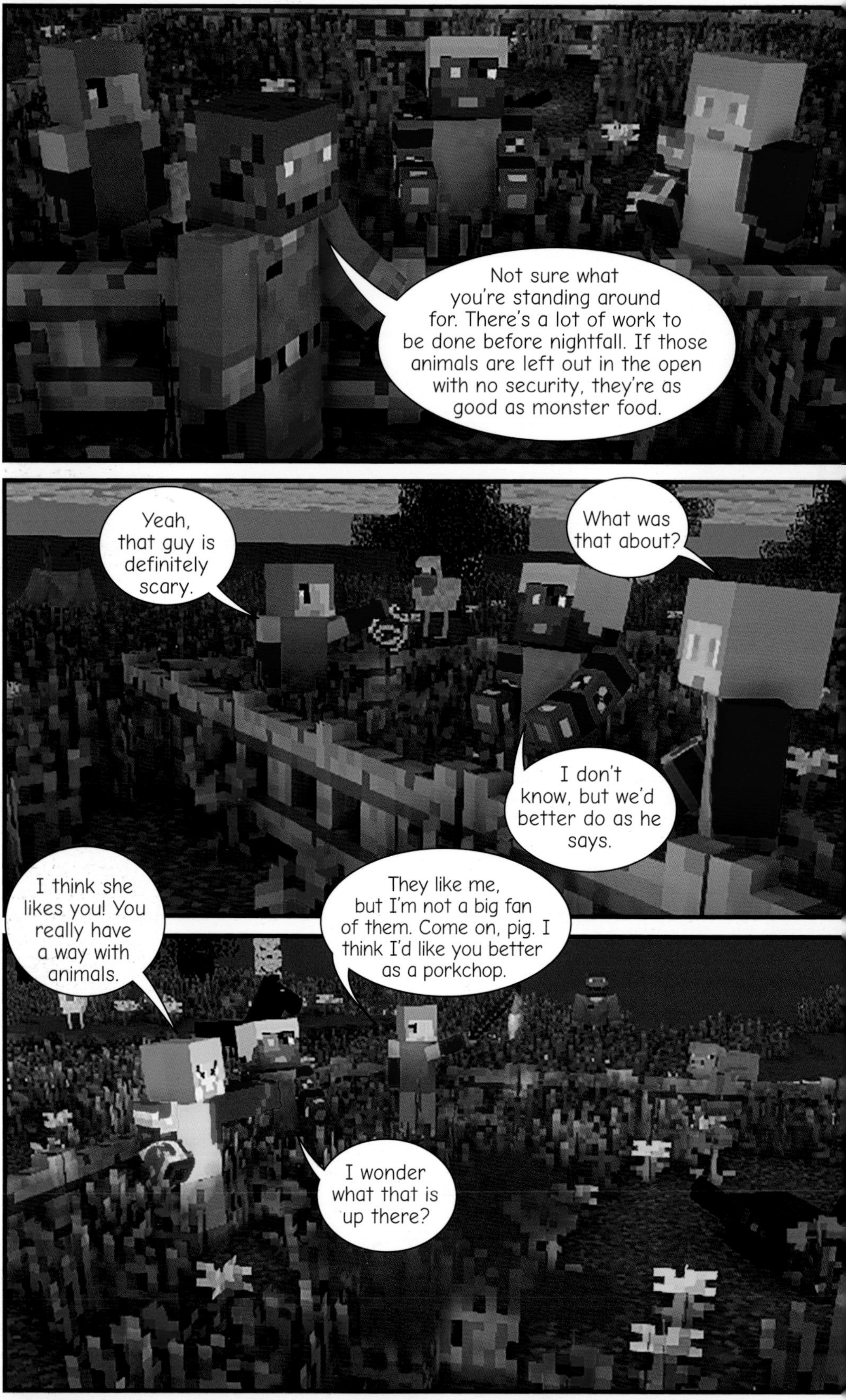

Not sure what you're standing around for. There's a lot of work to be done before nightfall. If those animals are left out in the open with no security, they're as good as monster food.
Yeah, that guy is definitely scary.
What was that about?
I don't know, but we'd better do as he says.
I think she likes you! You really have a way with animals.
They like me, but I'm not a big fan of them. Come on, pig. I think I'd like you better as a porkchop.
I wonder what that is up there?

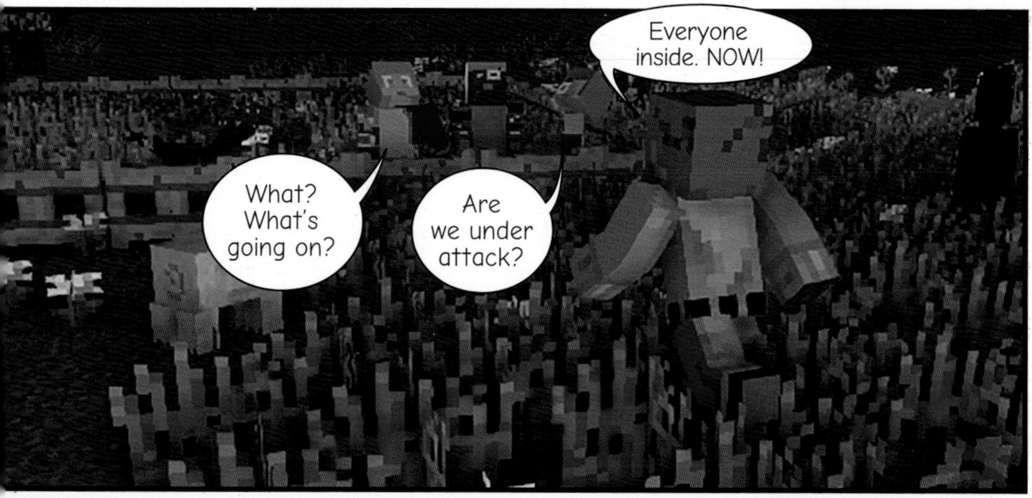
Everyone inside. NOW!
What? What's going on?
Are we under attack?

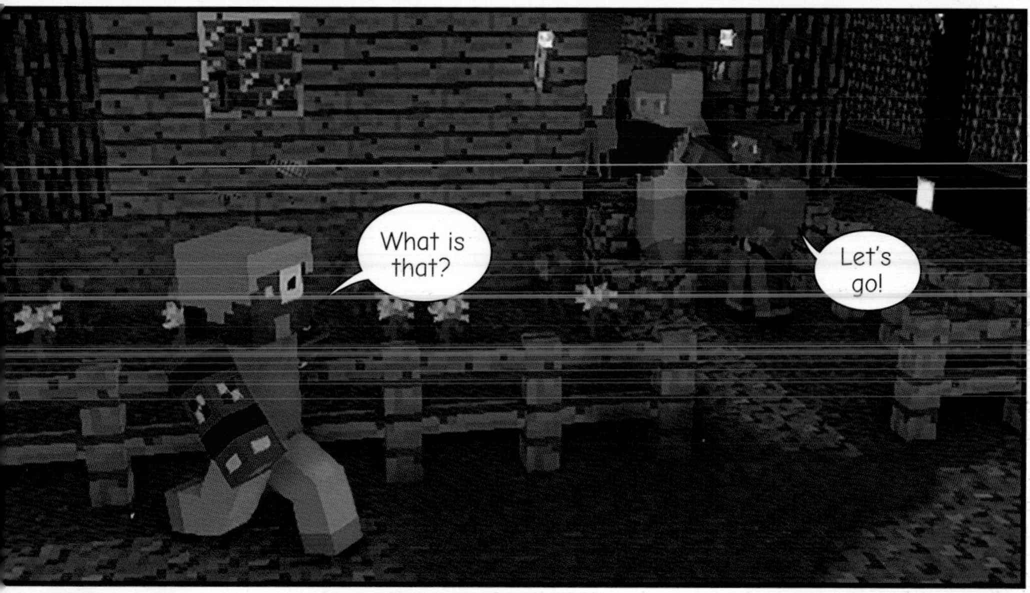
What is that?
Let's go!

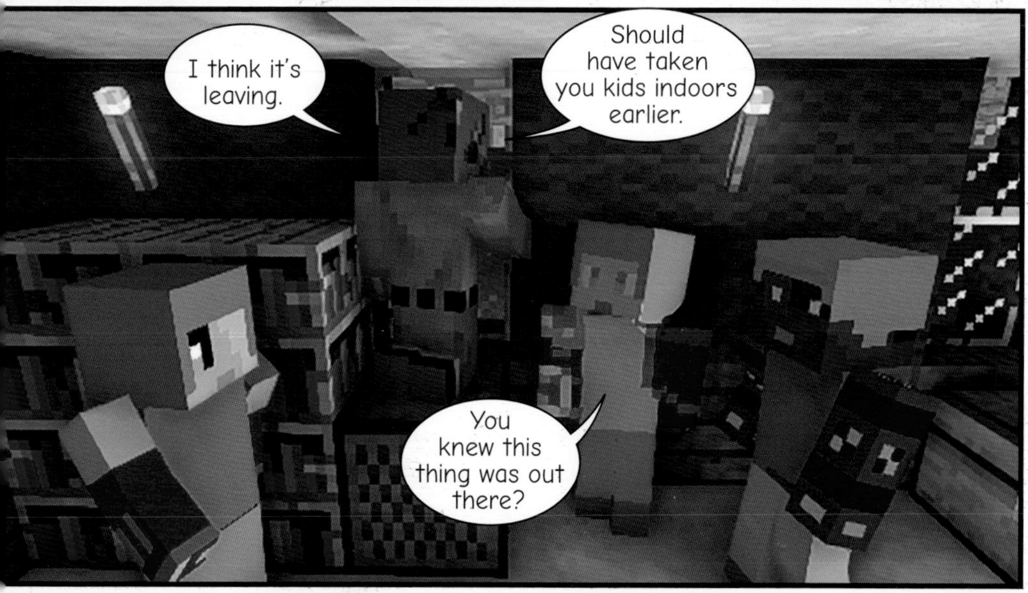
I think it's leaving.
Should have taken you kids indoors earlier.
You knew this thing was out there?

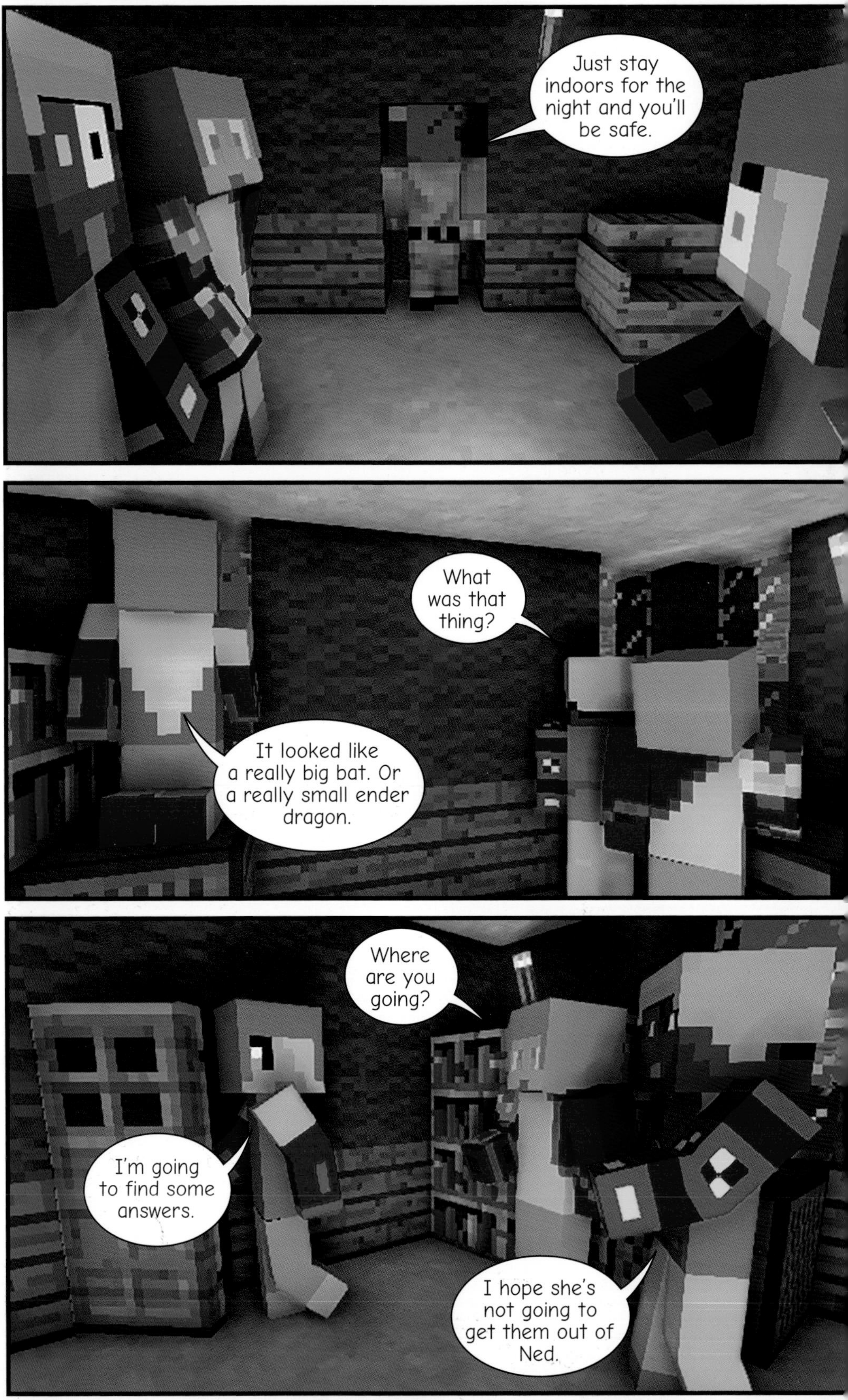
Just stay indoors for the night and you'll be safe.
What was that thing?
It looked like a really big bat. Or a really small ender dragon.
Where are you going?
I'm going to find some answers.
I hope she's not going to get them out of Ned.

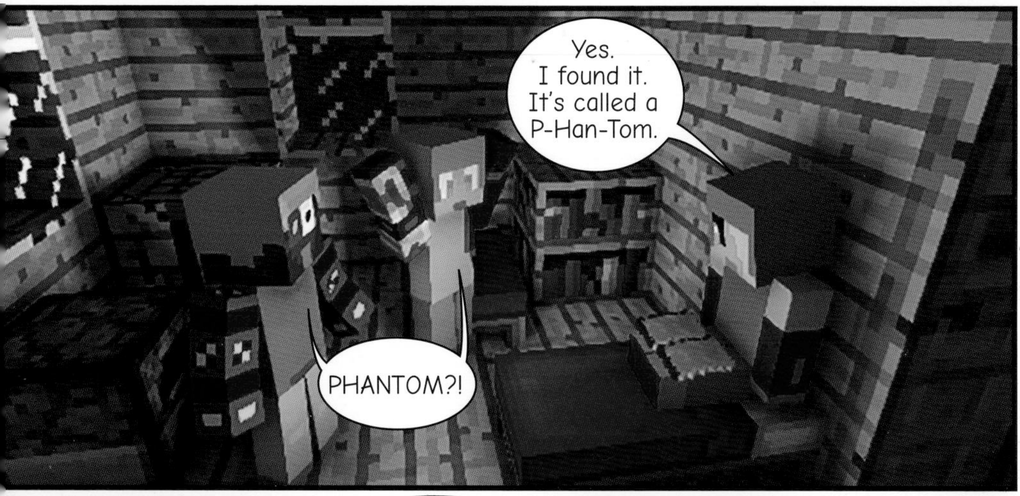
Yes. I found it. It's called a P-Han-Tom.
PHANTOM?!

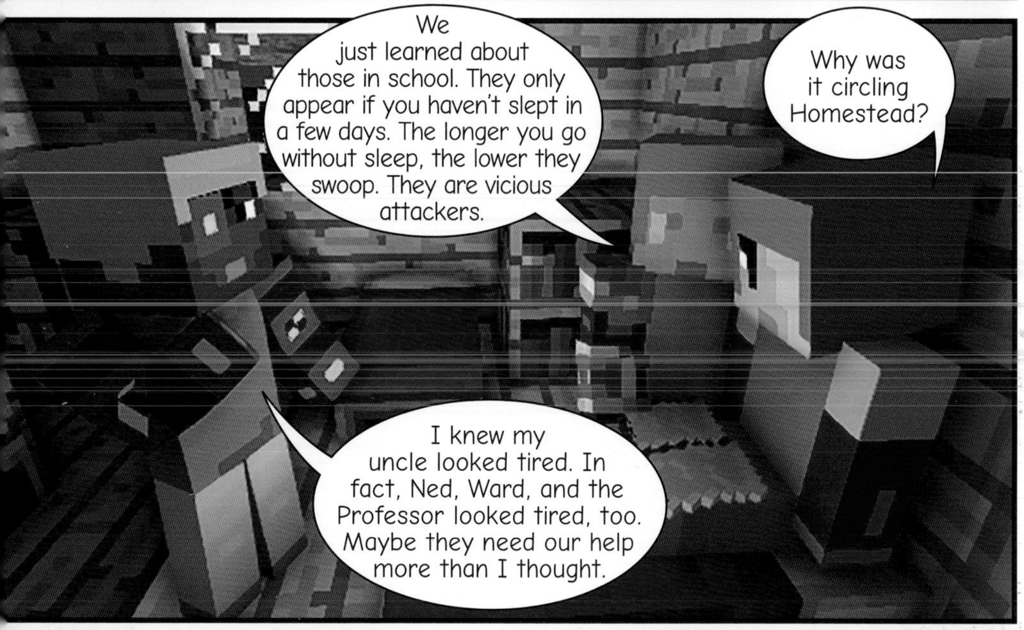
We just learned about those in school. They only appear if you haven't slept in a few days. The longer you go without sleep, the lower they swoop. They are vicious attackers.
Why was it circling Homestead?
I knew my uncle looked tired. In fact, Ned, Ward, and the Professor looked tired, too. Maybe they need our help more than I thought.

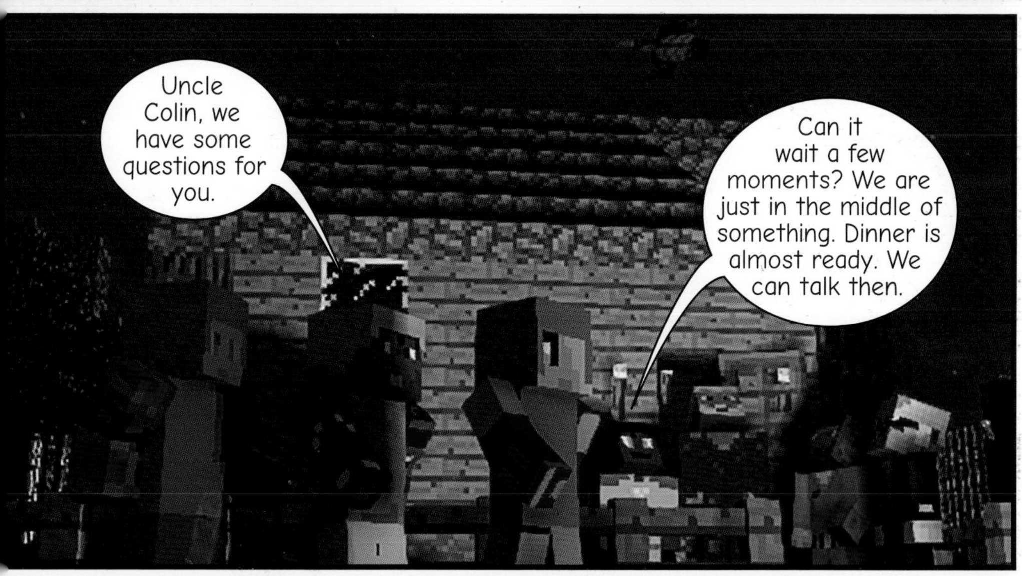
Uncle Colin, we have some questions for you.
Can it wait a few moments? We are just in the middle of something. Dinner is almost ready. We can talk then.

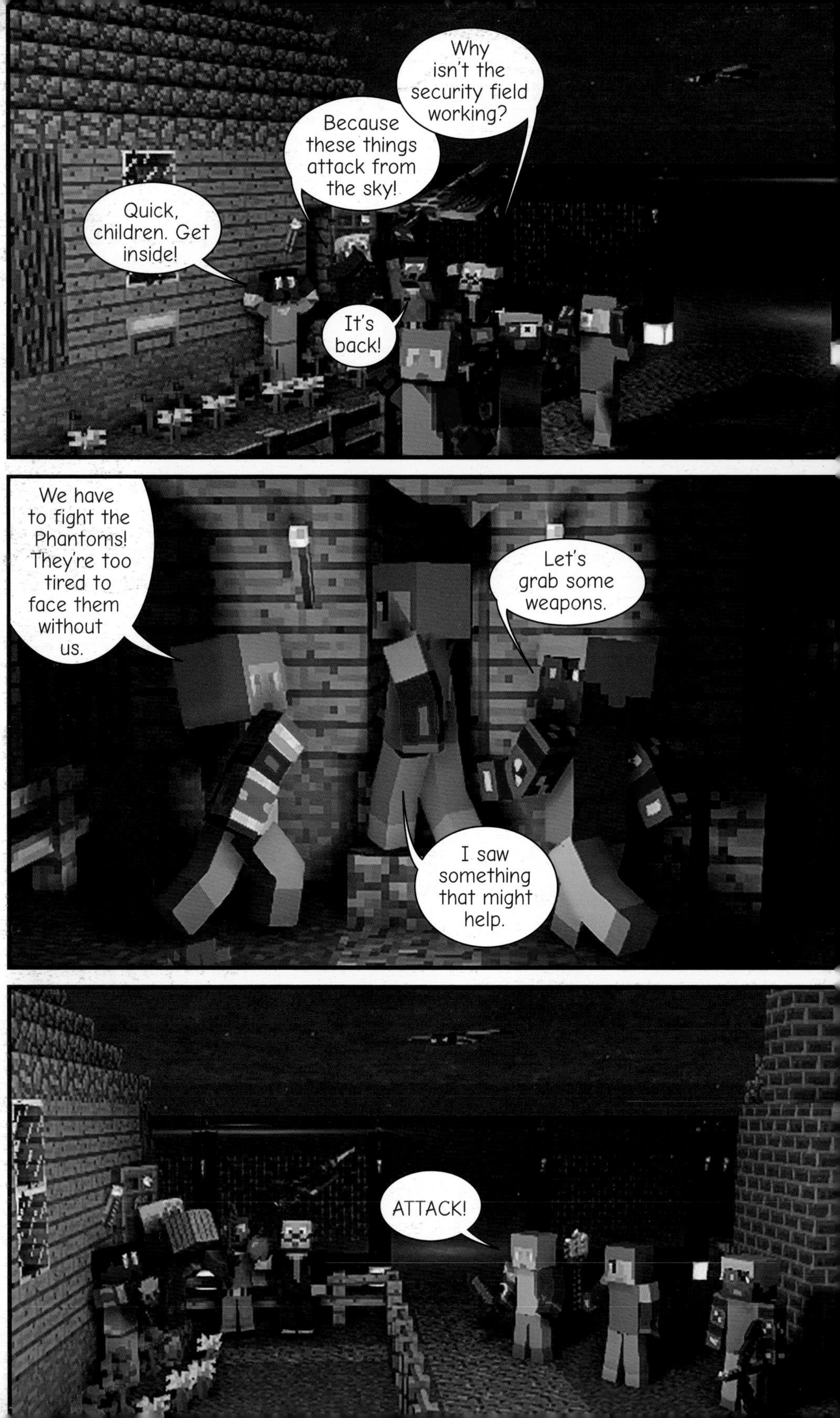
Quick, children. Get inside!
Because these things attack from the sky!
Why isn't the security field working?
It's back!
We have to fight the Phantoms! They're too tired to face them without us.
Let's grab some weapons.
I saw something that might help.
ATTACK!

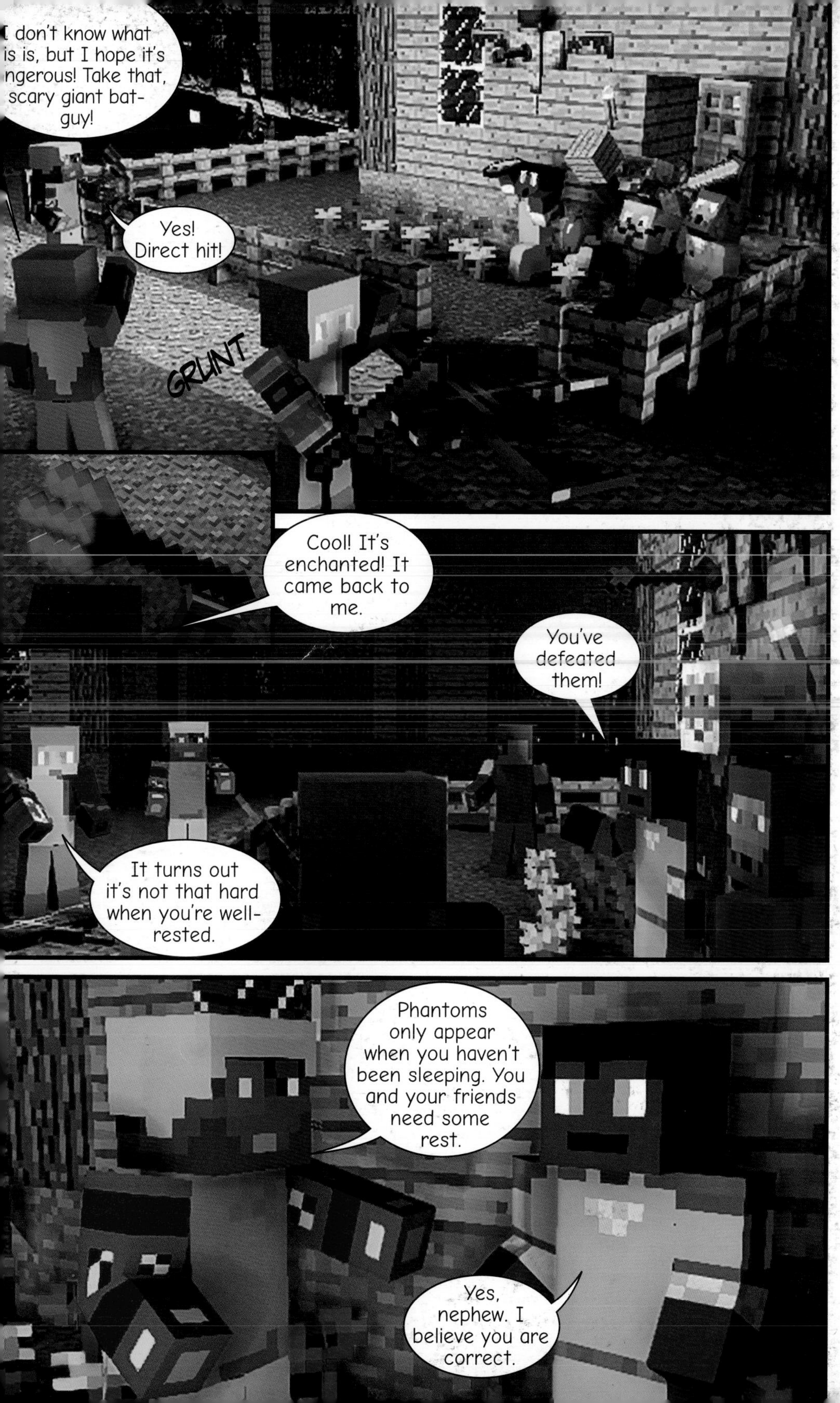
I don't know what is is, but I hope it's ngerous! Take that, scary giant bat-guy!
Yes! Direct hit!
GRUNT
Cool! It's enchanted! It came back to me.
You've defeated them!
It turns out it's not that hard when you're well-rested.
Phantoms only appear when you haven't been sleeping. You and your friends need some rest.
Yes, nephew. I believe you are correct.

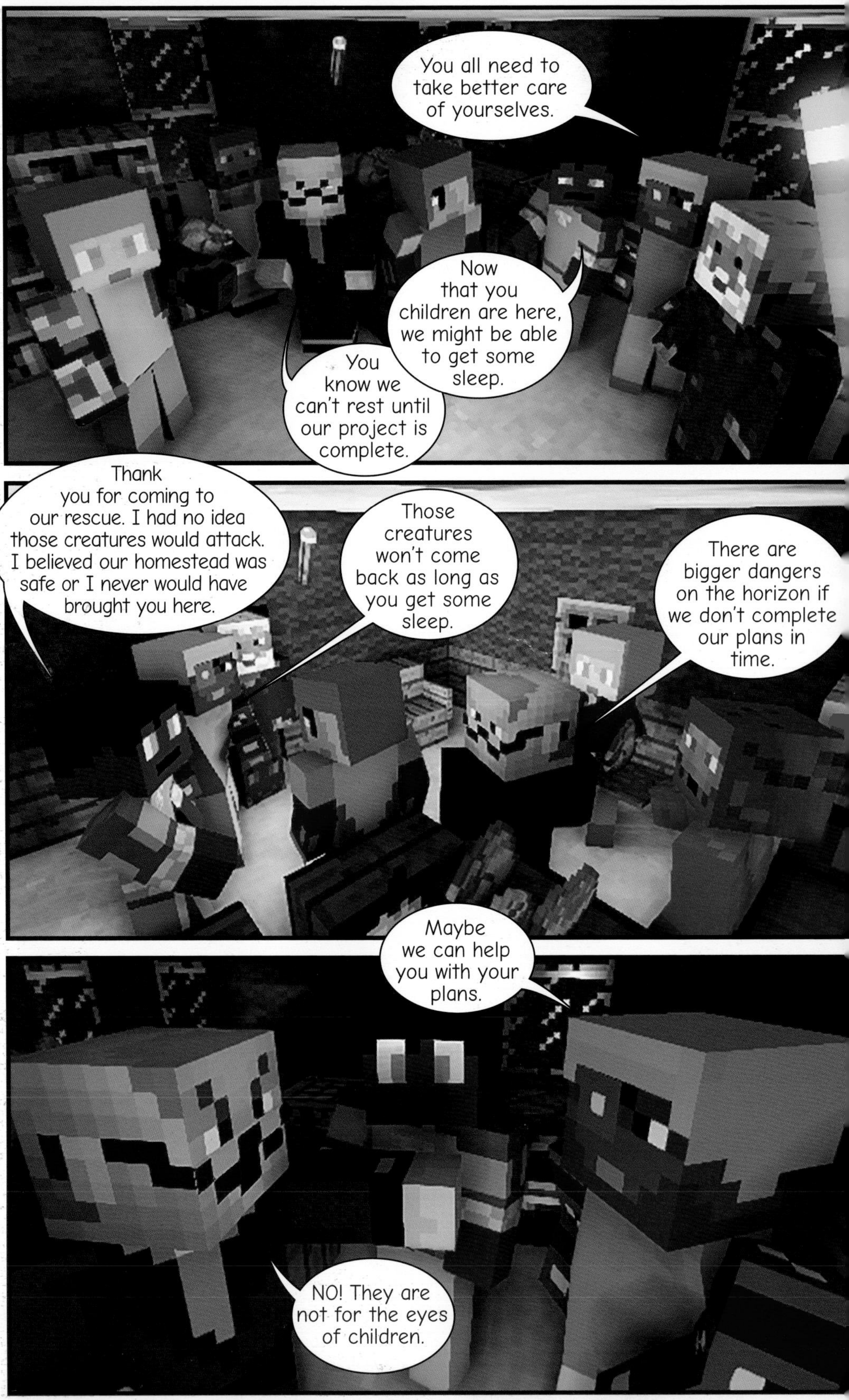
You all need to take better care of yourselves.
Now that you children are here, we might be able to get some sleep.
You know we can't rest until our project is complete.
Thank you for coming to our rescue. I had no idea those creatures would attack. I believed our homestead was safe or I never would have brought you here.
Those creatures won't come back as long as you get some sleep.
There are bigger dangers on the horizon if we don't complete our plans in time.
Maybe we can help you with your plans.
NO! They are not for the eyes of children.

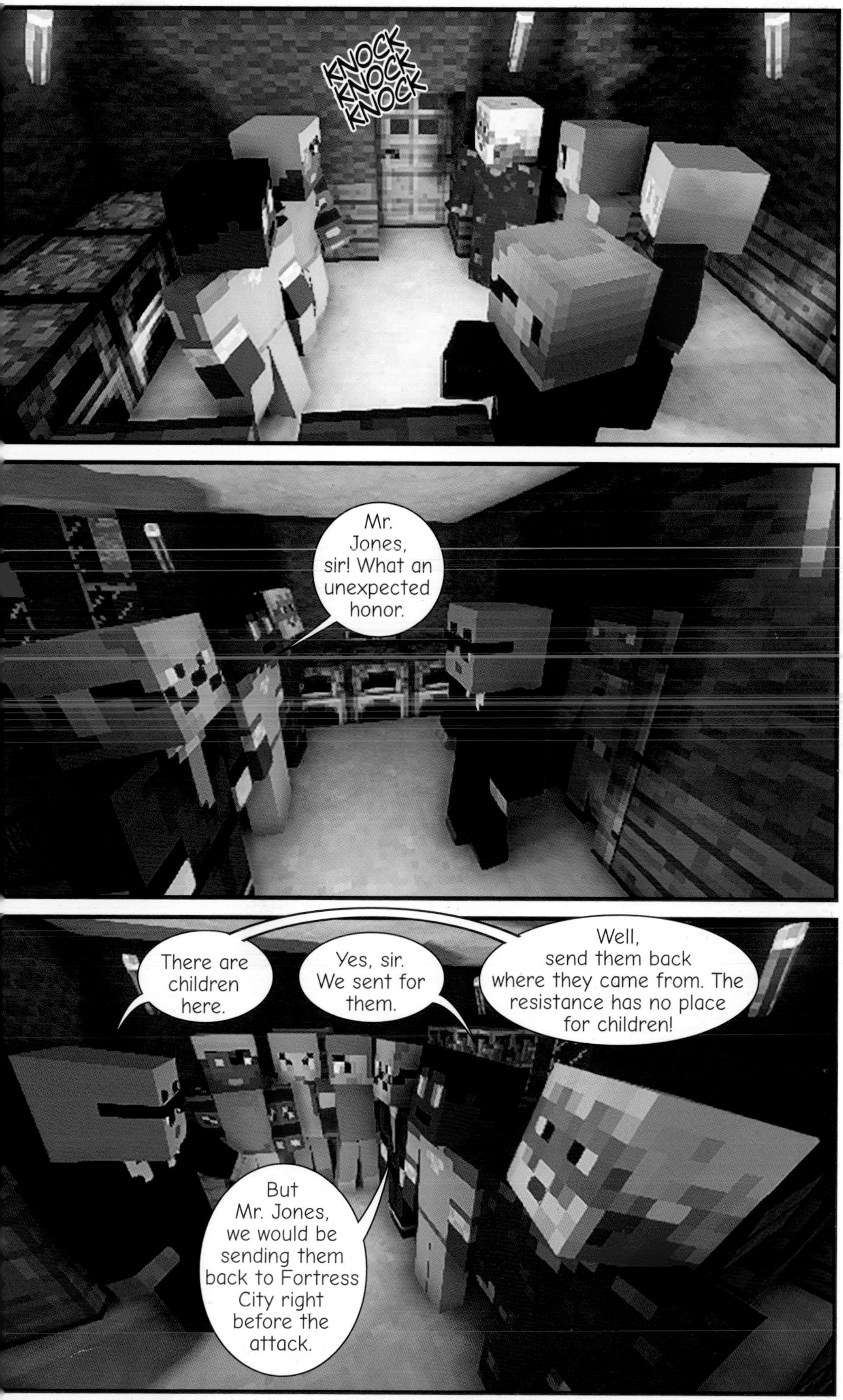
KNOCK KNOCK KNOCK
Mr. Jones, sir! What an unexpected honor.
There are children here.
Yes, sir. We sent for them.
Well, send them back where they came from. The resistance has no place for children!
But Mr. Jones, we would be sending them back to Fortress City right before the attack.

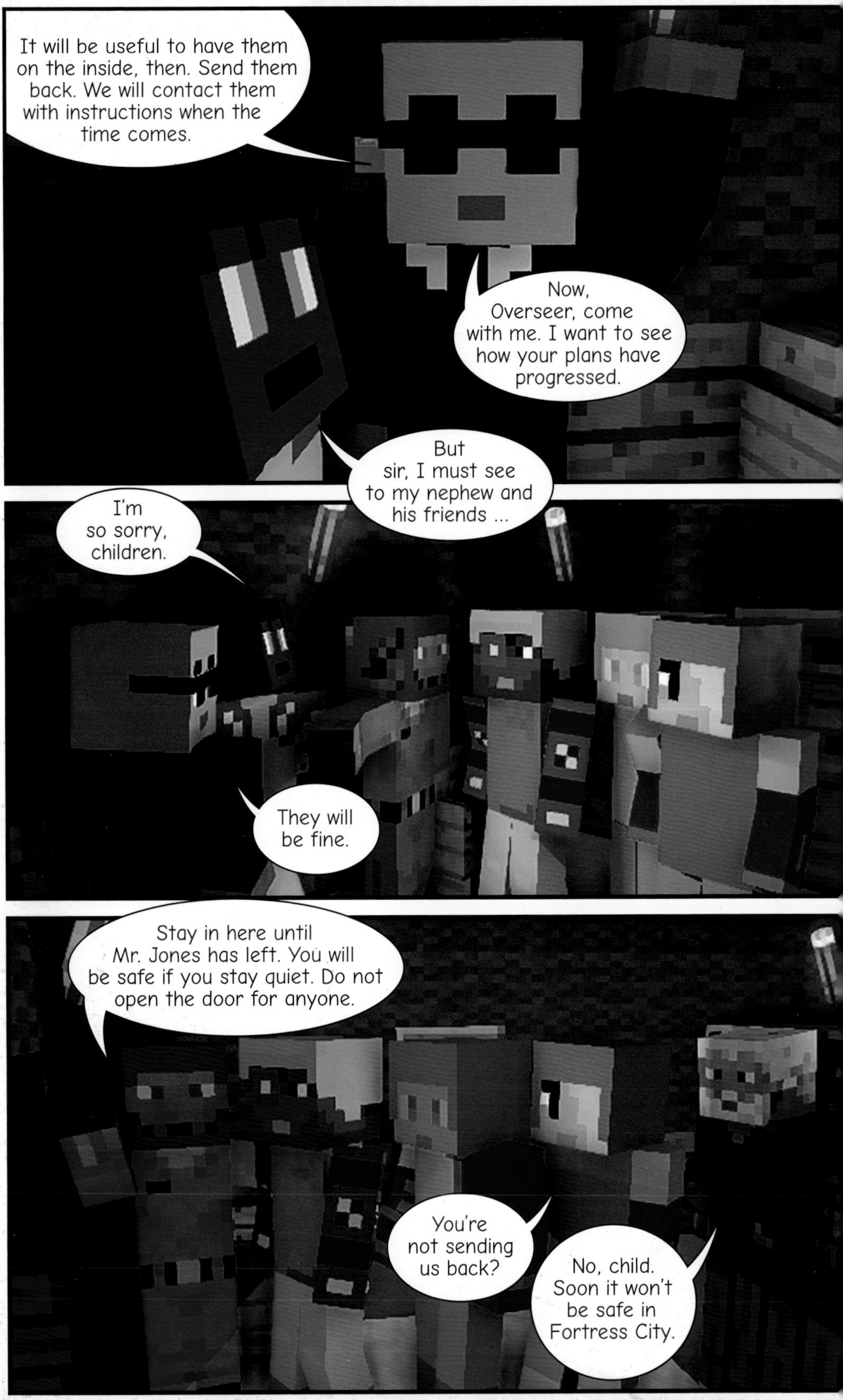
It will be useful to have them on the inside, then. Send them back. We will contact them with instructions when the time comes.
Now, Overseer, come with me. I want to see how your plans have progressed.
But sir, I must see to my nephew and his friends ...
I'm so sorry, children.
They will be fine.
Stay in here until Mr. Jones has left. You will be safe if you stay quiet. Do not open the door for anyone.
You're not sending us back?
No, child. Soon it won't be safe in Fortress City.

CHAPTER 10

UN-WELCOME HOME

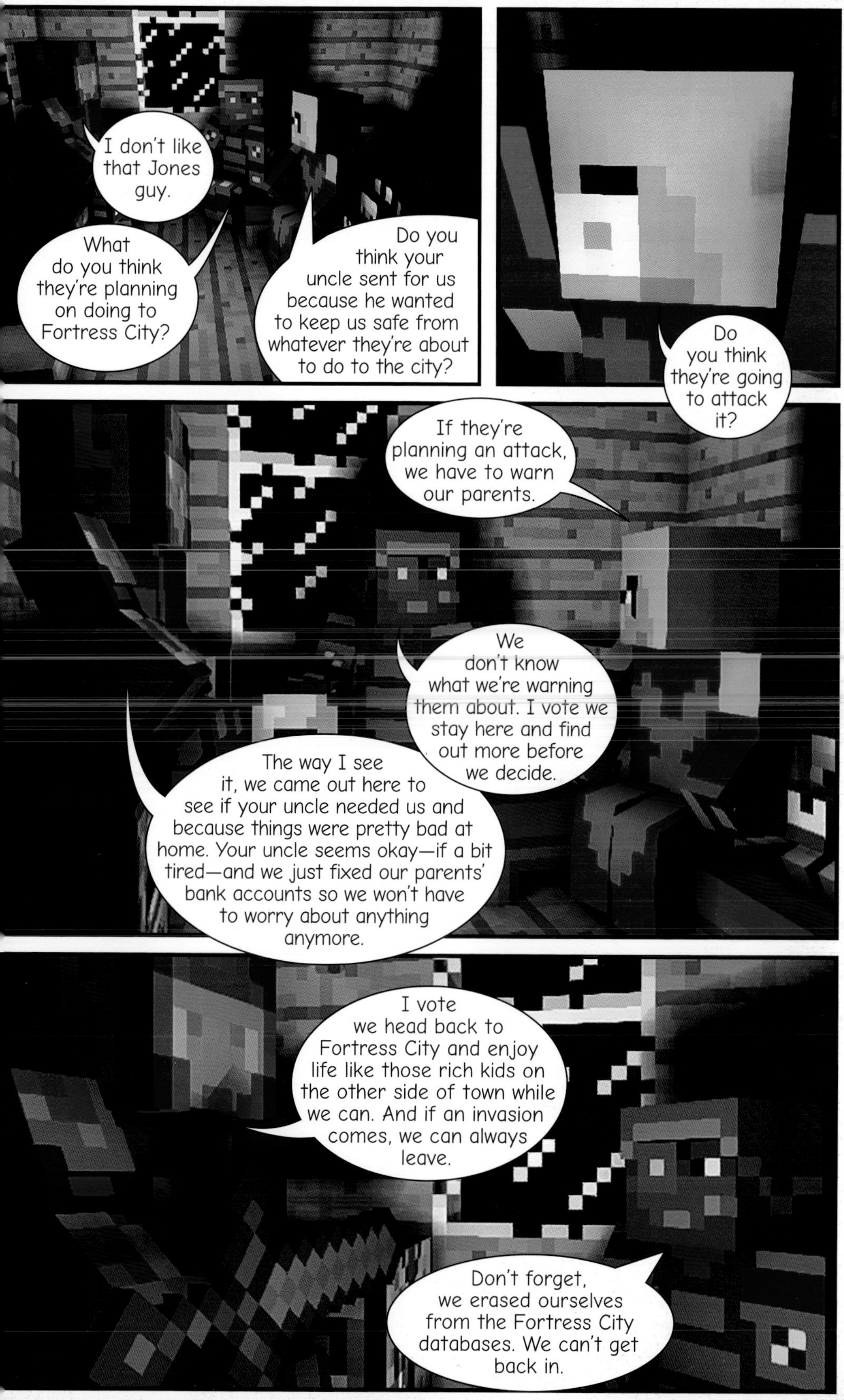
I don't like that Jones guy.
What do you think they're planning on doing to Fortress City?
Do you think your uncle sent for us because he wanted to keep us safe from whatever they're about to do to the city?
Do you think they're going to attack it?
If they're planning an attack, we have to warn our parents.
We don't know what we're warning them about. I vote we stay here and find out more before we decide.
The way I see it, we came out here to see if your uncle needed us and because things were pretty bad at home. Your uncle seems okay—if a bit tired—and we just fixed our parents' bank accounts so we won't have to worry about anything anymore.
I vote we head back to Fortress City and enjoy life like those rich kids on the other side of town while we can. And if an invasion comes, we can always leave.
Don't forget, we erased ourselves from the Fortress City databases. We can't get back in.

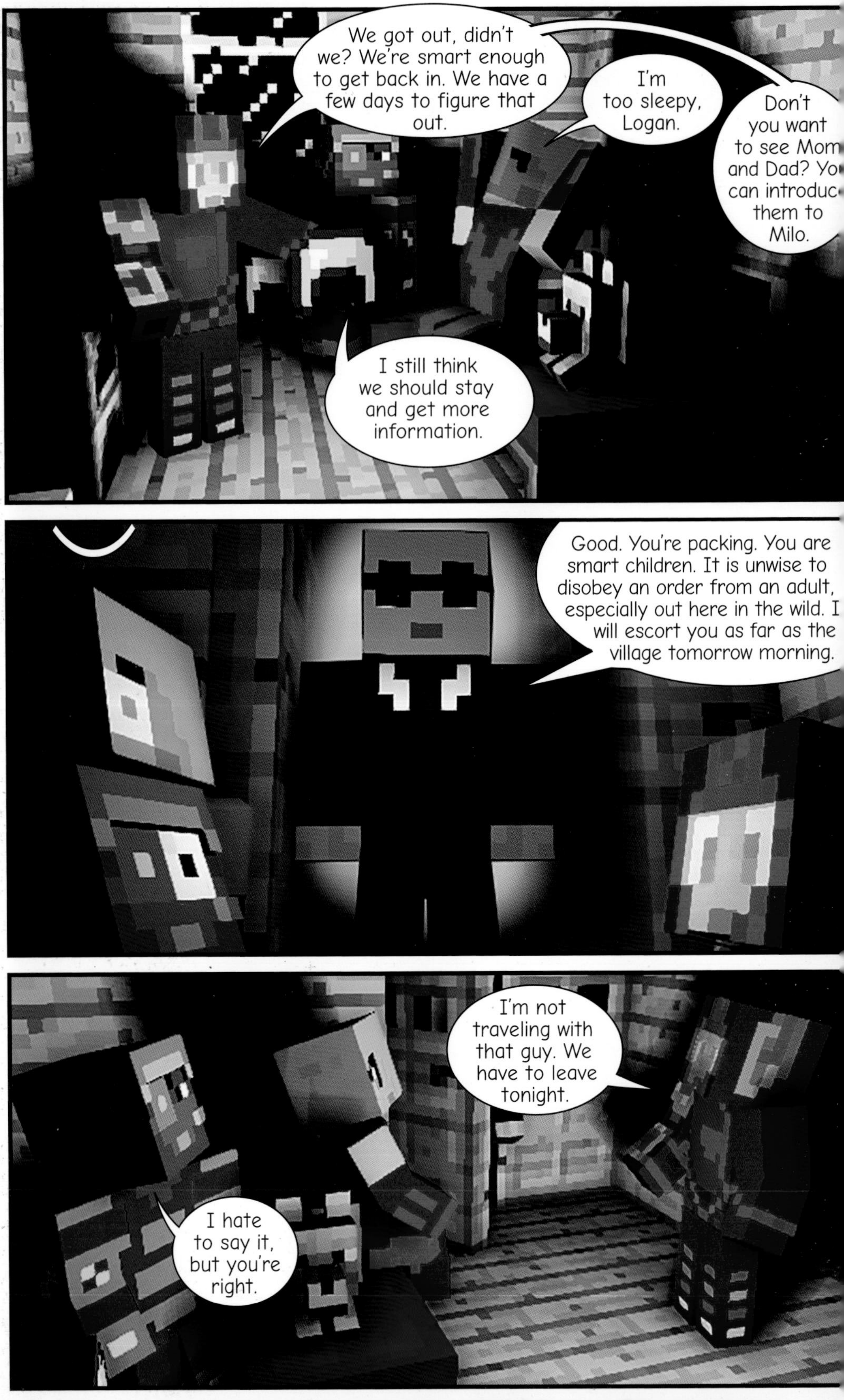
We got out, didn't we? We're smart enough to get back in. We have a few days to figure that out.
I'm too sleepy, Logan.
Don't you want to see Mom and Dad? Yo can introduc them to Milo.
I still think we should stay and get more information.
Good. You're packing. You are smart children. It is unwise to disobey an order from an adult, especially out here in the wild. I will escort you as far as the village tomorrow morning.
I'm not traveling with that guy. We have to leave tonight.
I hate to say it, but you're right.

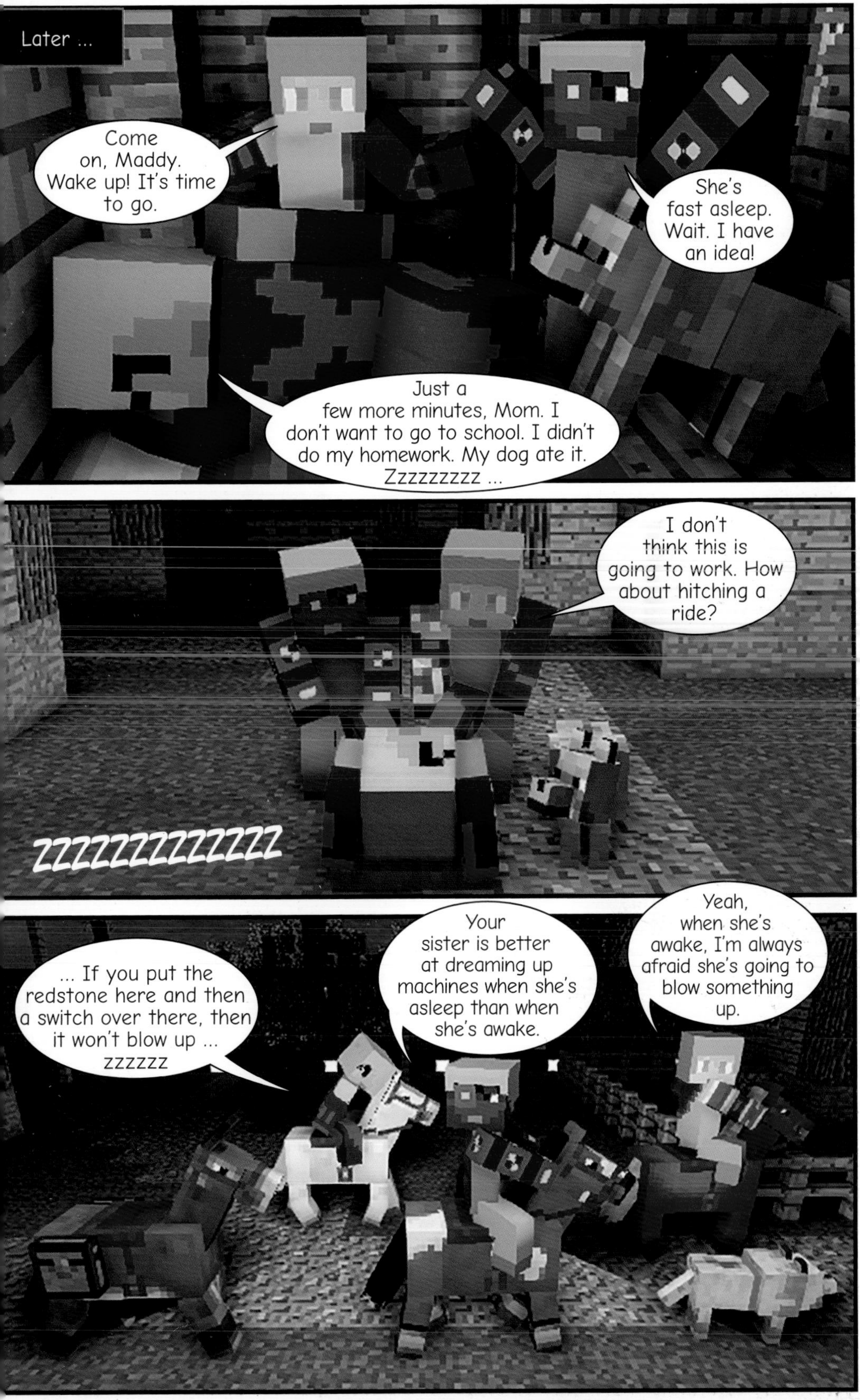
Later ...
Come on, Maddy. Wake up! It's time to go.
She's fast asleep. Wait. I have an idea!
Just a few more minutes, Mom. I don't want to go to school. I didn't do my homework. My dog ate it. Zzzzzzzzz ...
I don't think this is going to work. How about hitching a ride?
ZZZZZZZZZZZZZZ
... If you put the redstone here and then a switch over there, then it won't blow up ... zzzzzz
Your sister is better at dreaming up machines when she's asleep than when she's awake.
Yeah, when she's awake, I'm always afraid she's going to blow something up.

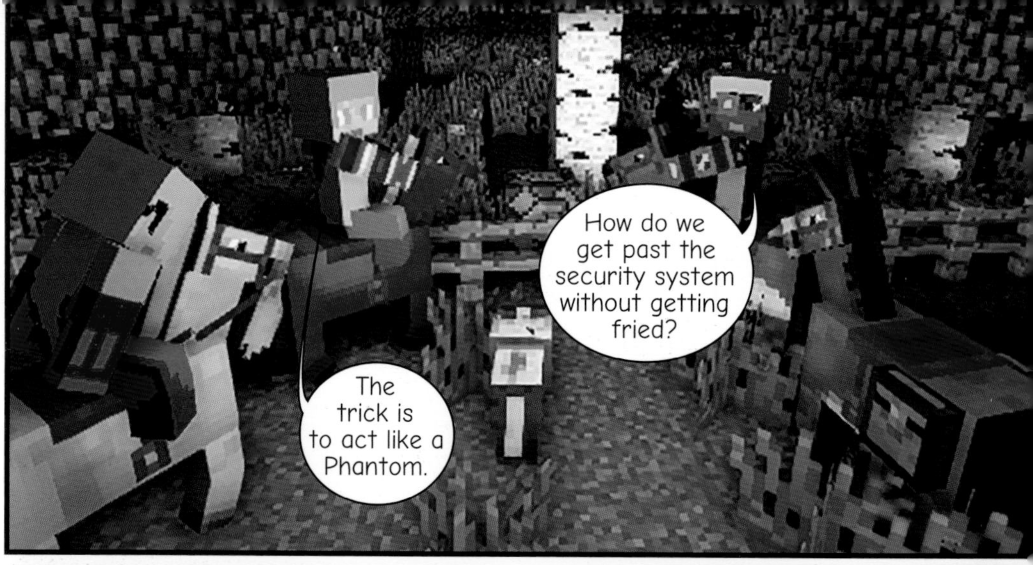
How do we get past the security system without getting fried?
The trick is to act like a Phantom.

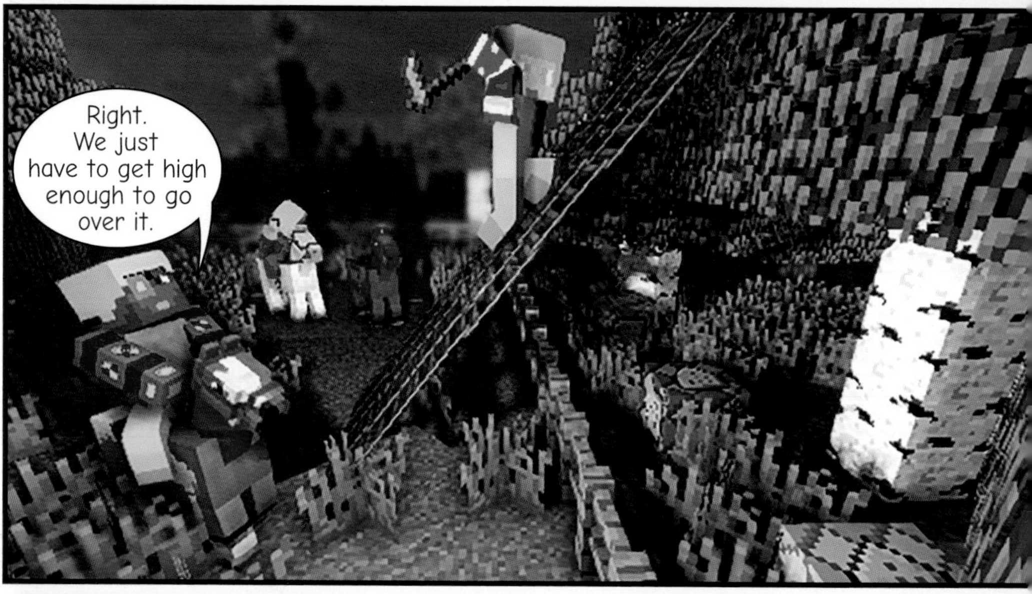
Right. We just have to get high enough to go over it.

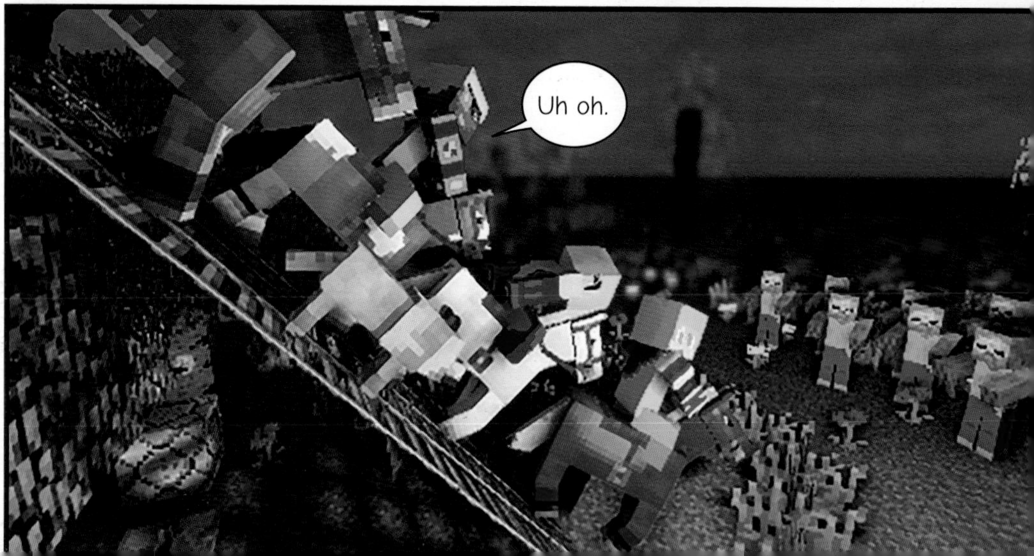
Uh oh.

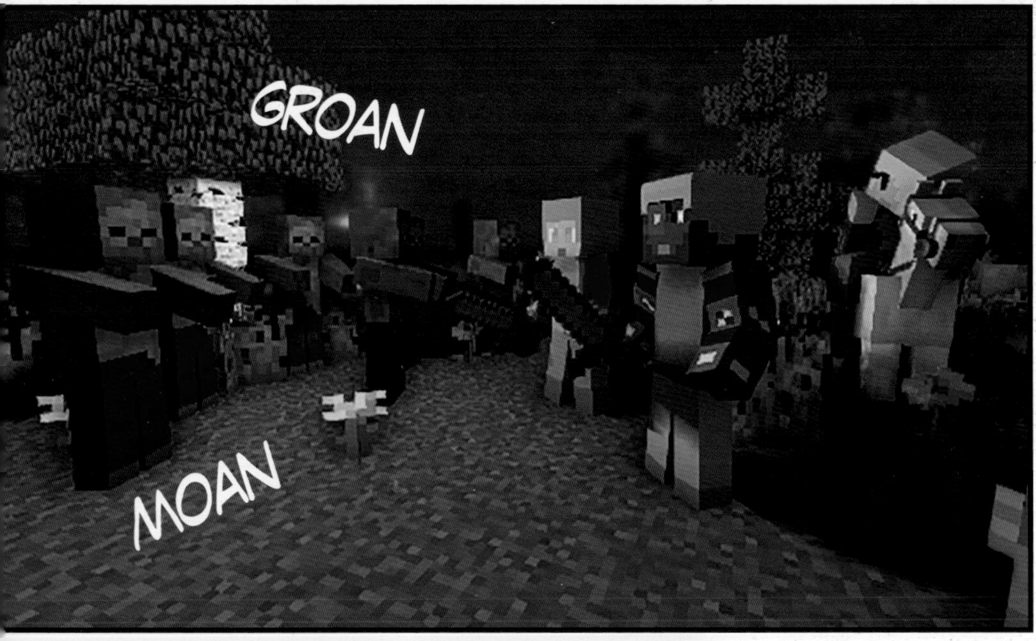
GROAN
MOAN

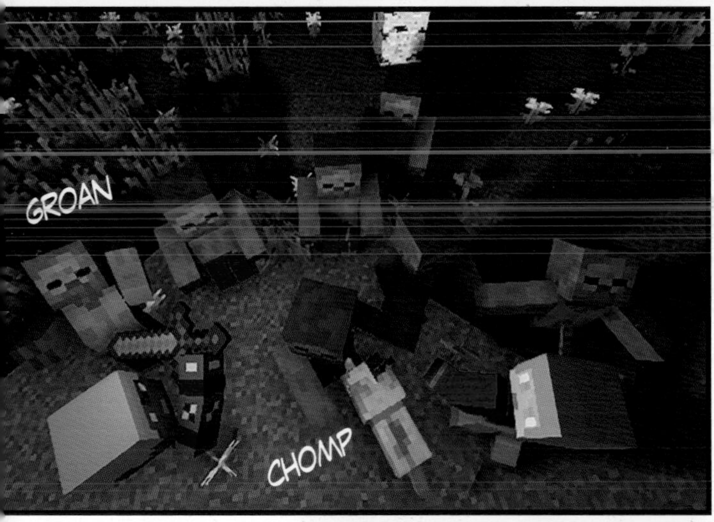
GROAN
CHOMP

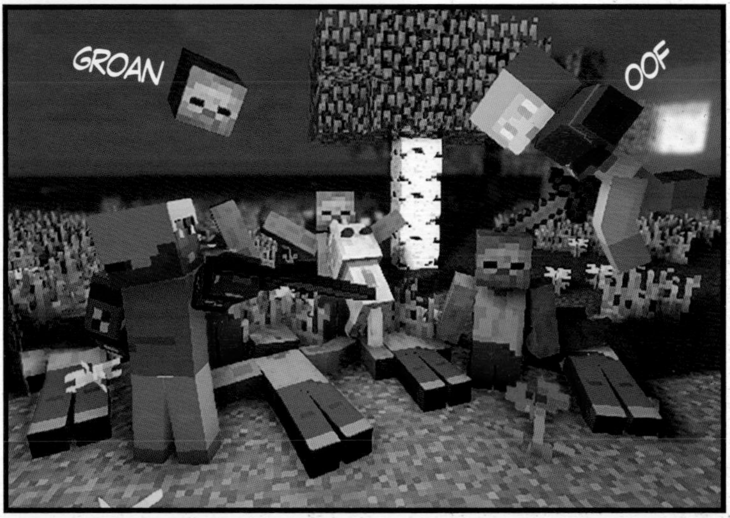
GROAN
OOF

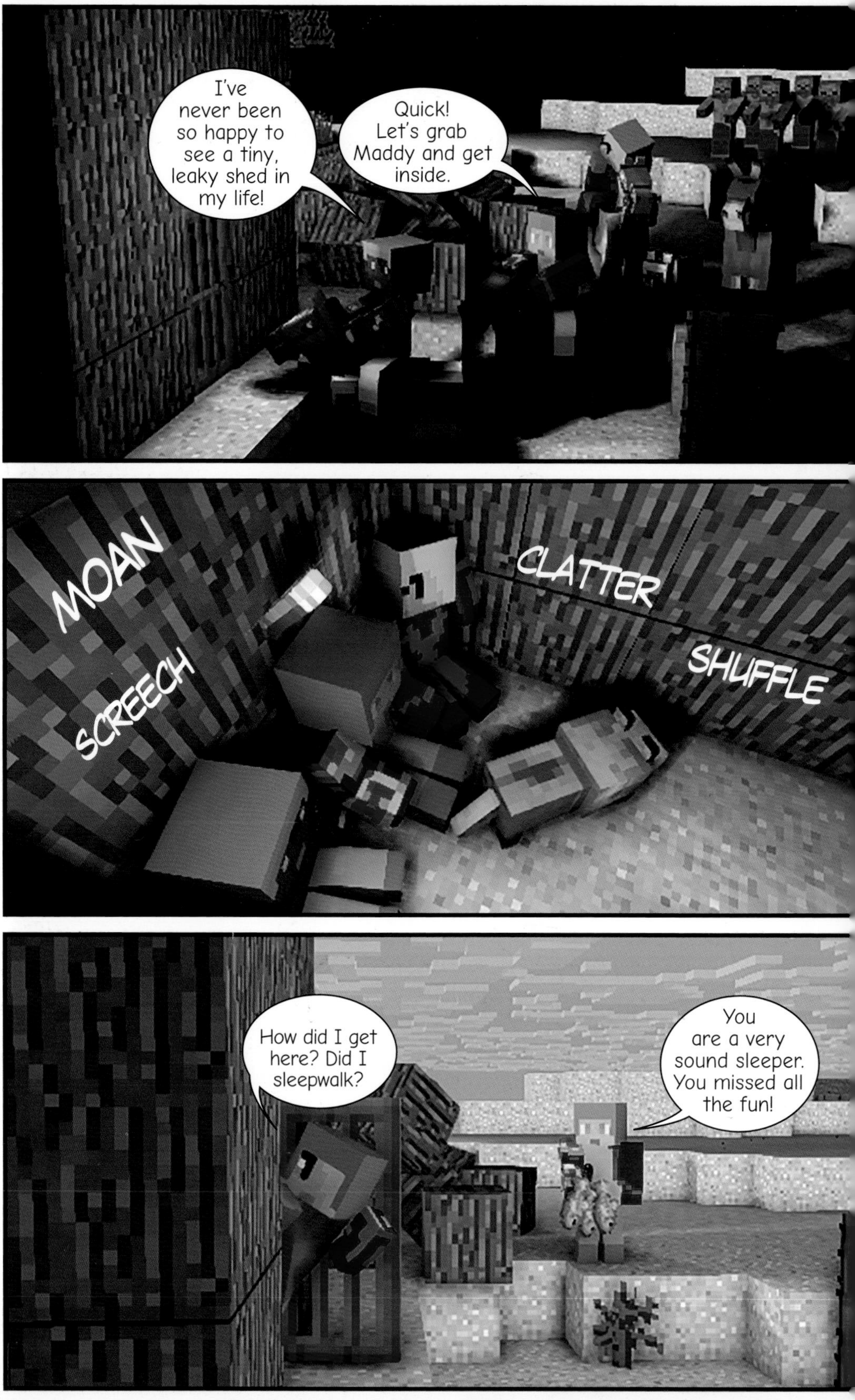
I've never been so happy to see a tiny, leaky shed in my life!
Quick! Let's grab Maddy and get inside.
MOAN
SCREECH
CLATTER
SHUFFLE
How did I get here? Did I sleepwalk?
You are a very sound sleeper. You missed all the fun!

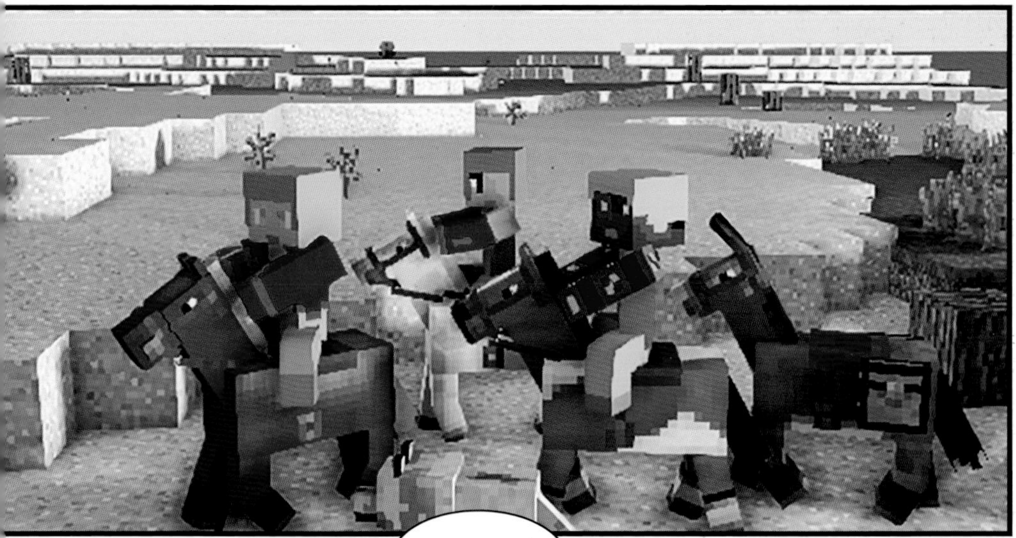

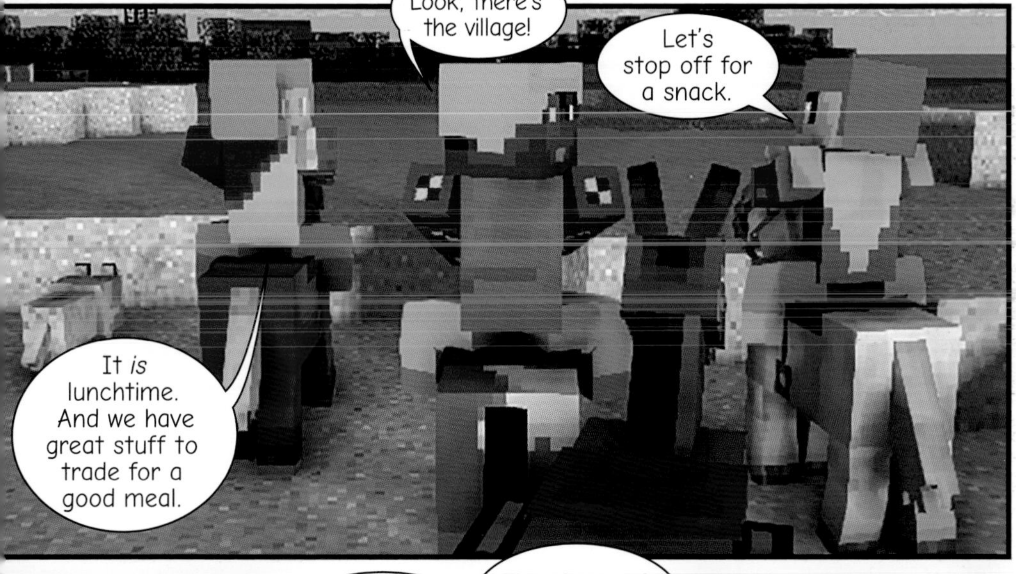

Look, there's the village!
Let's stop off for a snack.
It *is* lunchtime. And we have great stuff to trade for a good meal.

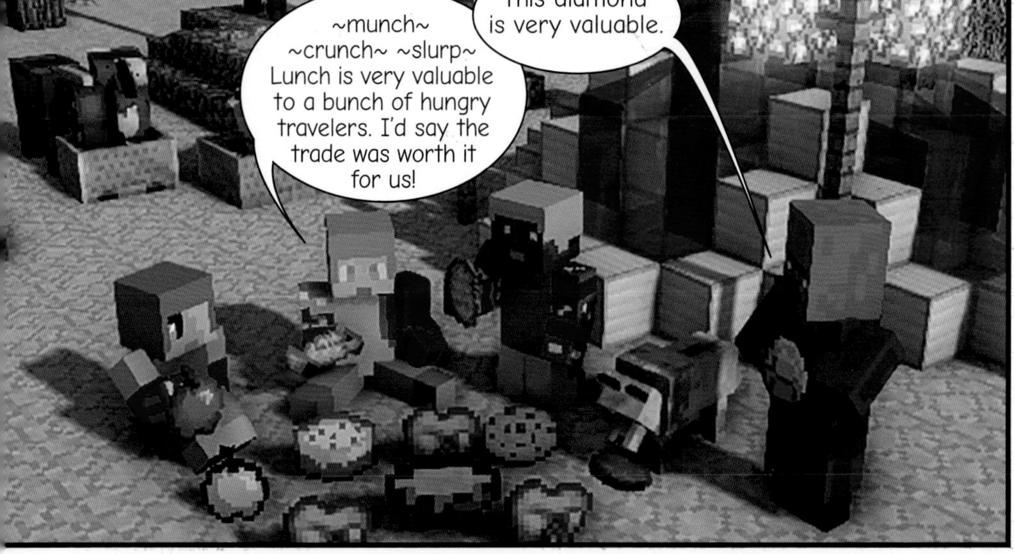

This diamond is very valuable.
~munch~ ~crunch~ ~slurp~ Lunch is very valuable to a bunch of hungry travelers. I'd say the trade was worth it for us!

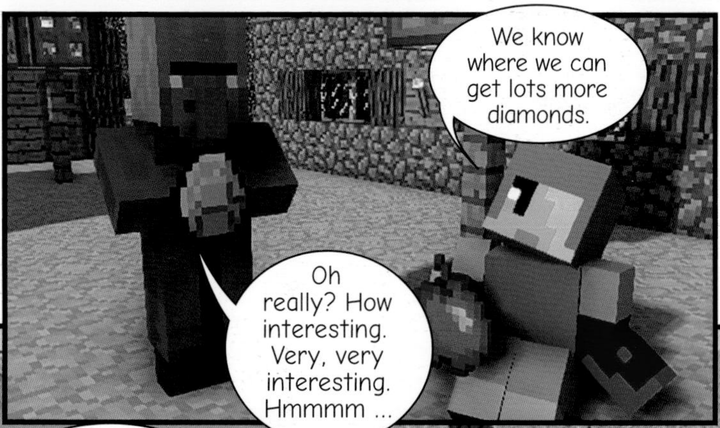
We know where we can get lots more diamonds.
Oh really? How interesting. Very, very interesting. Hmmmm ...

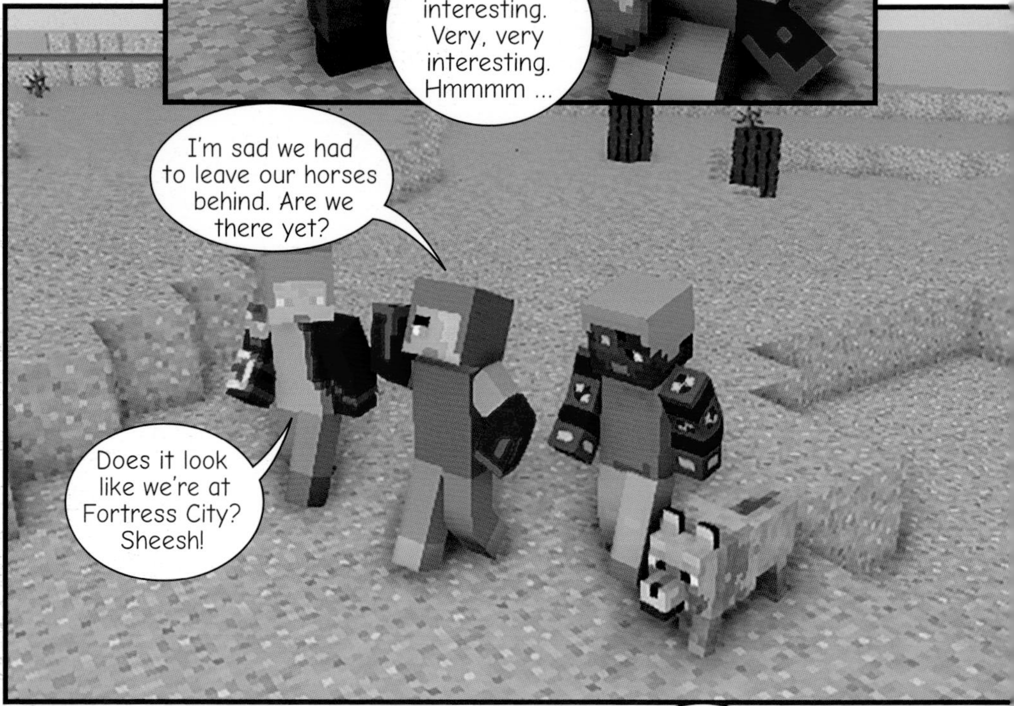
I'm sad we had to leave our horses behind. Are we there yet?
Does it look like we're at Fortress City? Sheesh!

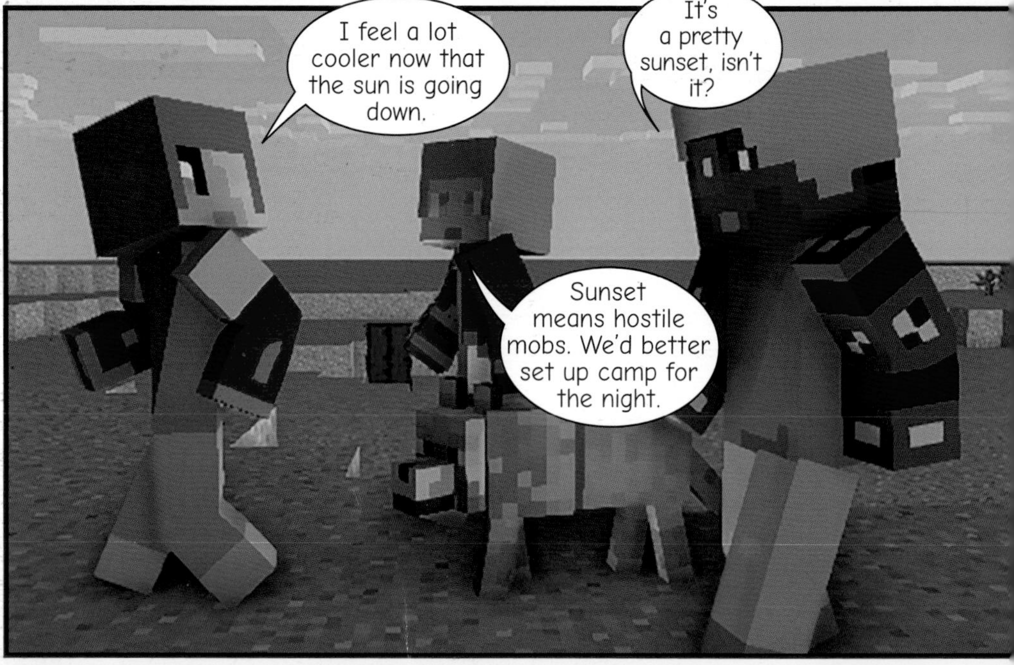
I feel a lot cooler now that the sun is going down.
It's a pretty sunset, isn't it?
Sunset means hostile mobs. We'd better set up camp for the night.

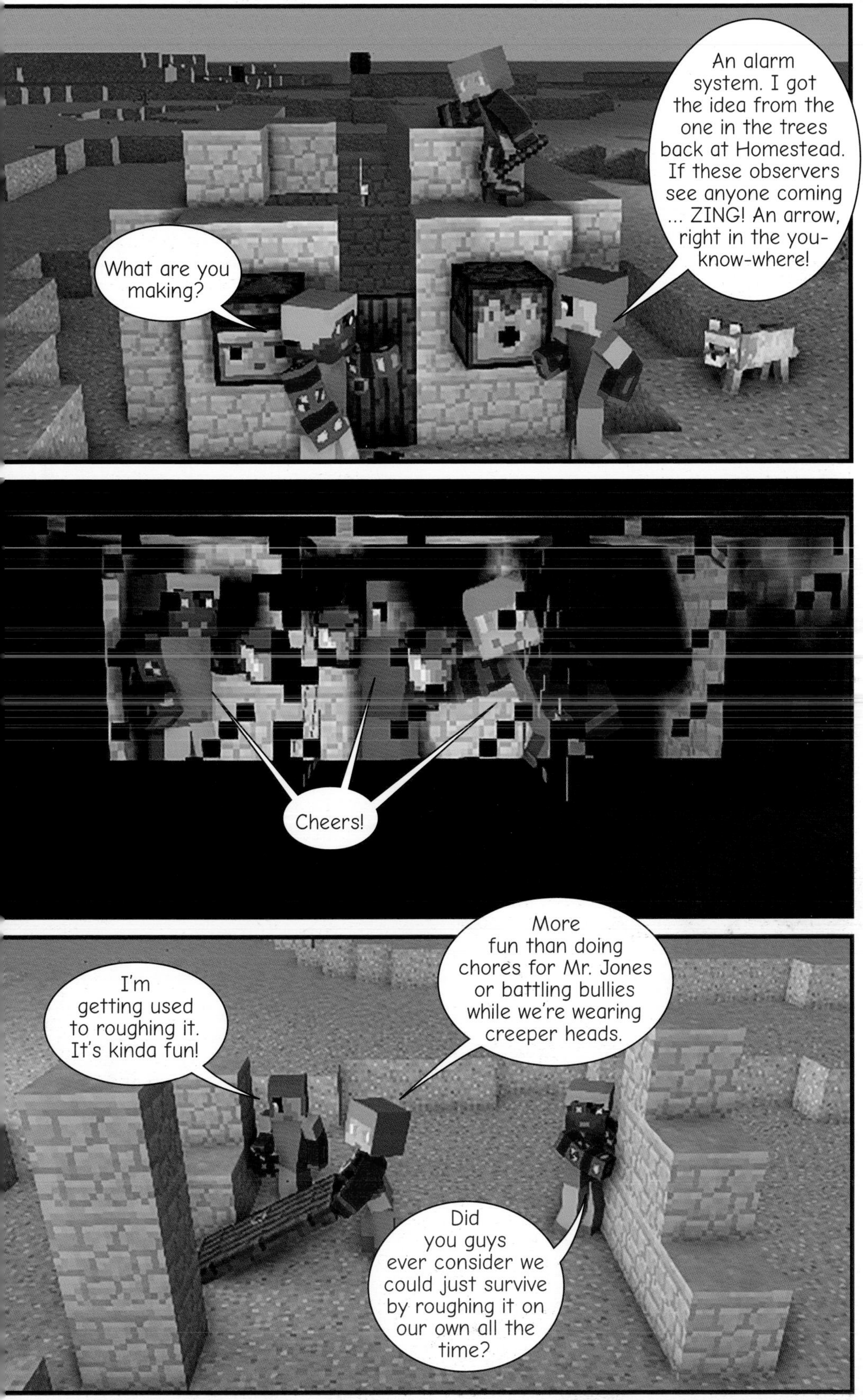
What are you making?
An alarm system. I got the idea from the one in the trees back at Homestead. If these observers see anyone coming ... ZING! An arrow, right in the you-know-where!
Cheers!
I'm getting used to roughing it. It's kinda fun!
More fun than doing chores for Mr. Jones or battling bullies while we're wearing creeper heads.
Did you guys ever consider we could just survive by roughing it on our own all the time?

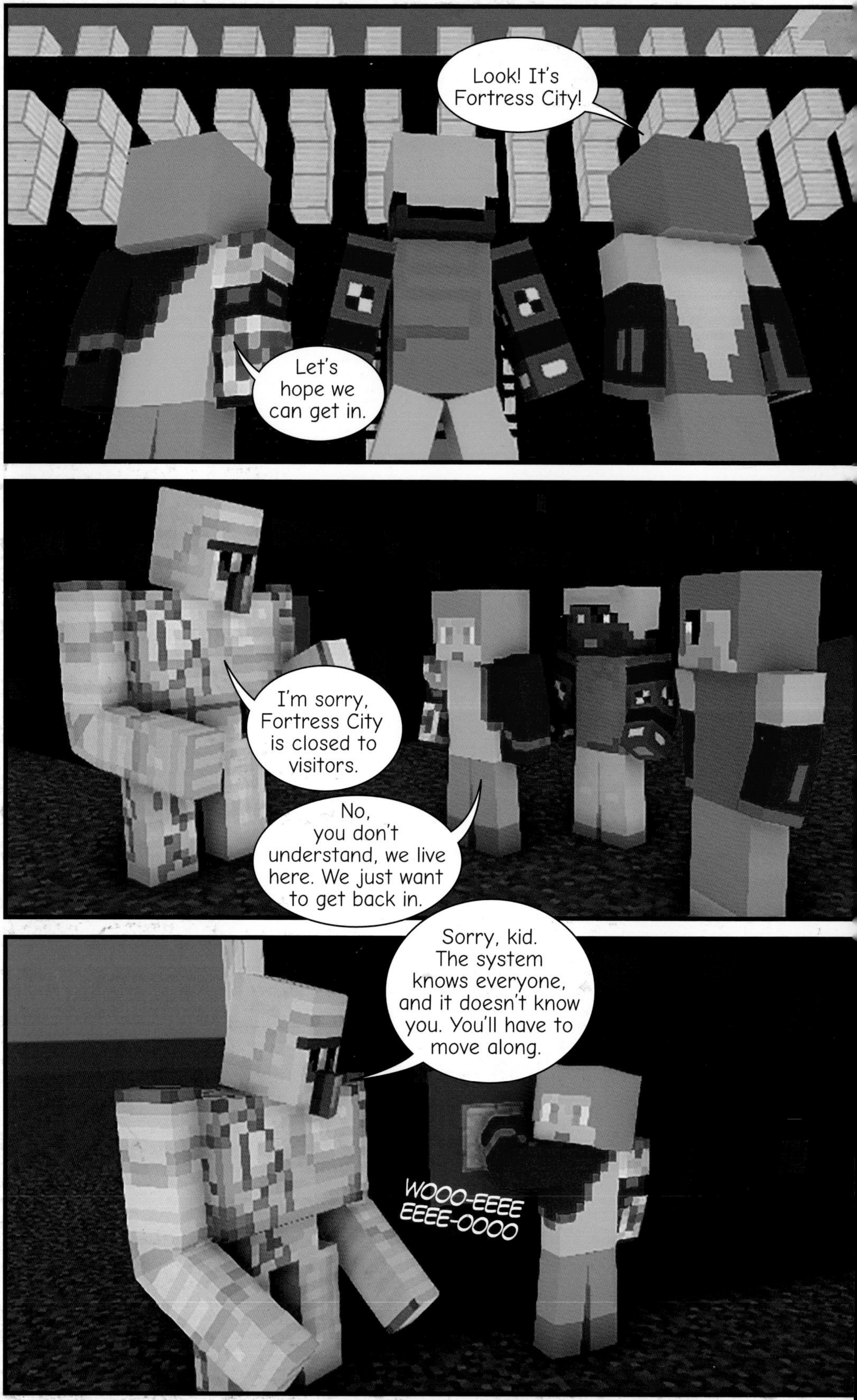
Look! It's Fortress City!
Let's hope we can get in.
I'm sorry, Fortress City is closed to visitors.
No, you don't understand, we live here. We just want to get back in.
Sorry, kid. The system knows everyone, and it doesn't know you. You'll have to move along.
WOOO-EEEE EEEE-OOOO

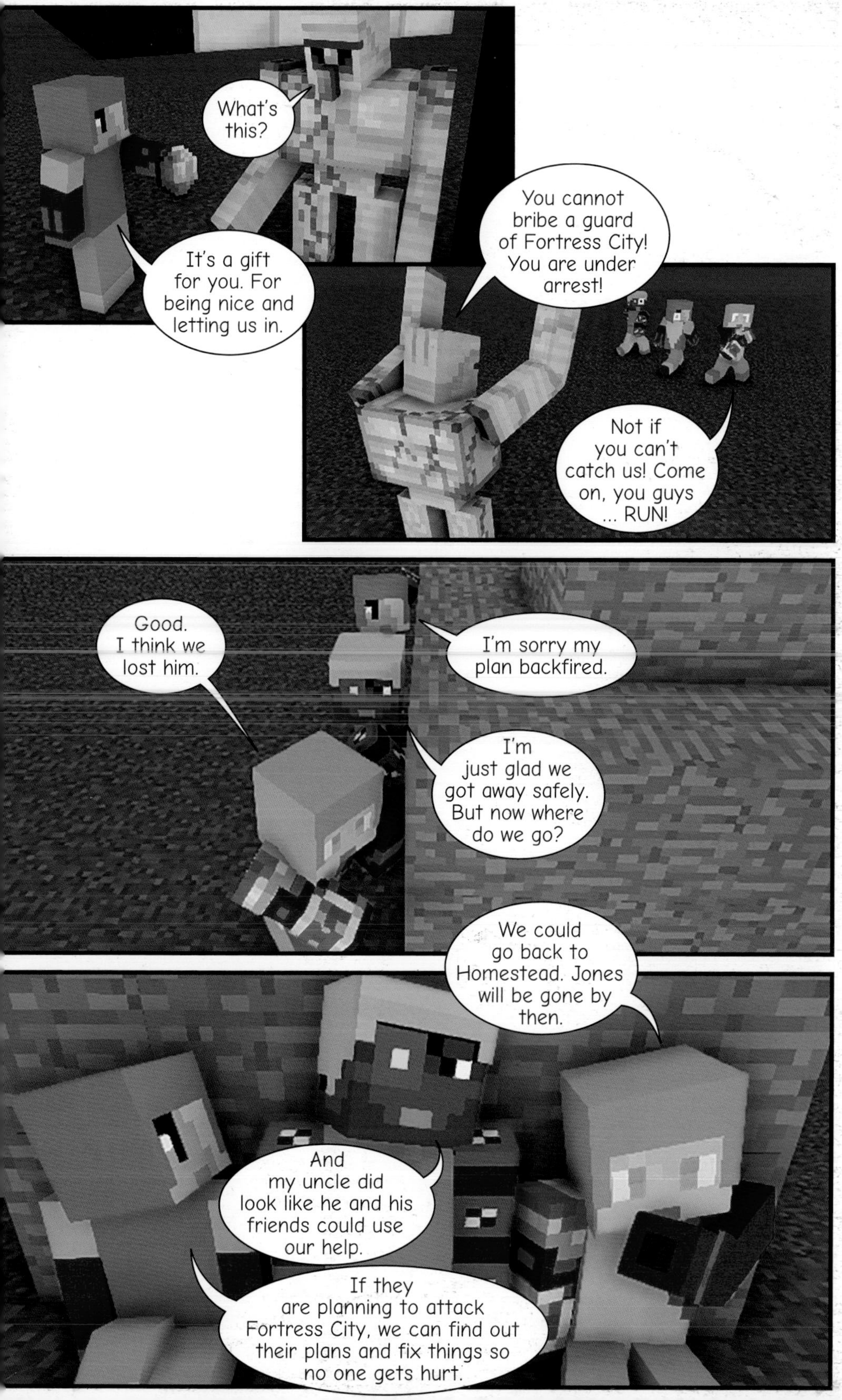
What's this?
It's a gift for you. For being nice and letting us in.
You cannot bribe a guard of Fortress City! You are under arrest!
Not if you can't catch us! Come on, you guys ... RUN!
Good. I think we lost him.
I'm sorry my plan backfired.
I'm just glad we got away safely. But now where do we go?
We could go back to Homestead. Jones will be gone by then.
And my uncle did look like he and his friends could use our help.
If they are planning to attack Fortress City, we can find out their plans and fix things so no one gets hurt.

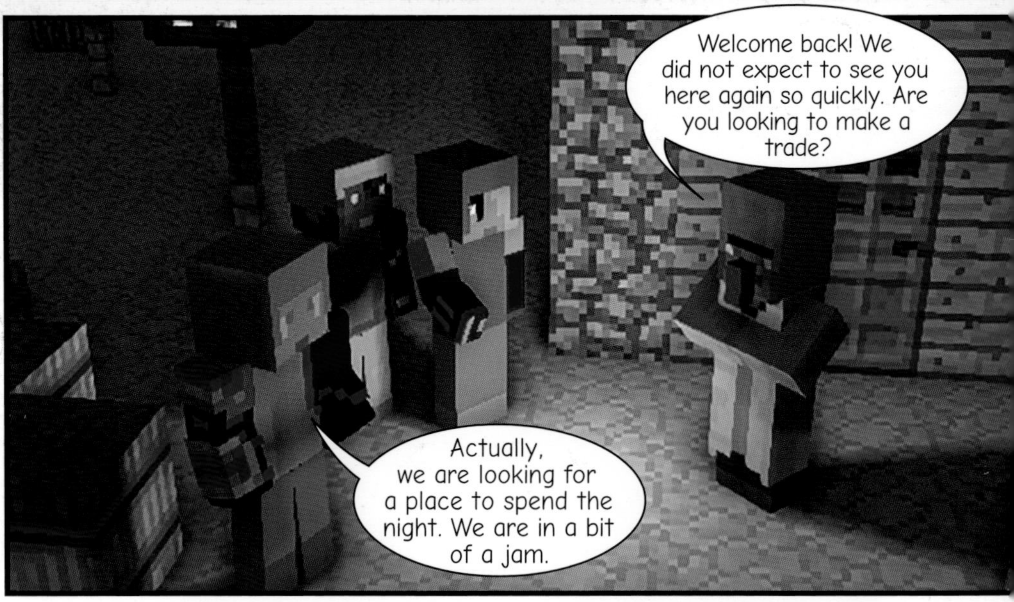
Welcome back! We did not expect to see you here again so quickly. Are you looking to make a trade?
Actually, we are looking for a place to spend the night. We are in a bit of a jam.

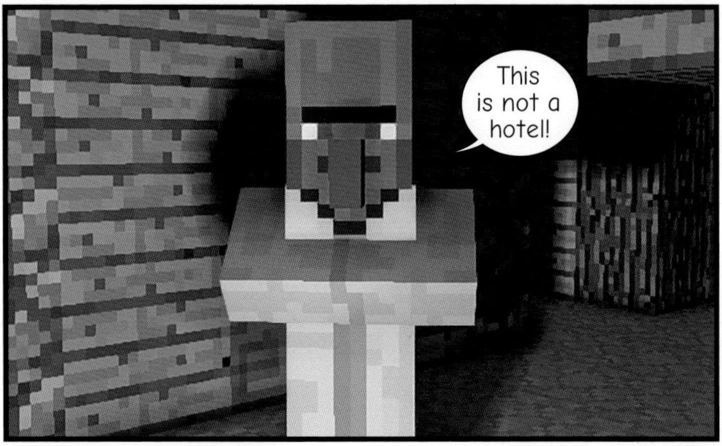
This is not a hotel!

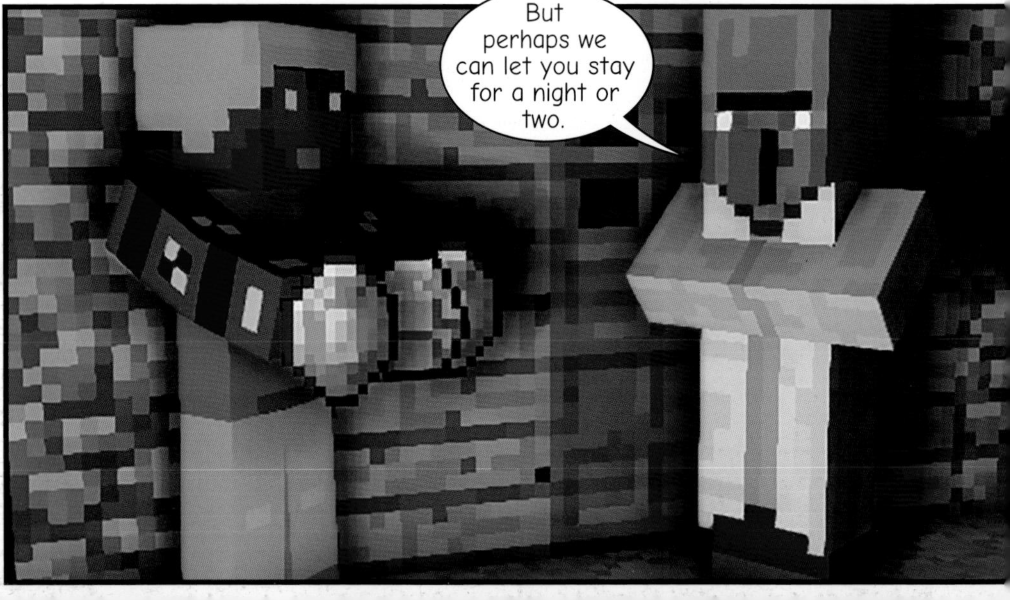
But perhaps we can let you stay for a night or two.

CHAPTER 11

KIDNAPPED

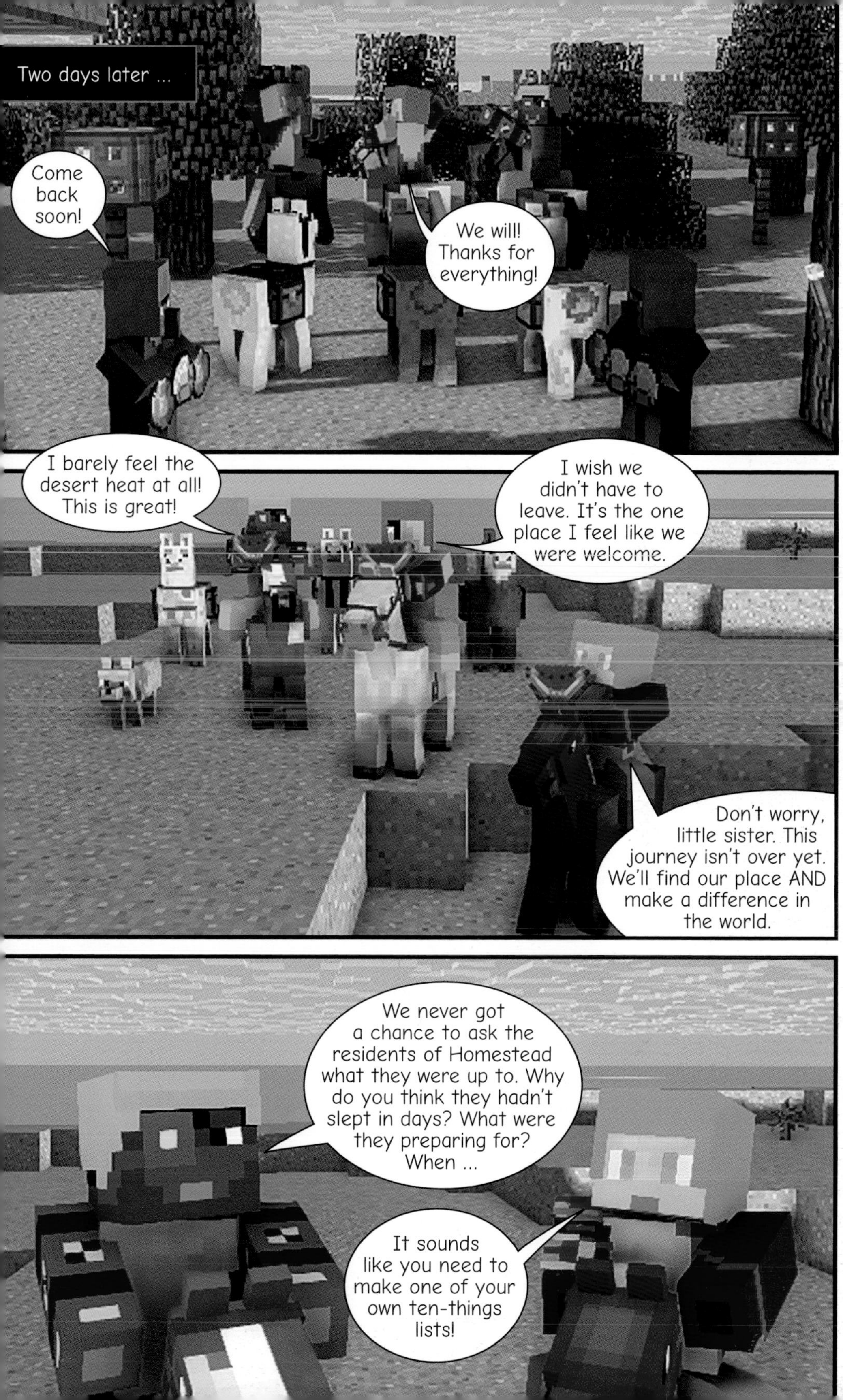
Two days later ...
Come back soon!
We will! Thanks for everything!
I barely feel the desert heat at all! This is great!
I wish we didn't have to leave. It's the one place I feel like we were welcome.
Don't worry, little sister. This journey isn't over yet. We'll find our place AND make a difference in the world.
We never got a chance to ask the residents of Homestead what they were up to. Why do you think they hadn't slept in days? What were they preparing for? When ...
It sounds like you need to make one of your own ten-things lists!

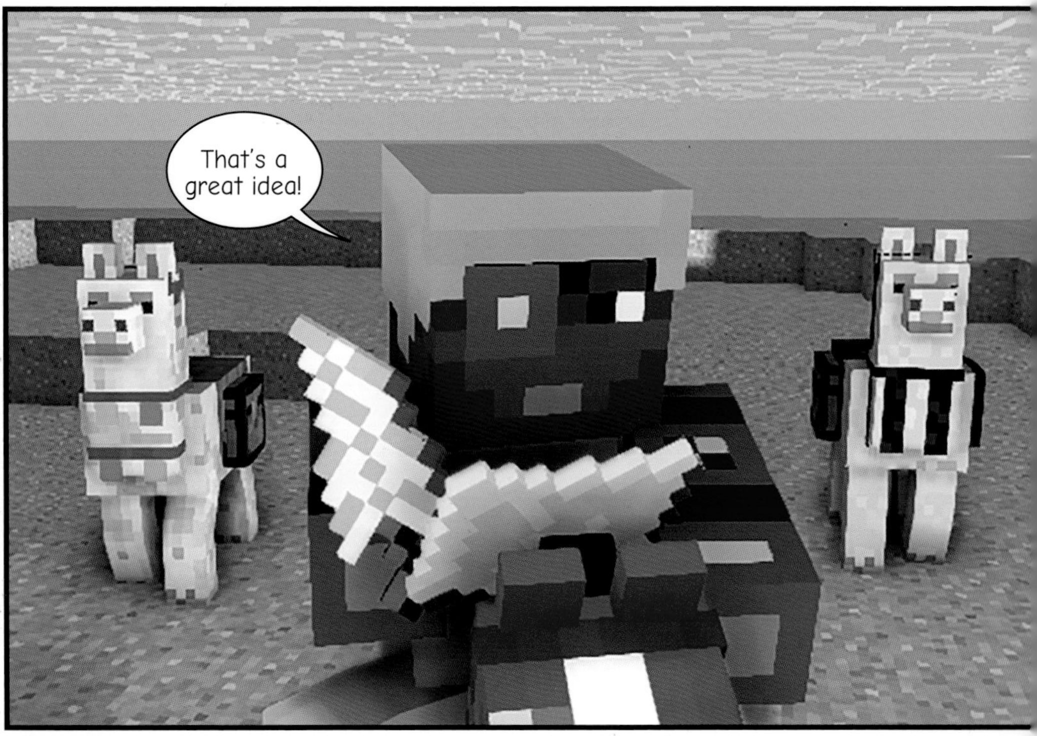
That's a great idea!

1. Why no sleep?
2. What's the plan?
3. Are they good guys?
4. When will they attack?
5. How will they attack?
6. Why will they attack?
7. Why is Ned in prison clothes?
8. How is he such a good cook?
9. Do they want our help?
10. Do we want to help them?

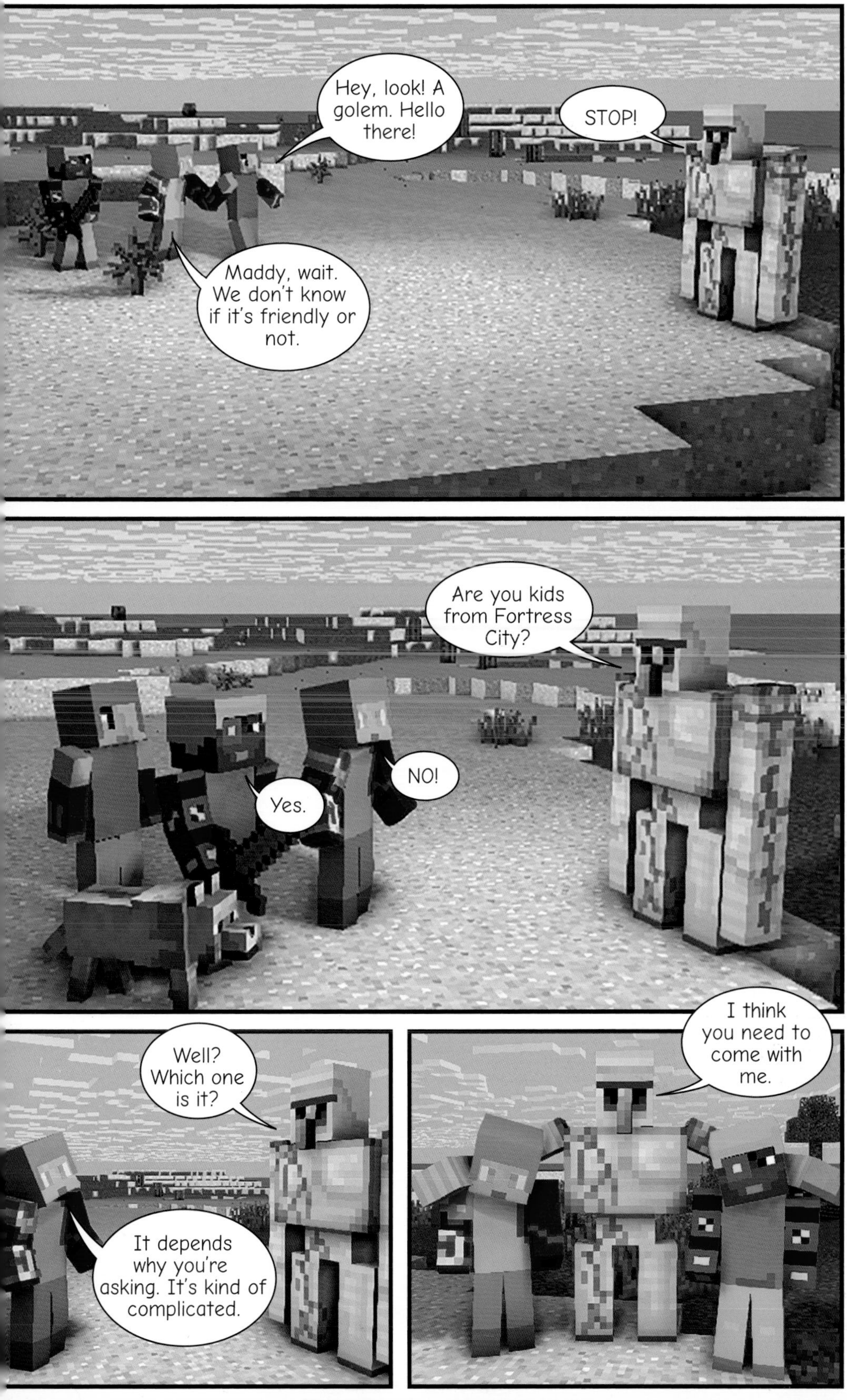
Hey, look! A golem. Hello there!
STOP!
Maddy, wait. We don't know if it's friendly or not.
Are you kids from Fortress City?
Yes.
NO!
Well? Which one is it?
It depends why you're asking. It's kind of complicated.
I think you need to come with me.

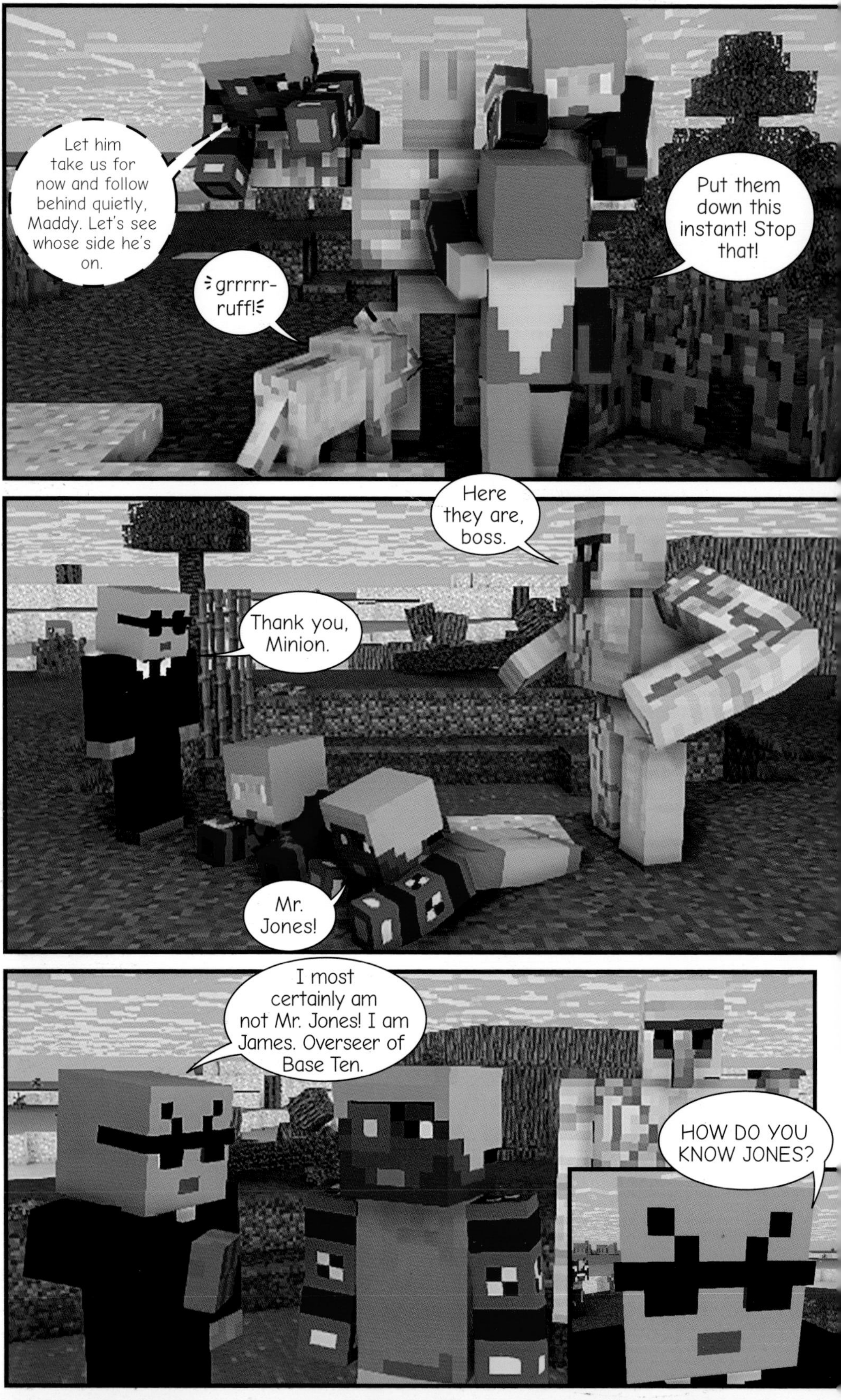
Let him take us for now and follow behind quietly, Maddy. Let's see whose side he's on.
grrrrr-ruff!
Put them down this instant! Stop that!
Here they are, boss.
Thank you, Minion.
Mr. Jones!
I most certainly am not Mr. Jones! I am James. Overseer of Base Ten.
HOW DO YOU KNOW JONES?

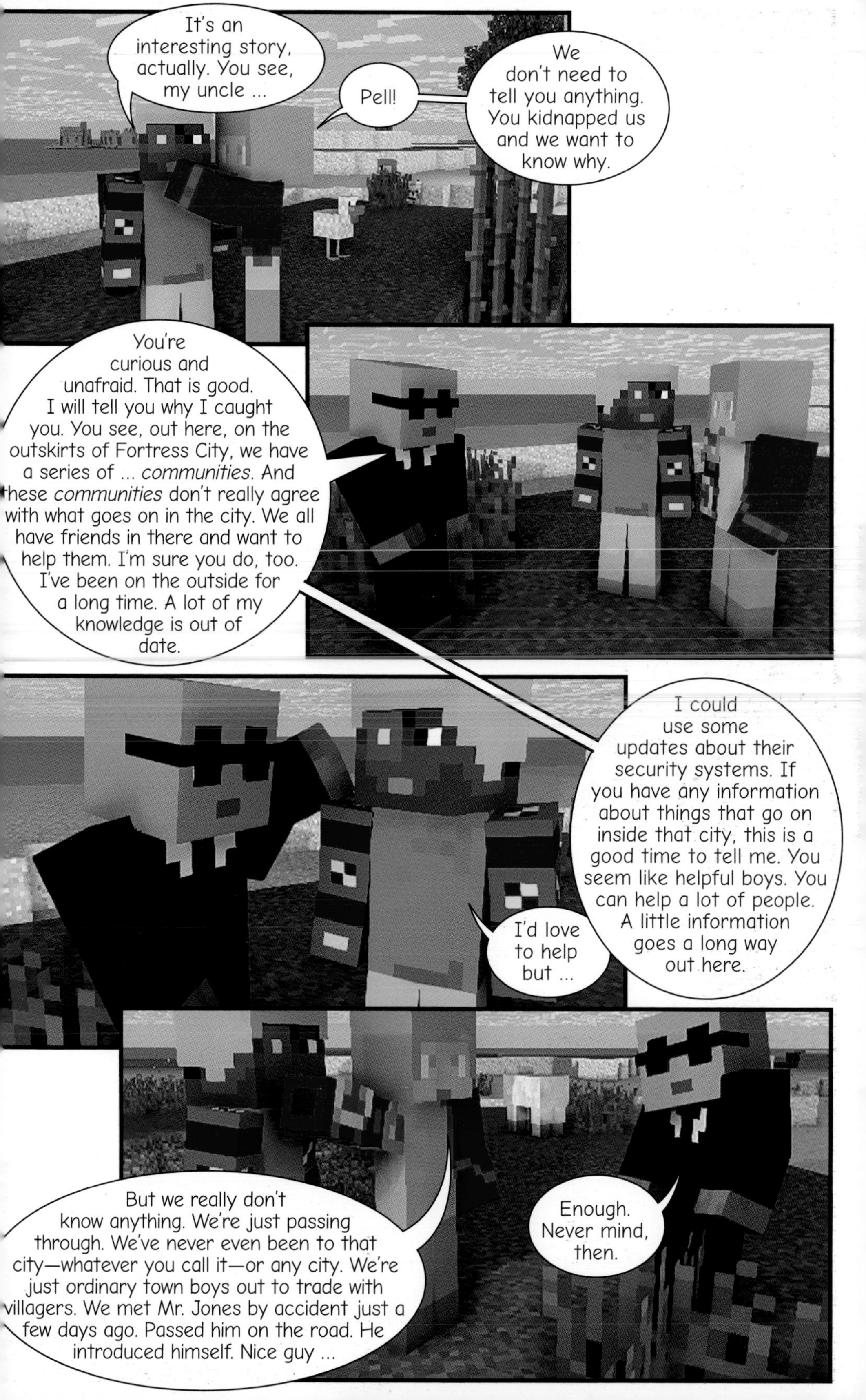
It's an interesting story, actually. You see, my uncle ...
Pell!
We don't need to tell you anything. You kidnapped us and we want to know why.
You're curious and unafraid. That is good. I will tell you why I caught you. You see, out here, on the outskirts of Fortress City, we have a series of ... *communities*. And these *communities* don't really agree with what goes on in the city. We all have friends in there and want to help them. I'm sure you do, too. I've been on the outside for a long time. A lot of my knowledge is out of date.
I could use some updates about their security systems. If you have any information about things that go on inside that city, this is a good time to tell me. You seem like helpful boys. You can help a lot of people. A little information goes a long way out here.
I'd love to help but ...
But we really don't know anything. We're just passing through. We've never even been to that city—whatever you call it—or any city. We're just ordinary town boys out to trade with villagers. We met Mr. Jones by accident just a few days ago. Passed him on the road. He introduced himself. Nice guy ...
Enough. Never mind, then.

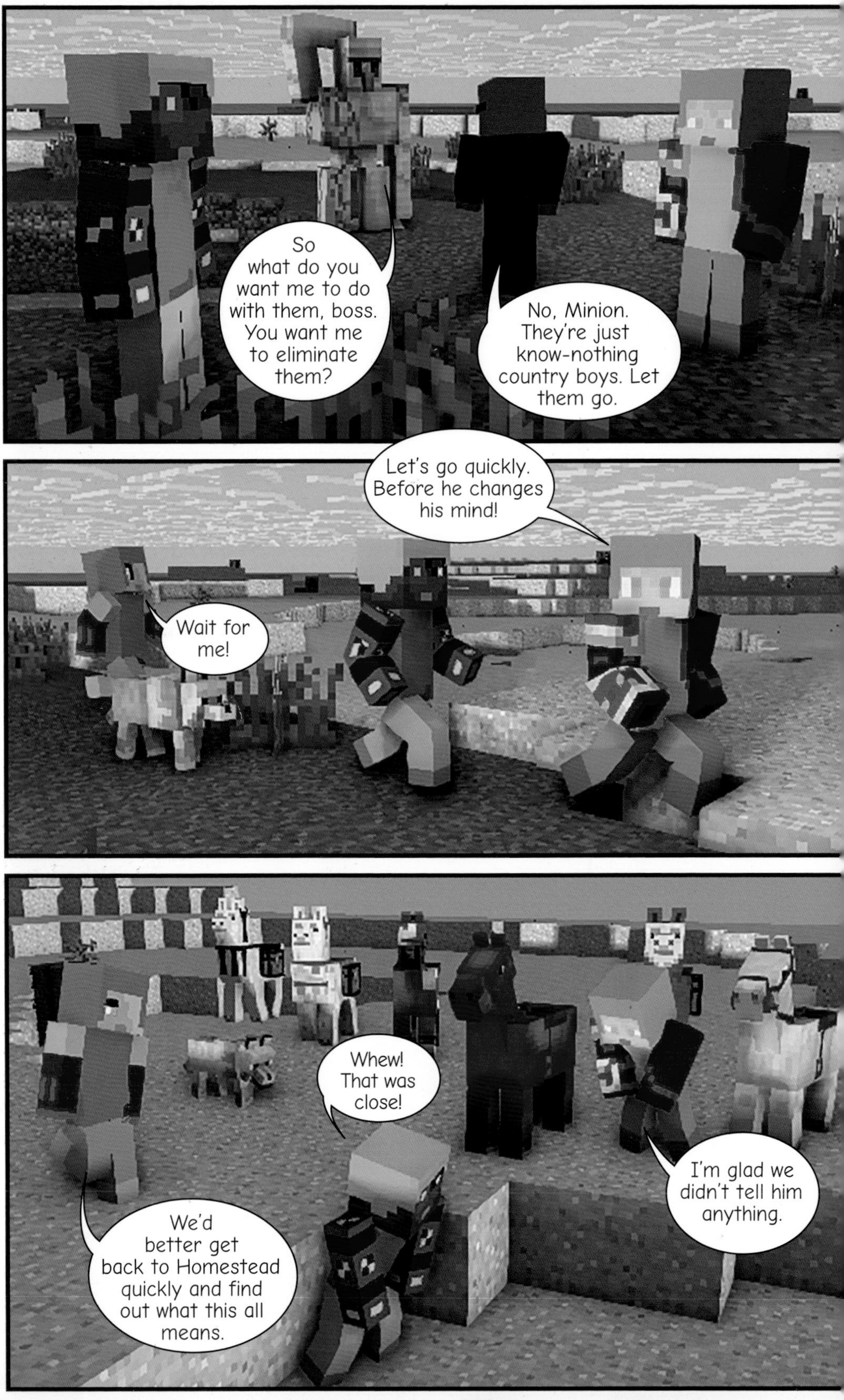
So what do you want me to do with them, boss. You want me to eliminate them?
No, Minion. They're just know-nothing country boys. Let them go.
Let's go quickly. Before he changes his mind!
Wait for me!
Whew! That was close!
I'm glad we didn't tell him anything.
We'd better get back to Homestead quickly and find out what this all means.

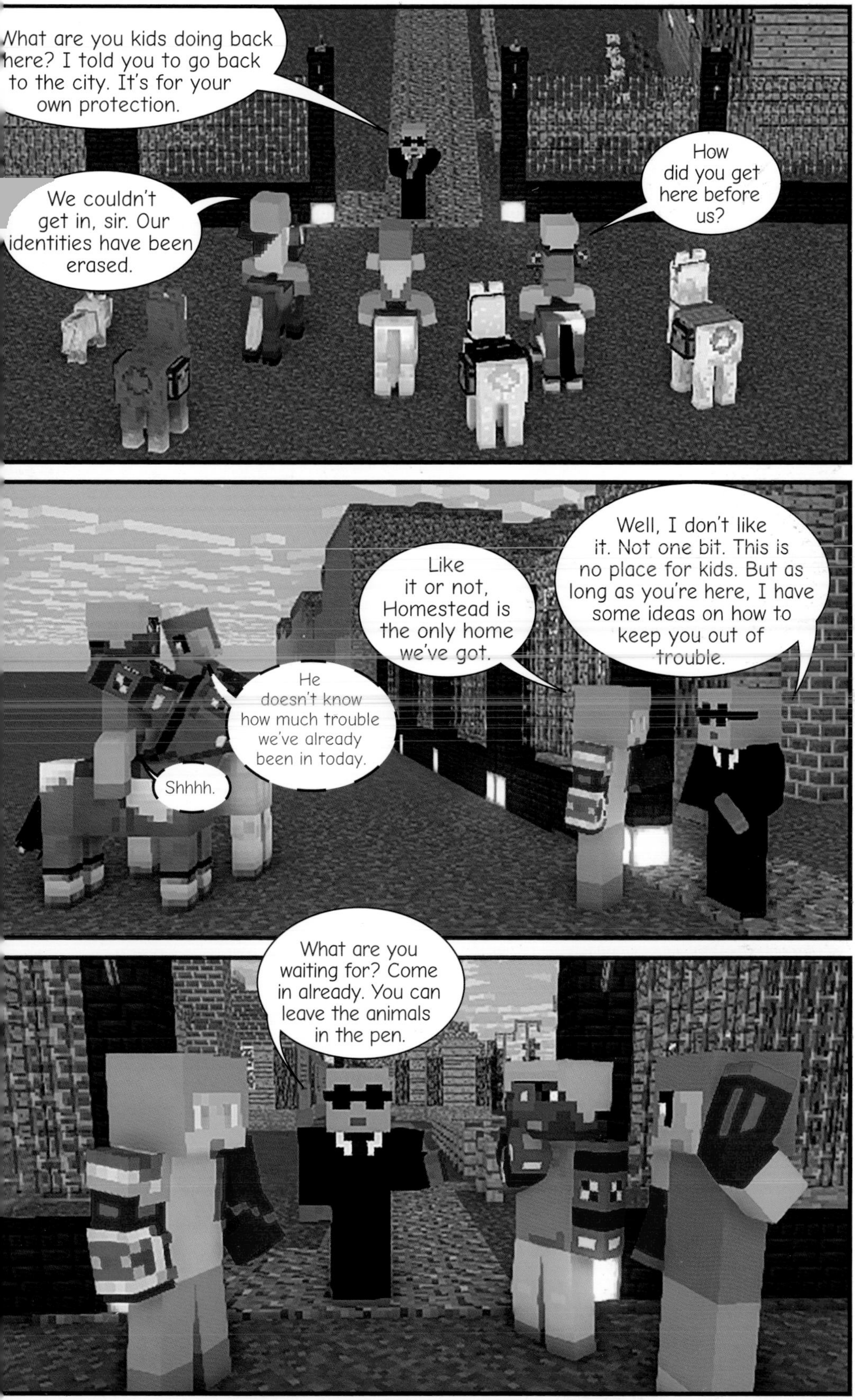
What are you kids doing back here? I told you to go back to the city. It's for your own protection.
We couldn't get in, sir. Our identities have been erased.
How did you get here before us?
Like it or not, Homestead is the only home we've got.
Well, I don't like it. Not one bit. This is no place for kids. But as long as you're here, I have some ideas on how to keep you out of trouble.
He doesn't know how much trouble we've already been in today.
Shhhh.
What are you waiting for? Come in already. You can leave the animals in the pen.

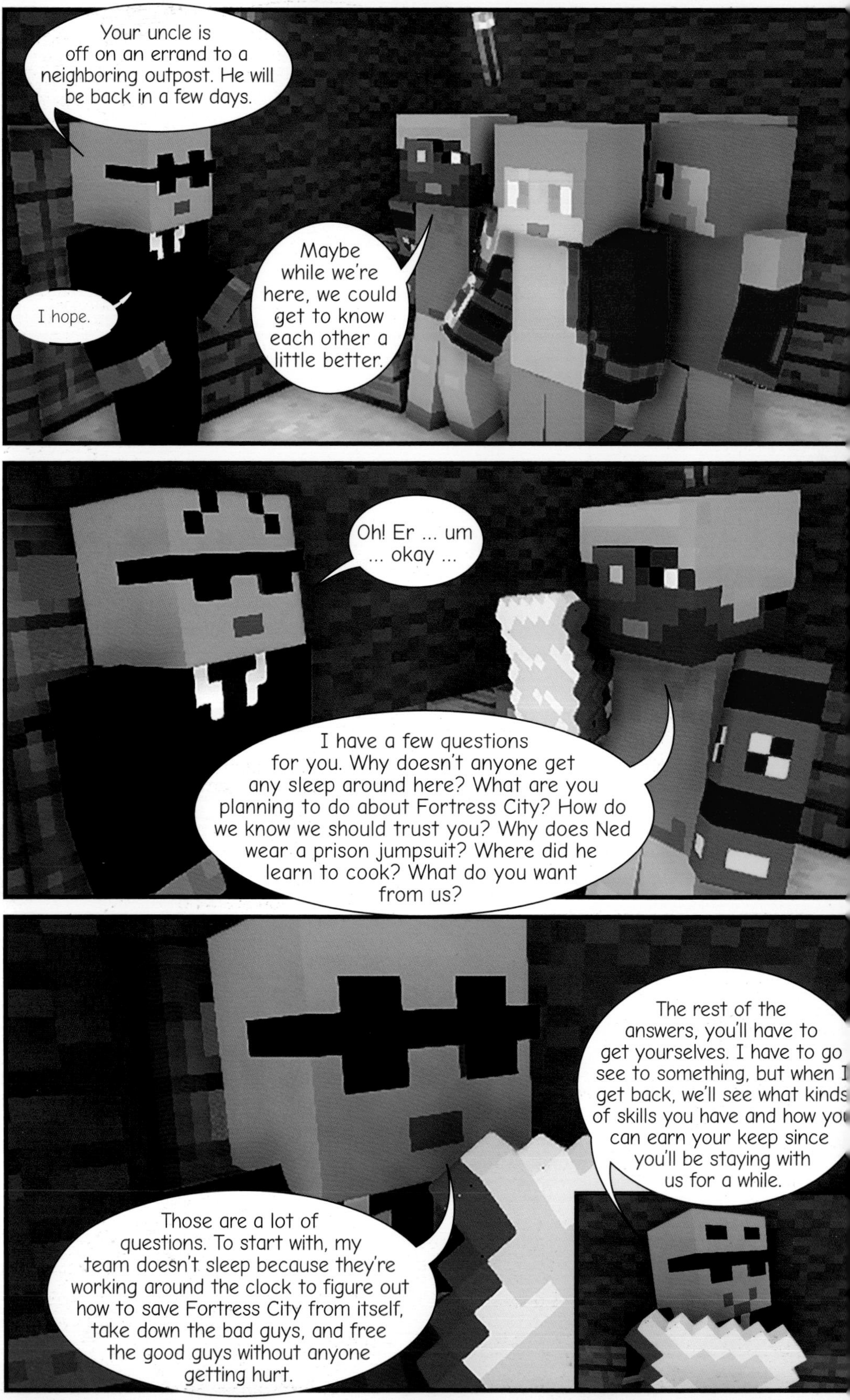
Your uncle is off on an errand to a neighboring outpost. He will be back in a few days.
I hope.
Maybe while we're here, we could get to know each other a little better.
Oh! Er ... um ... okay ...
I have a few questions for you. Why doesn't anyone get any sleep around here? What are you planning to do about Fortress City? How do we know we should trust you? Why does Ned wear a prison jumpsuit? Where did he learn to cook? What do you want from us?
Those are a lot of questions. To start with, my team doesn't sleep because they're working around the clock to figure out how to save Fortress City from itself, take down the bad guys, and free the good guys without anyone getting hurt.
The rest of the answers, you'll have to get yourselves. I have to go see to something, but when I get back, we'll see what kinds of skills you have and how yo can earn your keep since you'll be staying with us for a while.

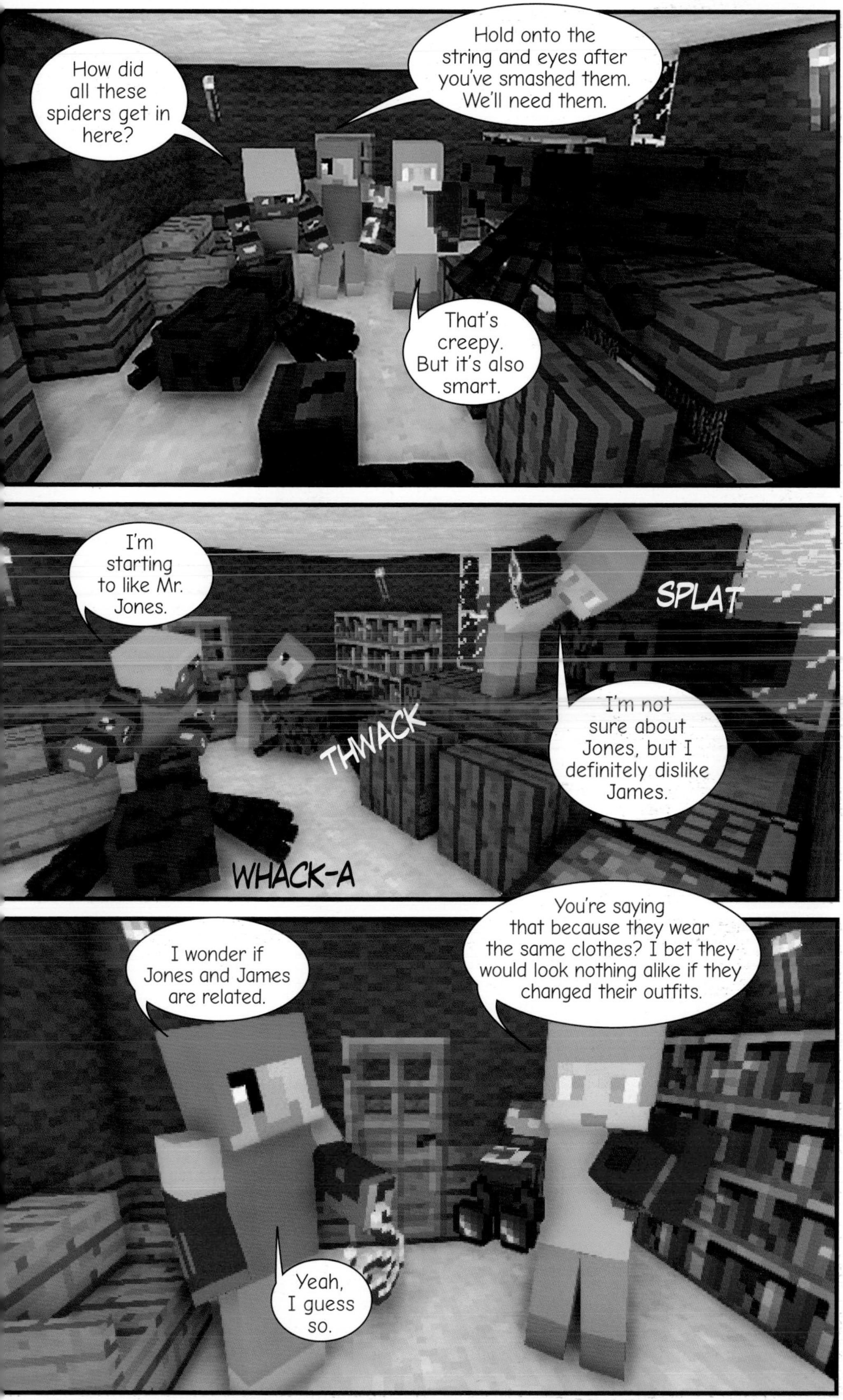
How did all these spiders get in here?
Hold onto the string and eyes after you've smashed them. We'll need them.
That's creepy. But it's also smart.
I'm starting to like Mr. Jones.
SPLAT
THWACK
I'm not sure about Jones, but I definitely dislike James.
WHACK-A
I wonder if Jones and James are related.
You're saying that because they wear the same clothes? I bet they would look nothing alike if they changed their outfits.
Yeah, I guess so.

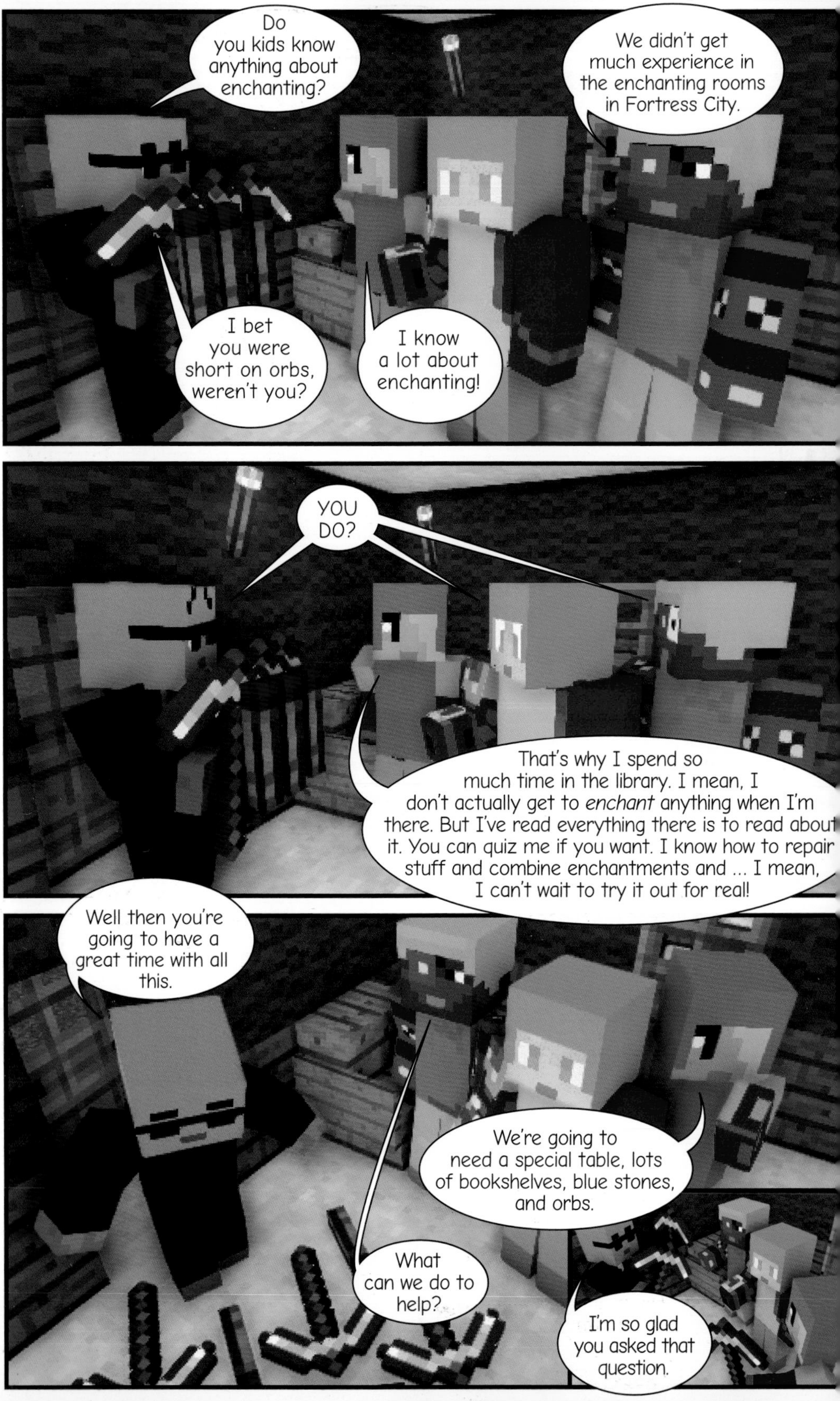
Do you kids know anything about enchanting?
We didn't get much experience in the enchanting rooms in Fortress City.
I bet you were short on orbs, weren't you?
I know a lot about enchanting!
YOU DO?
That's why I spend so much time in the library. I mean, I don't actually get to *enchant* anything when I'm there. But I've read everything there is to read about it. You can quiz me if you want. I know how to repair stuff and combine enchantments and ... I mean, I can't wait to try it out for real!
Well then you're going to have a great time with all this.
We're going to need a special table, lots of bookshelves, blue stones, and orbs.
What can we do to help?
I'm so glad you asked that question.

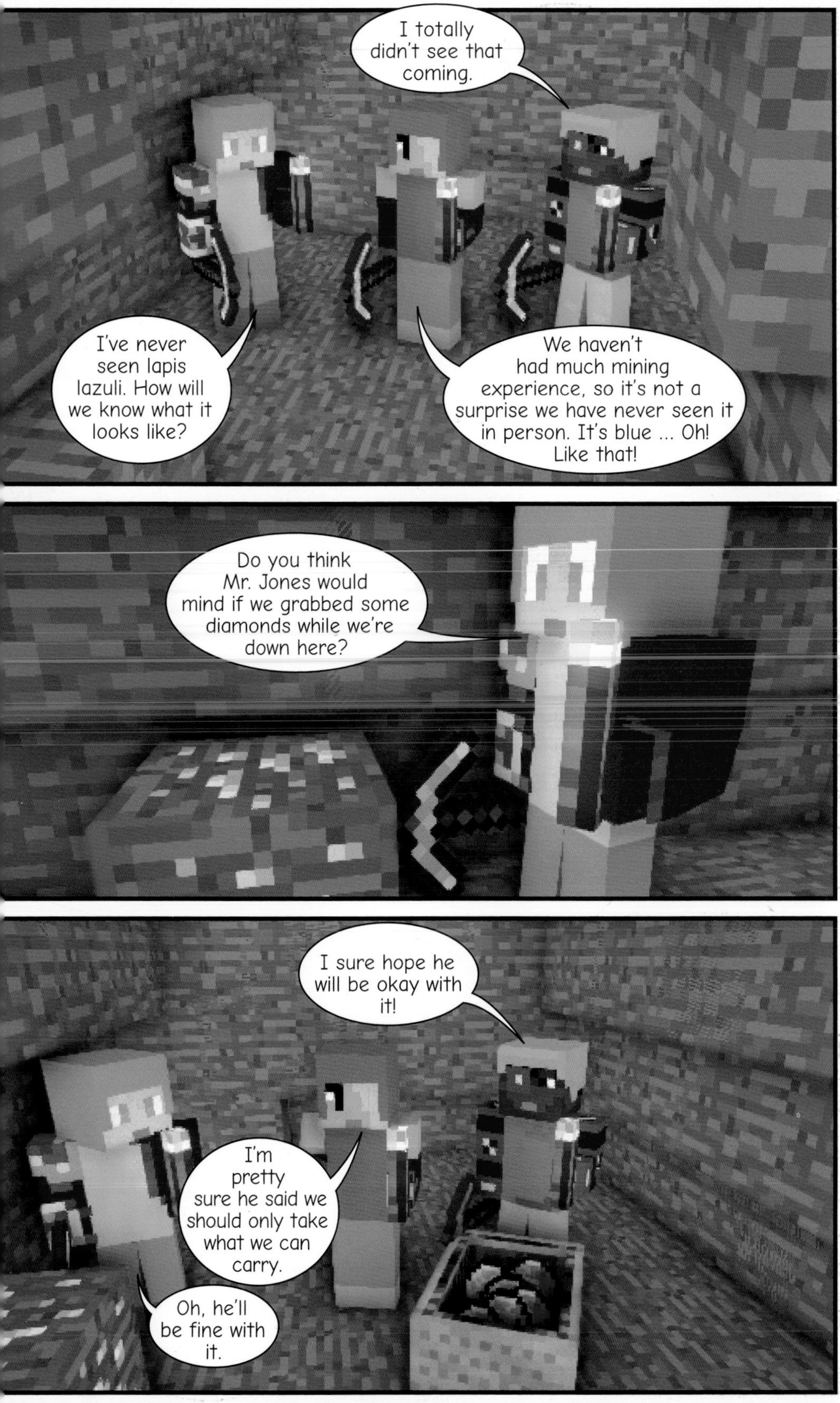

I totally didn't see that coming.
I've never seen lapis lazuli. How will we know what it looks like?
We haven't had much mining experience, so it's not a surprise we have never seen it in person. It's blue ... Oh! Like that!
Do you think Mr. Jones would mind if we grabbed some diamonds while we're down here?
I sure hope he will be okay with it!
I'm pretty sure he said we should only take what we can carry.
Oh, he'll be fine with it.

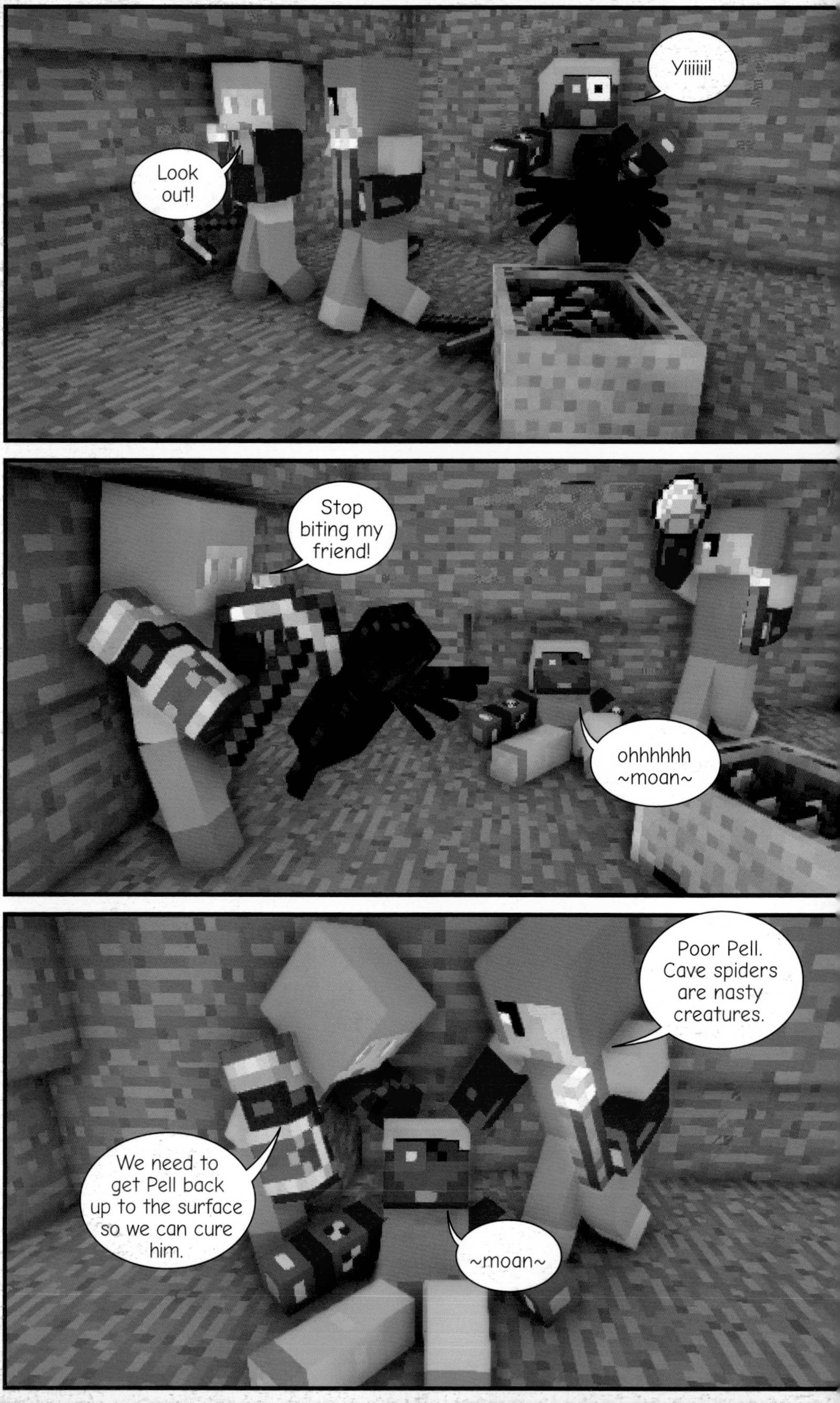
Look out!
Yiiiiii!
Stop biting my friend!
ohhhhhh ~moan~
Poor Pell. Cave spiders are nasty creatures.
We need to get Pell back up to the surface so we can cure him.
~moan~

CHAPTER 12

TEN THINGS REBELS DO

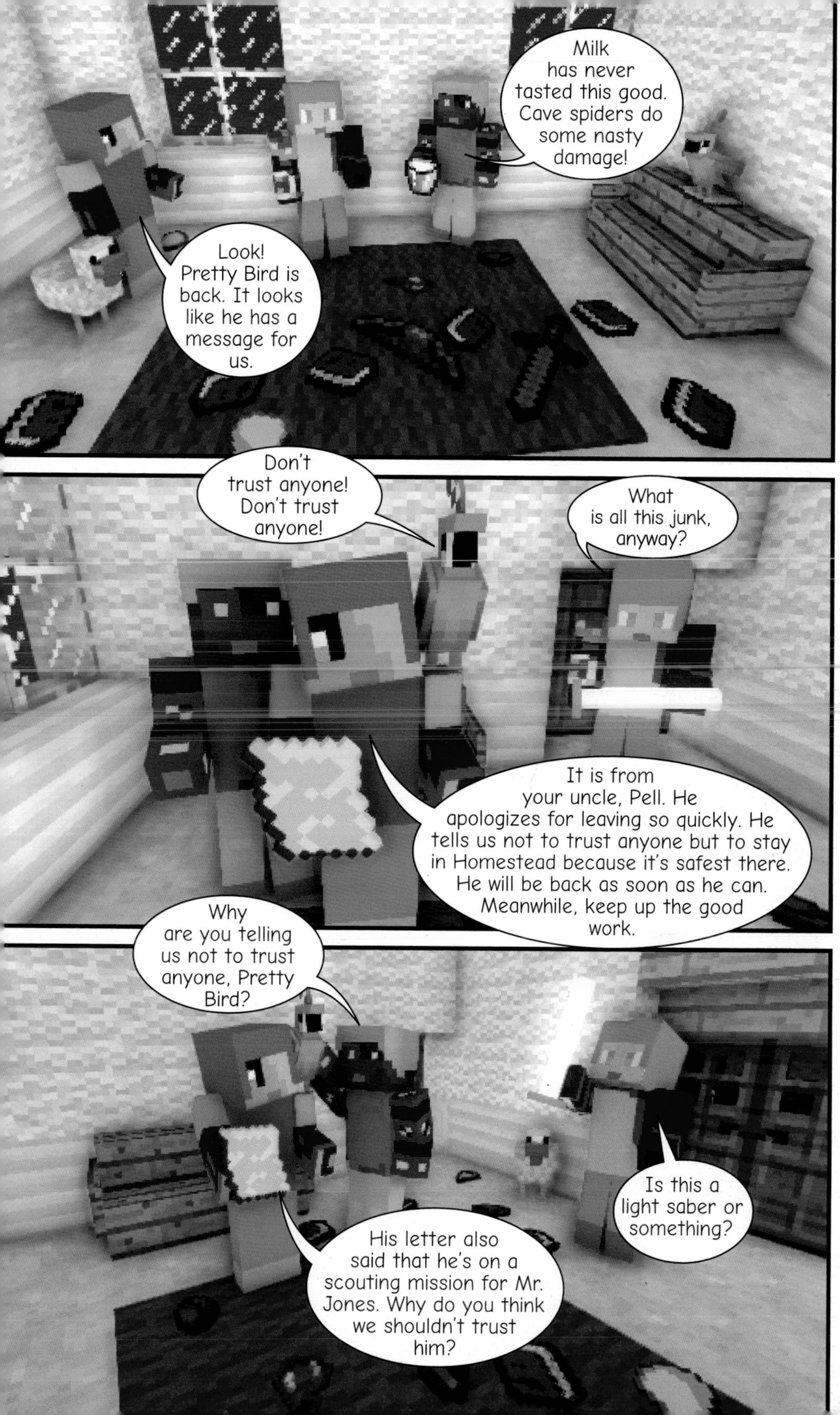
Milk has never tasted this good. Cave spiders do some nasty damage!
Look! Pretty Bird is back. It looks like he has a message for us.
Don't trust anyone! Don't trust anyone!
What is all this junk, anyway?
It is from your uncle, Pell. He apologizes for leaving so quickly. He tells us not to trust anyone but to stay in Homestead because it's safest there. He will be back as soon as he can. Meanwhile, keep up the good work.
Why are you telling us not to trust anyone, Pretty Bird?
Is this a light saber or something?
His letter also said that he's on a scouting mission for Mr. Jones. Why do you think we shouldn't trust him?

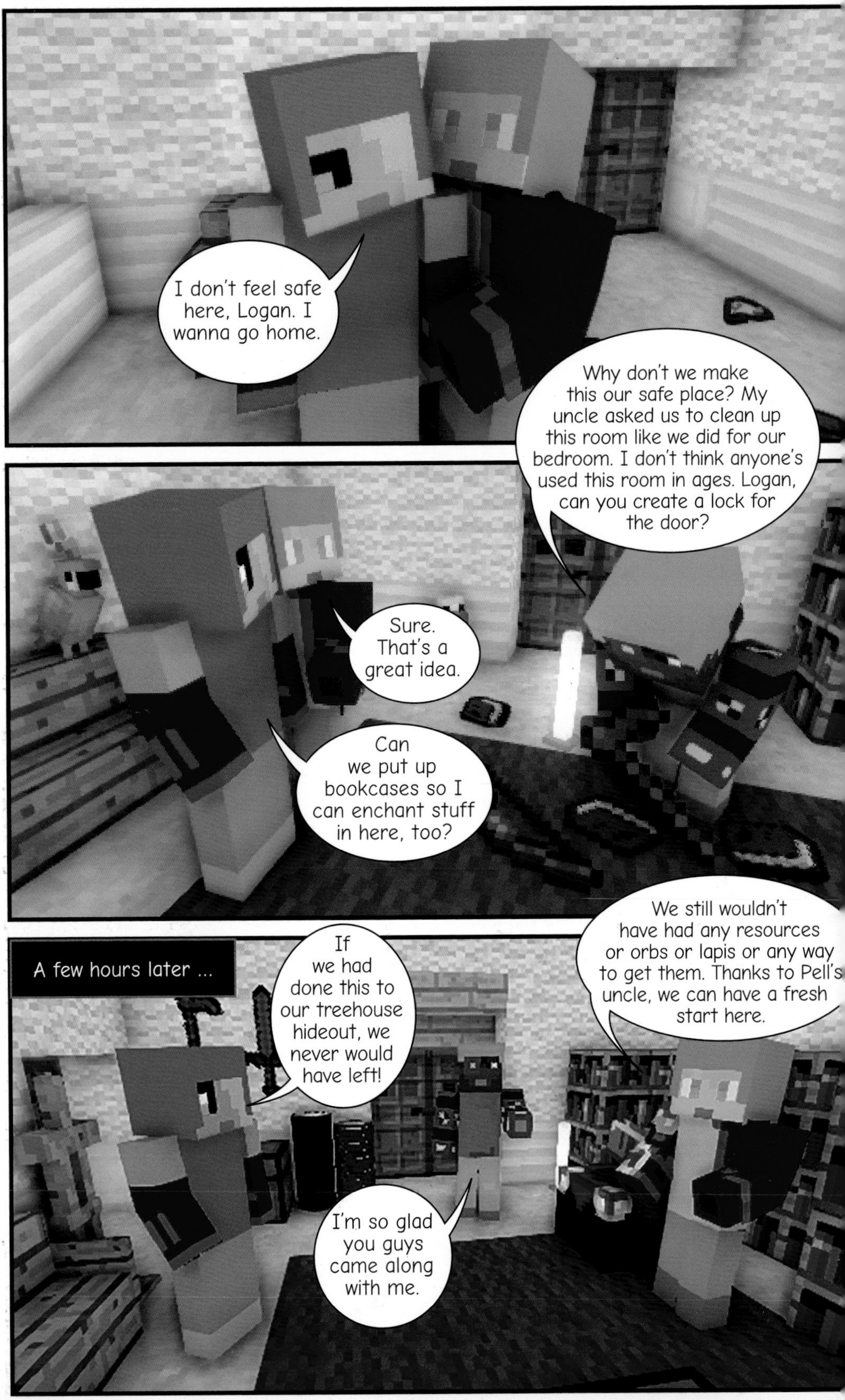
I don't feel safe here, Logan. I wanna go home.
Why don't we make this our safe place? My uncle asked us to clean up this room like we did for our bedroom. I don't think anyone's used this room in ages. Logan, can you create a lock for the door?
Sure. That's a great idea.
Can we put up bookcases so I can enchant stuff in here, too?
A few hours later ...
If we had done this to our treehouse hideout, we never would have left!
We still wouldn't have had any resources or orbs or lapis or any way to get them. Thanks to Pell's uncle, we can have a fresh start here.
I'm so glad you guys came along with me.

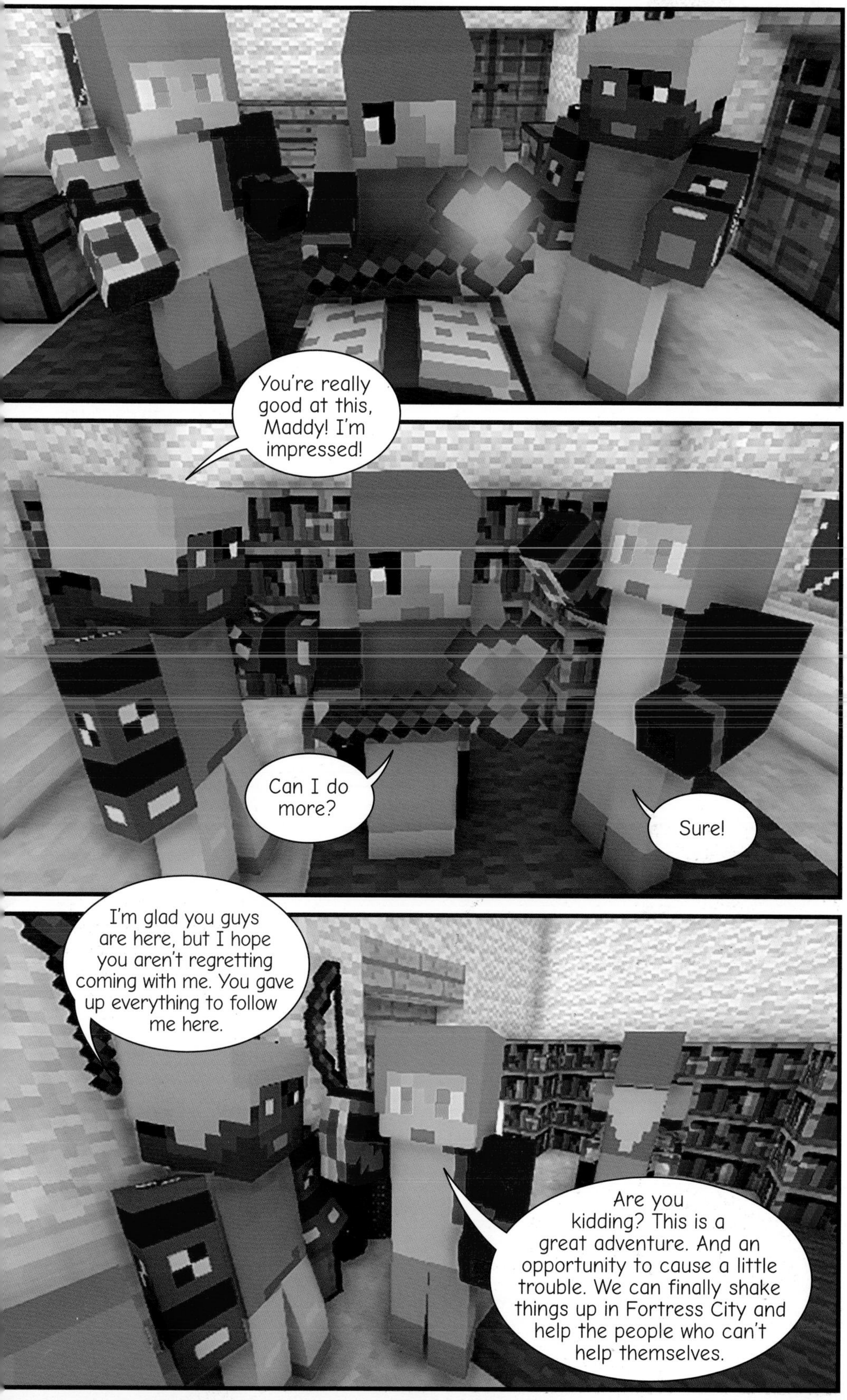
You're really good at this, Maddy! I'm impressed!
Can I do more?
Sure!
I'm glad you guys are here, but I hope you aren't regretting coming with me. You gave up everything to follow me here.
Are you kidding? This is a great adventure. And an opportunity to cause a little trouble. We can finally shake things up in Fortress City and help the people who can't help themselves.

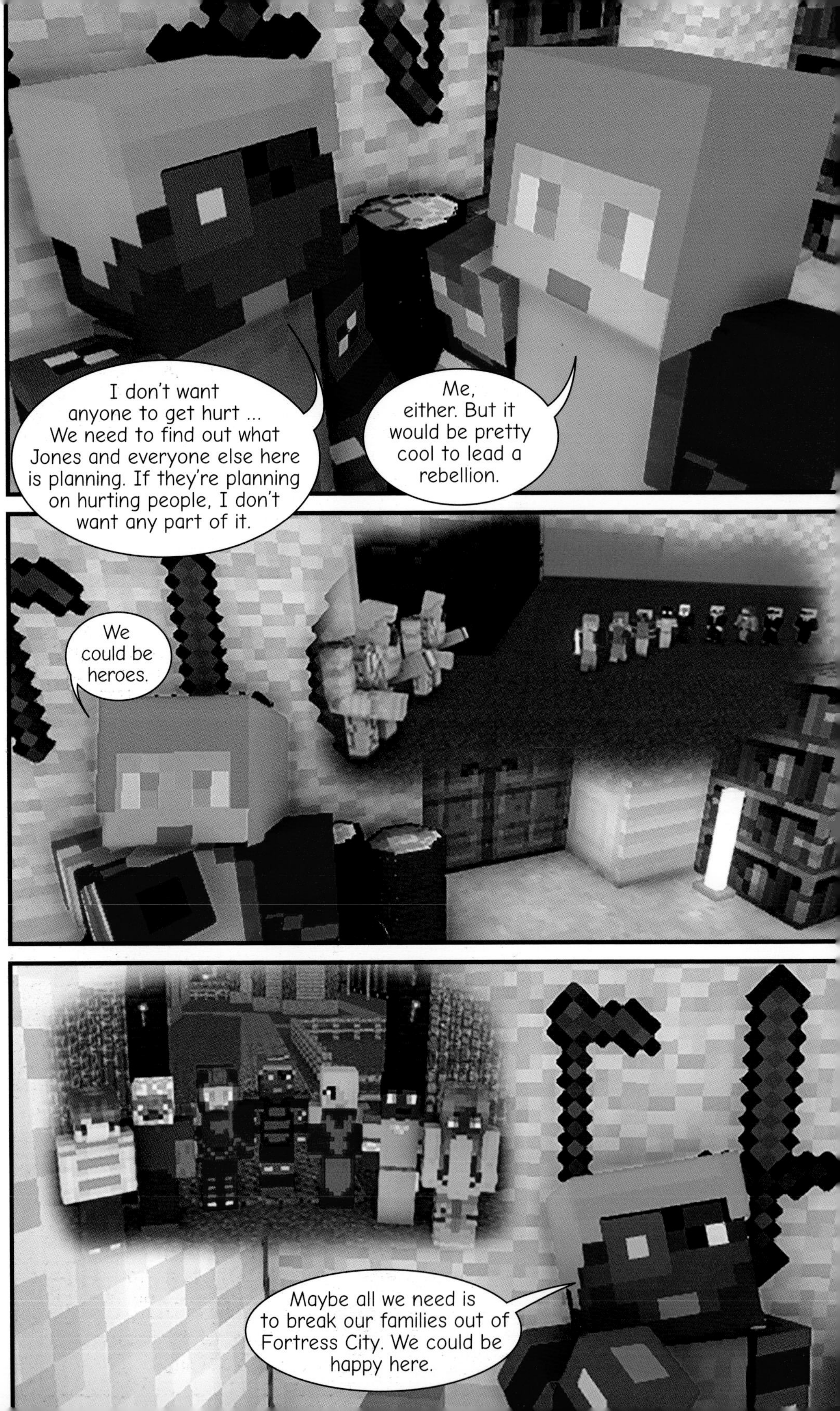
I don't want anyone to get hurt ... We need to find out what Jones and everyone else here is planning. If they're planning on hurting people, I don't want any part of it.
Me, either. But it would be pretty cool to lead a rebellion.
We could be heroes.
Maybe all we need is to break our families out of Fortress City. We could be happy here.

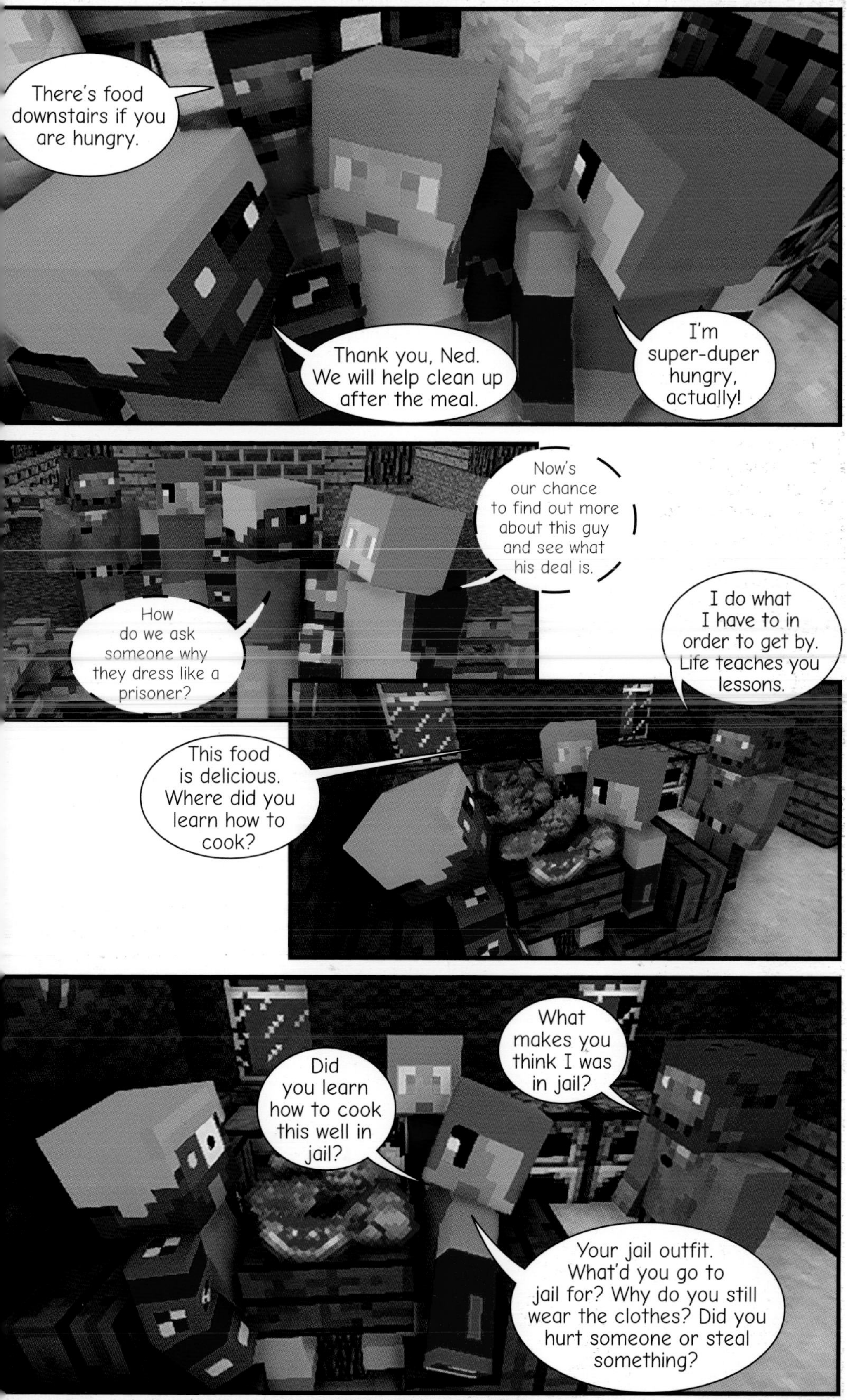
There's food downstairs if you are hungry.
Thank you, Ned. We will help clean up after the meal.
I'm super-duper hungry, actually!
Now's our chance to find out more about this guy and see what his deal is.
How do we ask someone why they dress like a prisoner?
I do what I have to in order to get by. Life teaches you lessons.
This food is delicious. Where did you learn how to cook?
Did you learn how to cook this well in jail?
What makes you think I was in jail?
Your jail outfit. What'd you go to jail for? Why do you still wear the clothes? Did you hurt someone or steal something?

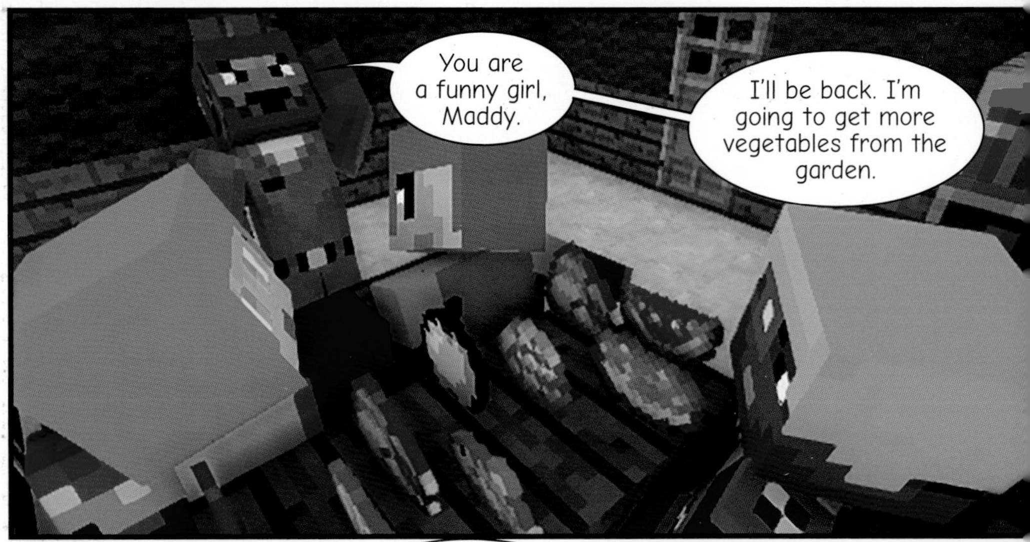
You are a funny girl, Maddy.
I'll be back. I'm going to get more vegetables from the garden.

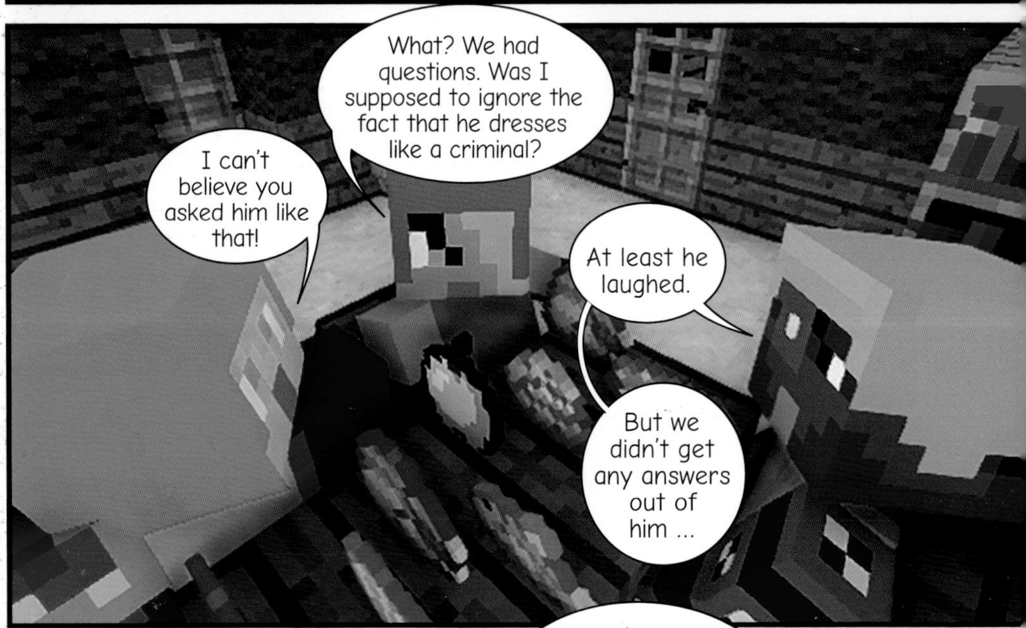
What? We had questions. Was I supposed to ignore the fact that he dresses like a criminal?
I can't believe you asked him like that!
At least he laughed.
But we didn't get any answers out of him ...

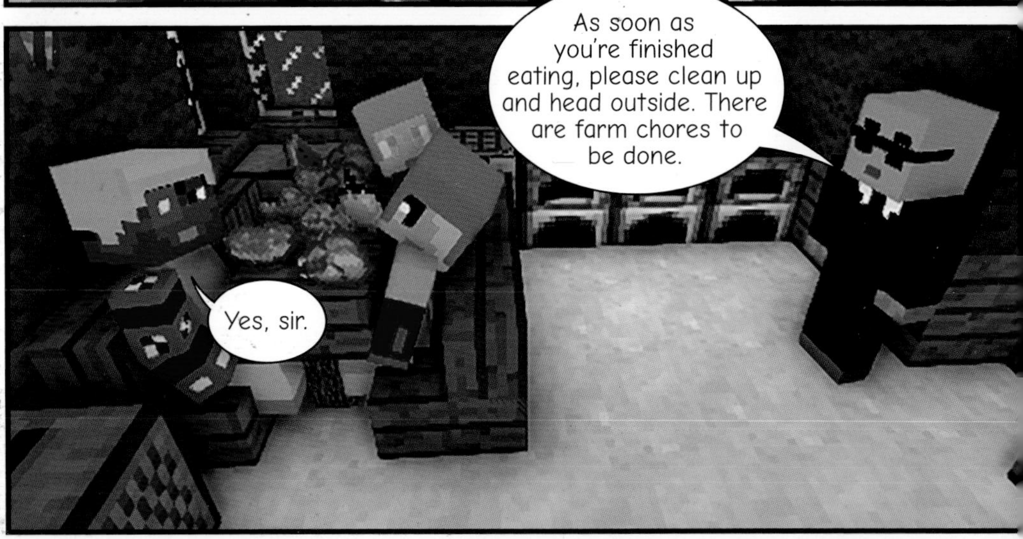
As soon as you're finished eating, please clean up and head outside. There are farm chores to be done.
Yes, sir.

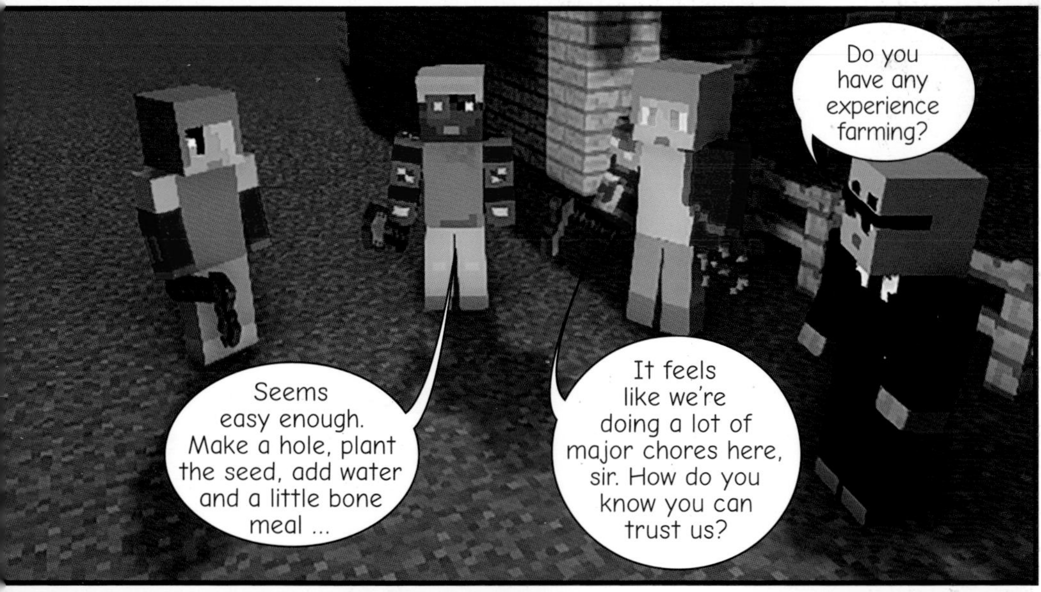
Do you have any experience farming?
Seems easy enough. Make a hole, plant the seed, add water and a little bone meal ...
It feels like we're doing a lot of major chores here, sir. How do you know you can trust us?

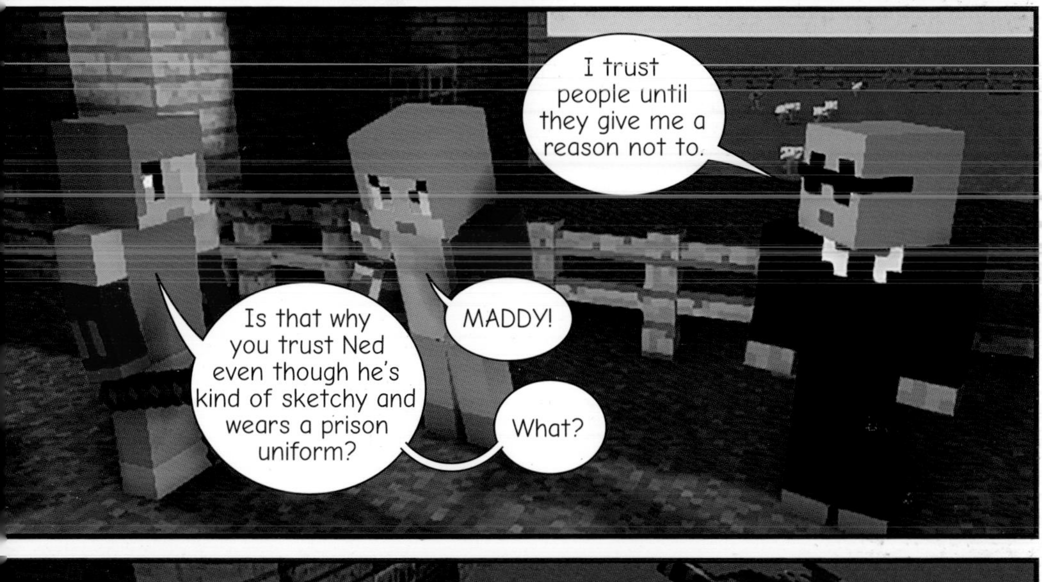
I trust people until they give me a reason not to.
Is that why you trust Ned even though he's kind of sketchy and wears a prison uniform?
MADDY!
What?

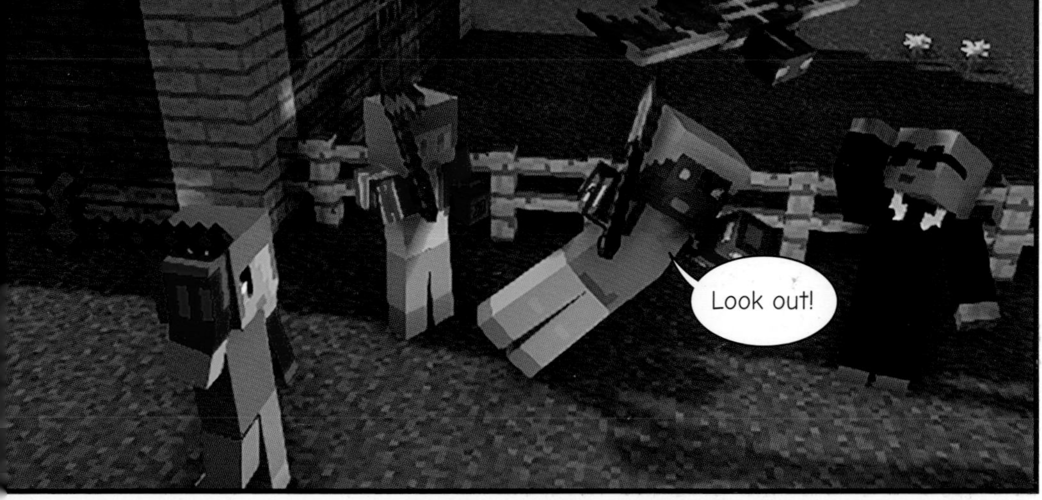
Look out!

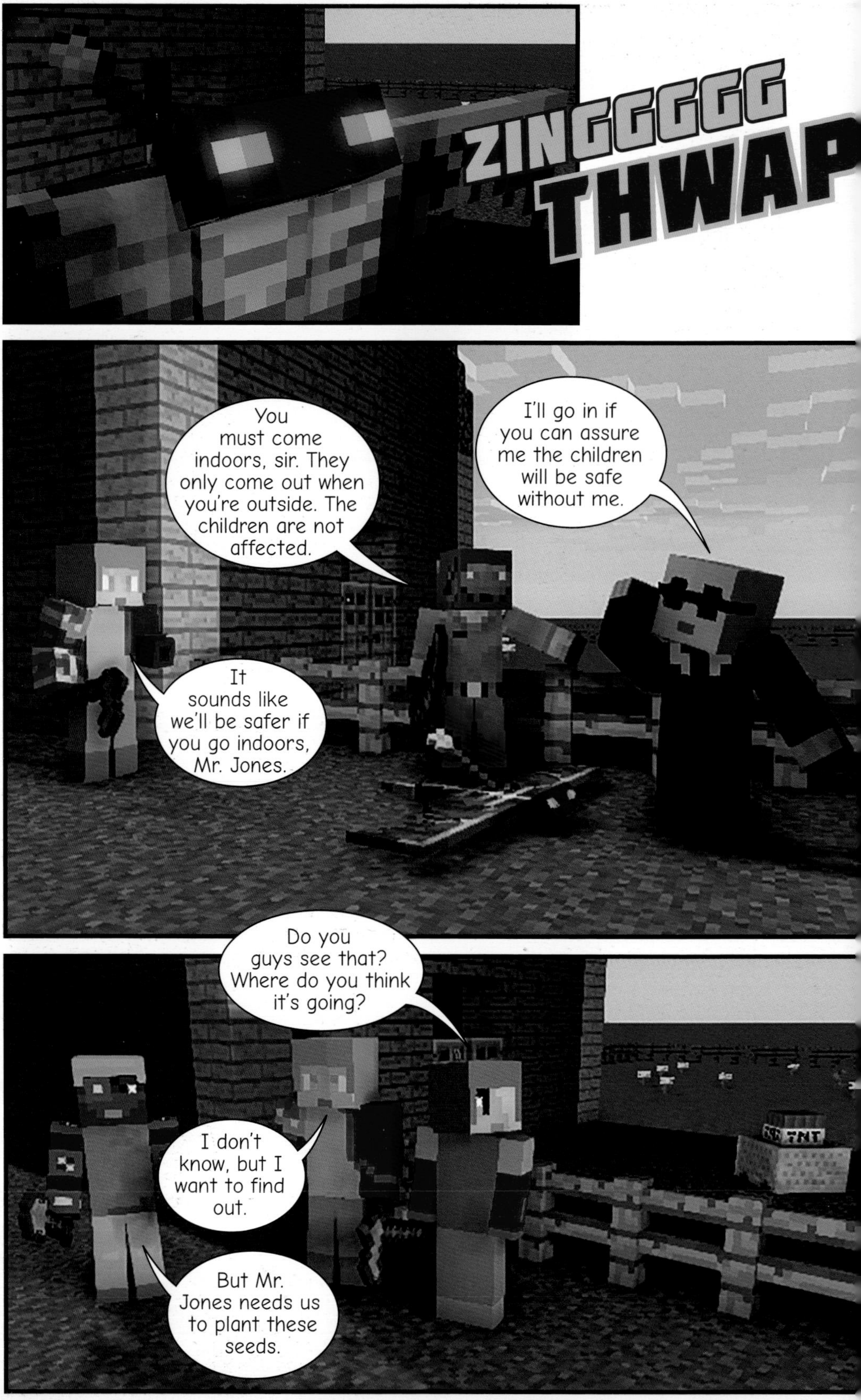
ZINGGGGG
THWAP
You must come indoors, sir. They only come out when you're outside. The children are not affected.
I'll go in if you can assure me the children will be safe without me.
It sounds like we'll be safer if you go indoors, Mr. Jones.
Do you guys see that? Where do you think it's going?
I don't know, but I want to find out.
But Mr. Jones needs us to plant these seeds.

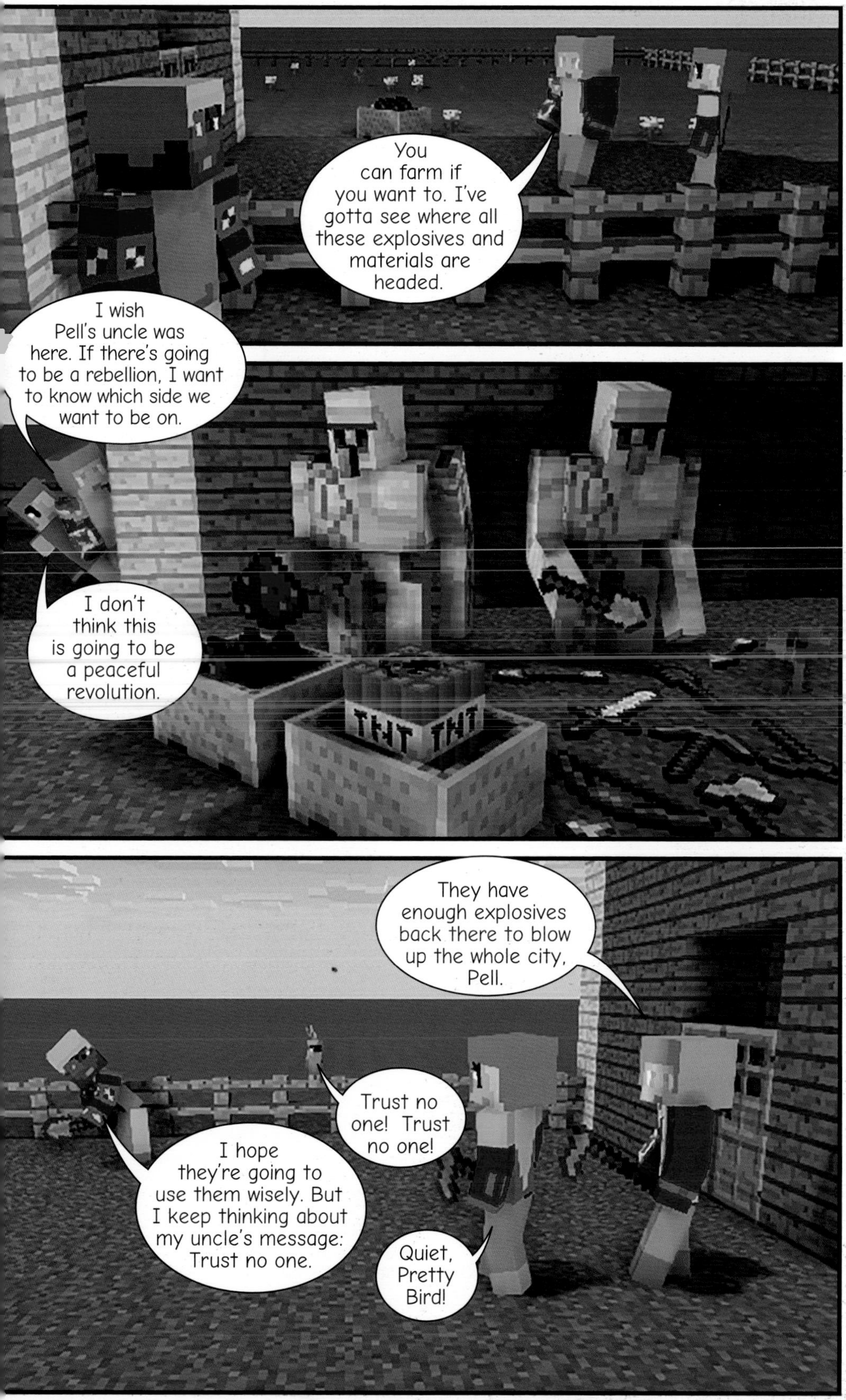
You can farm if you want to. I've gotta see where all these explosives and materials are headed.
I wish Pell's uncle was here. If there's going to be a rebellion, I want to know which side we want to be on.
I don't think this is going to be a peaceful revolution.
They have enough explosives back there to blow up the whole city, Pell.
I hope they're going to use them wisely. But I keep thinking about my uncle's message: Trust no one.
Trust no one! Trust no one!
Quiet, Pretty Bird!

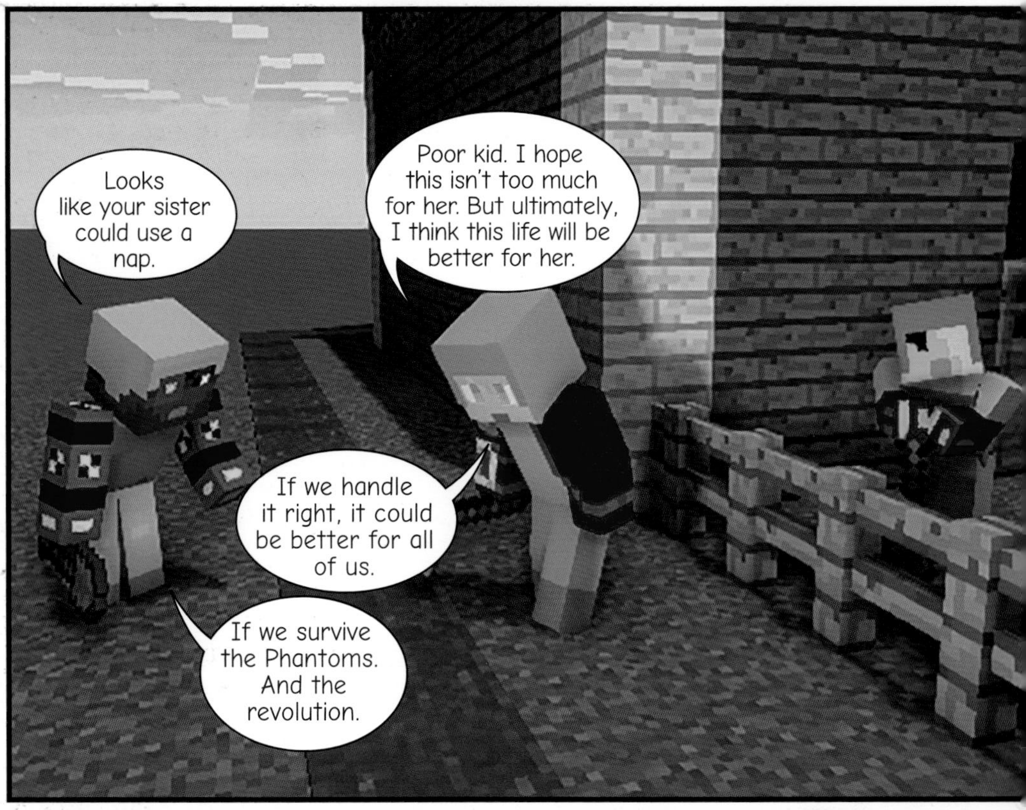
Looks like your sister could use a nap.
Poor kid. I hope this isn't too much for her. But ultimately, I think this life will be better for her.
If we handle it right, it could be better for all of us.
If we survive the Phantoms. And the revolution.

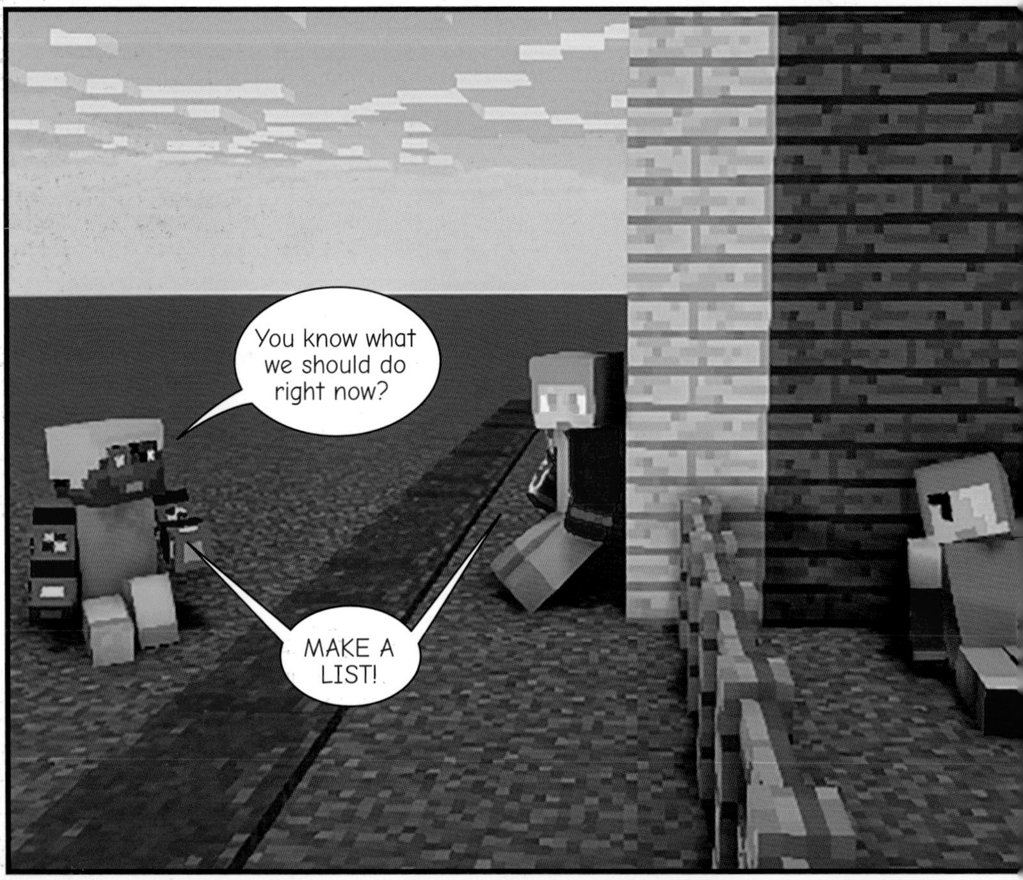
You know what we should do right now?
MAKE A LIST!

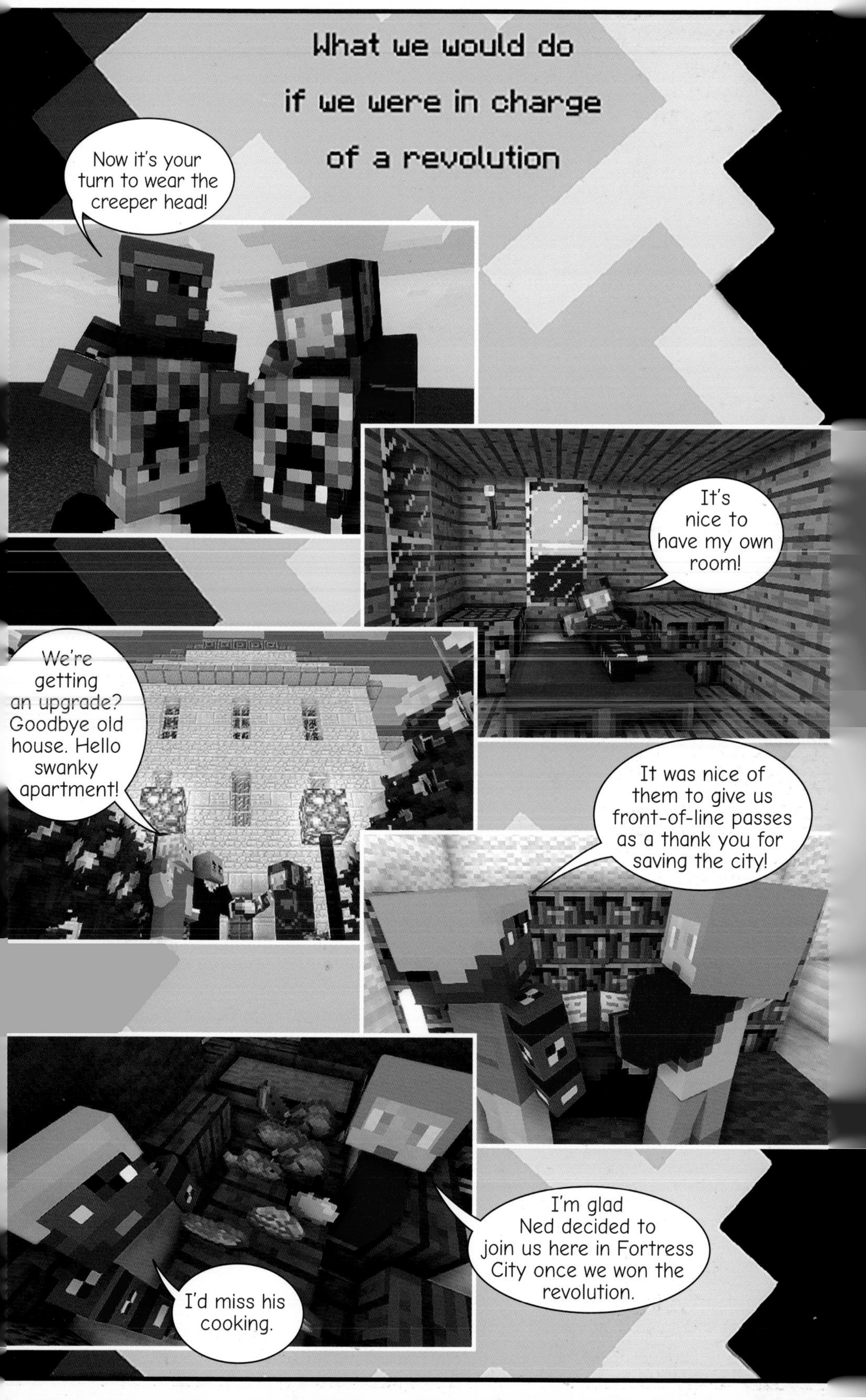
What we would do
if we were in charge
of a revolution
Now it's your turn to wear the creeper head!
It's nice to have my own room!
We're getting an upgrade? Goodbye old house. Hello swanky apartment!
It was nice of them to give us front-of-line passes as a thank you for saving the city!
I'm glad Ned decided to join us here in Fortress City once we won the revolution.
I'd miss his cooking.

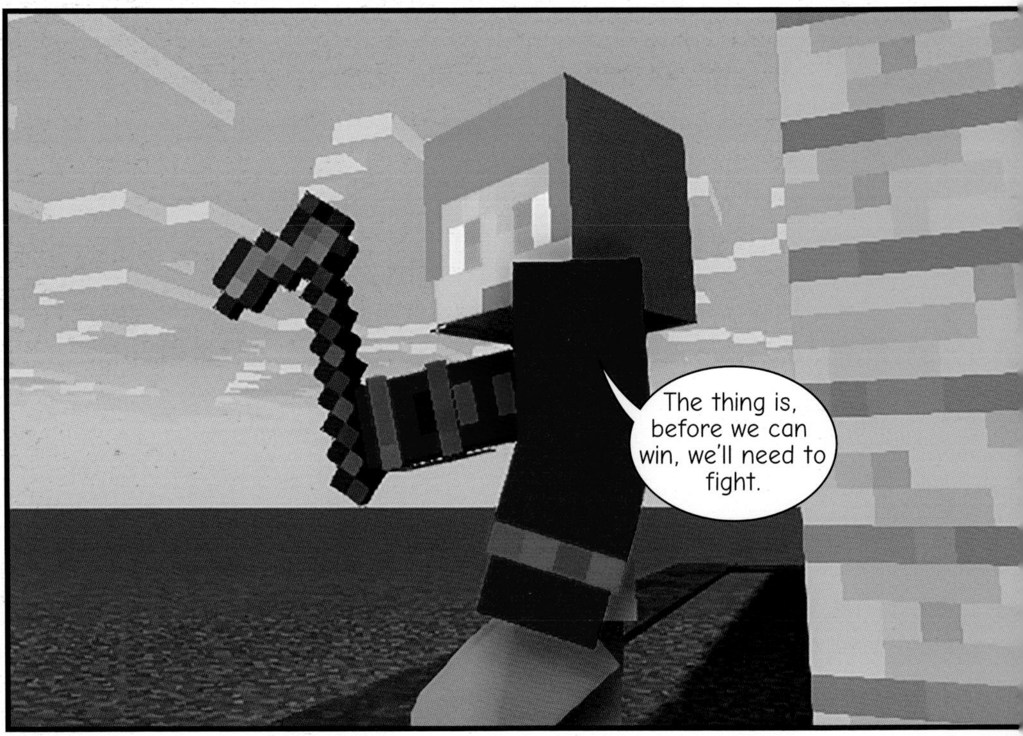
The thing is, before we can win, we'll need to fight.

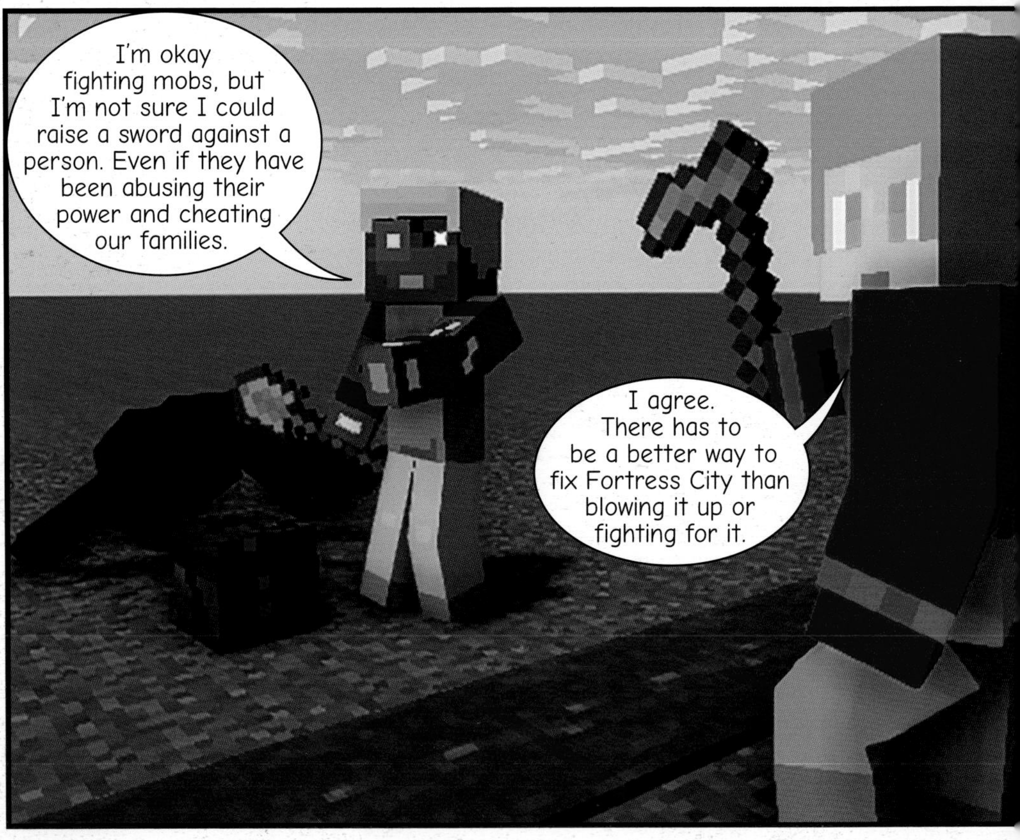
I'm okay fighting mobs, but I'm not sure I could raise a sword against a person. Even if they have been abusing their power and cheating our families.
I agree. There has to be a better way to fix Fortress City than blowing it up or fighting for it.

CHAPTER 13

REUNITED

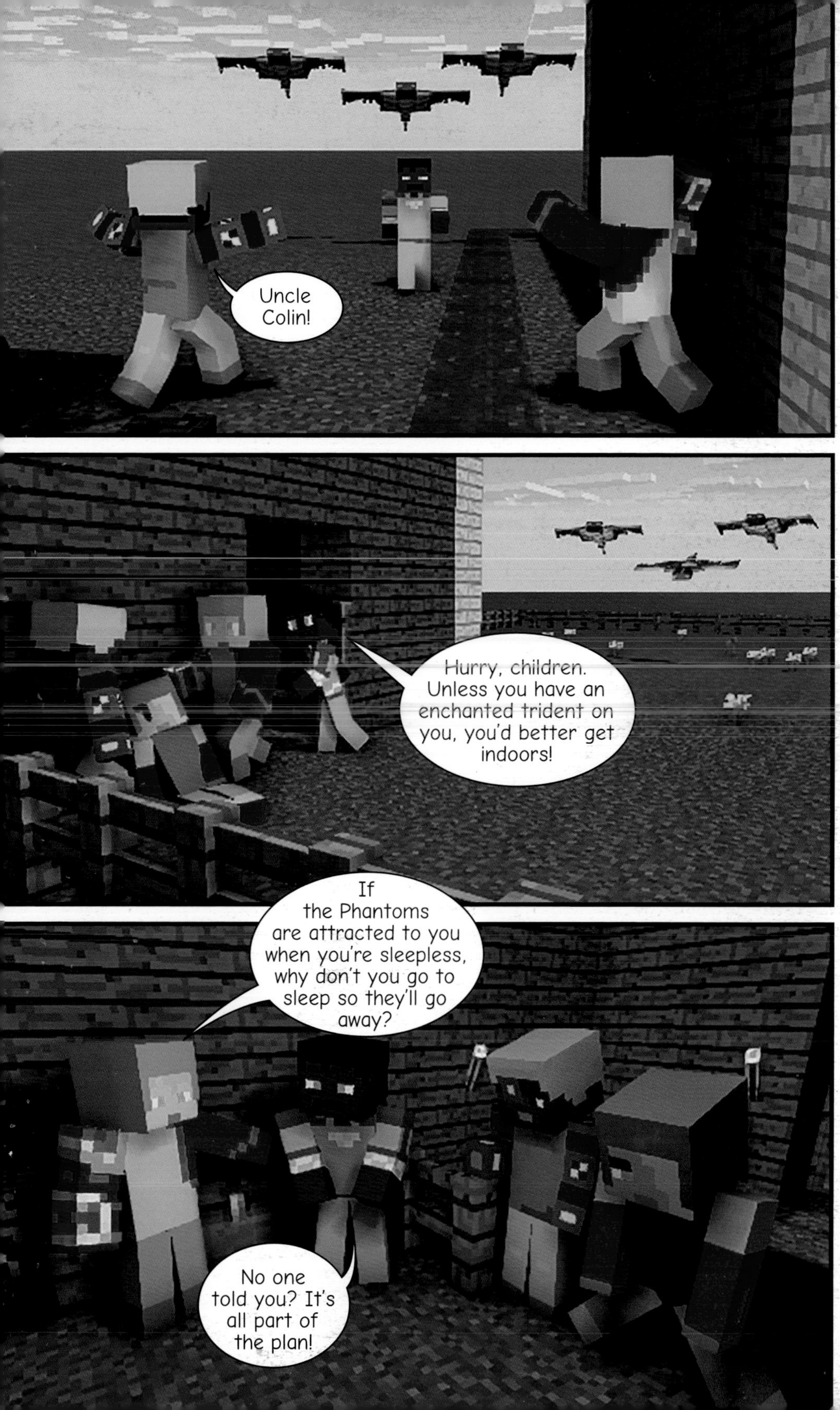
Uncle Colin!
Hurry, children. Unless you have an enchanted trident on you, you'd better get indoors!
If the Phantoms are attracted to you when you're sleepless, why don't you go to sleep so they'll go away?
No one told you? It's all part of the plan!

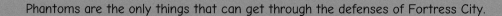

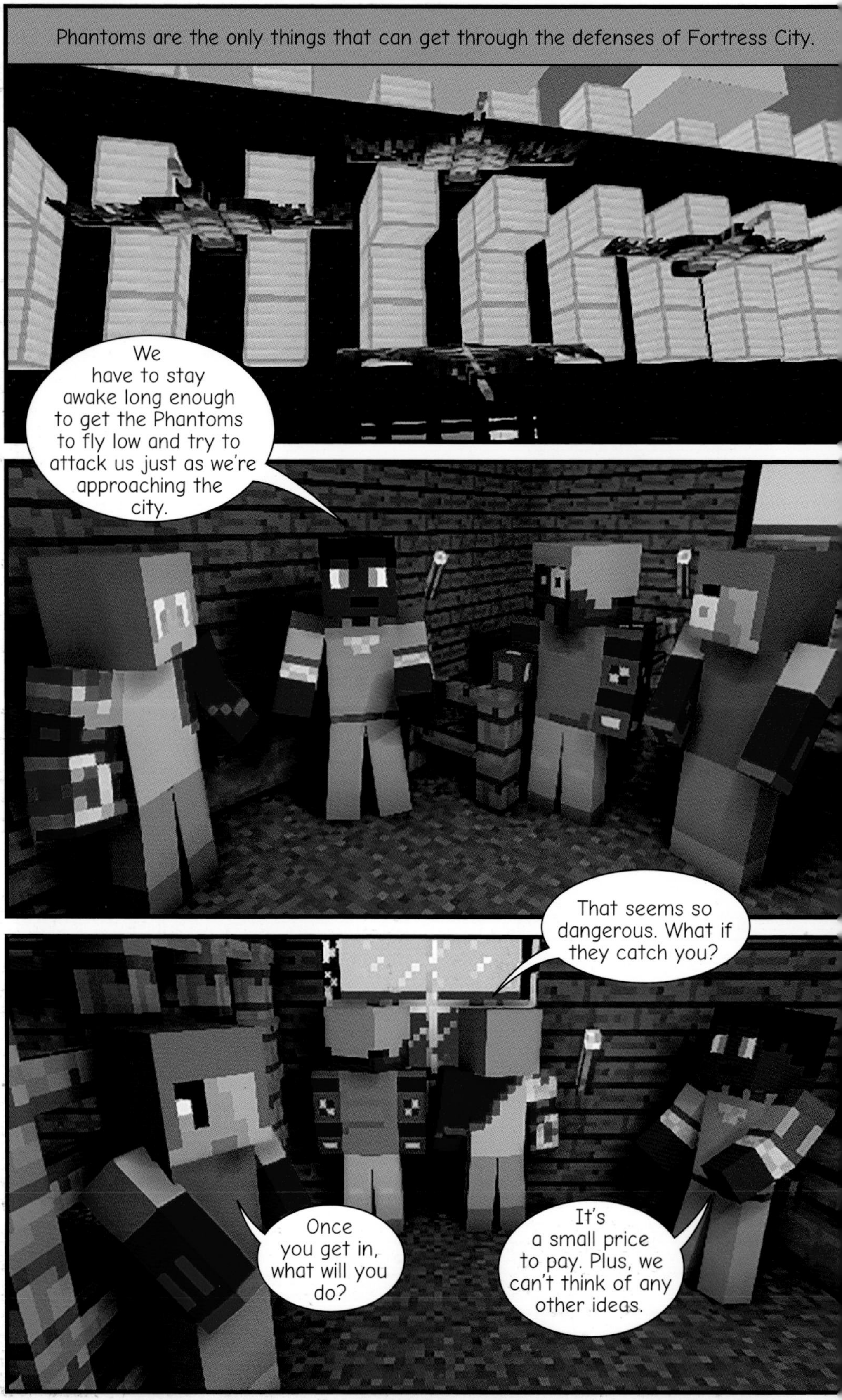

Phantoms are the only things that can get through the defenses of Fortress City.
We have to stay awake long enough to get the Phantoms to fly low and try to attack us just as we're approaching the city.
That seems so dangerous. What if they catch you?
Once you get in, what will you do?
It's a small price to pay. Plus, we can't think of any other ideas.

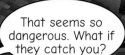

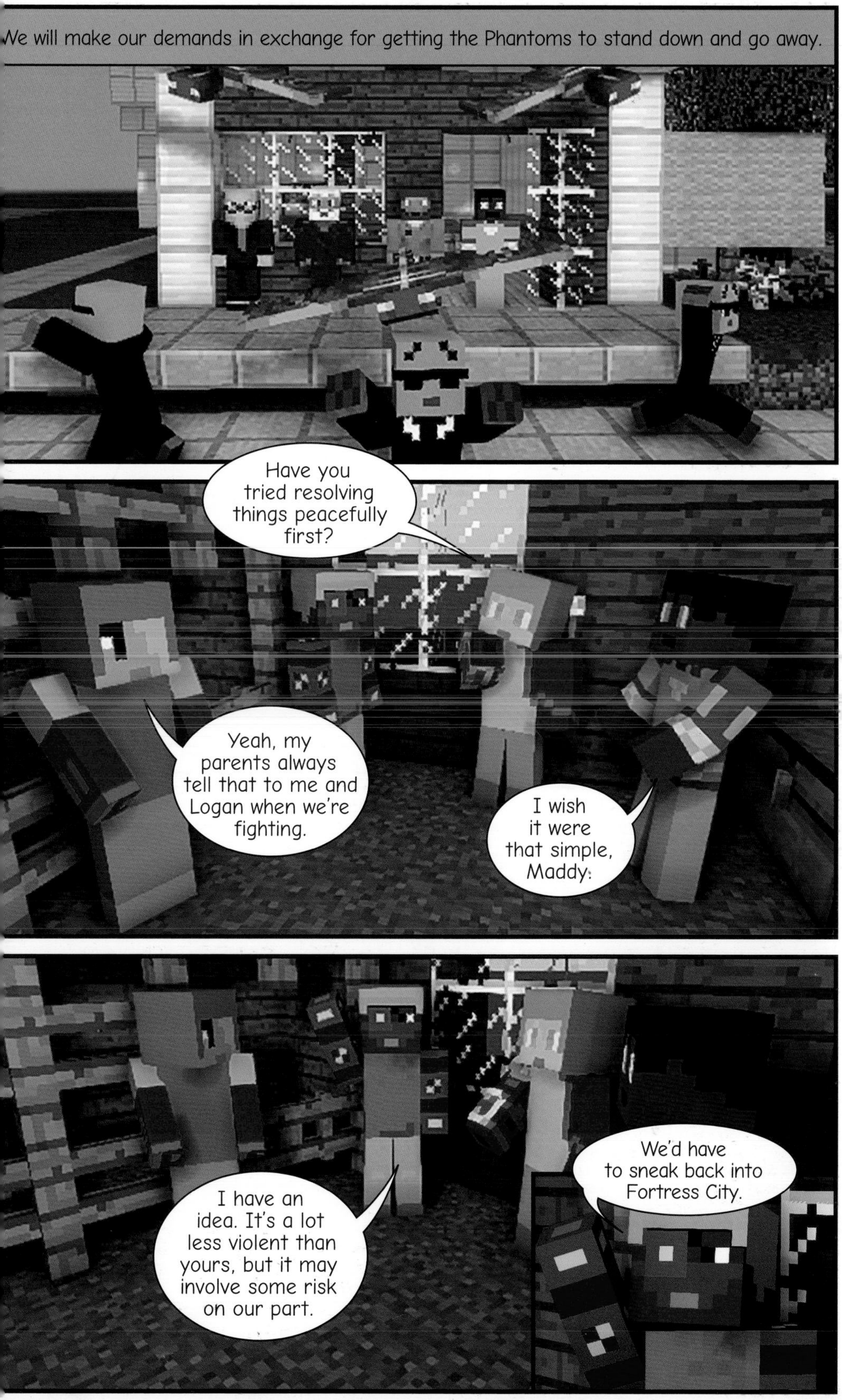
We will make our demands in exchange for getting the Phantoms to stand down and go away.
Have you tried resolving things peacefully first?
Yeah, my parents always tell that to me and Logan when we're fighting.
I wish it were that simple, Maddy.
I have an idea. It's a lot less violent than yours, but it may involve some risk on our part.
We'd have to sneak back into Fortress City.

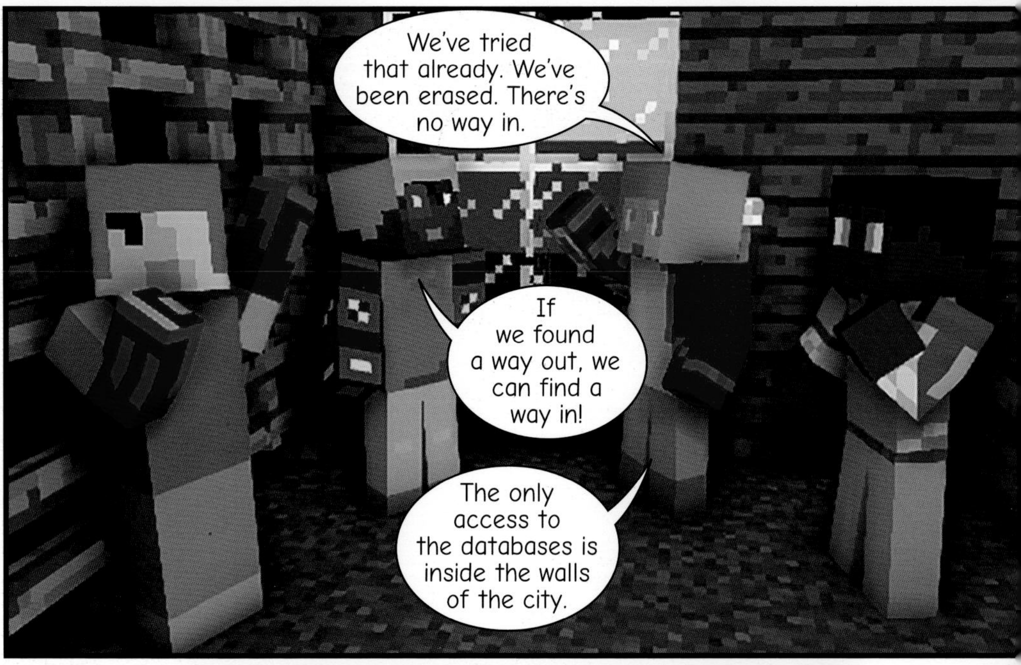
We've tried that already. We've been erased. There's no way in.
If we found a way out, we can find a way in!
The only access to the databases is inside the walls of the city.

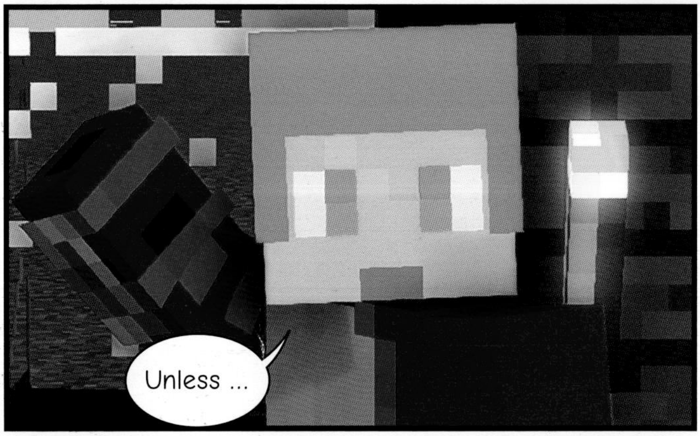
Unless ...

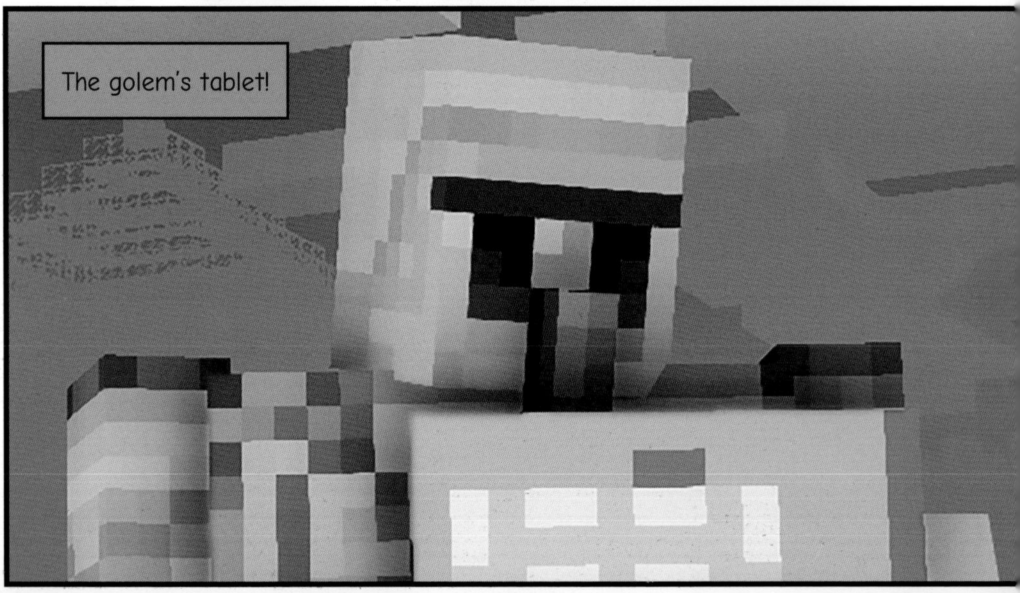
The golem's tablet!

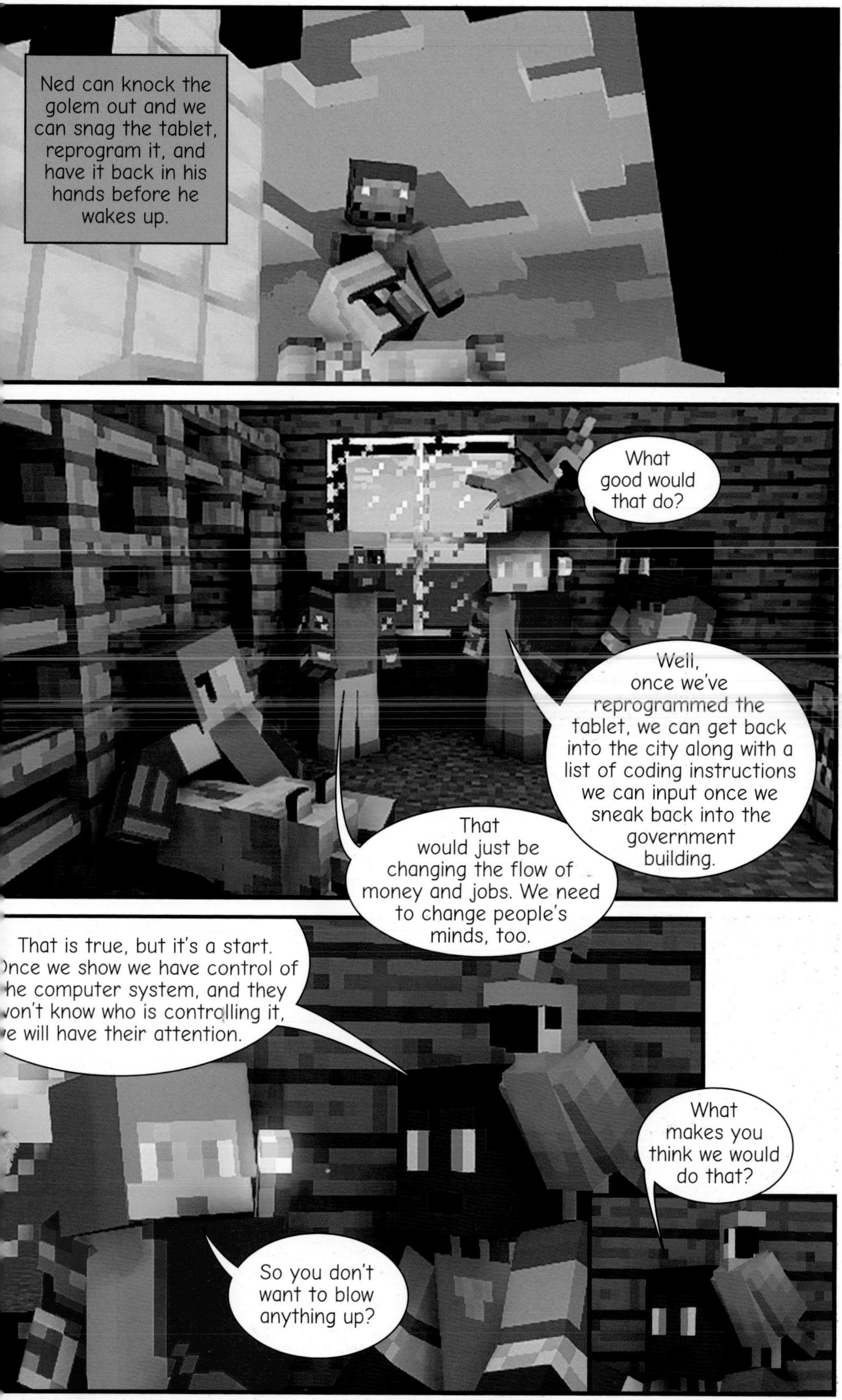

Ned can knock the golem out and we can snag the tablet, reprogram it, and have it back in his hands before he wakes up.
What good would that do?
Well, once we've reprogrammed the tablet, we can get back into the city along with a list of coding instructions we can input once we sneak back into the government building.
That would just be changing the flow of money and jobs. We need to change people's minds, too.
That is true, but it's a start. nce we show we have control of he computer system, and they on't know who is controlling it, e will have their attention.
What makes you think we would do that?
So you don't want to blow anything up?

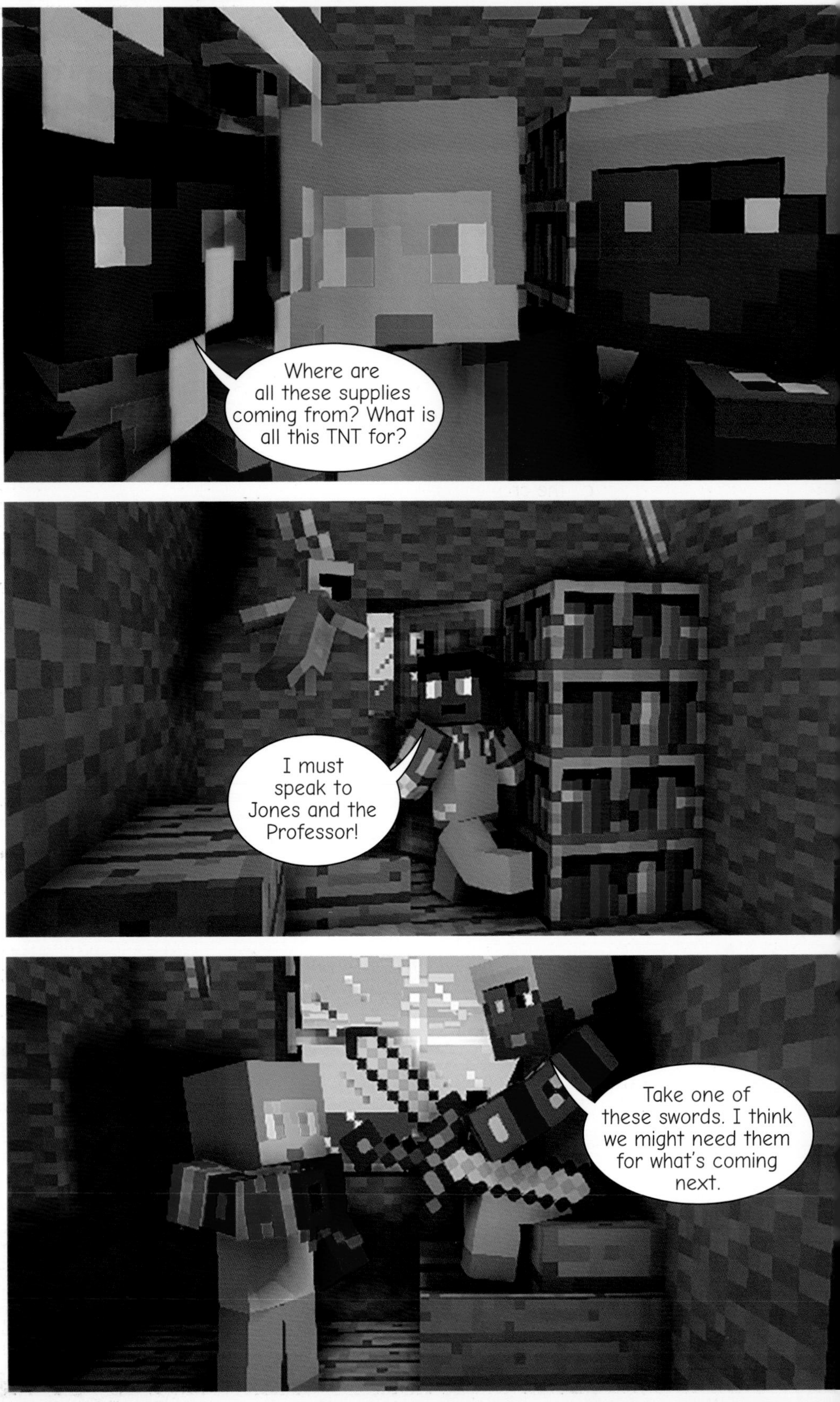
Where are all these supplies coming from? What is all this TNT for?
I must speak to Jones and the Professor!
Take one of these swords. I think we might need them for what's coming next.

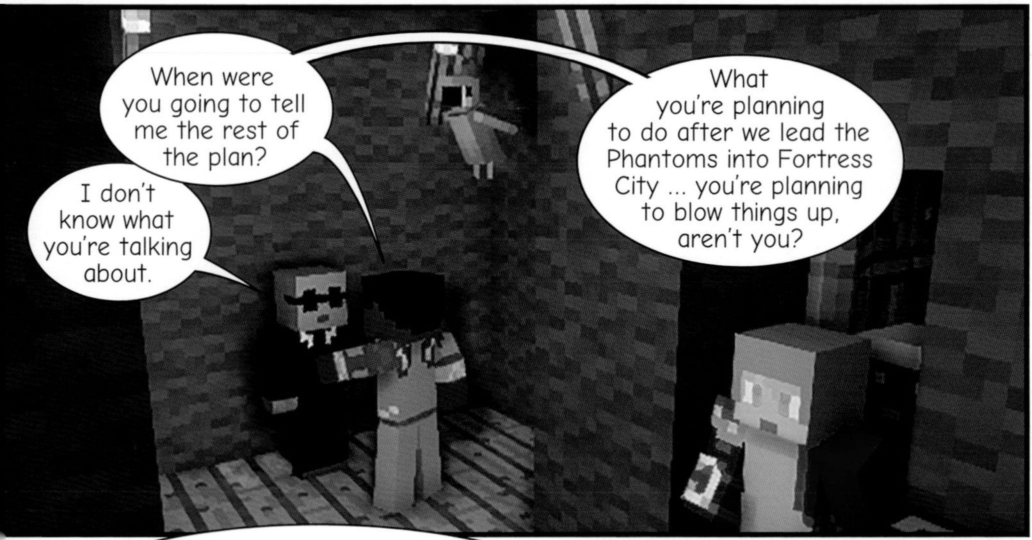
When were you going to tell me the rest of the plan?
I don't know what you're talking about.
What you're planning to do after we lead the Phantoms into Fortress City ... you're planning to blow things up, aren't you?

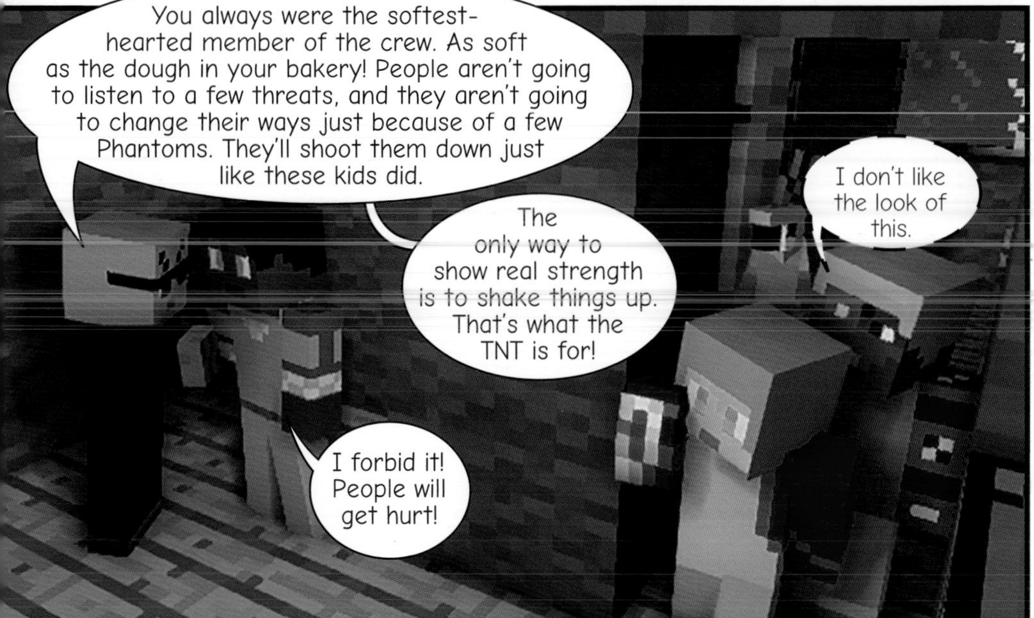
You always were the softest-hearted member of the crew. As soft as the dough in your bakery! People aren't going to listen to a few threats, and they aren't going to change their ways just because of a few Phantoms. They'll shoot them down just like these kids did.
The only way to show real strength is to shake things up. That's what the TNT is for!
I don't like the look of this.
I forbid it! People will get hurt!

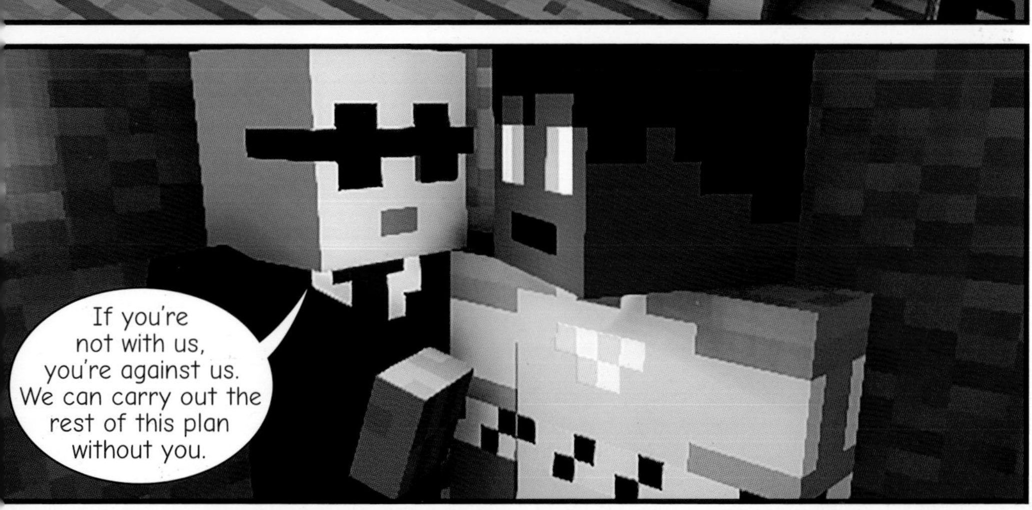
If you're not with us, you're against us. We can carry out the rest of this plan without you.

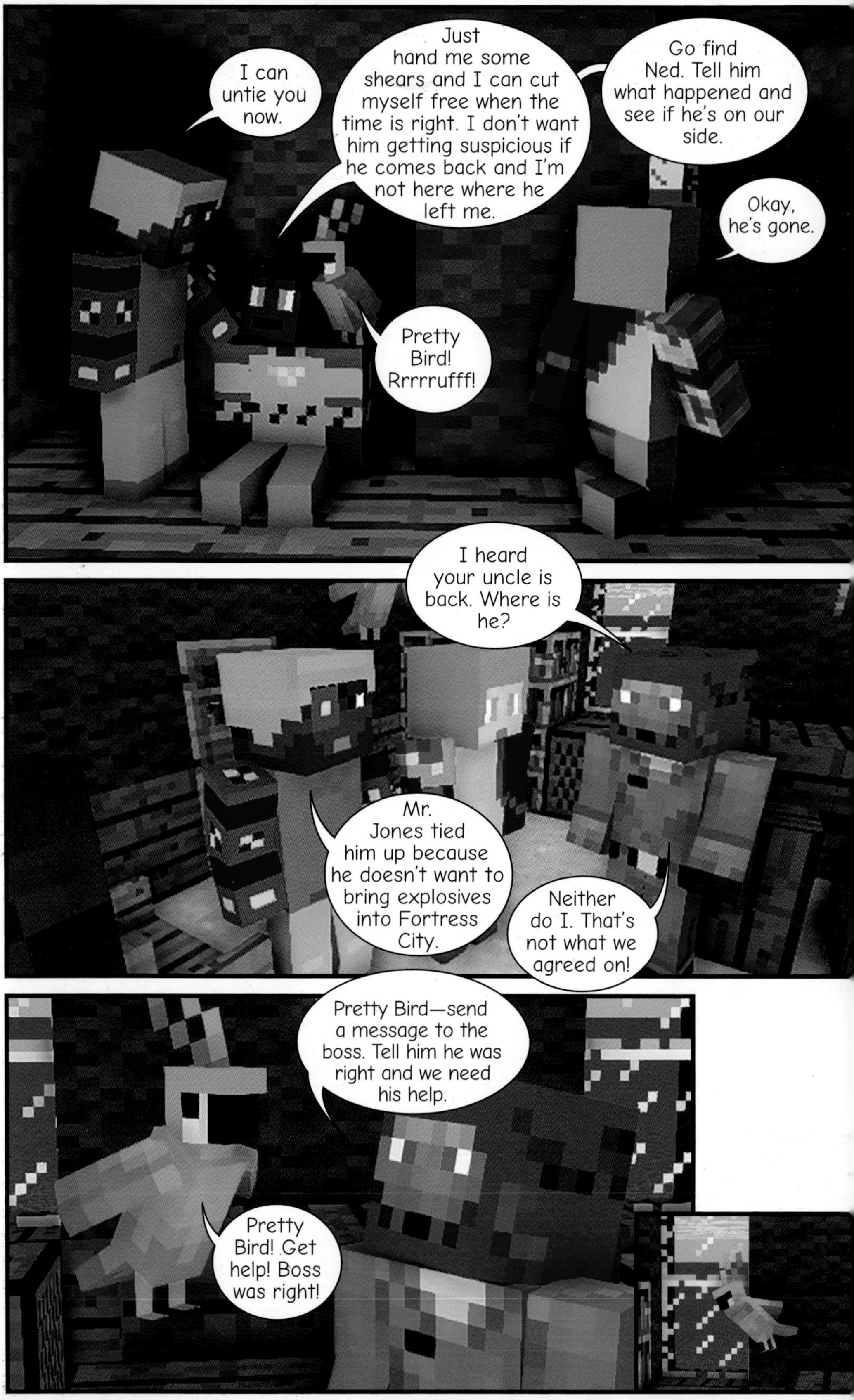
I can untie you now.
Just hand me some shears and I can cut myself free when the time is right. I don't want him getting suspicious if he comes back and I'm not here where he left me.
Go find Ned. Tell him what happened and see if he's on our side.
Okay, he's gone.
Pretty Bird! Rrrrrufff!
I heard your uncle is back. Where is he?
Mr. Jones tied him up because he doesn't want to bring explosives into Fortress City.
Neither do I. That's not what we agreed on!
Pretty Bird—send a message to the boss. Tell him he was right and we need his help.
Pretty Bird! Get help! Boss was right!

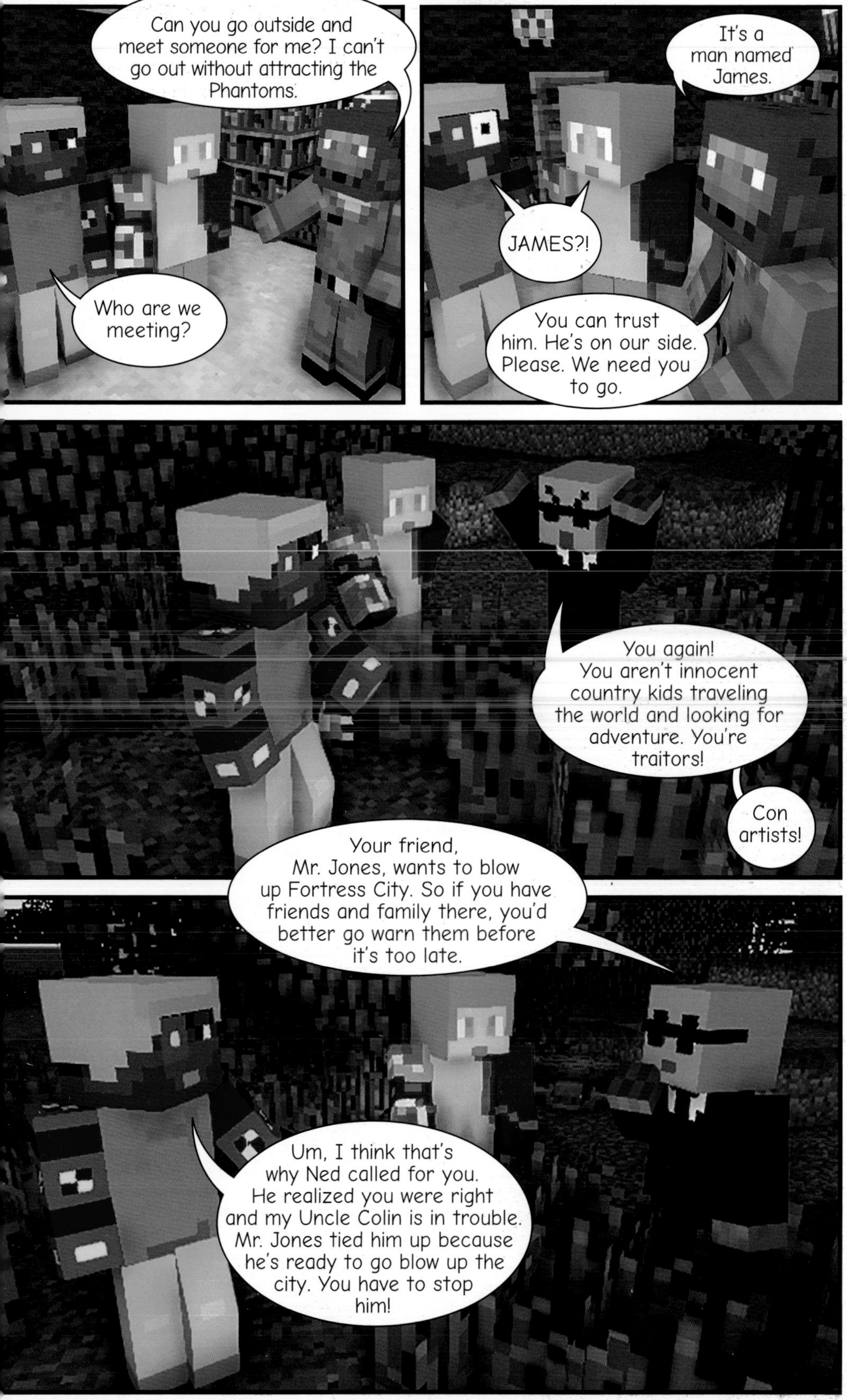
Can you go outside and meet someone for me? I can't go out without attracting the Phantoms.
Who are we meeting?
It's a man named James.
JAMES?!
You can trust him. He's on our side. Please. We need you to go.
You again! You aren't innocent country kids traveling the world and looking for adventure. You're traitors!
Con artists!
Your friend, Mr. Jones, wants to blow up Fortress City. So if you have friends and family there, you'd better go warn them before it's too late.
Um, I think that's why Ned called for you. He realized you were right and my Uncle Colin is in trouble. Mr. Jones tied him up because he's ready to go blow up the city. You have to stop him!

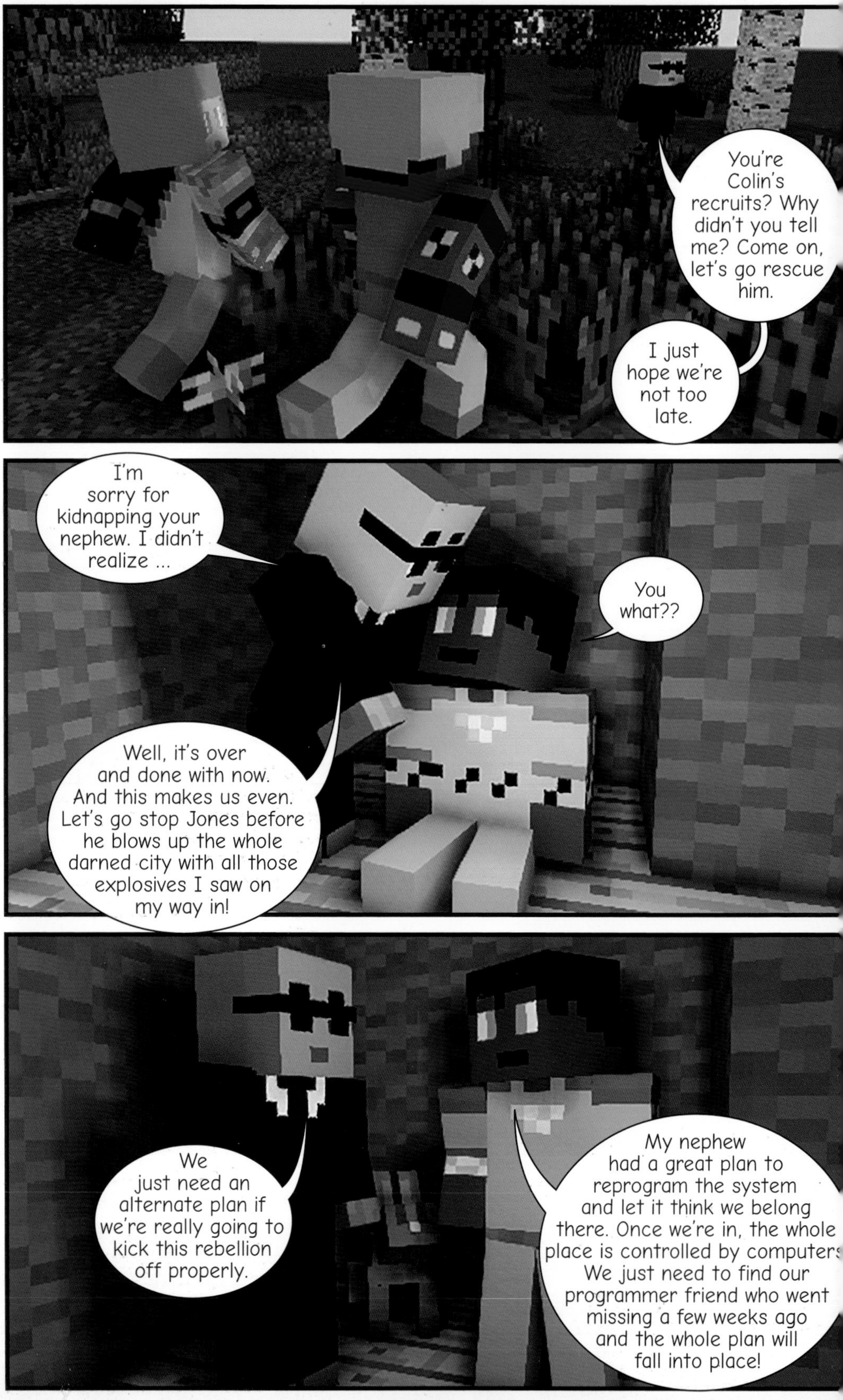
You're Colin's recruits? Why didn't you tell me? Come on, let's go rescue him.
I just hope we're not too late.
I'm sorry for kidnapping your nephew. I didn't realize ...
You what??
Well, it's over and done with now. And this makes us even. Let's go stop Jones before he blows up the whole darned city with all those explosives I saw on my way in!
We just need an alternate plan if we're really going to kick this rebellion off properly.
My nephew had a great plan to reprogram the system and let it think we belong there. Once we're in, the whole place is controlled by computers. We just need to find our programmer friend who went missing a few weeks ago and the whole plan will fall into place!

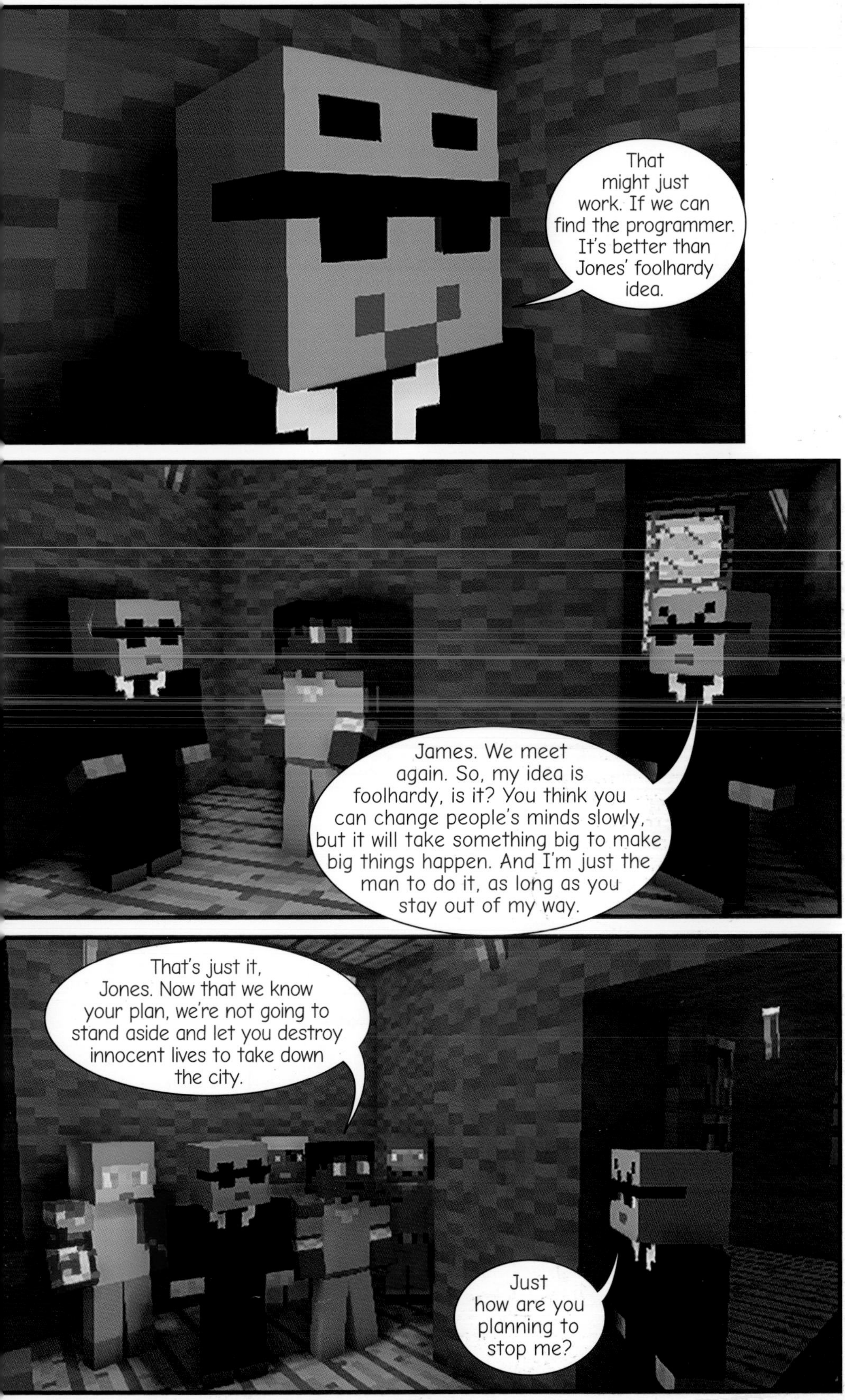
That might just work. If we can find the programmer. It's better than Jones' foolhardy idea.
James. We meet again. So, my idea is foolhardy, is it? You think you can change people's minds slowly, but it will take something big to make big things happen. And I'm just the man to do it, as long as you stay out of my way.
That's just it, Jones. Now that we know your plan, we're not going to stand aside and let you destroy innocent lives to take down the city.
Just how are you planning to stop me?

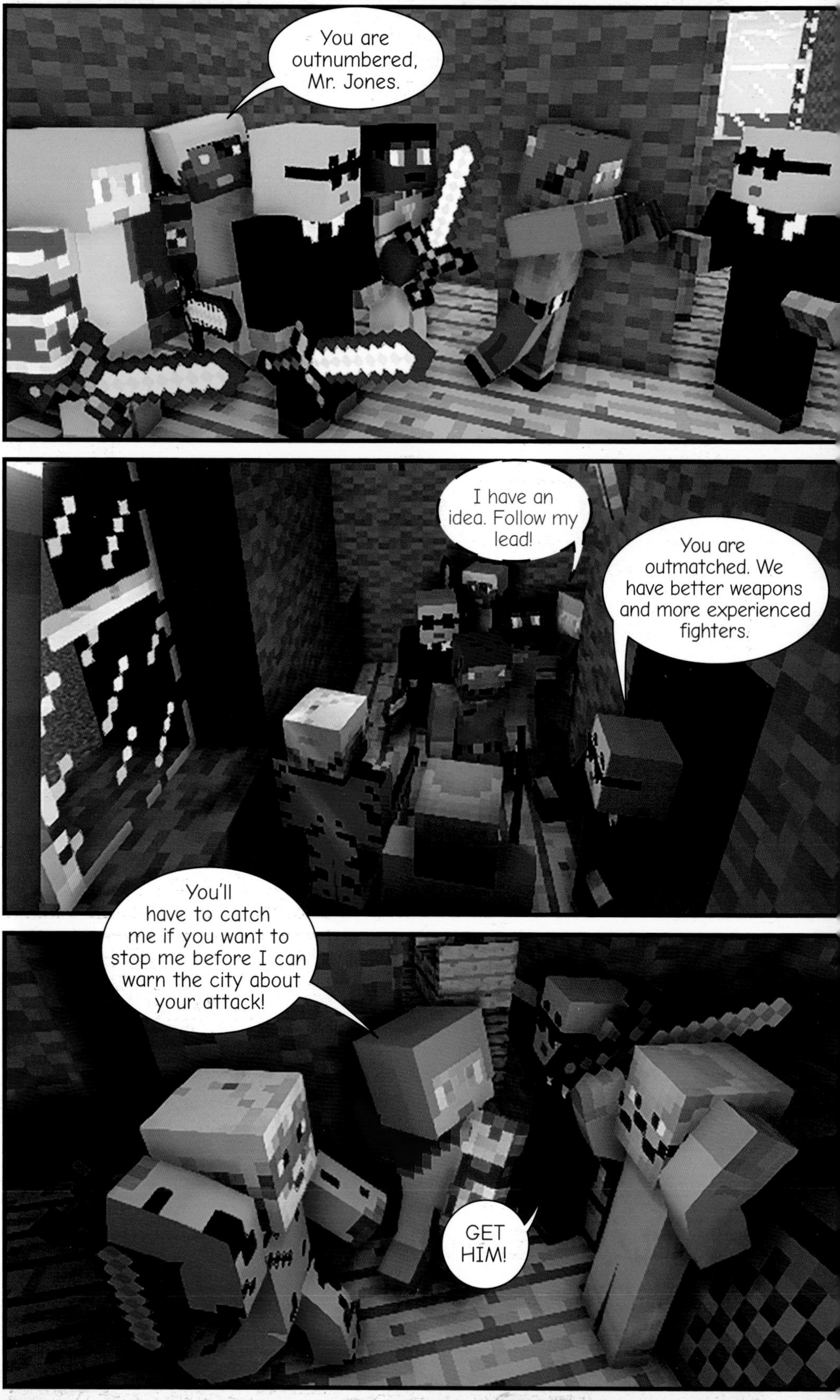
You are outnumbered, Mr. Jones.
I have an idea. Follow my lead!
You are outmatched. We have better weapons and more experienced fighters.
You'll have to catch me if you want to stop me before I can warn the city about your attack!
GET HIM!

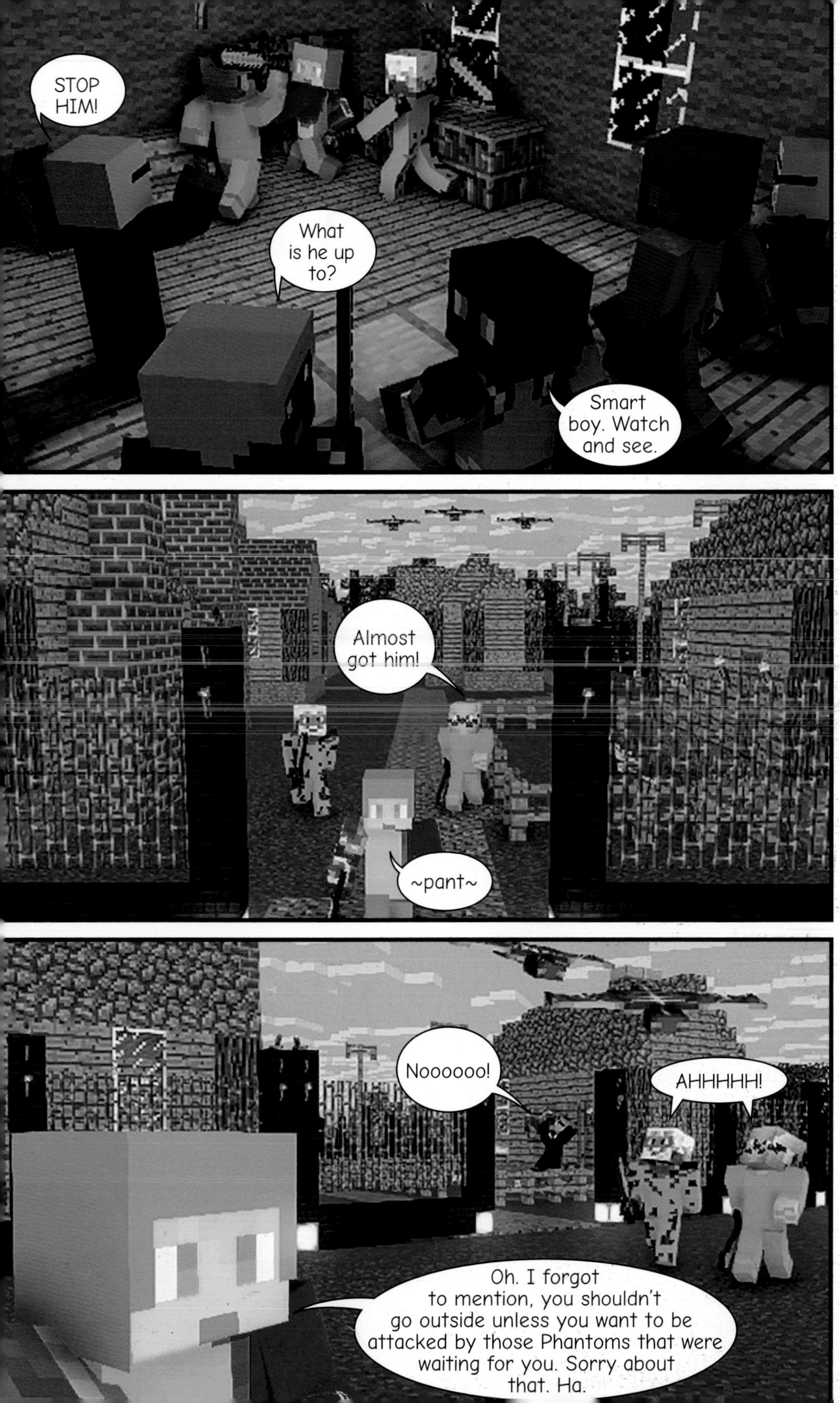
STOP HIM!
What is he up to?
Smart boy. Watch and see.
Almost got him!
~pant~
Nooooooo!
AHHHHH!
Oh. I forgot to mention, you shouldn't go outside unless you want to be attacked by those Phantoms that were waiting for you. Sorry about that. Ha.

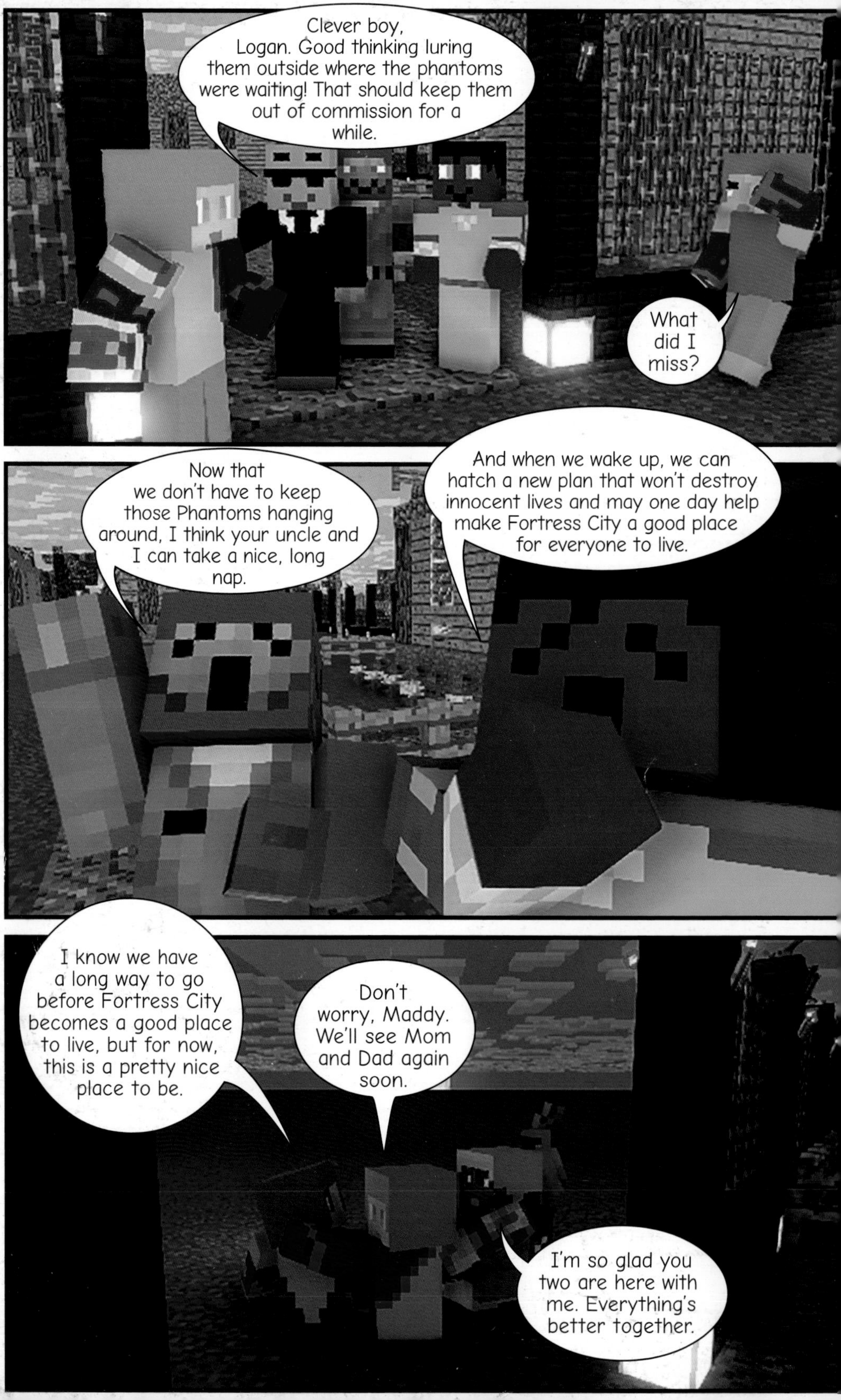
Clever boy, Logan. Good thinking luring them outside where the phantoms were waiting! That should keep them out of commission for a while.
What did I miss?
Now that we don't have to keep those Phantoms hanging around, I think your uncle and I can take a nice, long nap.
And when we wake up, we can hatch a new plan that won't destroy innocent lives and may one day help make Fortress City a good place for everyone to live.
I know we have a long way to go before Fortress City becomes a good place to live, but for now, this is a pretty nice place to be.
Don't worry, Maddy. We'll see Mom and Dad again soon.
I'm so glad you two are here with me. Everything's better together.